DANCE OF HEARTS

Dancing with the Earl [illegible] disconcerting to Miss We[illegible] cident with her fan, ear[illegible] never waltzed in public be[illegible] hand resting disturbingly [illegible] dark eyes looking down at her, [illegible] her with such confusion that she could scarcely concentrate upon the steps of the dance.

"Your strategy is working admirably, Miss Wentworth."

"What strategy?"

"Why, your strategy to make Russelton jealous, of course. He's looking daggers at me this very minute."

Miss Wentworth stole a glance in Lord Russelton's direction. "Yes, he does look annoyed, doesn't he?" she said with satisfaction.

"And we could make him even more annoyed." The Earl's eyes rested on her speculatively, and the hand on her waist seemed to tighten. "If Russelton's this upset, seeing you dance with me, imagine how jealous he'd be if he saw you kissing me! Come, what do you say, Miss Wentworth? Don't you think it a splendid notion?"

"Certainly not, my lord!"

"What, don't you want to kiss me?" The Earl's face assumed a hurt expression that was belied by the laughter in his eyes. "Not even out of curiosity?"

"No!" Yet Miss Wentworth was aware of a definite stirring of curiosity. What would it be like to kiss the Wicked Earl? The thought was exciting, like forbidden fruit: tantalizing, but out of the question, of course.

An Inconvenient Engagement

Joy Reed

ZEBRA BOOKS
KENSINGTON PUBLISHING CORP.

For Gayle

ZEBRA BOOKS are published by

Kensington Publishing Corp.
475 Park Avenue South
New York, NY 10016

First Printing: January, 1994

Printed in the United States of America

Chapter One

"Did you have a pleasant drive, my dear?"

"No, Mama." Miss Rebecca Wentworth pretended to be very busy untying the ribbons of her bronze green French bonnet, and she kept her back to the other two occupants of the elegant drawing room. "No, it was not a pleasant drive." Angry words trembled on the tip of Miss Wentworth's tongue, but with an effort she held them back. The drive had, in fact, been perfectly miserable; her escort (who was also her fiancé) had spent the entirety of the outing gazing with admiration upon every halfway well-looking woman who had crossed his path. The only times he had bothered to speak during the drive were to praise here a particularly neat ankle, or there an especially pretty figure that had caught his eye. Miss Wentworth had been justly incensed by this behavior, and she had no intention of letting it go unpunished, but she was afraid that if she tried to discuss the outrage now, while it was still fresh in her mind, she would more than likely burst into tears. "Not a pleasant drive at all . . . there was rather a cold wind blowing," she offered, at her mother's surprised look.

"Yes, there is an east wind today." Lady Wentworth,

Miss Wentworth's aunt, spoke with her usual air of authority. Lady Wentworth was a tall, majestic woman with iron grey hair, and it was her habit to speak as though she was issuing statements rather than merely making conversation. "I would not myself care to venture out in an open carriage, with an east wind blowing."

"I hope you didn't take a chill, Rebecca," said Mrs. Wentworth, regarding her daughter anxiously. "You look rather flushed. Dear Frederick would have done better to have taken his town carriage rather than that curricle of his, on such a cold day. Why did not you invite him to come in, my dear? I expect he could have used a cup of tea and a chance to warm himself a bit, before driving back."

"He could not keep his horses standing, Mama," said Miss Wentworth in an expressionless voice. This had also been her fiancé's excuse for letting her scramble down from the curricle unassisted, notwithstanding the fact that his groom could have very well held the horses if Lord Russelton had really wanted to perform this courtesy. The remembrance brought a fresh flush of anger to Miss Wentworth's cheeks. "I think I will go upstairs and lie down for a while before dinner, Mama," she said, and escaped from the drawing room before her mother could pose further awkward questions.

Once she had reached the refuge of her bedchamber, Miss Wentworth indulged herself in a hearty bout of tears. Her heart was not precisely broken, but her pride was definitely smarting. That she, who had been one of the season's belles, should have been reduced to this! She splashed cold water on her face and glared at herself in the glass, as though her fiancé were mirrored there rather than her own tear-stained reflection.

Even with reddened eyelids, the face in the mirror was a most attractive one. There might be those who could see beauty only in blondes, or others who preferred the more fashionable dark coloring, but Rebecca Wentworth had still received admiration enough to earn herself the title of a Diamond of the First Water, and she was universally acknowledged to be one of the Season's prettiest girls. She had a mass of glossy, honey brown hair, a peaches-and-cream complexion, and large, wide-set eyes of a vivid green untouched by the slightest hint of hazel. Her nose was little and straight, her face a pure oval, and her mouth adorable; when she smiled, her teeth were like the proverbial match-pearls, and an entrancing dimple was seen to appear. As for the rest of her person, it was as pleasing as her face: she had a pretty figure, and her movements were held to be particularly graceful. Launched into London society during the Little Season of the previous year, Miss Wentworth had enjoyed a considerable success despite the disadvantages of a very modest marriage portion. She had acquired a whole circle of admirers, but it was Frederick Russelton who had successfully wooed and won her.

Like Miss Wentworth, Lord Russelton was also in the midst of his first London Season, and was enjoying a similar degree of social success. He was a handsome young gentleman, holding the title of Baron Russelton, and he prided himself as much on dressing in the highest kick of fashion as on his family's impeccable lineage. He had met Miss Wentworth soon after her arrival in London and had immediately singled her out for his attentions, showering her with pretty gifts and even prettier compliments until her head was quite turned. It was the most romantic thing possible. To Miss

Wentworth's dazzled eyes, he had appeared a veritable Prince Charming, the lover she had always dreamed of.

Surprisingly, Miss Wentworth's mother had opposed the match, at least in the beginning. She thought Lord Russelton too young to be a suitable *parti*. He was, in fact, several months younger than Miss Wentworth herself, although that young lady had been quick to point out that he was exactly the same age as herself at the moment: namely, eighteen. Mrs. Wentworth shook her head and said that young men were inclined to be volatile. She would have preferred to have seen her daughter betrothed to a man a little older, and possibly a little wealthier as well. But Miss Wentworth would have none of it. She loved Frederick Russelton, and he loved her, and in the end Lord Russelton succeeded in charming even the reluctant Mrs. Wentworth into wholehearted approval. The engagement had been publicly announced at the end of the Little Season. Several of Miss Wentworth's other suitors had behaved with a flattering amount of jealous outrage, and she had gone off in a blaze of glory to celebrate the Christmas season at the country home of her cousin, Sir Richard Wentworth.

Miss Wentworth was unable to pinpoint exactly when the tide of her love affair began to turn. Lord Russelton had been unable to accompany her to her cousin's home at Christmastime, for he had already accepted an invitation to spend the holidays at the estate of one of his own relations. Miss Wentworth had happily agreed that of course he must go with his family. It was only a few weeks, after all, and what were a few weeks, when they would be spending the rest of their lives together? Christmas had come and gone. In January, Lord Russelton had come to visit Miss Wentworth at her own home in Derbyshire. He had met her father, the marriage settlements had been arranged, and the wedding date set for the end of June. At that time, all had seemed to be going smoothly.

Miss Wentworth had seen little of Lord Russelton during the months of February and March. She was still in Derbyshire, and he was at his own home in Norfolk. He had written her often, however, and his letters had certainly seemed to indicate that he found her as beautiful and lovable as ever. Miss Wentworth left off staring in the mirror and went over to her writing table. Yes, here they were, Frederick's letters, bound up with a blue ribbon. She turned them over for the hundredth time, searching for some sign of cooling, some hint that her betrothed's feelings had changed. But there was nothing; the letters breathed ardor and a suitably loverlike impatience for their coming marriage. No, there had been no clue in the letters.

Miss Wentworth had first sensed a change when she returned to London at the end of March. It was only little things at first. When he was courting her, Frederick had sent her flowers nearly every day; she had been well-nigh inundated with bouquets during the Little Season. Now he never gave her so much as a blossom. Of course, Lord Russelton's means were not large. He had inherited only an independence along with his title. It was true that he had additional expectations from his grandmother, Lady Cassandra, but those monies would not come to him until some indeterminate future date, and in his present financial situation it had perhaps been unnecessarily extravagant of him to have sent flowers on a daily basis.

Miss Wentworth told herself that she did not mind not receiving flowers anymore. What she did mind was the way Lord Russelton appeared to ignore her when she spoke to him, the perfunctory way he kissed her hand when he took leave of her, and—worst of all—the way his eyes lingered upon every pretty female around, in a fashion that was little better than an open insult to herself. In particular, Lord Russelton's eyes had been lingering lately upon Miss Clarissa Barrow.

Miss Barrow was a sturdy blonde, comely without being in any way a beauty. Miss Wentworth would never have been jealous of her in the normal course of things. But beside Miss Barrow's more visible attractions there loomed the appeal of a marriage portion rumored to be in the vicinity of eighty thousand pounds: she was the granddaughter of a gentleman who had made a fortune in the shipping business. This taint of the commercial had not prevented Miss Barrow from penetrating into the best circles. She had been presented at court, was seen at all the most fashionable parties, and had even received a coveted voucher to Almack's Assembly Rooms.

Miss Wentworth was barely acquainted with the shipping heiress, but when Lord Russelton had first begun to show signs of interest in Miss Barrow, Miss Wentworth had taken the time to look the other girl over closely. She simply could not believe that Frederick thought Miss Barrow prettier than herself. It was perfectly possible that he found the shipping heiress more lovable than the clergyman's daughter, of course, but Miss Wentworth was strongly of the suspicion that Lord Russelton had begun to regret tying himself to a young woman without fortune. Apparently love was no longer enough.

Had Lord Russelton come to Miss Wentworth and explained his change of heart—or even the change in his financial circumstances—she felt she could have forgiven him. It would still have been a painful blow, but she could have at least arranged matters so as to save face, telling the curious world that she and Lord Russelton had decided they would not suit. By preserving an appearance of amiability on all sides, the affair would have attracted little attention, and gossip could have been kept to a minimum. Instead of coming to her in an open, aboveboard manner, however, and leaving her some salve for her wounded pride, Lord Russelton was making it more and more obvious that he was trying to humiliate her into crying off. The rules of polite society forbade gentlemen from openly ending engagements; Lord Russelton seemed determined, by a kind of guerilla warfare, to shame and infuriate his fiancée into giving him his freedom.

At first, Miss Wentworth had been unable to believe her Prince Charming capable of such behavior. She made excuses for him, and shrugged off the smaller snubs and slights, but as time went on she was forced to recognize the truth. The signs were all too plain to see. Lord Russelton had not come to call upon her more than a handful of times since the beginning of the new Season. When Miss Wentworth met him in public, he greeted her coolly and left her side as soon as possible. He flirted with other girls before her eyes, and admired them loudly when she was alone in his company. Most damning of all, he had waltzed twice with Miss Barrow at Almack's the evening before.

This was carrying matters from a conflict in private to a far more public arena. There had been a number of raised eyebrows at Lord Russelton's devotion to the shipping heiress; by the time Miss Wentworth realized what was happening, the damage had already been done. It was useless to hope that such a thing could go unnoticed at Almack's. She had overheard enough gossip to know that it was an immediate *on-dit,* and one or two catty remarks had even been addressed to herself, which she had been obliged to swallow with the appearance of complaisance.

Miss Wentworth recognized that her position was fast becoming untenable. If she were to cry off now, there were plenty of people who would gleefully put two and two together and snicker because the lovely Rebecca Wentworth had been thrown over by her fiancé. Her reputation as a belle would be irretrievably damaged. The more serious of her other suitors had taken themselves off after the announcement of her engagement to Lord Russelton; the remainder dangled after her only to be fashionable, and she would not long remain fashionable after being as good as jilted. Miss Wentworth felt quite certain that no gentleman of her acquaintance would make her an offer if she found herself free again under such circumstances. It was a terrible situation, and Miss Wentworth was furious with Lord Russelton, whose cowardly, ungentlemanly behavior was bidding fair to ruin the whole Season, and probably her whole life as well.

Miss Wentworth had rapidly progressed from a state of melancholy to a state of indignation, and she was now fast progressing to a state of dangerous anger. She vowed that such Turkish treatment would not go unpunished. Frederick thought to force her to end the engagement; well, Rebecca Wentworth resolved to make it just as difficult as possible for him to obtain his freedom, and after the humiliation she had endured at Almack's last night she had begun to rack her brains for a really suitable revenge as well.

She had returned home the evening before in a mood

to consider such drastic measures as poison and hired assassins; as she lay awake that night, she had whiled away the sleepless hours by imagining Lord Russelton upon his deathbed, with his last breath gasping out an apology for his ill-use, when she, Rebecca Wentworth, had been good enough to accept his own unworthy offer rather than marrying Lord Wallace (who would have made her a viscountess) or Mr. Dewlap (who would have made her one of the wealthiest widows in the kingdom, once he expired, which at the age of eight-and-eighty he might have been expected to do without delay). In this fantasy, Miss Wentworth could not decide if she would spurn Lord Russelton's deathbed apology, or accept it with a Christian charity that would bring tears to his eyes. Miss Wentworth's papa was a clergyman, so her upbringing urged charity, but Miss Wentworth was in the grip of a very unchristian resentment just then. She rather thought she would prefer to let her errant fiancé go to his grave without the satisfaction of knowing himself forgiven.

It was a gratifying picture, and did much to relieve her overburdened feelings, but the cold light of day and her own common sense forced Miss Wentworth to abandon such melodramatic ideas. Whatever means she found to punish Lord Russelton would undoubtably have to be far more subtle. Humiliating, yes, but subtle.

She went down to dinner that evening in a subdued mood. Besides her aunt and mother, her cousin Richard was at the table. He was Sir Richard Wentworth now; he had succeeded to the title upon the death of his father a little more than two years ago. Sir Richard was dark-haired, heavy-set, and a few years older than Miss Wentworth; he had his mother's fine grey eyes but none of Lady Wentworth's awe-inspiring majesty. Sir Richard strove rather after the reputation of a Corinthian, preferring all the lower forms of sport to the polite entertainments of the *haut ton.* At the dinner table, he attempted in vain to convince his mother that a cockfight at the Archangel in Tufton Street was a more eligible way to spend the evening than a ball at Lady Sefton's.

"But you are forgetting, Richard. Henrietta will be there," said Lady Wentworth, her dark brows arching in a faint, well-bred reproof.

Sir Richard looked embarrassed. "Oh, Henri knows I don't care for that sort of thing. Dash it, I'm no hand at dancing, and as for sitting around making pretty conversation—" He received a look from his mother that made him sigh, but he continued to argue, albeit with an air of knowing the battle to be already lost. "I'll bet Henri wouldn't mind if I cried off from Sefton's, Mama. She don't care much for doing the fashionable, either. After we're married, we plan to live in the country and not bother ourselves with the London nonsense at all."

"That may be so, Richard, but I have already informed Henrietta's mother that you are to be present tonight, and Lady Ingleside will think it very odd if you do not appear. Moreover, you are forgetting that you agreed to escort Rebecca to the Seftons' tonight. Amelia and I have already accepted invitations to Mrs. Hawley's musicale, or we would be able to do it; since we cannot, however, Lady Ingleside very kindly offered to act as Rebecca's chaperone, so you must see that it is your duty to accompany your cousin tonight. It will do you no harm to polish your dancing and conversation, Richard," said Lady Wentworth, with the faintest hint of a smile on her austere features. "Certainly you are more likely to do so at the Seftons' than at the Archangel!"

"Oh, well, if I have to take Beck along to Sefton's, then there's no question, of course," agreed Sir Richard good-humoredly, helping himself to a dish of almond custard.

"My name is Rebecca, Richard! I wish you would try to remember, and not call me by that childish—"

"Dash it, I try to remember, Beck—Rebecca—but—"

"Such a shame that the young people can't ride to the ball with their fiancés," said Mrs. Wentworth, paying no heed to an argument that had been going on since nursery days. "I spoke with Frederick's mother, dear Lady Russelton, yesterday. She told me that she, Lady Cassandra, and Frederick are all going to the Seftons' tonight. If we had only been thinking, we might have arranged for Rebecca to go with the Russeltons, and Richard to go with the Inglesides. Then he could have been with Henrietta, and Rebecca could have been with Frederick. I'm surprised Frederick didn't suggest the idea himself when you were out driving today, Rebecca."

Miss Wentworth said nothing. She happened to meet her cousin's eye, however, and encountered there such a look of sympathy that her pride at once bristled. She returned his look with a defiant lift of her chin. Sir Richard cleared his throat. "Never would have worked, Aunt Amelia," he said. "Lady Cass still wears a hoop, y'know. Wouldn't have been room in the carriage for Beck—Rebecca, I mean."

"Yes, that is so," said Mrs. Wentworth, smiling indulgently. "Dear Lady Cassandra, such a delightful eccentric."

"A dashed quiz, is more like it. I wouldn't want the old—I wouldn't want her as *my* grandmama-in-law, Beck." Sir Richard shook his head, and again his eyes met those of his cousin with awkward sympathy. "You should have seen her at the theater the other night. Must've had a dozen plumes on her head. Looked for all the world like a dashed Red Indian, demmed if she didn't."

"It's time I got dressed for the Seftons' ball," announced Miss Wentworth, pushing away her half-finished plate. "I'll meet you in the drawing room when I am ready, Richard." The knowledge that even her cousin was aware of her humiliation had quite taken away her appetite.

Chapter Two

"I say, Beck." Sir Richard ran a finger around his starched neckcloth, donned under protest for the Seftons' ball; a Belcher handkerchief was his more usual adornment. Doubtfully, he eyed his cousin Rebecca sitting across from him in the Wentworth town carriage. Miss Wentworth's honey brown hair was worn in clusters of loose curls about her face, with the back hair twisted up into a knot. A wreath of white roses encircled her head. Her ball gown was white net over satin, trimmed with a triple flounce, and each flounce had been edged in lace and festooned with a cluster of white roses. She looked very lovely, but it struck Sir Richard that her face was rather grim for a young lady about to embark upon what was supposed to be an evening of pleasure. "I say, Beck," he said again. "I couldn't help noticing: have you and Russelton quarreled? Seems to me I haven't seen him around the house much, here lately."

"Why, no, Richard. Frederick and I haven't quarreled." Miss Wentworth's face became even more forbidding. "You must know that it is not at all the thing for an engaged couple to live in each other's pockets!"

"Yes, I know," retorted her cousin. "But it's struck me lately that Russelton's been behaving dashed chilly to you, the last few times I've seen him. Not just to you, either; I thought he was going to cut *me* the other day in Tattersall's, indeed I did! And I've been hearing a bit of talk about him and Clarissa Barrow." Sir Richard eyed his cousin again. "Mean to say, there's a deal of difference between not living in each other's pockets, and the way Russelton's been . . . well, I know Henri would have my head if I went about with some other girl half as often as Russelton's seen with the Barrow chit. But then, Henri's not a beauty like you, Beck," he added fair-mindedly.

Miss Wentworth's face relaxed a bit. "Indeed, Henrietta is very pretty, Richard, and I like her extremely," she said, smiling at her cousin.

"Yes, she's pretty, right enough. Thought so the minute I laid eyes on her." For several minutes Sir Richard sat smiling at nothing in particular, presumably dwelling with satisfaction upon his betrothed's many excellences. Watching his face, Miss Wentworth felt a stab of jealousy. "But that's neither here nor there. What I'm trying to say, Beck, is that if you'd like me to drop a word in Russelton's ear . . . well, chances are he doesn't realize how queer it looks, and how the old cats gossip about the least little thing. If he's to be at this ball tonight—"

"On no account must you speak to him, Richard," said Miss Wentworth firmly. "I am quite able to manage my own affairs."

"Maybe you are, but it strikes me you've been looking dashed peaked lately, all the same." Miss Wentworth looked offended. "It's true, Beck. Right this minute, you look as though you've got the headache and were only going to the Seftons' because you were being made to.

And there's no reason why we have to go to this dashed ball, y'know. We could turn around this minute . . . send our excuses to the Seftons . . ." Sir Richard thought longingly of the cockfight at the Archangel. If they went directly home, and he scrambled out of his evening toggery and into more suitable garments, he still might not miss too much of the sport. "Be more than happy to go back, Beck," he offered. "Wouldn't mind in the least."

"Certainly not." Miss Wentworth gave Sir Richard a glittering smile. "Why, my betrothed will be at the Seftons' tonight! I wouldn't dream of missing this ball."

Conversation within the carriage was scanty after this *non sequitur.* The drive was not a long one, however, and soon a crush of other carriages warned the two cousins that they were nearing the Seftons' town house. Miss Wentworth bestirred herself to gather up shawl, fan, and reticule. She and Sir Richard were eventually delivered to the entrance of the great house, ablaze with lights from cellars to attic. After being admitted, they made their way through the crowd toward their hostess, who was receiving at the entrance to the ballroom. A minute or so was spent exchanging civilities with Lady Sefton, and then they turned their attention toward finding Lady Ingleside, Henrietta's mother. Miss Wentworth also searched the ballroom for the face of Lord Russelton. She was relieved not to see him, and drew an involuntary sigh of relief; really, things were coming to a sad pass when one rejoiced at the absence of one's own betrothed! Presently, Sir Richard spied Lady Ingleside. They jostled their way through the throng to where she and her daughter sat, at the edge of the dance floor.

Lady Ingleside was a plump, jolly-looking lady with a round, good-natured face. Her daughter, the Honourable Miss Henrietta Ingleside, was a pretty blue-eyed brunette, with a suspicion of her mother's tendency toward plumpness. While Sir Richard and Henrietta greeted each other affectionately, Miss Wentworth seated herself beside the Inglesides and kept an anxious watch on the doors of the ballroom.

"And where is Lord Russelton tonight, Miss Wentworth?" Lady Ingleside inquired of her playfully. "Surely he doesn't intend to let you out of his sight with all these other handsome young bucks about. Serve him right if one of them stole you away!"

"I believe Frederick will be attending tonight, Lady Ingleside, but he is coming later, with Lady Russelton and Lady Cassandra."

Henrietta gave Miss Wentworth a curious, rather knowing look that made Miss Wentworth rage inwardly. Every day her situation was growing obvious to more and more people. She must think of something to do about her farce of an engagement, and think of it fast! Fortunately, she was not put to the trouble of thinking up more replies to Lady Ingleside's questions. The first dance began; Miss Wentworth's hand was at once solicited, and she and her partner took their places in the set along with Sir Richard and Henrietta. It was a relief to be dancing, and to know that her reputation had not yet sunk so low that she could not obtain a partner.

Miss Wentworth continued to keep a sharp watch on the ballroom doors while she danced. Lord Russelton failed to appear, but during the course of the dance her attention was caught and held by an unfamiliar face among the later arrivals entering the room. She examined the newcomer out of the corner of her eye with a good deal of interest. When the dance ended, she sought information from Henrietta, who was in her third Season and therefore an authority on London society, in Miss Wentworth's less-experienced eyes.

"Who? Over where?" Henrietta scanned the faces by the ballroom doors. Her blue eyes widened. "Oh, my dear! Why, that's Lord Stanford, the one they call the Wicked Earl. Imagine seeing him here. He doesn't go much into society anymore. Polite society, that is!"

"The Wicked Earl?" Miss Wentworth looked curiously at the gentleman standing near the doorway. "Why do they call him that, Henrietta?"

"Well, they *used* to call him the Dark-Haired Adonis, when he first came to London years ago. He is a handsome creature, isn't he?"

"Yes," agreed Miss Wentworth fervently. And knows it, too, she added to herself, watching the arrogant way the Earl was surveying the ballroom and its occupants.

"They do say, although it happened before *my* time, of course—" Henrietta embarked on a long and scandalous tale of the Earl's wrongdoings, to which Miss Wentworth lent only half an ear; she was absorbed in watching the Earl himself as he made his way through the crowd. He was tall, taller than most of the other gentlemen in the ballroom, and his shoulders were broad, tapering to narrow hips. His build was that of a member of the Corinthian set, and there was an athletic grace about the way he moved, suggestive of powerful force held in check. Yet self-restraint was not a quality generally associated with the Earl of Stanford, if Henrietta was to be believed.

"—and Belinda Satterthwaite, a few seasons before I was presented! My dear, it was such a *scandal*—"

His hair was heavy, and black as a raven's wing, and his face was wonderfully attractive, strong and square-jawed with handsome, clear-cut features. At least, he would have been attractive, had his face not been disfigured by that look of arrogant boredom, Miss Wentworth decided.

"—and they ended up marrying her off to some cousin in the country, but of course everyone *knew*—"

He was dressed in black evening clothes, and the severe simplicity of his attire made every other gentleman in the room look positively shabby.

"—but they say she ended up losing the baby after all, and really it's just as well, of course. And they say now that he and Lady Rosamund . . ." Henrietta raised her eyebrows expressively. "I expect that's why Lord Stanford's here tonight. Look at Lady Rosamund over there, staring at him."

Miss Wentworth dragged her eyes from the Earl of Stanford and looked at the lady whom Henrietta had indicated. Lady Rosamund was a statuesque, black-haired beauty robed in shimmering claret silk, and she was indeed staring at the Earl with painful intensity. She made an imperious gesture with her hand, beckoning him toward her. Miss Wentworth looked back at the Earl to see how he would react to the summons. If anything, he looked more disdainful than ever; he gave Lady Rosamund a cool nod and resumed his survey of the dance floor.

"Well, did you see that?" gasped Henrietta. "He practically cut her. She looks mad as fire about it, too!"

Sparks were quite visibly shooting from Lady Rosamund's dark eyes. Miss Wentworth was so intrigued by the little drama she was witnessing that she forgot her own concerns and never even noticed the arrival of the Russelton party. It was with a start, then, that she discovered her fiancé to be standing at her side, accompanied by his mother Lady Russelton and his grandmother, the redoubtable Lady Cassandra.

Tonight, Lady Cassandra was arrayed in an impressive toilette of stiff purple taffeta, worn over hoops and cut after the fashion of her youth, some forty years ago. Plumes nodded atop her turban of purple velvet. Lady Russelton, her daughter-in-law and Lord Russelton's mother, faded into insignificance beside Lady Cassandra's magnificence, though Lady Russelton was not a woman who would have drawn much attention in any setting; she was a small, mousy woman with a perpetually apprehensive look on her face.

Before her marriage to a mere baron, Lady Cassandra had been the daughter of a duke, and she greeted Miss Wentworth with all the condescension natural to one born to such great estate. "Ah, Miss Wentworth: you're looking well tonight, m'dear. That's a pretty dress you're wearing. Don't care much for this modern fashion of wearing your waist up to your armpits, but you carry it off very well. Very well indeed." Lady Cassandra nodded twice or thrice with lofty approval.

Lady Russelton took advantage of this temporary lull to murmur a greeting in her soft voice. She then began inquiring after the health of Miss Wentworth's aunt and mother, but was immediately interrupted by her mother-in-law.

"Yes, yes, May, but you don't need to bore poor Miss Wentworth with all that right now, prosing on forever in such a way. I daresay she and Frederick are itching to take the floor. I am, myself, and would, too, if I were only twenty years younger! I see Ella Darcy over there. Come along, May, we must find out if she really plans to marry her eldest daughter off to that old *roué* of a Haversham." The dowager hurried off in search of the latest *on-dit* with a rustle of purple taffeta skirts. The crowd parted respectfully before her as she advanced. Her hapless daughter-in-law trailed after, bearing shawls, fans, smelling bottles, and all the other accouterments of the *grande dame*.

"Well, Rebecca, I suppose we may as well dance," said Lord Russelton in a distant voice, his eyes fixed on a point somewhere over Miss Wentworth's head.

"Why, thank you, Frederick. I would be delighted to dance with you," said Miss Wentworth sweetly.

It was a country dance, for which Miss Wentworth was grateful. There was little opportunity for conversation amid the energetic movements of the dance; a good thing, too, as her partner made no attempt to converse at all. The affianced couple went through the figures in perfect silence. Miss Wentworth studied her fiancé throughout, wondering how things could have gone so wrong, so suddenly.

Lord Russelton was a handsome young man of medium height and slender build. His hair was dark and his eyes blue—a rather light, shallow blue, Miss Wentworth suddenly discovered, looking at him with critical eyes for the first time in their acquaintance. And how had she never noticed before that his eyes were set too close together? Tonight, as always, Lord Russelton was dressed in the height of fashion. His starched shirtpoints reached his ears, he sported a fearfully and wonderfully tied neckcloth, his blue coat had a nipped-in waist and large brass buttons, and a handful of fobs dangled from his waistcoat. In her present critical mood, it struck Miss Wentworth that all these extravagances (which she had rather admired at one time) appeared almost gaudy beside the quiet elegance of . . . well, say the Earl of Stanford, for instance.

Miss Wentworth abandoned her study of Lord Russelton and looked about the ballroom for the Wicked Earl. He was not among the dancers taking part in the country dance. She finally located him talking to another gentleman, on the fringes of the ballroom. Yes, he might be a terrible rake, but he certainly knew how to dress. He cast the other gentlemen around him into the shade, though being so very tall and handsome he naturally possessed something of an unfair advantage. The Earl's severely tailored black coat would not have flattered Lord Russelton; Miss Wentworth reflected with malicious satisfaction that poor Frederick really needed all that padding in the shoulders to cut any kind of a figure at all.

The country dance came to an end at last. Lord Russelton delivered Miss Wentworth back to Lady Ingleside and left her there without saying a single word. Miss Wentworth sat down beside her chaperone and fanned herself, trying not to look as angry as she felt.

"My dear, I couldn't help noticing," whispered Henrietta, leaning over to squeeze Miss Wentworth's arm. "Noticing that you and Frederick are at outs, I mean. Is it a lovers' quarrel?"

"No, I—" It occurred to Miss Wentworth that this would make a fine excuse for the visibly strained relations between Lord Russelton and herself. "Not exactly," she modified cautiously.

"I know precisely how you feel." Henrietta looked sympathetic. "You may not believe it, but even Richard and I have had our quarrels. We had one a few months back, about the stupidest thing! The costume I was wearing to a masquerade, if you can credit it, my dear. We didn't speak to each other for nearly a week. Men can be so trying. Just look at Frederick over there; I believe he's trying to make you jealous by flirting with that odious Clarissa Barrow. Well! I wouldn't let him get away with it if I were you."

"What would you do, Henrietta?" asked Miss Wentworth with interest.

"I'd flirt with the handsomest gentleman in the room, and show him that what's sauce for the goose is sauce for the gander!"

Miss Wentworth's eyes promptly flew off in search of the Earl of Stanford. She could not find him anywhere in the ballroom, however, and when she realized what she was doing, she took herself to task. He might be handsome—undoubtedly he was handsome—but he was also a complete stranger. You don't know him, she chided herself, and with his reputation it's probably just as well. Although there could be no question that he was the handsomest gentleman in the room, as Miss Wentworth concluded after scrutinizing every other gentleman with pretensions to the title. "There's Mr. Fanton," she said doubtfully. "He's handsome enough, but I don't think it would make Frederick jealous if I flirted with him. Everyone knows he's a perfect moonling."

"You try it and see," advised Henrietta. "Frederick's been taking you for granted, that's what the trouble is. If it looks as though you're slipping away from him, he'll realize how much he wants you and come after you. Men never know they want a thing until it looks as if they can't have it."

Miss Wentworth considered. If Lord Russelton was dissatisfied with her marriage portion, as she feared to be the case, then no amount of flirtation was likely to do any good. On the other hand, he had really seemed to love her at one time, and a spark of love might still remain unextinguished. Perhaps Henrietta's suggestion would help to fan the flames. But did Miss Wentworth really want her fiancé back?

She didn't, really, she assured herself, but it would be gratifying to have Frederick at her feet once more, if only to have the pleasure of turning around and spurning him once he was there. In any case, it could do no harm to encourage other gentlemen.

"I'll do it," she decided aloud. "If I can find someone who'll flirt with me, that is."

Henrietta snorted. "You goose! With your face, you need not worry. Just smile nicely at Mr. Fanton, and he'll be over here in a trice."

Mr. Jeremy Fanton was a youthful sprig of fashion, undeniably handsome but not renowned for intelligence. He had golden curls worn *à la chérubin,* a clefted chin, and eyes of a soft blue, and despite his lack of mental attainments he was rather a favorite with the ladies. Encountering a dazzling smile from Miss Wentworth, Mr. Fanton blinked and smiled back tentatively. Then an unsettling thought occurred to him. He looked around to see if perhaps the smile had been directed toward some other gentleman, but there seemed to be no other likely candidate about. Was it really he that was so honored? He looked back at Miss Wentworth and received a second, still more encouraging smile, accompanied by a gesture of the hand that even Mr. Fanton's feeble intellect recognized as a clear summons. As though pulled by a powerful magnet, Mr. Fanton was drawn across the ballroom to Miss Wentworth's side.

"Miss Wentworth," he said reverently. "Did you—was it me you wanted?"

"Mr. Fanton!" Miss Wentworth held out both her hands and bestowed another brilliant smile upon him. "I was hoping you might be here tonight. You're such a marvelous dancer, Mr. Fanton, and I did so enjoy dancing with you at Almack's last night!"

This heavy-handed hint found its object. Mr. Fanton immediately invited Miss Wentworth to be his partner in the cotillion that was about to begin. She accepted, and the two went out to take their places on the dance floor.

Mr. Fanton tried to think of what he could have done to earn such a signal honor. He knew his dancing to be nothing out of the ordinary; in fact, he still had difficulty remembering the figures of the quadrille, and he rather thought he had trod upon Miss Wentworth's foot once or twice the evening before. No, it couldn't be his dancing that had brought him this sudden admiration. It had to be his new coat. He'd never gone to Stultz for his coats before, and he'd had some doubts about the set of the shoulders when he'd put this new coat on tonight, but by Jove, if such an out-and-outer as Miss Wentworth was smiling at him and showering him with compliments—and she'd never noticed him to speak of, before tonight—well, he was dashed if he wouldn't order all his coats from Stultz from now on. "Do you like my new coat, Miss Wentworth?" he inquired with an ingratiating smile, congratulating himself upon his own powers of perception.

"What?" Miss Wentworth had been observing her fiancé for possible signs of jealousy.

"My coat—do you like it?"

"Oh. Oh, yes, very nice." Miss Wentworth wondered what Mr. Fanton was thinking of, maundering on and on about his coat, for heaven's sake. Really, it was hopeless to expect Frederick to be jealous of such an idiot. But Miss Wentworth was in general a kind-hearted girl, despite her recent thirstings for violent revenge. She listened with well-feigned interest as Mr. Fanton described the agonies he had suffered in weighing the relative merits of Bath cloth and superfine, and the exact size and style of buttons that had been decided upon after hours of soul-searching. Miss Wentworth was not sorry when the dance ended. As far as she could tell, Frederick had never even looked in her direction. He and Miss Barrow had sat out the cotillion together, and seemed to be involved in an intimate discussion that necessitated a great deal of hand pressing and the exchange of any number of meaningful looks. It would obviously take more than a cotillion with Jeremy Fanton to get his attention.

After the cotillion, Miss Wentworth dismissed Mr. Fanton kindly but firmly. He drifted away, disappointed without really being surprised. It was too much to expect such an unprecedented piece of good fortune to continue.

The next dance was a waltz. Being relatively new to London society, Miss Wentworth had not yet obtained the permission of Almack's autocratic patronesses to engage in that daring dance. Henrietta went out to waltz with Sir Richard, and she was left sitting beside Lady Ingleside, who was absorbed in conversation with the hatchet-faced dowager sitting at her left. Miss Wentworth had never felt more alone. During the Little Season of the year before, Lord Russelton had always sat with her during the waltzes, keeping her company and sharing her indignation at the unreasonable rules that kept young ladies from enjoying the most intoxicating dance of all. Now, without a word of apology, he was leading out Clarissa Barrow. Miss Wentworth's cup was dangerously close to overflowing. She looked about for a means to occupy herself; anything, so that the gossips wouldn't see her sitting alone and miserable while her fiancé waltzed with another woman.

Her desperate eyes fastened upon the broad-shouldered, black-coated figure of the Earl of Stanford moving through the crowd surrounding the dance floor. He would be directly behind her chair in a moment. Really, it looked remarkably like Providence.

Without further reflection, Miss Wentworth let her fan slide from her hand, to land at the Earl of Stanford's feet.

Chapter Three

The Earl stooped to retrieve the trifle of embroidered white silk lying on the floor. "I believe this is yours, ma'am?"

"Oh, yes!" Miss Wentworth rose to her feet and prepared her most dazzling smile. "I can't think how—"

The words died on her lips. The Earl was smiling at her—a rather ironic smile—and as his eyes met hers, she was conscious of a sensation like a physical blow, somewhere near the pit of her stomach. At the same time, she found her mind registering a whole array of distinct and conflicting emotions. Part of her was occupied in noticing that the Earl's eyes were brown, with golden flecks, and that with a smile on his face he was really indecently handsome, the handsomest gentleman she had ever seen or imagined; another part of her intellect was recognizing with indignation that there was a good deal of mockery in his smile; and an inner voice, possibly her conscience, was whispering, "*Now* you've done it." She became aware that the Earl was speaking to her and she gathered her scattered wits.

"You had better put it around your wrist."

"What?"

"Your fan," said the Earl patiently. Miss Wentworth looked down to where the fan still lay in her outstretched hand. "You had better put the cord around your wrist." The Earl repossessed himself of the fan and slipped the silken cord over Miss Wentworth's hand in its white kid glove. He is touching my hand, she thought, watching as his fingers deftly looped the cord around her wrist. The Earl laid the fan in her hand and closed her unresisting fingers over it. "It really wouldn't do to drop the handkerchief—or the fan—twice in one evening, you know," he said, with gentle mockery.

"Oh!" Miss Wentworth felt color suffuse her cheeks. "I thank you, sir," she said coldly. She seated herself beside Lady Ingleside with a flounce of anger, but though she steadfastly refused to look at him again, she was very much aware that the Earl lingered beside her for a moment longer before giving a short laugh and walking away.

The waltz ended. Henrietta and Sir Richard returned to Lady Ingleside, and Sir Richard invited his cousin to stand up with him in the dance that was forming. Miss Wentworth was still occupied in ruing her own behavior, and resenting that of the Earl of Stanford, but she roused herself from her meditations and accepted her cousin's invitation. She and Sir Richard took their places on the ballroom floor.

"I say, Beck—"

"My name is Rebecca!" snapped Miss Wentworth, whose nerves were still disordered after her encounter with the Earl.

Sir Richard looked a bit startled. "I mean Rebecca. Dash it, it's just a habit, Beck—Rebecca! Now you've gone and made me forget what I was going to say." He was silent for a moment as they went through the figures of the dance, his forehead wrinkled in thought. "Got it," he said at last. "Stanford: saw you talking to him while I was dancing with Henri. What's that fellow been saying to you?"

"I merely dropped my fan, and he was . . . *kind* enough to retrieve it for me."

"Don't you have anything to do with him, Beck! Rebecca, I mean," advised Sir Richard. "Not at all the sort of fellow you want to know."

"You need not worry, Richard. I don't want to know him. I thought him quite odious," said Miss Wentworth, with unnecessary violence.

Sir Richard looked relieved. "Well, that's all right, then. Didn't know but what—however, that's neither here nor there. Thought Russelton was looking mighty queer about it, though, and thought I'd drop a word in your ear."

"Frederick was looking upset?" The fan strategem had been expressly formulated to annoy Lord Russelton, but somehow Miss Wentworth had never once thought to look in his direction while the conversation with the Earl was taking place. Thinking again of Lord Stanford's mocking smile, she felt again a contraction in the pit of her stomach. "You think Frederick minded my speaking to Lord Stanford?"

"Lord, yes! Stands to reason. I'd have something to say if I saw Henri talking to him, I'll tell you that!"

Miss Wentworth began to feel a little better. The amusement on the Earl's face had been as infuriating as it was embarrassing; he obviously suspected her of setting her cap at him. Dropping the handkerchief, indeed! Nothing could have been further from the truth, thought Miss Wentworth indignantly. But if she had managed to annoy Frederick, perhaps it had been worth the mortification.

Without conscious thought, she once more looked around the ballroom until she finally discovered the Earl, now in conversation with Lady Sefton. As if he felt her regard, he looked up, and his eyes met hers for an instant. Much to her annoyance, she felt herself blush again.

John Gerald Cedric Collingwood, eighth Earl of Stanford, Viscount Southland, and Baron D'Amont, had almost decided that the evening was going to be a total loss. Even as he had dressed for the Seftons' ball, he had wondered at himself. The decorous entertainments of the *haut ton* weren't his usual choices for diversion, but Rosamund had been so insistent that—like a fool—he'd given in. There had been more than a hint of promise in her dark eyes, and more than a suggestion, too, that if he met her at this ball he might have her to himself all evening, and possibly longer . . . and then he'd arrived at the Seftons' to find Hallcroft already solidly established at her side, and with her husband in attendance as well, for God's sake. Rumor had it that Hallcroft was another supplicant for Lady Rosamund's favors. The Earl had a good mind to abandon the field, leaving Hallcroft in sole possession, and good luck to him; he himself had been laying siege to the lady for nearly two months, and damned little had he received to show for it. Really, Rosamund put altogether too high a value on her own charms.

It had been amusing at first, vying for her smiles, and he'd had reason to believe himself the favorite, but the way Rosamund was blowing first hot and then cold was beginning to pall upon him. After weeks of pursuit, the Earl felt he could reasonably expect a more tangible reward than smiles, half-promises, and a few stolen kisses. Rosamund needed a lesson. His blood boiled when he thought of the way she'd beckoned him across the ballroom as if he were a damned lackey. It had almost been enough to decide him to shake the dust of the Seftons from his feet then and there, and seek amusement elsewhere. Out of respect for his host and hostess, he had stayed on a little longer, but he had actually been on his way to the door when the green-eyed girl with the flowers in her hair had thrown her fan at his feet.

The Earl stood near the door of the ballroom, looking back across the floor to where Miss Wentworth sat beside her chaperone. That bit of byplay with the fan had been no accident, of course. He'd been on the town long enough to recognize a dead set when he saw it. But the girl would find herself catching cold at her game; at this late date he wasn't about to be caught by yet another miss in pursuit of his title, and he made it a point not to amuse himself with girls out of the schoolroom, even when they were beauties.

And there was no doubt about the girl's beauty.

She had the most amazing eyes . . . the thought of green eyes struck a chord of recognition in his memory, and the Earl frowned. Surely the girl must be Miss Wentworth, the one they called the Green-Eyed Incomparable? Several of his acquaintances had bored him very much last season on the subject of the divine Miss Wentworth. There'd been some talk about an engagement, too. Young Russelton, wasn't it? He surveyed the crowded ballroom and soon espied Lord Russelton waltzing with Miss Barrow. The Earl smiled, the first genuine amusement he had felt all evening. He thought he could judge pretty accurately the emotions surging behind Miss Wentworth's lovely face. Being fresh out of the schoolroom, she was still at the mercy of the stiff-necked Almack's patronesses and forbidden to waltz. It must be galling for such an out-and-out beauty to see her fiancé spinning around the floor while she was consigned to sit by with the dowagers. It seemed, too, that he'd heard some talk at the club about Russelton trying to sheer off from the match and take up with some heiress or other instead. Well, that explained it: the business with the fan had been an effort to make the fiancé jealous.

The Earl eyed Miss Wentworth speculatively. He had half a mind to oblige her at the game. It would suit his own purposes as well, for it hadn't escaped him that Rosamund had looked sick with jealousy even during the short time it had taken him to return the Wentworth girl's fan. Rosamund had already shown signs of jealousy on earlier occasions, and it now struck the Earl that this possessiveness was annoying, and premature, too, under the circumstances. Yes, it would definitely be worthwhile to follow up Miss Wentworth's invitation. He'd be killing several birds with one stone: teaching Rosamund a salubrious lesson about playing fast and loose with the Earl of Stanford, obliging a damsel in distress, and incidentally furthering an acquaintance with a more than usually attractive young lady. The Earl set off in search of his hostess.

"The Wentworth girl?" Lady Sefton frowned. "Now, Stanford, what do you want with her? She's just out of the schoolroom, not your style at all. If you mean to—"

"I only want to dance with her, Maria." The Earl gave Lady Sefton his most winning smile. "I feel sorry for her, sitting by while other young ladies waltz.

You're a patroness; you need only say the word to grant her permission. Will you do it, Maria?"

"Her chaperone wouldn't thank me." Lady Sefton continued to regard the Earl sternly. "And she's engaged to young Lord Russelton, you know. Surely you don't—"

"My intentions are honorable, I assure you." The Earl laughed at his hostess's look of skepticism. "Truly, a dance—a waltz—is all I want of the young lady, if you will only present me as a desirable partner."

"This isn't Almack's, Stanford. I doubt I should oblige you. The other patronesses will think it odd."

"I am persuaded that if you give the nod, Maria, all will be well."

"Hm . . ." Lady Sefton looked unconvinced. "Well . . . she has always seemed a well-behaved girl, to be sure . . . her manners are as pretty as her face. I really don't have any objection to giving her the sanction to waltz, I suppose."

"I thank you, Maria."

"But I still have doubts about your intentions, Stanford!"

"You need not. I promise to be a pattern-card of propriety on this occasion. Please, Maria? Oblige me in this, and I will be your slave for life."

Stronger women than Lady Sefton had succumbed to the Earl's smile. She hesitated, sighed, and then smiled back. "Well, I'll do it, Stanford, but as I said, her chaperone won't thank me. Kindly refrain from doing anything to make me regret my good nature! And since I am doing you a favor, you must agree to do me one in return."

"Anything!"

"You must honor us at Almack's with your presence now and then."

"Done," said the Earl promptly. "I will be there Wednesday night, and I promise to dance with all the plainest damsels in the room."

Lady Sefton laughed, and dealt the Earl a playful rap across the knuckles with her fan. While they waited for the dance in progress to come to an end, the Earl looked about for Miss Wentworth. He eventually located her on the dance floor with her cousin, and observed with amusement that she blushed when he caught her eye. Really, it promised to be an enjoyable evening after all.

The dance ended at last. After Richard had returned her to her chaperone, he and Henrietta had gone off together, and Miss Wentworth was left sitting beside Lady Ingleside, abandoned once more. Lord Russelton had sat beside Clarissa Barrow during the last dance, and now he was leading Miss Barrow onto the floor for a second waltz, just as he had done at Almack's the night before. Miss Wentworth was distracted from her fiancé's treacherous behavior, however, by the sight of Lady Sefton and the Earl of Stanford bearing down upon her.

"Miss Wentworth?"

Miss Wentworth rose to her feet, an uncertain smile on her face. She fixed her gaze upon Lady Sefton, having no wish to meet again the Earl's mocking dark eyes, but she was uncomfortably aware of those eyes all the same. "Yes, Lady Sefton?"

"Miss Wentworth, I would like to introduce to you a friend of mine, Lord Stanford: a great scamp, I fear, but he has faithfully promised to behave himself this evening. Stanford, allow me to present Miss Wentworth."

Lady Sefton leaned forward and addressed Miss Wentworth in a loud stage whisper. "Should he fail to keep his word, only let me know, my dear, and I'll have him thrown out on his ear!" Lady Sefton's words were accompanied by a threatening gesture with her fan; the Earl raised one hand as though to ward off the blow and grinned broadly. "There is a waltz beginning now, and you children have my permission to join it. Remember, Stanford, you are in my debt." Lady Sefton smiled, rapped the Earl across the knuckles again by way of reminder, and bustled off to greet some late arriving guests.

"Shall we dance, Miss Wentworth?"

As if in a trance, Miss Wentworth took his arm and let him lead her onto the floor. Lady Ingleside half rose to her feet, looking after Miss Wentworth with a ludicrous mixture of alarm and perplexity on her round face. What was Maria Sefton about, introducing Stanford of all people to little Miss Wentworth? Lady Ingleside very much feared she had just failed in her duty as chaperone. Images of lambs and wolves ran through her mind, followed by an equally disturbing vision of Constance Wentworth's probable reaction.

Still, it was only a dance after all, and Miss Wentworth safely betrothed to that nice young Lord Russelton, so perhaps it didn't much matter; Maria Sefton had done the introductions, too, making it awkward to interfere. Lady Ingleside shrugged her plump shoulders, settled comfortably back in her chair, and hoped news of the incident would never reach Lady Wentworth's fastidious ears.

Dancing with the Earl of Stanford proved even more disconcerting to Miss Wentworth's feelings than the incident with the fan, earlier that evening. She had never waltzed in public before. Her sole experience had been with the dancing master at her school, and since that gentleman was in his sixties there had been nothing terribly exciting about waltzing with *him.* But waltzing with the Earl of Stanford was an entirely different proposition. She was aware of his hand resting disturbingly on her waist, and of his dark eyes looking down at her, filling her with such confusion that she could scarcely concentrate upon the steps of the dance. She wondered why the Earl had chosen her as his partner. After the way he had spoken to her when he had returned her fan, she had been certain that he thought her disgustingly forward. Even the remembrance made her cringe; she found she could not bear to have him think it had been done as a gambit to get his attention. Drawing a deep breath, Miss Wentworth raised her eyes to the Earl's face.

"Lord Stanford! I daresay you wondered at me earlier, when I . . . when my fan . . ."

"When your fan landed at my feet? Yes, I'll admit I did wonder at the time if you might not have had an ulterior motive!"

"Well, I did. But it was not what you think, my lord! Indeed, I really was not trying to—trying to scrape an acquaintance, although I can see it may have looked that way."

"You devastate me, Miss Wentworth." The Earl grinned down at her. "But this confession actually comes as no surprise to me. I believe I have a tolerably clear idea of the situation. Your fiancé—Russelton, is it not? Lord Russelton was not being properly attentive, and I was the instrument you chose to recall him to a sense of his duty."

Miss Wentworth bit her lip. It was bad enough to be

thought bold, but even worse to have her private affairs appear so obvious to a perfect stranger. "Yes," she admitted. "It was a stupid, ill-natured thing to do, I suppose."

The Earl studied Miss Wentworth, his eyes flickering over her in a way that made her face grow warm. "You don't look stupid, Miss Wentworth . . . and you certainly don't look ill-natured. Under the circumstances, I think you were perfectly justified in your actions. Russelton's a fool, neglecting you for that bucolic blond charmer he's been flirting with all evening." The Earl turned his head to look at Miss Barrow, then resumed his inspection of Miss Wentworth. "You're far prettier than she is. And your figure is better, too."

Miss Wentworth regarded the Earl for a moment. "Thank you?" she said doubtfully.

"No, no! You must not thank me for such a shocking piece of impertinence. A heavy setdown is what I deserve."

Miss Wentworth laughed. The Earl observed with interest the dimple that flickered beside her mouth. "First you say something shockingly impertinent . . . then you *tell* me it was shockingly impertinent . . . and then you advise me to give you a setdown? I don't understand your reasoning, my lord."

"I was trying to make you blush," explained the Earl, and was delighted to see Miss Wentworth's cheeks turn pink. "Yes, exactly like that. Your strategy is working admirably, Miss Wentworth."

"What strategy?" said Miss Wentworth, confused.

"Why, your strategy to make Russelton jealous, of course. He's looking daggers at me this very minute."

Miss Wentworth stole a glance in Lord Russelton's

direction. "Yes, he does look annoyed, doesn't he?" she said with satisfaction.

"And we could make him even more annoyed." The Earl's eyes rested on her speculatively, and the hand on her waist seemed to tighten. "If Russelton's this upset seeing you dance with me, imagine how jealous he'd be if he saw you kissing me! Come, what do you say, Miss Wentworth? Don't you think it a splendid notion?"

"Certainly not, my lord."

"What, don't you want to kiss me?" The Earl's face assumed a hurt expression that was belied by the laughter in his eyes. "Not even out of curiosity?"

"No!" Yet Miss Wentworth was aware of a definite stirring of curiosity. What would it be like to kiss the Wicked Earl? The thought was exciting, like forbidden fruit: tantalizing, but out of the question, of course. Miss Wentworth shook her head in an unconscious effort to rid herself of the idea. "You will force me to give you that setdown after all, my lord," she said.

The Earl laughed, showing white teeth in his devastating smile, and again Miss Wentworth felt a distinct lurch in the region of her stomach. What was there about the man that elicited such a powerful response? The sensation was unsettling, and it should have been a relief when the waltz ended, but it was not: Miss Wentworth was conscious only of disappointment. The Earl led her back to Lady Ingleside and bowed over her hand.

"A delightful dance, Miss Wentworth," he said, smiling down at her. Miss Wentworth dreamily noted the way the corners of his eyes crinkled up when he smiled, not a mocking smile as before, but a friendly, rather conspiratorial smile, infinitely attractive. He carried her gloved hand to his lips and kissed it, then stood aside as another gentleman of her acquaintance claimed her for the quadrille that was forming.

Miss Wentworth heard scarcely a word of her partner's conversation during that quadrille. Her mind was busy going over and over what the Earl had said, and how he had looked, during their waltz together. Undoubtably Lord Stanford was an outrageous flirt, but Miss Wentworth was acquainted with several other flirts equally outrageous, and dismissing the whole episode as meaningless flirtation did not account for the turmoil that arose in her breast whenever the Earl of Stanford so much as looked at her. It was a sensation hitherto unknown in her experience. Even Lord Russelton, when he was still Prince Charming, had never affected her in such a way. Such a physical way . . .

Rather shocked by the trend of her thoughts, Miss Wentworth determined not to think about the Earl of Stanford anymore. She made an attempt to concentrate instead upon what her partner was saying, but her mind kept losing the thread of the conversation and returning to the same absorbing subject.

One way and another, the Earl had given her a good deal to think about. She had found his quickness of understanding nearly as impressive as his outstanding good looks. From the very first he had seemed to see right through her; her motives had been detected and dragged out into the open before she could so much as open her mouth to explain. It was humiliating to have had her schemes laid bare in so unceremonious a manner, but it had also been almost a relief not to have had to pretend for once; why, the Earl had even indicated a willingness to assist her in straightening her tangled affairs, although it was unlikely that his motives were altogether selfless. Miss Wentworth wondered what exactly his motives might be. Did he think to use her as he had used Belinda Satterthwaite, the girl Henrietta had told her about? Well, if that was his intention, he would find Rebecca Wentworth to be made of sterner stuff. There was no harm in flirting a bit with the Earl of Stanford, but she was not about to let his very considerable charm lead her into mischief.

While Miss Wentworth was formulating these strong-minded resolves, her cousin Sir Richard was making repeated attempts to catch her eye. Happening to glance his way at last, Miss Wentworth encountered a darkling look that warned her a lecture was in the offing. She sighed heavily, causing her partner to wonder anxiously if he was boring her. Richard must have noticed her waltzing with Lord Stanford; she recalled, too late, her cousin's instructions to have nothing to do with the Earl. Miss Wentworth's thoughts took a different turn now, as she began to prepare her defense. She had been the recipient of one or two of Sir Richard's lectures in the past, but fortunately there were several points in her favor on this occasion. Lady Sefton herself had introduced her to the Earl, and surely there was nothing scandalous about dancing one dance with him if an Almack's patroness could think it an eligible thing to do. The quadrille ended, and Miss Wentworth's partner took her back to Lady Ingleside. Sir Richard was waiting for her there.

"Beck, I want a word with you," he said in a forbidding voice. "Let's take a walk to the refreshment saloon, shall we?"

"Oh, Richard, that's a splendid idea," cried Miss Wentworth, sinking into her seat and fanning herself vigorously. "But really, I am quite fatigued after that endless quadrille. If you are going to the refreshment room, perhaps you would be so kind as to fetch me back some punch?"

"Yes, Richard, I'm thirsty, too, now that I think of it," said Henrietta. "This ballroom is stifling."

Lady Ingleside thought that she, too, could use a glass of punch, since Sir Richard had been kind enough to suggest it. Sir Richard champed his teeth for a moment and then stomped off to the refreshment saloon. As soon as he had returned with the punch, Miss Wentworth seized a glass, drained it, and handed it back to her cousin with a sweet, apologetic smile.

"That was delicious, Richard. But . . . would you mind very much, refilling my glass? I seem to be exceedingly thirsty this evening."

Her cousin's jaw tightened ominously. He looked at Miss Wentworth, and then at the empty glass in his hand, and after a moment a trace of reluctant amusement appeared on his face. Without a murmur he left the ballroom, returning presently with the refilled glass. "You win, Beck," he said in a low voice, placing it in her hand. "I won't rake you down right now. I haven't time, for one thing, because I promised this next dance to Lucy Waite. But mind you save me a dance later on. I have something to say to you, as you very well know!"

"Yes, Richard," said Miss Wentworth submissively, resigning herself to the prospect of a most disagreeable dance.

Henrietta, meanwhile, had engaged the empty-headed Mr. Fanton in conversation, and presently the two of them went out to take their places in the set that was forming. Sir Richard was already on the dance floor with Lucy Waite. Miss Wentworth looked about to find herself a partner and saw Lord Russelton leading out

Miss Barrow. Her eyes widened. Surely this was the third time he'd danced with Clarissa Barrow this evening? She calculated rapidly: yes, two waltzes, and now this cotillion. Miss Wentworth's breast swelled with indignation. To dance three times with the same partner was outrageous behavior, certain to raise a storm of criticism. Already a number of dowagers were gazing at Lord Russelton and Miss Barrow with marked disapproval. It was only a matter of time before eyes turned toward Miss Wentworth, to see how she was enjoying the sight of her fiancé going beyond the bounds of all propriety and making a spectacle of himself with the shipping heiress.

Miss Wentworth knew a craven urge to turn and flee the ballroom. Or would it be better to find a partner and act as though nothing out of the ordinary was happening? She was frantically trying to decide, when she felt a tap on her shoulder.

"Would you care to dance again, Miss Wentworth?" asked the Earl of Stanford, smiling down at her.

"Yes!" Miss Wentworth sprang to her feet. "Yes, my lord. I would be delighted to dance with you again."

The Earl began to lead her toward the dance floor, but stopped midway. He looked pointedly at Lord Russelton and Miss Barrow, and then back at Miss Wentworth.

"Or perhaps you would prefer not to dance this set, Miss Wentworth," he said. "The floor seems . . . overcrowded. We might explore the Seftons' conservatory instead." He regarded her blandly. "Or perhaps you would prefer to go out on the terrace for a moment?"

Looking into those dark eyes, Miss Wentworth felt something stir within her. "I believe I could do with some fresh air, my lord," she said demurely.

"The terrace, then. I'll fetch your shawl." The Earl's

words and manner were those of any polite gentleman, but the look in his eyes made Miss Wentworth drop her own. A thrill of excitement went through her. If the Earl tried to kiss her on the terrace—and judging by the look in his eye, she was pretty sure he intended to try—she rather thought she might let him.

The sane, sober part of her knew perfectly well that she was behaving with an imprudence bordering on actual folly, but that strange excitement was there to urge her on, and Miss Wentworth was very angry at her fiancé just then; she had also drunk two glasses of champagne punch in quick succession. None of these circumstances was enough to make her forget that what she was doing was scandalous, but in combination they were enough to make her decide she did not care.

The Earl returned with her shawl. Laying her hand on his arm, Miss Wentworth left the ballroom by his side without a backward glance. She sincerely hoped Frederick Russelton was taking note of her departure.

The Earl steered her down a hallway and past a saloon that held a few elderly couples playing cards, until they came to a set of double doors that led onto the terrace. The Earl held one of the doors open for Miss Wentworth to pass through, and then followed her outside, shutting the door behind him.

The sound of music and laughter from the ballroom grew muffled once the door was shut; only a faint breath of melody came fitfully with the night breeze that stirred the leaves of the trees in the garden. A half moon hung in the sky overhead. The Earl took Miss Wentworth's arm and led her a little way down the terrace. Miss Wentworth searched for something to say to break the silence, but commonplaces about the moon or the Seftons' garden seemed trite now that she was alone with the Earl in the darkness, away from the lights and noisy revelry of the ballroom. She gave a little shiver, not entirely from the cold. The Earl immediately draped the shawl around her and then let his arm rest lightly across her shoulders as they stood together, looking down into the shadowy garden beyond the terrace. Miss Wentworth shivered again, and the arm slid to her waist. When she made no protest, the Earl gently drew her around to face him.

"About that kiss we were discussing earlier," he said.

Miss Wentworth waited, her face upturned. The Earl's mouth came down on hers, lightly at first, and then became demanding in a way that took her by surprise.

Miss Wentworth had been kissed before. There had been a youthful incident with a boy back home in Derbyshire, and since her engagement had been made official she had been kissed several times by her fiancé, as was perfectly proper. She had always thought the pastime overrated, and had secretly wondered what all the fuss was about; now she realized where the danger lay. Clearly there were kisses and kisses! What the Earl was doing to her mouth seemed not so much a kiss as a violation.

Miss Wentworth was so shocked that she was stunned into immobility. When at last she made an effort to pull away, the Earl's arms merely tightened around her, while his mouth continued to assault her own in the same unspeakable manner. Panic arose within her and then, just as abruptly, the panic began to subside, for it had begun to dawn upon her that the sensation was not altogether an unpleasant one. Her own mouth began to respond, hesitantly and then wholeheartedly. At this point, the Earl's hands began to run up and down her back, and Miss Wentworth became aware of a rising excitement within herself, a melting sensation spreading through her body that seemed at the same time to melt away all thought of further resistance. She was filled with warmth, and conscious of a yearning like an aching hunger, which the Earl's kisses had aroused but could not now satisfy. The resulting frustration was unbearable and exquisite at the same time.

She ran her hands experimentally over the Earl's broadcloth-clad back and shoulders, solid and masculine beneath her touch; she twined her fingers in his hair, thick and heavy and yet soft as silk. Even the way he smelled was exciting: clean, as of soap and starched linen, without the sickly scent of the eau-de-cologne that she associated with Frederick. Shamelessly, she cast aside all thought of betrothed and betrothal, and insinuated herself closer within the Earl's arms, aware only of the feel of his body against hers and a rather confused but insistent desire to feel him closer still.

The terrace door squeaked and began to swing open. Miss Wentworth drew in her breath sharply. The Earl at once released her. She watched as he bent down to pick up her shawl, which had slipped to the ground early on and had been lying abandoned ever since. Once more he draped it around her shoulders, and the hands that had been holding her so intimately only a moment before, now touched her as impersonally as if the whole episode had never happened. She looked up at him, her eyes wide and uncertain.

"Alas, my role is played, Miss Wentworth," said the Earl, with regret and a touch of mischief in his voice. "Here is Russelton come to collect you, and not a moment too soon!" Raising his voice for Lord Russelton's benefit, he added, "Now that your escort is here, I'll take myself off. Your servant, Miss Wentworth." He bowed and kissed her hand, nodding casually to Lord Russelton who had come up to stand beside his fiancée. Miss Wentworth watched the Earl walk back into the house through the terrace doors.

"Really, Rebecca!" Lord Russelton's voice was scathing. "What the deuce were you thinking of, coming out here with him? Pretty behavior, upon my word!" He grasped Miss Wentworth's arm none too gently and led her back toward the ballroom, delivering along the way a speech calculated to make any young lady of spirit rebel and break off her engagement forthwith. "Do you understand me, Rebecca?" he demanded, at the conclusion of a fairly thorough denunciation of his fiancée's manners and morals. "By God, I won't tolerate it, and you had better learn now rather than later if we are to go on together."

"What?" Miss Wentworth looked at him blankly.

"I asked if you understood me," said Lord Russelton, with pardonable exasperation. Miss Wentworth continued to look blank. "Did you hear nothing of what I said, then?" he demanded, his voice rising.

"I'm sorry, Frederick." An odd little smile hovered on her lips. "I'm afraid I wasn't listening. What was it you were asking me to understand?" Seeing that Lord Russelton was regarding her with disbelief, Miss Wentworth made an effort to recollect herself and her surroundings. "Was it about your dancing with Clarissa Barrow three times?" she suggested helpfully. "You need not apologize, Frederick. I think it is a silly rule anyway, about not dancing more than twice with the same person. The quizzes were all scandalized, I suppose, but I am not so easily shocked." The smile she gave him was perfectly kindly, but there was an abstracted quality in her voice that made it clear her thoughts were elsewhere.

Lord Russelton was so disgusted that he made no further attempt to berate his betrothed. He escorted her back to her chaperone with an air of strong disapproval that she scarcely seemed to notice.

The evening had gone badly for Lord Russelton. Once more, he had failed in his object. He had thought to be free of his engagement to Rebecca Wentworth long before now, and by this time perhaps even betrothed to Clarissa Barrow, although he rather doubted if Mr. and Mrs. Barrow would allow a second engagement to be announced so soon after his first had been broken off. But they could have had an informal understanding, at least—if it had not been for the obstacle of that first engagement.

It was proving to be a serious obstacle. Naturally, desperate situations called for desperate measures, but from time to time Lord Russelton felt a twinge of guilt over his conduct. It really was a pity about Rebecca. A nice little thing, and pretty as could be, but no dowry to speak of; the way his creditors were hounding him lately, Lord Russelton had come to realize he couldn't afford to tie himself to a nearly portionless girl.

He had reached that conclusion some weeks back, after a particularly painful session with his man of affairs. That gentleman had as good as threatened to reveal the extent of his indebtedness to his grandmother. Horrified, Lord Russelton had protested. In a reasonable but uncompromising voice, the man had pointed out that as a minor, he was legally absolved from paying gambling debts, just as though anyone in their senses could think of not paying debts of honor! Lord Russelton knew he had to pay those vowels; he also knew he had to do it without his grandmother getting wind of his predicament. Lady Cassandra was certain to kick up a fuss if she found he had run so deeply into debt, and if she happened to be in the mood to work herself into one of her occasional towering rages it was possible she might even disinherit him. That would spell financial ruin for him; yet social ruin was equally certain if he failed to pay his debts of honor. The problem boiled down to the difficulty of paying his debts without having recourse to Lady Cassandra. Very delicately, his man of business had suggested that marriage to an heiress might be a possible solution. Lord Russelton had stared at him for a moment, and then had left the office, his head whirling with conjecture.

As though fate had decided to take a hand in his affairs, Clarissa Barrow had driven past in her phaeton as he was walking away from the interview with his man of business. She took him up beside her, and a half hour spent in her company was sufficient to show him that here indeed was a solution, if only he could free himself somehow from that first, rash commitment to Rebecca Wentworth.

This Lord Russelton had steeled himself to do with all possible speed, owing to the urgency of the situation. He had thought out his strategy and had decided that with only a little calculated neglect Rebecca could easily be brought to end the engagement herself. Lord, there'd been a dozen bucks dangling after her last Season; such a beauty would surely turn to one of them instead, if she found her original choice unsatisfactory. Unfortunately, she'd hardly seemed to notice his neglect, and Lord Russelton had been forced to use stronger measures.

This business tonight, for instance, dancing with

Clarissa three times. Lord Russelton was uneasily aware that he might have overstepped the line there. His grandmother had already told him as much, and he winced at the remembrance of her acid tongue and forthright speech. It wouldn't do to fall foul of Lady Cassandra over such a thing. He stood to come in for something truly handsome when the old girl cut up; even with Clarissa's marriage portion in the offing, he wasn't fool enough to whistle his grandmother's fortune down the wind. But it was proving almost impossible to rid himself of Rebecca, further his suit with Clarissa, and all the while keep his grandmother in ignorance of both activities, not to mention the state of his purse.

Nearly at wits' end, Lord Russelton decided it might be time for a change of strategy. Removing himself from London altogether was the best idea he could come up with. His creditors could be fobbed off with promises of payment when he returned, and in his absence Rebecca might get the hint and cry off. It wasn't a perfect solution; Clarissa would be displeased to have him leave town, but he could write to her every day, and he thought he had her firmly enough hooked to risk it. In any event, it seemed a greater risk to remain in London at present. He had already tied himself up with social engagements for the next few weeks, but if Rebecca hadn't made any move by then toward ending the engagement, he'd remove to Norfolk for a while and see how that served.

Already much exercised in mind, Lord Russelton had found a fresh source of worry at Lady Sefton's ball. He had watched with great agitation as Miss Wentworth left the ballroom with the Earl of Stanford. In theory, he was glad to see her encouraging the attentions of other gentlemen, but Stanford, for God's sake! No one could think of the Earl of Stanford as anything like a serious suitor. Seeing them together, Lord Russelton had become possessed of an appalling suspicion, and after finding them in such a suggestive attitude on the terrace, he was unable to banish it from mind.

Was it possible that Rebecca intended to go through with the betrothal, marry him, and then play him false with Stanford after they were wed? Lord Russelton thought it entirely possible, given the character of the parties involved. Everyone knew the Earl of Stanford preferred married flirts. It did seem a trifle incredible to think of Rebecca Wentworth doing such a thing, but Lord Russelton was beginning to think he'd never really known Rebecca. He could have sworn she'd had too much pride to sit by all this time and watch him single out Clarissa.

How simple it would be if only he could do the crying off himself! But it would finish him socially if he tried it, not to mention losing him his grandmother's blunt. Lord Russelton decided to stick with his original strategy for a few weeks longer, after which time he'd retire to Norfolk for a while if things hadn't worked out. He hoped with all his heart that further desperate measures wouldn't be necessary.

Chapter Four

The Earl of Stanford thought it politic to quit the Seftons' ball immediately after Lord Russelton's arrival on the terrace. He took leave of Maria Sefton a bit cautiously, but she had seemed her usual cordial self, so he concluded that she hadn't seen him leave the ballroom with Miss Wentworth. He reflected with amusement that he hadn't exactly lived up to his promise to be a pattern-card of propriety. But it had only been done to oblige the young lady, as the Earl assured himself. Pique, pure and simple: Miss Wentworth had been piqued to see Lord Russelton neglecting her for another girl, and had kissed the Earl of Stanford by way of retaliation. The Earl didn't flatter himself that she gave a rap for him. He was only the means to her ends, and when he had left her on the terrace it had looked as though she had been in a fair way toward achieving those ends. Russelton had come after her hotfoot, and doubtless they were making up their differences even now.

The Earl found himself speculating about the cause of their falling out; had it merely been the usual lovers' quarrel, or was there any truth in the rumor that

Russelton was after an heiress? If he was, Miss Wentworth was likely to find herself grassed. No amount of jealousy would serve her ends under those circumstances, although the Earl thought he would be happy to oblige her if she had further need of his assistance. Really, it had been a very enjoyable kiss . . .

Oh, no, you don't, he reminded himself. After the Belinda Satterthwaite fiasco, he had sworn off unmarried girls forever. He'd paid dearly for that episode, though not as dearly as Belinda herself, poor thing. The Earl wondered if she had found happiness married to her country cousin. He hoped she had; it was incredible to think that what amounted to a moment's madness could have had such far-reaching consequences.

Certainly he himself had paid a high price for his own part in the madness. A number of his acquaintances had cut him after the news became known, and London had been a most uncomfortable place for some time afterwards. He had managed to weather the storm, however, and though he had never ceased to regret the initial misdeed, he could not really regret his subsequent behavior. Any amount of social ostracism was better than being tied for life to Belinda. Pretty, but featherheaded, and wild to a fault; he hadn't been the first by any means, no matter what she had sworn to her parents. It had all been a painful lesson to the young Earl of Stanford. Thereafter he had restricted himself to professional Cyprians and such married ladies as were willing to bestow their favors on men other than their husbands, a sufficiently wide field in itself.

This recalled to mind the Lady Rosamund. The Earl was surprised to realize that he hadn't given a thought to Rosamund for the better part of the evening. She must have been mad enough to spit when he'd left the ballroom with Miss Wentworth, and even angrier when he took leave of the Seftons without so much as a word to her own beautiful, bad-tempered self. The Earl grinned to himself. The lady would likely be in one of her passions tonight, and he was just as glad he wouldn't be there to witness it. Rosamund's tantrums, her jealousy, and above all the niggardly way she was doling out her favors had decided him: he was done with her. If she tried to bring him back around, he would tell her why, and that in no uncertain terms.

The breeze that had been scarcely perceptible on the sheltered terrace struck him with a colder, sharper force as he stood waiting for his carriage in front of the Seftons' town house. The moon above was alternately revealed and concealed by wisps of cloud that drifted across its face; lamps and flambeaux flickered as a gust of wind swept through the ranks of carriages waiting in the square. The Earl's topcoat was caught and billowed by another gust as he stepped into his carriage. He hesitated for a moment before giving orders to the coachman. Since his plans for the evening had fallen through, he was at something of a loss for ideas, but there was an odd restlessness pervading his spirits, and the night was still young.

The Earl decided to take a look-in at White's. Upon his arrival there, he was immediately hailed by a party of his boon companions and was made to take up a hand of whist. For once, his luck seemed to be in. He won a considerable sum, but in spite of this—or because of it—the cards bored him tonight. He soon made an excuse to leave the club. After quitting White's, he found he still felt restless, yet he could not think of a single thing to do in all London that sounded more appealing than returning to his lodgings and going to bed. In the end, this was what he did, surprising his valet very much by appearing at such an early hour, though that imperturbable individual never betrayed his shock by so much as a flicker of an eyelash.

There was a letter resting on the mantelpiece of the Earl's bedchamber, a highly scented letter sealed with a quantity of pale blue sealing wax. The Earl's lip curled when he saw it. He opened the missive and perused it appreciatively; Alicia's spelling and punctuation tended to be original, to say the least. Of course, originality was a highly desirable asset in her profession, but Alicia was also beginning to show signs of an alarmingly rapacious nature beneath her admittedly lovely exterior. The letter was carefully worded, for Alicia. The Earl read it twice. As he had expected, it contained yet another plea for that damnably ugly and damnably expensive emerald necklace she'd seen at Rundell and Bridge's some time back. He had given Alicia a set of sapphires not two weeks ago, and now here she was, dunning him for emeralds.

The Earl frowned and thought of the Stanford emeralds, an impressive set of jewelry that had been in his family for generations. Was it possible that Alicia had somehow learned of their existence, and had decided to hint for emeralds in hopes of getting her hands on them? If so, her luck was out, for he didn't intend to give the family emeralds to a lightskirt, no matter how pretty or how coaxing. Nor did he intend to buy her that necklace at Rundell and Bridges's. What was Alicia about, wanting emeralds anyway? Sapphires, yes, but emeralds would look very much amiss around the neck of a flaxen blonde who never dressed in anything but blue. The whole idea irritated him. Alicia's constant demands were becoming tiresome—he'd been more than generous, by any standards—and now her taste was shown to be flawed, definitely flawed.

Then, too, it had struck him lately that she was giving Broxton a deal more encouragement than she had any right to give when she was being paid by the Earl of Stanford for her undivided attention. Clearly it was time to give Alicia her *congé;* let the sapphires serve as a farewell gift.

Before going to bed, the Earl sat down and penned a letter to that effect, which he sent off that very night. It was as carefully written as Alicia's own billet (though the spelling was considerably better), and it expressed all the conventional regrets, worded in such a way as to make the fair recipient gnash her teeth with impotent fury. Although veiled sarcasm was probably wasted on Alicia, as the Earl reflected philosophically. She would take the letter at face value, write him off as a bad bargain, and waste no time in finding another fool to take his place.

With Alicia disposed of, he fell again to thinking of Miss Wentworth and that kiss on the terrace. A pity Russelton had interrupted, just as things were getting interesting. But perhaps it was as well that he had. The Earl had no mind to involve himself seriously with a schoolroom miss, and at one point he had been in some danger of forgetting his own strict rules about unmarried girls. Fortunately, no mischief had actually been done, and it had been quite a pleasant experience, getting up a flirtation with Miss Wentworth. She was even prettier than he had been led to believe. Perhaps later, after she was married, it might be worthwhile to look her up again. . . .

* * *

On the following day, the Earl received a caller in the person of the Honourable Mr. Giles Collingwood. Giles was really the Earl's uncle, but their relationship was more cousinly in nature, as the Honourable Mr. Collingwood was only a few years the Earl's senior. Giles had been born more than two decades after the seventh Earl, the present Earl's father; the seventh Earl, in turn, had set up his nursery some half-dozen years later, presenting his young brother with a nephew little older than himself.

"Jack!" The Honorable Mr. Collingwood, a tall, thin, dark gentleman with something of the Earl's cast of countenance, rose to seize his nephew by the hand. "You're looking devilish, Jack," he announced, favoring the Earl with a sharp scrutiny. "Burnt to the socket. I'm not surprised, mind; you're going the pace altogether too hard, if half what I hear is true."

"I thank you, Giles," said the Earl, with mingled exasperation and affection. "Do you dare visit me, then, without a physician in attendance? Given my advanced state of decrepitude, you know!" The Earl's eyes flickered over his uncle's figure, and he grinned suddenly. "And if we're to talk of looking devilish, that waistcoat of yours. . . ."

The Honourable Mr. Collingwood looked down at his pink-and-green striped waistcoat with a fond smile. "Pretty, ain't it? I don't expect it would please you, Jack, but then I ain't one of you high sticklers. I like a bit of color in a waistcoat, myself! No, seriously, my boy, you do look a trifle white around the gills. Sure you're feeling quite the thing?"

"Never better, Giles," said the Earl. "You'll be glad to hear my gout troubles me scarcely at all nowadays.

Only see how well I can hobble about! Can I get you a glass of Madeira? Or there's sherry, if you prefer it."

"Madeira for me, thanks." Mr. Collingwood watched as his nephew filled two glasses from a decanter standing on a nearby table. The Earl handed him a glass and came around to seat himself in one of the blue leather chairs grouped in front of the fireplace in his parlor.

"To what do I owe this honor, Giles?" inquired the Earl presently, after a moment or two had gone by and Mr. Collingwood began to show signs of sinking into a brown study. "I trust it isn't solely the state of my health that brings you here."

"No, though I must own it did give me a nasty start when I saw you. Not surprising, though, with the pace you go, and if what I've been hearing is true."

"That's the second time you've alluded to talk about my affairs. Just what exactly have you heard?"

"Alicia," said Mr. Collingwood succinctly. "Heard she was in your keeping now. She'll ruin you, my boy, same as she did Howell."

"I reached the same conclusion some time ago, Giles. I believe you will find that Broxton has stepped into my shoes."

"Well, I'm devilishly glad to hear it! Wouldn't want to see you end up in the same case as Howell. They gave out it was a hunting accident, but no such thing, of course: blew his own brains out, poor fellow."

"And you think I am likely to do the same? Much obliged."

"No, but you've been playing deep—never mind how I know, but I do know, and what with that, and the company you keep . . . I'm dashed fond of you, Jack. I don't usually try to play uncle, particularly not the Dutch variety, but it's time somebody gave you the word with no bark on it. You're what, now—thirty?"

"Twenty-nine."

"Old enough to stop chasing after the skirts and start thinking about marrying and setting up your nursery."

"What, worrying about the succession, Giles?" The Earl cocked a satirical eyebrow. "I see no cause for concern. Should I stick my spoon in the wall prematurely, the title would devolve into your own capable hands."

"I don't want it," said Mr. Collingwood frankly. "Wouldn't care for the fuss. They'd all be after me to marry—"

"I know exactly what you mean," sympathized the Earl, in a voice that held a quiver of laughter. "They'd be telling you to—er—stop chasing after the skirts and—"

"The difference is, I'm a confirmed bachelor," said Mr. Collingwood severely. "Never been one for the petticoats." He hesitated and eyed his nephew's face. The Earl was frowning a little now, staring into the empty grate of the fireplace. "Well, I didn't come here to lecture you, Jack. Only seeing you look so—well, never mind." Mr. Collingwood cleared his throat and took another sip of Madeira. "Nearly forgot the real reason I came by. Almeria's going to the Italian Opera tonight, and she's expressed a desire to see your phiz. Sent me to tell you she'd be very much obliged if you could make up one of the party."

"Has she some nice girl she wants me to meet?"

"No, no, I think she's given up on that score. Just a family party: you, me, Almeria, and Jane—Almeria's youngest, you know. Almeria thinks she's got Croftley on the string for Janey, and she's in high croak. Pretty good for a girl just out of the schoolroom."

"Yes, indeed, if Jane's the one I'm thinking of. Tallow-faced girl, with nothing to say for herself . . . that should suit Croftley, though. He does enough talking for any three people." The Earl spoke absently, busy considering his aunt's invitation from every angle. He had originally planned to go to the opera tonight with Rosamund. The plans had been arranged before the dustup last night, however, and he had already made up his mind to stay away. Showing up in his aunt's party instead was sure to infuriate Rosamund, but the Earl did not feel inclined to spare her on that account. "Yes, I'll go. I'll send a note around to Almeria and let her know."

"Not necessary, my boy. I'm dropping by her house later today, and I'll deliver the word." Mr. Collingwood drank off his Madeira and stood up, preparatory to taking his leave. "As I said, I didn't mean to lecture you, Jack. I don't usually try to put my oar in—you know that—but I'm dashed fond of you and hate to see you go to the devil without making a push to stop you. Although if you've broken off with Alicia, I can see you've got your affairs in hand better than I supposed."

"I trust I do," said the Earl, smiling faintly. "But pray don't apologize. It's extremely diverting to hear you distributing all this sage advice as if you were eons older than I. Have you no other advice for me before you go, O greybeard?"

"Well, since you've asked, I'd advise you to stay away from that hell in Pall Mall I saw you coming out of, the other day. Stick to White's and Watier's. You can ruin yourself there just as easily, and in the best company, too," retorted Mr. Collingwood, and took his leave.

After he had accompanied his uncle to the door, the

Earl returned to the parlor and resumed his seat in front of the fireplace. He finished drinking his Madeira with the appearance of being deep in thought; amusement, annoyance, and anger passed in turn across his face. At last, he abandoned his meditations and stood up, addressing the bellrope in a peremptory manner. His valet, arriving in response to the summons, was instructed to have my lord's curricle and greys sent round, and then, only moments later, was issued contradictory instructions that the curricle and greys would not be required after all. These vacillations were accepted with no visible signs of surprise or displeasure on the part of my lord's valet. The Earl spent the remainder of the afternoon irritably struggling with various matters relative to his estate and tenantry, a task he had been postponing for several weeks. But he remembered to have his valet lay out formal dress that evening, and he called for his carriage in good time to take him around to his aunt's at the appointed hour.

That same evening, while the Earl of Stanford was on his way to his aunt's house, Miss Wentworth was engaged in making her own preparations for the opera.

She and her cousin had left Lady Sefton's ball the night before, soon after the Earl's departure, but first she had been made to listen to a gentle lecture from Lady Ingleside on the impropriety of leaving the ballroom with the Earl of Stanford. The drive home with her cousin had been enlivened with another lecture on the same subject, delivered much more forcibly.

Miss Wentworth had listened meekly enough, and had agreed with every word, but she could not help thinking a good deal about what had taken place on the terrace. Her own behavior astonished her far more than that of the Earl. How could she have lived eighteen whole years without once suspecting that she was really a wanton at heart? Miss Wentworth had never thought of herself as a fast girl, but there was no denying that she had done nothing to discourage the Earl's advances. If one were to be strictly truthful, in fact, one would have to admit her guilty of positively encouraging him! Annoyance with Frederick might have had something to do with her decision to leave the ballroom with a man she knew to be a notorious rake, but once she was alone with the Earl, Frederick had been forgotten as totally as though he had never existed. It had been a shock to find her own well-behaved self capable of such behavior. Both mind and body had been in a state of turmoil after the Earl had left her on the terrace; thinking about it, even now, had a disturbing tendency to revive the turmoil. On the whole, Miss Wentworth thought it prudent to try to forget the incident.

Thoughts of the Earl were not uppermost in her mind as she made her toilette for the opera. She was more concerned about the prospect of spending a whole evening in an opera box with her sullen fiancé. Fortunately, Sir Richard and Henrietta would be there, to leaven what promised to be an uncomfortable ordeal, but their presence also ensured that there would be witnesses if Frederick chose to treat her badly. Miss Wentworth found herself not a little apprehensive about the evening ahead.

There was some comfort to be found in her appearance, at least. When she had gone shopping for a new opera dress a few weeks before, she had been downcast because her mother had been unable to accompany her to the modiste; instead, Lady Wentworth had been appointed her escort. She'll make me get something cut up to the collarbones, Miss Wentworth had thought miserably, well aware of her aunt's opinions about the style of dress suitable for girls just out. But when Miss Wentworth had stood before her aunt, there in Hélène's modish salon, robed in the most gorgeous dress imaginable, Lady Wentworth surprised her by not rejecting the dress out of hand.

"Isn't it lovely, Aunt Constance?" said Miss Wentworth, trying to speak naturally but unable to keep a note of supplication out of her voice. "Hélène says it is just the thing for the opera."

"Mademoiselle est ravissante—absolument ravissante!" cried Hélène, rolling her eyes heavenward and clasping her hands in rapture. *"Elle vous va à merveille* . . . the dress becomes her to a marvel!"

Lady Wentworth ignored the modiste's noisy transports and turned her fine grey eyes upon her niece. Every detail of the dress was subjected to an intense scrutiny. Miss Wentworth waited nervously. "You look very well, Rebecca," said Lady Wentworth at last. "To be sure, the corsage is a touch more *décolletée* than your other gowns, but for the opera a moderate *décolletage* is perfectly unexceptionable. Then, too, now that you are engaged to be married your change in station entitles you to a less conservative mode of dress than that proper to unmarried girls. I believe that gown will do very well indeed."

So here she was tonight, wearing her lovely new dress, although Miss Wentworth felt gloomily certain that Lord Russelton wouldn't appreciate it in the least. The dress was of emerald green silk shot with gold and trimmed with delicate gold embroidery along skirt, neckline, and tiny off-the-shoulder sleeves. The green overgown was worn open, over a slip of ivory satin. Her mother had lent her her own pearl necklace, and at the last minute Lady Wentworth had contributed a very pretty pearl tiara for Miss Wentworth to set in her hair. The gold in the tiara and the clasp of the necklace nicely picked up the gold in the trimming of the dress. She had braided and looped up her honey brown hair, with a few loose curls about her face, and her eyes appeared greener than ever with the green of her dress to set them off.

Miss Wentworth felt the end result was all she could have hoped for, but the girl she saw reflected in the cheval glass wore an anxious, rather unhappy expression in spite of her gala attire. She pinched her cheeks to give them more color, and turned to pick up her shawl and small ivory fan lying ready nearby. Before leaving her bedchamber, she gave a final tug to the corsage of her gown. There was, she discovered, a difference between wearing a dress in the privacy of Hélène's salon, and appearing in public in the same dress. Even with Lady Wentworth's sanction, the amount of her bosom on display made her slightly uncomfortable; she had never worn such a low-cut gown before. Miss Wentworth resolved to keep her shoulders well back throughout the evening and sailed downstairs to join her party.

Chapter Five

The Earl of Stanford sat in his aunt's opera box in a relaxed attitude, silk-stockinged, black knee-breeched legs crossed negligently at the ankle. His appearance was that of a gentleman very much at his ease, and his mood one of extreme boredom. He wondered what the devil he had been thinking of, to commit himself to such a tedious evening. He had a fondness for his aunt, but her seemingly inexhaustible flow of social chitchat grew wearisome after a short time. Once she was launched, the conversation had a way of developing into a monologue about the doings of her own set of friends. His cousin Jane was now a pretty girl, improved all out of recognition from the stammering, giggling schoolgirl he remembered, but she seemed to have become tongue-tied in the bargain. All his efforts to make conversation with her died a swift death, met only by a shy "Yes" or "No," with an occasional "I'm sure I could not say" for variety. In truth, a large part of her speechlessness was occasioned by the presence of her handsome, rakish cousin the Earl of Stanford, but the Earl naturally made no allowance for this and thought her merely painfully shy. When the talk between Mr. Collingwood and his sister turned to a discussion of the Prince Regent's latest antics, the Earl groaned inwardly, thrust his hands in his pockets, and wished himself elsewhere. Idly, he surveyed the occupants of the other opera boxes around them.

The Lady Rosamund glared at him from across the way. The Earl had already derived a good deal of amusement from the expression on her face when she had first noticed him in his aunt's box. He gave her an offhand nod now, and laughed to himself at the fury in her dark eyes, fury that was visible all the way across the opera house. An ill-tempered jade—he was well rid of her.

A glitter of jewelry in a box farther down caught his attention next. The Earl's eyebrows rose. So Alicia had already found someone to give her those emeralds! They looked frightful on her, too, just as one might expect. Alicia's pale blue gown suited her fair hair and ivory skin—nearly everything she wore or owned was blue—but the green glitter around her neck could not be said to enhance the overall effect. The Earl shook his head over the folly of women. What a blue-eyed blonde wanted with emeralds in the first place . . . his eyes moved a little farther along the tier of boxes, and then stopped in recognition.

Now there was the lady who should have been wearing emeralds! Miss Wentworth, in her green dress, sat beside Lord Russelton in the Wentworth opera box, her eyes fixed straight ahead and her hands restlessly opening and closing her ivory fan. The Earl sat up a little straighter in his seat, ennui forgotten. He had thought Miss Wentworth extraordinarily pretty the evening before, but now he realized she was downright beautiful, a Diamond of the First Water, and not just in the common style, either. Emeralds would have suited her down to the ground, with those green eyes of hers. He caught himself wondering how the family emeralds might look upon her. The idea came as something of a shock, but he considered it dispassionately and decided they would become her very well indeed. Far better than the trumpery pearls she was wearing tonight . . . nevertheless, his eyes dwelt appreciatively for some time on the pearls lying against the creamy swell of Miss Wentworth's bosom, displayed to advantage against the green and gold of her dress.

As Miss Wentworth had foreseen, the evening was turning out to be perfectly wretched. On the drive to the opera house, Lord Russelton had been silent and moody, responding curtly to every attempt made by Henrietta to get some kind of general conversation going. Now that they were settled in Lady Wentworth's opera box, he slouched in his seat, shifting impatiently from time to time and maintaining a sullen silence broken only by an occasional sigh. In contrast, he had bowed with great courtesy toward a box across the hall, where Miss Barrow sat in a heavily trimmed white gown with an impressive number of diamonds sprinkled about her stout person. It was a relief when the curtain rang up on the first act. Miss Wentworth fastened all her attention on the stage, hoping to distract herself for a time from her fiancé's boorish behavior.

At the end of the first act, Henrietta and Sir Richard rose from their seats. "We're going down to the saloon to get ices," explained Henrietta. She eyed Lord Russelton in a questioning way. "Would you care to come along with us, Frederick? Rebecca?"

"No, I thank you," said Lord Russelton curtly, not bothering to ascertain whether or not his companion would have liked an ice. Miss Wentworth fumed as Sir Richard and Henrietta left the box. Now she was doomed to sit through the interval alone with Frederick, and doubtless he would be even worse company in the absence of the others, if such a thing were possible.

Miss Wentworth's temper began to rise. Just as she opened her mouth to make a cutting remark, Lord Russelton stood up. He muttered something under his breath that might have been an excuse and walked out the box, shutting the door behind him with a slam.

Miss Wentworth looked after him in disbelief. She knew a moment of blinding fury. Fortunately, most of the people in the other boxes were either absent or too busy conversing to notice her solitary state, but a lady alone in an opera box was certain to find herself a very public spectacle before long.

Miss Wentworth had never been more embarrassed and angry in her life. She wondered if she ought to go in search of her cousin, but the idea of shouldering her way alone through the inevitable crowds of ogling bucks daunted her. Staying and brazening the situation out seemed the lesser of the two evils. Miss Wentworth sat with her eyes cast down, hands folded in her lap.

Throughout the first act of the opera, the Earl's eyes had been repeatedly drawn to the Wentworth opera box. Admittedly, the greater part of his scrutiny had been directed toward the region of Miss Wentworth's neckline, but he had also made note of her discontented expression, and Lord Russelton's sullen face, and had deduced without too much difficulty that the betrothed couple were still at odds. When Lord Russelton had abandoned his fiancée, the Earl of Stanford had been an interested observer; he had seen Miss Wentworth's look of shock and outrage, and he had watched with dawning comprehension as Lord Russelton reappeared a short time later in the box where Clarissa Barrow sat. The Earl made a hasty excuse, cutting off his aunt in midsentence, and went to the rescue.

"Come in," said Miss Wentworth in a rather brittle voice, in answer to his tap on the door.

"Good evening, Miss Wentworth," said the Earl, entering the opera box. "May I sit down?" He did not wait for an answer, but seated himself in Lord Russelton's vacant chair with an impudent smile.

"You!" Miss Wentworth found herself gazing at him stupidly, as stupidly as she had when he had returned her fan the night before. "What brings you here, my lord?" she asked faintly, after a moment of stunned silence.

"Beauty in distress. All my instincts of chivalry were aroused when I saw you heartlessly abandoned, and once again I resolved to come to your aid. What the devil is Russelton about, Miss Wentworth, deserting you for the likes of that blond charmer across the way . . . what's her name?"

"Miss Barrow."

"Ah, yes, the shipping heiress." The Earl cast a curious glance at Miss Wentworth's tight face. "That's the second time Russelton's played you this trick, isn't it? Well, that settles it: we must put our heads together and come up with a fitting punishment. I'm quite sure we can think of something!"

Miss Wentworth looked into the Earl's laughing dark eyes and smiled in spite of herself. "I think not, my lord," she said primly.

The Earl studied with appreciation the dimple that was flickering around Miss Wentworth's mouth. It struck him that she had a singularly lovely smile. "Do you know,

Miss Wentworth," he said deliberately, "do you know, I'm beginning to think this engagement of yours highly unsuitable. If Russelton is neglecting you now, it stands to reason he'll be even worse once you're actually married." The Earl looked toward the Barrows' opera box and saw with amusement that Lord Russelton was scowling back at him. "And he apes the dandy set, I see: yet another failing! Though that, at least, might conceivably wear off with time." He returned the youthful peer's regard blandly, taking in the buckram wadded shoulders, florid waistcoat, and elaborate neckcloth with which Lord Russelton had chosen to adorn himself. "Just how old is Russelton, Miss Wentworth? He looks the veriest schoolboy in that get-up."

"Eighteen, my lord. And you needn't look so shocked, for I am exactly the same age myself," said Miss Wentworth defensively.

"Eighteen? Good God, on no account must you marry him. There's a deal of difference between the male and female animal at that age. I remember my own youth very well, and I can assure you that few, if any, eighteen-year-old males are anywhere near ready to—er—settle down to the married state. Do believe me, Miss Wentworth, for I speak with some experience on the subject!"

"A great deal of experience, my lord, from what I have been given to understand," said Miss Wentworth sweetly.

"Now I wonder what can have given you that idea." The Earl regarded her with a smile that was distinctly wicked. "Has someone been blackening my reputation behind my back, Miss Wentworth? Or do you speak from your own personal observations on the subject?"

The reference to that kiss on the terrace was too

pointed to be missed. Miss Wentworth decided the conversation had better be diverted to safer channels. "Oh, I didn't exactly—that is, I only heard a bit about you from one of my friends. She told me that you used to be called the handsomest gentleman in London—that the ladies used to call you the Dark-Haired Adonis—"

"They used to call me that, did they? I'm glad I didn't know, for I fear I'd have been nauseated rather than gratified. Dark-Haired Adonis, indeed . . . dare I ask what they call me now?"

Miss Wentworth looked him over doubtfully. The Earl's voice had been amused, but she thought there had been a flash of anger in his eyes. "Oh, how rude of me!" she gasped, as the import of her own words finally came home to her. "I didn't mean to imply that you aren't handsome anymore, my lord. Why, the only reason I dropped my fan at your feet last night was that a friend of mine suggested I should punish Frederick by flirting with the handsomest gentleman in the room. I thought that if anything would vex him, it would be seeing me talking to you."

The Earl's lips twitched a bit at this artless confidence, but his eyes continued to bore into her own with an uncomfortably penetrating expression. "I'm flattered, Miss Wentworth, but you still haven't told me what the gossips call me nowadays, you know. Skirting the issue, I see . . . it must be something pretty bad. Please tell me. I won't be angry with you, I promise."

"The Wicked Earl was the name *I* heard," said Miss Wentworth with reluctance. "But—"

"Oh, Lord, that's even worse than the other. Sounds like a villain in one of Mrs. Radcliffe's novels. I wonder you dared to be seen in my company last night, if that's how I was represented to you."

"Oh, I wasn't afraid," Miss Wentworth assured him kindly. She had begun to regain her composure and found herself conversing quite easily with the Earl, even with the memory of that kiss hanging about in the air. "I only heard it said of you once, and—and I daresay it is mostly exaggeration, just as everything becomes exaggerated once the gossips take it up." She thought the Earl still looked rather offended and she decided to change the subject again. "How do you enjoy the opera, my lord?"

"To tell the truth, not much, but then opera has never been one of my enjoyments. I probably wouldn't have come tonight, had not my aunt requested my company. I am very glad I did come, however, since it gives me a chance to renew our . . . our acquaintance? No, our friendship; I feel sure we will be friends! What do *you* think of the performance thus far, Miss Wentworth? You looked quite rapt during the first act."

"Yes, it's very beautiful, I think, although—" Miss Wentworth caught herself on the verge of admitting that she had chosen to concentrate upon the action onstage in preference to her escort's behavior. "Although I don't understand Italian very well," she finished instead.

"No, nor do I, but I am surprised to hear *you* say so. I had thought that you, like every other fashionable young lady, would have studied Italian, French . . . perhaps even Spanish and German as well."

The fascinating dimple flickered into being once more. "Well, I did *study* them, but that's not to say I *understand* them," admitted Miss Wentworth, with a gurgle of laughter.

Sir Richard and Henrietta, bearing ices, reentered the box at that moment. The Earl politely stood up. Miss Wentworth, rather flustered, rose to make introductions.

Henrietta returned the Earl's greeting cordially, and regarded him with great interest, but Miss Wentworth's cousin acknowledged his presence with only the slightest of bows. "Lord Stanford and I are already acquainted, I believe," said Sir Richard stiffly. His eyes went from Miss Wentworth to the Earl, with patent disapproval. "Ahem . . . would you care to accompany me for a turn up and down the lobby, Rebecca?"

"No, Richard, I don't care to go, and I wouldn't dream of putting you to so much trouble. Why, you haven't yet finished your ice! And I do believe the second act is about to begin." Miss Wentworth resumed her seat and fixed her eyes on the stage, ignoring her cousin's deepening frown.

"I'll bear you company then, until your escort returns, Miss Wentworth," said the Earl, much enjoying the situation. "No doubt he will return any moment now."

Miss Wentworth stole a look across the opera house. Lord Russelton was still seated in the Barrows' box, even though the second act was clearly about to begin. Miss Wentworth decided he could stay there through the rest of the opera for all she cared; the Earl had as good as promised to remain with her as long as he was needed, and certainly he was a more agreeable companion than Lord Russelton had been.

She stole another look at her fiancé and noted with pleasure that he appeared disturbed to see her in the Earl's company. He kept looking rather anxiously across the opera house, but Miss Barrow seemed to be holding him in check. Congratulating herself on this satisfactory state of affairs, Miss Wentworth prepared to enjoy the second act.

"There now, my lord! Even if you do not care overmuch for opera, you must have thought *that* beautiful," she challenged the Earl, as the soprano on-stage finished her aria. "Why, there are actually tears in my eyes."

There was indeed a liquid look about Miss Wentworth's eyes. "Yes, very pretty," said the Earl, thinking privately that the music was no more beautiful than those wonderful green eyes. "But I must confess I understood very little of the lady's plaint. Something about her heart?"

"Yes, she is telling her heart not to beat for his sake, because he is wicked and it would be wrong to relent. But alas, she cannot efface his image from her heart!"

"A pity, under the circumstances." The Earl joined in the general laughter as the other characters onstage proceeded to exploit the unfortunate soprano's tenderness in the most shameless way. "Poor girl . . . you can see how badly her trust is being betrayed!"

"Yes, it is very bad," agreed Miss Wentworth, smiling. "She must love him very much, to let herself be hoaxed again by that villain."

The Earl looked at Miss Wentworth. There was no trace of self-consciousness on her face. He wondered if she loved her fiancé very much and was surprised to feel something like jealousy at the thought. It was pretty unforgivable of Russelton to abandon her publicly in a crowded opera house. Even if it was only a lovers' quarrel . . . "Perhaps it will be a lesson to her in the future, not to trust the rogue," he said, striving for a light tone but unconsciously giving the words a rather pointed significance.

Miss Wentworth, in turn, studied the Earl from under her lashes. Was he trying to warn her not to trust him? By now, Miss Wentworth had all but forgotten Lord Russelton's existence; she was surprised by the Earl's words and wondered that a rake should warn his victim in advance. Not that she needed a warning. The shockingly intimate way he had kissed her last night should have been enough to put her on her guard. Instead, here she was, encouraging him for all she was worth! Miss Wentworth marveled at her own gullibility. Then the Earl looked over at her and smiled, and the mystery was explained. If he had chosen to take her in his arms and kiss her, right there in the opera box, she felt she would have been quite powerless to resist him.

The first scene of the opera's second act had ended before Lord Russelton made a tardy reappearance. The Earl relinquished his seat unwillingly. He recognized, with some surprise, that he had never enjoyed any part of any opera more than he'd enjoyed that single scene spent in Miss Wentworth's company. He thought, too, that the lady herself looked less than pleased to see her original escort again, and found himself extremely gratified by this circumstance.

Rising to his feet, he executed a general bow to the whole company that began by expressing—to Miss Wentworth—his reluctance to leave, and ended with a challenge—to the gentlemen present—lest they fancy they had played any part in his decision to do so.

"Your servant, Miss Wentworth," he said, pressing a kiss on her gloved hand. He continued to hold it in his own quite a bit longer than was strictly necessary. She did not attempt to withdraw it, but only smiled at him; looking into those wide green eyes he felt a nearly overpowering urge to kiss her again, then and there, and not on the hand, either.

At last he released her hand and became aware that the other three occupants of the box were watching this prolonged leave-taking with a variety of emotions. Sir

Richard looked disapproving; Miss Ingleside's expression was interested and rather speculative; Lord Russelton was exhibiting a fine dog-in-the-manger attitude and looked as though he would have liked to plant a facer on the Earl's classic features. The Earl gave him stare for stare, and then permitted a slight smile to appear upon his lips. Lord Russelton's hands clenched into fists. The Earl's smile widened into a grin; he shut the door of the opera box gently behind him and made his way back to his aunt's party.

Miss Wentworth and her fiancé sat through the remainder of the second act in chilly silence.

Chapter Six

When at last he took leave of his aunt's opera party, the Earl of Stanford was in a state of mind akin to exhilaration. It had been famous sport, putting young Russelton's nose out of joint by flirting with his pretty fiancée. What a beauty she was, and uncommonly good company, too. Opera generally bored him stiff, but tonight—well, possibly it had been an above average performance, but the Earl was inclined rather to ascribe full credit to his companion, disregarding entirely such trivial factors as the performers' skill, the librettist's wit, and the composer's genius. It was refreshing to be in the company of a young lady unaffected enough to show real enthusiasm, who neither simpered nor (the Earl thought of his cousin Jane) found herself tongue-tied in his presence. And Miss Wentworth might have been forgiven a touch of discomfort. In the Earl's experience, young ladies were prone to blush and look arch when confronted by gentlemen who had kissed them as he'd kissed Miss Wentworth last night. Had it really been only last night? It seemed unreal, in retrospect, but about the reality of that kiss the Earl had no doubts, and he was only sorry there had been no opportunity to repeat it during the course of the evening. In his euphoric mood, he decided on an impulse to dismiss his carriage and walk to White's instead. The night was not far advanced, in the Earl's reckoning; doubtless he could find some kind of convivial party at his club to while away the remainder of the evening.

The exhilaration had begun to fade before he had gone halfway to White's. Thoughts of Miss Wentworth led to a recollection of their conversation together, and certain phrases that had fallen artlessly from her lips he discovered to be lodged like thorns in his side. That absurd nickname, the Wicked Earl, had touched a particularly sore spot. The Earl was no longer young enough to think such a title glamorous; being acquainted with real wickedness, he was resentful at being classed with the likes of those gentlemen who considered the entire female sex fair game for their sport. Whatever his own misdeeds, he had never indulged in such pastimes as the debauching of innocent maidens, willing or otherwise. Nor had he made conquests for the purpose of amassing a collection, as did certain of his acquaintances who vied with one another to add numbers to totals already impressive. It had never been his practice to boast of his amatory adventures, though he was forced to admit he'd never made any secret of them, either.

When he had first come to London years ago, fresh out of Oxford, he had plunged at once into the round of amusements indulged in by nine out of ten young gentlemen new on the town. The Earl smiled to think what a rackety character he had been in those days. But it had all been high spirits; nothing worse than an occasional run-in with the Watch. It wasn't until after the death of his father that he had fallen into worse excesses.

The Belinda Satterthwaite affair, for instance. The

Earl was heartily glad his father hadn't been around when that storm broke. The seventh Earl had been a stern parent in many ways, but his son had genuinely loved and respected him, and the present Earl knew it would have cut his father to the heart to see his heir the center of such a scandal. Moreover, his father might well have compelled him to marry Belinda . . . yes, it was as well the seventh Earl hadn't lived to witness that particular transgression.

His father's death had marked a turning point in his career. Part of the change had undoubtably been caused by his own succession to the title upon his father's demise. An earl must always be acceptable to London society, and an earl who also enjoyed the advantages of wealth and considerable good-looks had been embraced with an enthusiasm that might have turned the head of a far more stable character than he had possessed at the time. Society had looked indulgently on his exploits, exploits that would have been condemned in other gentlemen. He had fallen into the way of believing that the combination of title and wealth—and the popularity that went with them—was sufficient excuse for anything he cared to do. As London's more decorous entertainments palled upon him, by degrees he had begun to frequent other, less savory circles for amusement. And he had allowed himself to be drawn into that disastrous intimacy with beautiful, reckless Belinda, older than himself both in years and experience; a young lady of respectable lineage but doubtful reputation, whose behavior throughout their brief, unhappy liason had led him to believe her to be considerably more in command of the situation than had subsequently proved to be the case.

Once his name had been tarnished by that scandal, the descent had been swift, and perhaps inevitable. It had seemed necessary at the time to demonstrate to the members of the *ton* how little he cared for their condemnation. Looking back, he could see that he had more or less tailored his conduct to suit his newfound bad reputation, and had ended by confirming what everyone had been only too eager to believe in any case.

Yet it was unjust that society had denominated him as wicked on those grounds alone. His behavior was no worse than that of a dozen others he could name. Of course, that was a paltry excuse; again he thought of his father, and of how grieved that gentleman would have been to see his son saddled with such a character. The seventh Earl had displayed a surprising degree of tolerance for his son's youthful follies, but he would have certainly condemned the Earl's current style of life out of hand. In his present mood, it struck the earl that an existence spent gaming, drinking, and making love to other men's wives did indeed have something ignoble about it. Worst of all, there was beginning to be remarkably little satisfaction in that existence.

By this time, the Earl's high spirits had degenerated to such an extent that he decided to forgo White's altogether and turned his steps toward his lodgings instead. He felt discontented with himself, and with life in general, and in a mood to do something desperate. A pair of footpads lying in wait observed his face as he passed and unanimously agreed to let him proceed unmolested. There was that in his expression that made even the watchman on his rounds give him a wide berth, as a gentleman whom it would not pay to cross that night.

The Earl's valet greeted his appearance with outward composure but inward speculation. My lord seldom returned home before dawn, and was not infrequently out for days at a time, and here he was, returning home shortly after midnight for the second night in a row! Roberts scrutinized the Earl covertly as he folded away his master's evening raiment. Could he be falling ill? In his experience, when a gentleman deviated from his usual habits it was a sign of trouble. Not financial trouble, Roberts thought, although along with the rest of the household he had heard rumors of recent heavy losses at the gaming table. Could it possibly be a woman? During his employment with the Earl, he had seen that gentleman invariably display an attitude of insouciance toward the fair sex, and it was an attitude that seemed to serve him extremely well . . . probably not a woman, then. Roberts decided that whatever the explanation for such unprecedented behavior, the Earl did not really appear to be ill, although there was no denying that my lord appeared a trifle pulled, now that he really looked at him.

Much the same kinds of thoughts were revolving in the Earl's head. He would have been surprised to hear himself described as conceited, but years of adulation and flattery had left their mark, and a certain amount of self-satisfaction had crept in over time. The Earl was accustomed to take his face as much for granted as he took his title and fortune: an asset that could be turned to advantage and might be depended on to obtain nearly anything he fancied. Miss Wentworth's disclosure that he "used to be" thought handsome disturbed him more than he cared to admit; counting his uncle's remarks, it made two references to physical deterioration in the space of a single day. Curiously, he studied his own face in the mirror.

There was a sprinkling of silver hairs around the temples. That was nothing new; he'd even joked to several friends about his advancing old age when he had first discovered them years ago. But it seemed to him now that the silver was growing more prominent, and there were lines on his face he had never noticed before. Taken altogether, however, it was still an agreeable face, and he hadn't expected to stay young forever, had he? In fact, he had; it was disconcerting to see visible evidence that youth was slipping away. Ten years ago he would have thought thirty to be quite middle-aged, and his thirtieth birthday was now less than a year away. It gave him an odd feeling of loss.

He finished removing his clothing, down to his underlinen, and the sight of himself in the mirror again gave him pause. He regarded his reflection with disbelief. Was it possible that he was getting fat as well as old? Surely there was a thickening at the waist . . . he looked toward his valet, wanting to receive reassurance that such an awful fate could not be overtaking him, but his own eyes could see the truth plainly enough. The change was small but unmistakable. It wasn't surprising, given his lifestyle in recent years; he had made something of a reputation for himself as a Corinthian when he had first come to London, but over time he had largely abandoned sporting pursuits for other pastimes. Sitting up night after night, knocking down several bottles at a sitting, was not calculated to improve the physique. The Earl scowled at himself in the mirror. He couldn't help growing old, but he was damned if he'd let this kind of thing continue. He wasn't yet thirty, after all. It shouldn't take much to repair the damage.

Lying in bed, his head resting on his folded hands, the Earl stared at the canopy of bedcurtains above him and considered the problem. It was customary to rusticate in the country when one felt in need of a repairing lease. Certainly there would be plenty to keep him busy at Stanford Park; he was assailed by yet another pang of guilt as he thought of how long it had been since he'd visited the family estate. His father would have been grieved beyond measure to see the well-tended lands of which he had been so proud, slipping into disrepair. The Earl knew he had been unforgivably remiss in that direction, as frequent, urgent messages from his bailiff all too plainly attested. Perhaps when the Season ended he would devote some time to setting things straight at Stanford Park, but he was unwilling to quit London at the height of the Season. A change of regime was really all that was needed at present: more exercise, and less late nights and drinking.

"Roberts, I believe I'll go riding tomorrow morning. See that I am wakened early," said the Earl, turning his head to address his valet, who was bustling about, setting the room in order for the night.

His servant's face betrayed no shock at this revolutionary request. "Very good, my lord. At what hour do you wish to be called?"

The Earl thought. He had a suspicion that rising early might be less appealing when morning actually rolled around. "Say around seven-thirty," he temporized. "Tell Ned to have Leonidas saddled and brought around no later than eight-thirty."

"I shall do so, my lord," said Roberts, and withdrew to spread the news that the master was in the throes of a brainstorm of some kind.

The Earl was awakened the next morning by sunlight streaming through the windows. His valet had drawn the bedcurtains and the window draperies of his bedchamber, and was engaged in setting out hot water and shaving apparatus. The Earl groaned.

"You did ask to be called at seven-thirty, my lord," said Roberts, with an apologetic air.

"Yes, I believe I did, now that you mention it. Lay out my riding dress, would you, Roberts?"

"I have already done so, my lord," said his valet reprovingly, and left the bedchamber.

The Earl lay in bed for a few minutes longer. He was tempted to roll over and go back to sleep, but the remembrance of his burgeoning waistline galvanized him into action. He rose and began to prepare for his ride, albeit with a noticeable lack of enthusiasm.

Yet once he was actually cantering through the park, he began to be glad he had forced himself to come. It was rather refreshing to be out at an hour when fashionable London was still asleep, and when he himself might well have still been up from the night before. The tradesmen going about their duties and the nursemaids in the park with their infantile charges struck him as pleasant, wholesome sights; the wind in his face brought back a trace of the exhilaration he had felt the night before. It would be no very disagreeable thing after all, to make a regular habit of morning rides. The Earl returned home in excellent spirits, and with more appetite for breakfast than he had felt for many weeks.

Sitting at the breakfast table, however, he was reminded once again of his waistline. He looked long at the York ham, and the rashers of bacon, and partook of toast and coffee instead.

"Roberts, if a person were desirous of ridding himself of some—er—excess weight, what kind of reducing regime might he follow?" he asked his valet, who was passing through the parlor bearing an armful of starched cravats.

"Ah," said Roberts, enlightened. He considered the question gravely. "I believe that some form of physical exertion, perhaps in combination with an avoidance of rich food, is held to be the most successful means of reducing flesh."

"Yes, of course, but I meant . . . well, what specifically? Do you know of any particularly successful regimen?"

"I have heard that young Lord Byron—the gentleman who writes the poetry—successfully rid himself of a considerable amount of weight by subsisting on dry biscuits and soda water."

"Oh." The Earl looked down at the marmalade pot, the contents of which he had been about to convey to the single square of toast remaining upon his plate. "Thank you, Roberts." He set both aside, and finished his coffee in meditative silence.

That afternoon, he decided to pay a visit to Jackson's Boxing Saloon. At one time he had been considered an amateur pugilist of great promise, but in common with most other Corinthian pursuits, his visits to Jackson had grown less frequent of late. After making a few calculations, the Earl was surprised to find it had been close to a year since he'd set foot in Jackson's. No doubt he would be rusty, but sparring a few rounds with Jackson would be first-rate exercise. It shouldn't take long to bring himself back into top condition.

He soon found he had been overly optimistic. "Ah, you were a bit slow bringing back your left after throwing that jab, my lord. You want to watch leaving your face open to your opponent's right," he was told, at the conclusion of an especially humiliating encounter.

"Damn you, Jackson," said the Earl resentfully, daubing blood from his handsome nose and breathing hard.

"Bless you, I could have drawn your cork a dozen times before now, what with the way you're carrying your hands so low," said the great ex-champion, his habitual good humor unimpaired. "You're a bit out of condition, my lord, that's the trouble. If you was wishing to bring yourself back into trim, now—"

"I am," stated the Earl grimly.

"Then you'd better be coming to me more regular, like. You aren't a youngster anymore, my lord! Still, it shouldn't take much to shape you up as long as you're willing to work. You showed a deal of promise as a stripling, if I remember aright, and you haven't entirely lost your form."

"Damn you, Jackson," said the Earl again, but without rancor. "And I suppose you consider that being encouraging. Well, you may look to see my face again tomorrow, back for more of the same rough treatment!" He returned his late antagonist's grin with a rueful smile, and took himself off to be rubbed down.

Driving home from Jackson's in his curricle, he was in such a thoughtful mood that his groom was forced to point out that, unless he was wishful to embroil himself with a landau that was awkwardly blocking the flow of traffic ahead, it would be as well if he reined in his horses a bit.

"What? Oh, yes, Ned." The Earl turned his attention to his greys. Once the obstacle had been successfully bypassed, he cast a sideways look at his groom. "You used to work for Barclay years ago, didn't you, Ned?" he asked, in a diffident voice.

"Yes, my lord, I was with the Captain close on twenty years, afore coming to you."

"That's what I thought. I wonder . . . do you have any idea what kind of regimen he ran his fighters through? Jackson says I'm out of condition, and I daresay he's right."

"Well, my lord, properly speaking it weren't really

my job to help with that part of the business, seeing as my sphere of duties was in the stables," said Mr. Deane, rather dampeningly. Seeing that the Earl looked properly chastened, he relented and went on, more encouragingly, "But I expect I could tell you as well as another what the Captain did to put his bruisers in fighting trim, if you give me a minute to recollect myself." The groom meditated for a moment and then began to outline a blood-curdling regime of purgings and sweatings, together with a schedule of exercise that struck dismay into the Earl's heart. "Five o'clock, that's when they'd have to wake . . . run a mile or so at top speed . . . walk half-a-dozen miles at a moderate pace, breakfast, and then another half-a-dozen miles. A rest at noon, and then a few more miles, moderate-like. After dinner, he'd put 'em through another half mile at top speed and then a half-dozen miles at the slower pace. And then sparring matches, of course, and your work with the heavy bag—"

"Good God," said the Earl. "And—er—what about diet?"

"Red meat," said his groom firmly. "No cheese or milk. Milk's likely to curdle in the stomach, they say. Raw egg yolks—"

"Raw?" said the Earl, revolted.

"Raw egg yolks. Stale bread and strong ale. That, and your red meat, is what Captain Barclay particularly held with, when he was training Cribb for the Molyneaux fight."

"I see. Thank you, Ned," said the Earl, and relapsed into silence.

By the time the dinner hour arrived, the Earl found that with so much unaccustomed exercise and only a scanty breakfast he was very sharp-set indeed. He felt so much thinner already that he thought he could afford to indulge in a beefsteak and a bottle of burgundy at his club that evening. Of course, he felt fat, guilty, and disgusted at himself immediately afterwards, and was convinced he had undone all his labors by this momentary weakness. A single bottle was much less than he customarily consumed of an evening, however, and he played only briefly at Macao after dinner, with the thought of rising early again the next morning for another ride. It occurred to him that he seemed to have more time on his hands than usual, now that Alicia was out of his life. Rosamund, too . . . he hadn't made any provision for women in this new regimen, but that matter could be left to take care of itself. It generally did, in his experience.

Though the Earl's first efforts toward rehabilitation met with less than total success, the occasional setback did not serve to deter him from the course he had chosen to pursue, a course that included neither of the extreme measures recommended by his servants. Wise enough to see the folly of going from one extreme to another, he decided that a moderate course would serve him best.

After a few weeks of morning rides, regular sessions at Jackson's, relative early nights and comparatively abstemious libations, he felt much better and was pleased to note that the offending flesh at his waistline was beginning to recede. Even his face had lost some of the pallor and look of strain his uncle had remarked upon. It felt good to rise clear-headed of a morning, and to be fit once more; he began to aspire toward landing Jackson a facer in the not-too-distant future, to revenge himself for that bloody nose! The Earl was relieved to see that he was not so very far gone after all, in the physical sense, at least.

As for the moral, he was at first too busy—and too fatigued—to give any thought to finding a replacement for Alicia. When the matter did occur to him, after a week or so had gone by, the face that inexplicably sprang to mind was such an ineligible one that the Earl shelved the whole issue and concentrated instead upon the task at hand.

He reflected with amusement that hard physical exertion was a well-known substitute for the lack of other excitements.

Chapter Seven

Miss Wentworth had not enjoyed an easy time of it since the night of the opera. Her pride would not allow her to admit that she had been abandoned—actually abandoned—by her fiancé that night, before the Earl had shown up to keep her company. Naturally enough, Sir Richard took it for granted that Lord Russelton's departure from the Wentworth opera box had taken place sometime after the Earl of Stanford's entrance therein, although Sir Richard was at a loss to explain such patently inexplicable behavior.

"Russelton must be about in his head," he said emphatically. "Going off and leaving you alone with the greatest rakehell in town! You and Russelton been quarreling again, Beck?"

"Frederick and I have never quarreled, Richard."

Sir Richard shook his head. "Must have said something to him, to send him off in a pelter like that. I don't say it was all your fault, mind. Russelton had no business to leave, but that's not to say you had any business flirting with Stanford like you was doing all evening!"

"Lord Stanford was only in our box for the interval and part of the second act," said Miss Wentworth indignantly. "And as he was kind enough to bear me company—"

"Don't you go thinking it was kindness he had in mind! I believe I'd best have a word with Russelton."

"No!"

"Dash it, Beck, somebody had better tell him to his head what's going on, since he doesn't have the wit to see it himself. You're supposed to be marrying him, here in a couple of months, and if Stanford means to make a nuisance of himself, hanging about—"

"I am persuaded that Lord Stanford means to do no such thing. And Frederick knows it, too, or he would not have left me with Lord Stanford and gone off to Miss Barrow's box," said Miss Wentworth, improvising rapidly. "I appreciate your concern, Richard, but if Frederick does not mind, I don't see why you need do so."

Sir Richard regarded his cousin narrowly. "Russelton went off with Clarissa Barrow again, did he?"

"Yes, why should he not? I am sure I had no objection, since I had Lord Stanford for company!"

Sir Richard could only shake his head in reply. Lord Russelton's behavior he found to be as incomprehensible as it was negligent, and he suspected, correctly, that his cousin had omitted some part of the details that might have explained why her future husband had chosen to leave her in the sole company of a libertine earl for the better part of an hour. After much coaxing, he agreed not to take Lord Russelton to task for this conduct, but he was still sufficiently alarmed by the incident to divulge it to Miss Wentworth's mother.

It caused a great flutter in the household. Miss Wentworth was made to repeat over and over the exact sequence of events that had led her to make so dangerous an acquaintance. Lady Sefton and Lady Ingleside were held to be very much at fault, but Mrs. Wentworth could not believe that her daughter would have been singled out for attention by such a notorious rake unless she had given him some kind of encouragement.

"I dropped my fan, Mama," said Miss Wentworth patiently. "And then Lady Sefton introduced us, and he asked me to dance. I saw no harm in it. You never told me I should not dance with the Earl of Stanford, Mama." No need to mention that Henrietta had told her enough to make such a precaution unnecessary!

"He does not usually frequent polite society," said Mrs. Wentworth with a sigh. "I would certainly have warned you, had I thought you might meet him somewhere. Well, I suppose you could not help dancing with him, but Richard tells me you also left the ballroom in his company?" She fixed her daughter with a gimlet eye.

"Yes, I told you. We went to the terrace. It was so hot in the ballroom that I felt quite unwell, and thought fresh air would make me feel better." With a twinge of contrition, Miss Wentworth assured herself that this could not really be accounted a lie. Certainly there had been something nauseating in the sight of Frederick dancing with Miss Barrow three times in a single evening.

"You should have told Lady Ingleside if you felt faint! Stanford did not—that is to say, he did not try to . . . he did not make any improper advances while you were alone together, did he, Rebecca?"

"He behaved just as one would have wished, Mama," said Miss Wentworth, studiously avoiding her mother's eye. Sir Richard was regarding her with deep suspicion, and she was hard put to keep from blushing. "And Frederick also came out on the terrace soon after, you know," she said defensively.

"Yes, it's as well he did. Since he took you back to the ballroom, perhaps no one realized you left it with Stanford. We must hope word of *that* does not get about, or people will be saying that you are fast, my dear."

"Yes, Mama," said Miss Wentworth, in a colorless voice.

As it happened, fortune favored Miss Wentworth. There were practically no repercussions from either of her encounters with the Earl. On the night of Lady Sefton's ball, all eyes had been riveted on Lord Russelton and Miss Barrow dancing together for a scandalous third time, rather than upon the interesting spectacle of Lord Russelton's fiancée exiting the ballroom with the Earl of Stanford. And few, if any, people seemed to have observed them together on the night of the opera; if the sight had been remarked, it gave rise to no more than the mildest speculation. Miss Wentworth's reputation remained intact.

She saw little of her fiancé during the next few weeks. Occasionally, Lord Russelton sent her a formal note inviting her to some entertainment, probably at the prompting of his autocratic grandmother, but Miss Wentworth made excuses to decline these invitations. Her abandonment at the opera still rankled. She was more than ever determined to break her engagement, just as soon as she could find some means of settling the score with Lord Russelton. Toward this end, she was giving a good deal of serious thought.

Preoccupation with her vexatious engagement did not prevent Miss Wentworth from continuing to think about the Earl of Stanford, however. He was in her thoughts more than was comfortable. Wherever she went, she found herself searching for his face. She was disappointed but not at all surprised when she consistently found him absent, for she knew he was seldom seen at *ton* parties such as she attended. Occasionally, she saw Lady Rosamund, but the Earl was never with her. Miss Wentworth wondered if there was truth in the rumors that linked his name with that lady. She hoped the gossip was not true, and then scolded herself for caring if it was.

The Earl of Stanford was nothing to her, or she to him, except for that single troublesome kiss that would not allow itself to be banished from mind. It was annoying, the way the Earl and that kiss kept intruding on her thoughts. Even the marble-backed novel she was reading found her picturing the hero with the Earl's dark, handsome face, when the author of the novel had plainly described her hero as having "leonine" golden hair and flashing eyes of a brilliant blue—not a mention of dark eyes with laughter lurking in their depths, or a smile to render one weak in the knees . . .

About three weeks after the night at the opera, Miss Wentworth went riding in the park with Henrietta and Henrietta's younger sister. It was the fashionable hour of the afternoon, when all London was out riding and driving, seeing and being seen. The young ladies were mounted on hired hacks; neither Lady Wentworth nor Lady Ingleside thought it necessary to keep riding horses, but the ladies were none of them such accomplished horsewomen as to feel this any great disadvantage. Miss Wentworth was indifferent to her mount's sluggish temperament, as long as she could rejoice in her modish riding habit of russet brown, corded with matching silk braid and worn with a russet brown hat whose rakish ostrich plume tickled her left ear. Miss Ingleside was loud in her admiration of this costume, while Miss Wentworth professed herself equally taken with Henrietta's own habit and hat, the latter a particularly dashing creation in the style of a man's high-crowned beaver, supplemented with a flowing veil.

Fancying themselves very much experienced women of the world, Miss Wentworth and Miss Ingleside discussed fashions and the latest *on-dits,* and exchanged greetings with friends and acquaintances. They also condescended to point out several notable personalities to the Honourable Miss Emma Ingleside, who looked on enviously. Emma was not yet out, but Lady Ingleside was an easygoing parent and had no objection to her youngest daughter riding in the park, even if Emma was still officially restricted to the schoolroom on other occasions.

"There's Mr. Fanton," said Henrietta, as they wended their way through the crowded park. "Shall we go over and talk to him for a minute?"

"Why not?" returned Miss Wentworth, smiling. "He is a sweet creature, even if he has no brains to speak of!"

The ladies rode over to greet the flattered Mr. Fanton. "Good afternoon, Miss Wentworth, Miss Ingleside." Mr. Fanton regarded Emma doubtfully and then lifted his hat with an air of inquiry. "And Miss . . .?"

"My sister Emma," explained Henrietta.

"Ah," said Mr. Fanton, looking pleased. "Thought she looked familiar, but couldn't put a name to the face. Very pleased to meet you, ma'am." He executed quite a neat bow, considering that he was also controlling a rather skittish bay hack at the same time. "And how are you enjoying the Season, Miss Emma? Dreadful squeeze last night at the Emberley's, wasn't it?"

"Emma isn't out yet," said Henrietta, giggling, while Emma smiled, extremely flattered at this assumption of worldliness on her part. "She won't be presented till the year after next."

"Still in the schoolroom, eh?" said Mr. Fanton. "Mathematics, geography, Latin grammar, all that?"

"French," corrected Emma, her face tragic. "And oh, how I detest it!"

"Terrible stuff," agreed Mr. Fanton with ready sympathy. "But now that we're not at war with the frogs anymore, no saying but it might be handy to be able to patter a spot of French. If you ever get over to Paris, you know," he explained painstakingly. "Understand that's all they speak over there."

The ladies, with tolerably straight faces, agreed that a knowledge of the French language might prove useful when visiting France. Mr. Fanton looked pleased. "Don't you go and study too much, though, Miss Emma," he went on to caution. "Wouldn't want to be thought a blue-stocking, you know. Fatal, that; mean to say, it's all very well to know a bit of bong-jaw and whatnot, but you don't want to go maudling your brain with too much education. Take your sister, or Miss Wentworth, here." Miss Ingleside and Miss Wentworth exchanged glances and prepared themselves for anything. "You copy them, Miss Emma, and you won't go wrong. All the crack, these two. You don't catch *them* spouting off in company about—about mathematics, and Shakespeare, and so forth." Feeling he had made his point, and paid a pretty compliment at the same time, Mr. Fanton bestowed his angelically sweet smile on the whole company. "Well, and look at me: never been a clever fellow, but here I am with the three prettiest ladies in the park. Just goes to show!"

Presently, Mr. Fanton was hailed by another acquaintance. He made his adieux and rode off, leaving the ladies to giggle over the more witless of his remarks as they made their way around the ring.

"Who is that, Henrietta?" asked Miss Wentworth gazing with wide eyes at a carriage that had just come into view. She thought she was regarding a fairy princess come to life. A lovely lady with the fairest of blond hair and large blue eyes was sitting in a cream-colored barouche drawn by four cream-colored ponies. The upholstery of the barouche was sky blue, the same color as the lady's rather low-cut dress and the liveries of her coachman and footmen.

"Don't look at her, my dear! She's not a lady, you know, but a—a—"

"Lightskirt?" said Miss Wentworth with interest. "Is she, really?" The lovely lady was surrounded exclusively by gentlemen, a circumstance which did seem to bear out the truth of Henrietta's statement, especially when taken in part with the cut of the lady's dress.

"Yes, she's quite notorious. They say she used to be the Earl of Stanford's mistress. Among others!"

"Lord Stanford's mistress?" repeated Miss Wentworth, with sinking heart. Then the rest of Henrietta's speech registered, and she added, more hopefully, "Used to be?"

"Yes, I'm sure I heard a rumor that she was . . . *consorting* with another gentleman now. Someone was saying something about it, just the other night. But I can't think who the other gentleman was." Henrietta frowned, thinking deeply. "Was it Sir Eustace? No . . ."

Miss Wentworth regarded the lady with fresh interest.

She was so very beautiful, and her carriage so magnificent and picturesque, that Miss Wentworth felt a twinge of violent envy, an envy that she suspected was derived at least in part from the lady's connection with the Earl of Stanford. Making an effort, Miss Wentworth averted her eyes from the lady in blue, only to see a spectacle still more unwelcome.

Henrietta saw it at the same time. "Why, there's Frederick, with Miss Barrow! What a smug creature she looks. Just because she's rich enough to drive her own phaeton . . . I detest the way she goes about, queening it over everyone and thinking herself all the crack. And I can't imagine why Frederick—" Henrietta stopped and looked apologetically at Miss Wentworth. "I'm sorry, Rebecca. I didn't mean to be tactless, but I can see . . . well, you still haven't patched things up with Frederick, have you? I'm not surpr— I mean, I expect he's still angry about that time you invited Lord Stanford to your aunt's opera box. Isn't it just like a man, to flirt with another girl and then get angry because you chose to flirt with someone else, too! And I thought Lord Stanford was charming . . . but Frederick must have been furious. Richard certainly was! To think of Frederick's going off and leaving you alone with Lord Stanford!"

Henrietta, like Sir Richard, had not been given an entirely truthful account of what had taken place at the opera, and Miss Wentworth was too mortified to enlighten her. "Yes, Frederick seemed to be very angry that night," she said, watching her fiancé. The phaeton, hampered by the heavy traffic in the park, was moving slowly toward the party on horseback; the sight of Lord Russelton smiling at Miss Barrow, as he had used to smile at her, made Miss Wentworth's heart sick. "Let's pretend we don't see them, Henrietta," she said abruptly. "I don't want to give Frederick the satisfaction." Suiting action to word, she wheeled her mount about and almost collided with a curricle that had drawn up alongside. "Oh, I beg your pardon, I—Oh!" she exclaimed, staring at the gentleman in the curricle.

"Yes, it's me, Miss Wentworth," said the Earl, reining in his greys and smiling at her astonishment. "Like a demon in a pantomime, I have a way of popping up unexpectedly. And just at the critical moment, too!" His eyes flickered toward Miss Barrow's phaeton and then back again, with a mischievous significance.

"Yes, indeed," said Miss Wentworth. Overcome by the timeliness of the Earl's appearance, she just sat there, smiling back at him foolishly, until Henrietta gave a gentle cough. Reminded of her friend's presence, Miss Wentworth was also reminded of her manners and exerted herself to perform the proper courtesies, making mention of the Earl and Henrietta's earlier acquaintance and introducing the Earl to Henrietta's little sister.

This last introduction bore a rather one-sided character. Emma could only goggle in response to the Earl's polite greeting, overwhelmed at meeting one whom she instantly recognized to be the embodiment of all her favorite storybook heroes.

Miss Wentworth could scarcely blame Emma for staring. The Earl, clad in blue topcoat, fawn-colored inexpressibles, and gleaming Hessian boots, was a magnificent specimen of manhood; even Miss Wentworth, at this, their third meeting, was experiencing a certain amount of shyness in his presence. For Emma, encountering him for the first time with a smile on his face, the impact was sufficient to deprive her of speech.

"It's a lovely day, isn't it, my lord? We have been enjoying our ride extremely," said Henrietta, taking the conversation in hand since both her companions seemed content to merely look at the Earl. "Shut your mouth, Emma," she hissed in an aside to her little sister. "I see you, too, have allowed the beauty of the day to persuade you to come here and be jostled along with the rest of us."

"Yes, a great crowd, but as you say, a lovely day," agreed the Earl. "So lovely that I wonder if I might persuade Miss Wentworth to drive around the ring with me in my curricle. We never finished our conversation the other night at the opera, you know, something I have since regretted very much. My groom is at your service and will hold your mount, Miss Wentworth, if you care to come."

"Yes, do, Rebecca," urged Henrietta, grimacing fiercely in the direction of Miss Barrow's phaeton. "Emma and I were just saying how much we would like to dismount and walk a little way down that path over there, where all the flowers are blooming. Now we may do so, if you or your man will be kind enough to help us remount when you bring back Rebecca, Lord Stanford."

"Certainly," said the Earl. He swung himself down from his curricle to help the ladies dismount, turned Miss Wentworth's hack over to his groom, and assisted Miss Wentworth in climbing into the curricle. Then he bowed politely to the Misses Ingleside and whipped up his horses. The shipping heiress's phaeton was now parked beside another carriage under a nearby clump of trees, and Miss Wentworth had the satisfaction of seeing her fiancé's eyes widen when the Earl's curricle came into view. As they threaded their way along the crowded carriageway, the Earl shot Miss Wentworth a swift, conspiratorial smile.

"Miss Wentworth, you really will have to teach that fiancé of yours a stern lesson, you know. Once again I find that Russelton has cast you aside for a young woman with not half your charms. I speak figuratively, of course: as far as your respective builds go, she would make two of you," said the Earl, regarding Miss Barrow's sturdy figure with a critical eye.

Miss Wentworth gave a choke of laughter, but did not immediately reply. She knew a sudden desire to confide the truth to someone. The Earl of Stanford might be an odd choice for a confidant, but he had already shown himself to be quick-witted enough to see through her pretenses and sympathetic enough to assist her twice before. By now, he must have some inkling that matters between her and Lord Russelton were not as they should have been.

"It is not exactly as it looks, my lord. I fear I may have misled you a trifle before, when we—when I—well, when you spoke as you did just now, of teaching Lord Russelton a lesson. . . ." It was unexpectedly difficult to find the proper words. Miss Wentworth tried again. "You see, I do not really consider that any engagement exists between Frederick Russelton and myself—"

"I beg your pardon?" The Earl's eyebrows rose. "But surely I am not mistaken in thinking that an announcement was made? Sometime last year, I believe . . . yes, I remember the occasion very well. Farnsworth was in a frenzy when he read of it in the *Morning Post.* He kept threatening to blow his brains out, until a couple of his friends led him off to drown himself in an ocean of brandy instead."

Miss Wentworth laughed. "Mr. Farnsworth is very silly," she said demurely, the dimple playing about her mouth. "I'm quite sure he cares for his dinner a great deal more than he ever cared for me!"

"It would be unchivalrous for me to agree with that statement, Miss Wentworth, though Farnsworth's size would tend to confirm it! But I can assure you he was a great bore on the subject of his poor broken heart for many weeks. Farnsworth wasn't the only sufferer, either, if I recall rightly. Why, there was talk at White's about donning mourning bands for the occasion!"

Miss Wentworth smiled, but having begun she was determined to finish her confession. "Yes, the engagement was announced, of course. The thing is, Frederick no longer wishes to marry me. Oh, he has not actually said so—I would think better of him if he had—but I'm quite certain he is behaving this way," she gestured toward Miss Barrow's phaeton, "he is behaving this way so that I will take offense and cry off. I've been aware for some time that his feelings have . . . changed. Even that night at Lady Sefton's ball . . ." Miss Wentworth swallowed. "I'm afraid I led you a trifle astray on that occasion, my lord. As you supposed, I was trying to make Frederick jealous, but it was really more a matter of . . . well . . . revenge."

"Oh, but I was happy to be of assistance, Miss Wentworth, whatever your motives," the Earl assured her solemnly, while his dark eyes laughed at her in the most reprehensible way. "Anything further along those lines that I might do to assist you—"

"No, no! I mean—" Miss Wentworth collected herself. "I mean, I don't expect you to help, my lord. I am very angry with Frederick, of course, but . . . well, that is between him and me." There was a slight quaver in her voice, and she stared at the distant waters of the Serpentine with an intensity that could not quite disguise a suspicious moisture about her eyes.

The Earl was silent for a moment. When he spoke again, his voice held an uncharacteristic note of gentleness. "I believe Russelton has been playing rather deep of late," he said. "No doubt the young fool has strayed into dun territory. I know it probably doesn't make it easier to bear, but it might be some comfort to your pride. If only you'd had the forethought to provide yourself with a grandfather in the shipping business!"

"Yes, I know." Miss Wentworth nodded resolutely. "And I can understand—a little—but it would have been so much better if Frederick had told me outright, instead of—instead of—"

"He has certainly behaved very badly. Would you like me to take him out and thrash him soundly? I would be more than happy to do so, Miss Wentworth."

A smile began to reappear above the gloom overshadowing Miss Wentworth's countenance. "I wish you would," she said wistfully. "But I suppose it would cause a great deal of talk. No, it would never do, of course. Thank you all the same, my lord, but I believe I will have to wait and take my revenge in my own time."

"So you do intend to revenge yourself?"

"I daresay it seems very petty," said Miss Wentworth, a little shamefaced.

"Not at all: a perfectly human reaction. I expect I should do the same in your position. What form will your revenge take?"

"Well, I am not precisely certain yet," admitted Miss Wentworth. "But I imagine it will be mostly a matter of holding off, refusing to let Frederick have his freedom.

He can't offer for Miss Barrow until he is through with me! Our wedding is—was—set for June. I don't intend to let things go on for that long, of course, but the longer I can stall, the more it will likely vex him."

"I see," said the Earl pensively. "A very good revenge, too, if his creditors are pressing him. And probably Miss Barrow as well; she looks the sort of female who would chafe at delay. Russelton will be well-served if he marries her. It could only be for her fortune, of course."

"Of course. I am not in the least jealous of her," said Miss Wentworth with dignity. Then she laughed out loud. "No, that's not quite true, my lord. I'll admit that I'm a trifle jealous of Miss Barrow's phaeton. It would be great fun to have one's own phaeton to drive in the park. Both Henrietta and I are terribly envious of her, on that account."

The Earl ran an eye appraisingly over Miss Barrow' phaeton, just visible rounding the barrier. "Not a bad rig, but I don't like her cattle. Those bays are showy but unsound, unless I miss my guess. And Miss Barrow handles her whip awkwardly. I expect you could outshine her easily, Miss Wentworth." Moved by a strange and powerful urge to please the lovely creature at his side, he spoke impulsively, "And there's no reason why you shouldn't, come to think of it," he said. "I have a phaeton I seldom use. You're most welcome to borrow it some afternoon, whenever you please. Imagine how shocked Miss Barrow would be to see a rival of your caliber! Come, Miss Wentworth, wouldn't you enjoy taking the wind out of the shipping heiress's sails?"

Out of the corner of his eye, the Earl examined Miss Wentworth's face to see how she liked the idea, and made a mental note to go out and buy a phaeton suitable for a lady's use at the earliest opportunity. He wondered if he was insane, or merely a fool. A third possibility occurred to him, which he put aside for examination at a later time.

Miss Wentworth was smiling, envisioning herself in the Earl's dashing phaeton—any phaeton he owned was sure to be dashing—sweeping past Frederick and poor Miss Barrow with her unsound bays. "It would not do, you know," she said with a sigh. "People would think it very odd to see me driving your phaeton."

"I never drive it myself, Miss Wentworth." Which at least was true, he thought. "No one would be likely to recognize it. You'd need a groom of your own to accompany you—my Ned's pretty well known—but that could easily be arranged. I myself would be nowhere in the picture."

"But I could not drive a pair of horses in any case," said Miss Wentworth regretfully. "I drive our gig, back home, but Richard says I'm cow-handed and could never manage a pair. He taught me to drive the gig, so I suppose he should know."

"Nonsense," said the Earl. "I'll wager I could teach you to handle a pair in no time at all. Let me be your instructor, Miss Wentworth, and in a few weeks you can burst upon the scene as the newest female whip."

"Mama would never let me out the door with you, my lord," said Miss Wentworth, with devastating frankness. "It's very kind of you to offer, but I don't suppose there's any use even asking."

The Earl blinked. This complication had not occurred to him. The females with whom he had dealt in recent years did not require their mother's permission for anything they might choose to do in his company.

"I daresay I could call upon your mother and tell her

our plan," he ventured. "Not the part about discomfiting Russelton, naturally, but only that I am willing to teach you to drive."

"No. Oh, no. You see . . . there was some awkwardness about my even dancing with you, the other night. . . ."

The Earl grinned, his face suddenly alight with mischief. "You do not give me enough credit, Miss Wentworth. Let me come to call upon your mama. I'm sure she'd allow me to take you out driving—with a groom along for propriety of course—if only the matter was explained to her in the proper light. And I am held to be uncommonly persuasive, you know!"

"You might be able to persuade Mama," allowed Miss Wentworth, unable to keep from smiling at this shameless assertion. "But I fear you would never convince Aunt Constance, my lord, and it is she who generally decides whom I may or may not drive out with. My aunt, Lady Wentworth, you know."

"A dragon, is she?"

"Well, not precisely a *dragon.*" Miss Wentworth considered the question. "Aunt Constance isn't old, or ugly, but she has a way of looking at one . . . she frightens *me* a little, and *I* have known her all my life!"

"Dragon or not, I am willing to try. I'll wager I can talk her around in a trice."

"You would lose your wager, my lord!"

"Very sure of yourself, aren't you, Miss Wentworth?" The Earl's eyes held a dangerous gleam. "Do you care to hazard something on the issue . . . say, another kiss? A kiss against whatever you care to demand of me. I, too, am sure of myself, you see! Come, Miss Wentworth, if you are so certain of success, what cause have you to hesitate? Will you stake me a kiss?"

"Anything you like, my lord!" The gleam in the Earl's eye became more pronounced, and Miss Wentworth sought to rectify her error. "That is, a kiss will do very well, since I shan't be required to pay it. And for your stake in the wager, you must undertake to buy yourself a prayer book, if you—*when* you lose, to give your thoughts a more proper direction!"

"What makes you think I don't already own a prayer book, Miss Wentworth?" inquired the Earl, looking the picture of grieved virtue.

"Even if you do, it will do you no harm to have two of them," said Miss Wentworth severely. Her dimple began to flicker. "And just think of how edified everyone will be, when it becomes known that the Earl of Stanford was in Hatchard's buying himself a prayer book."

The Earl's lip twitched. "A horrifying prospect, Miss Wentworth. I should certainly send my groom in to buy it for me."

"No, that must be part of the wager. You must go into Hatchard's, announce your name in a loud, clear voice, and ask to be shown the prayer books. But I leave the choice of styles open to your own decision, my lord."

"Very well," said the Earl at last, a smile playing about his lips. "You put me on my mettle, but never let it be said that I cried craven on a bet! I must have a little time to plan my strategy, however. Until Thursday? I will come to call upon your aunt Thursday afternoon, Miss Wentworth. Be sure to have your prettiest carriage dress laid out!"

"And you must be sure to decide what color of prayer book will suit you, my lord!"

The curricle had come nearly full circle around the ring, and they were approaching the barouche drawn by the cream-colored ponies. Miss Wentworth looked quickly toward the Earl, wondering how he would react to the sight. Henrietta had said the lady in blue was now safely attached to some other gentleman, but Miss Wentworth's reliance upon Henrietta's words was not so great that she would not have welcomed further confirmation. The blond beauty raised her big blue eyes to watch as the Earl drove past, but he did not so much as glance in her direction, being occupied instead in giving Miss Wentworth a few preliminary pointers about the management of a pair of horses. Miss Wentworth was so pleased to have her hopes confirmed that she overlooked this brass-faced certitude about the outcome of the wager, and accepted his instructions with a becoming meekness.

The Earl soon located the Misses Ingleside and reined in beside them. While his groom stood to the greys' heads, he came around to assist Miss Wentworth in leaving the curricle. Gathering the long skirts of her riding habit over one arm, she cautiously essayed the step to the ground, but before she could attempt it, the Earl reached up and lifted her down with as little show of effort as if he had been lifting a child rather than a fully grown, though not very large, young lady. There was a giddy moment in which she found herself between heaven and earth, with the Earl's hands on her waist and his eyes looking into her own; then he set her upon her feet and released her with no attempt to prolong the intimacy. It was done so neatly and over so quickly that it should have been the most trivial of incidents, yet Miss Wentworth was conscious of feeling breathless, and the warmth of her cheeks made her certain she was blushing.

The Earl had turned aside to help Henrietta and

Emma remount their hacks. Then it was Miss Wentworth's turn, and in a moment more she, too, was in the saddle, watching him climb into the curricle. The groom scurried around to take his seat behind, and the Earl prepared to whip up his horses. "Don't forget, I'll bring my phaeton around to Berkeley Square Thursday for your first lesson, Miss Wentworth," he said, with heavy significance and an audacious smile. The Earl's groom gave his master a startled look and choked slightly. The Earl turned to look at him. "Er—did you say something, Ned?"

"No, my lord," said the groom, recovering himself.

The ladies watched the Earl drive off round the ring once more. "I shall keep these gloves forever," announced Emma in thrilling accents. "He touched my hand, you know, when he helped me to remount."

"Goose," said Henrietta. She transferred her attention to Miss Wentworth. "What was that all about, him saying he would call in Berkeley Square?"

Miss Wentworth shook her head. "He has offered to teach me drive with a pair of horses, but of course Mama and Aunt Constance will never allow me to go with him."

"Or Frederick either, I should think!"

"Or Frederick," agreed Miss Wentworth absently. Her eyes followed the Earl's curricle until it disappeared from view.

Chapter Eight

"And what phaeton was you telling the young lady you'd be bringing around on Thursday?" demanded the Earl's groom, once they had passed out of earshot of the ladies.

"The phaeton I am going to buy, of course."

"My lord, you'll catch cold at that." The groom spoke earnestly, with the license of long and faithful service. "Miss is quality, my lord, not the likes of *her.*" He nodded toward Alicia, still surrounded by the court of her admirers. "If you was thinking to go offering that young lady a slip on the shoulder—"

"Certainly not! You misunderstand the situation, Ned. I am merely doing the young lady a favor, from motives of purest chivalry," said the Earl piously. His groom snorted. "What! Don't you believe my motives are pure?"

"I'd be a sight more likely to believe they was, if it was an ugly girl you was doing the favor for, my lord!"

"She is lovely, isn't she?" mused the Earl, a faraway look in his eyes. "I am to teach her to drive. I wonder, would these greys be too lively for her to handle?"

"Yes," said his groom uncompromisingly.

"Then I must buy a pair as well as a phaeton." The Earl turned to smile at his disapproving servant. "Aren't you going to favor me with your advice on the subject, Ned?" he asked, in a provocative voice.

"I've known you a good long time, my lord, and I know when I'd be wasting my breath! All I can say is, I hope you don't find yourself in the suds over this business, as I don't doubt you will."

"I shouldn't wonder if you're right, but not in the sense *you* mean, I trust. Come, cannot I depend on you to advise me upon the selection of my new cattle?"

"You can depend on me for that," said his groom grudgingly. "But don't you go thinking I approve of this start, my lord, for I don't, and so I tell you!"

The Earl had no intention of losing his wager with Miss Wentworth. It represented a new and delightful challenge, with a prize well worth the winning; so well worth winning, in fact, that he chose to disregard the possibility of failure altogether and set out on a course of lavish expenditure as if victory were assured. A trace of doubt did obtrude occasionally, however. The Earl grinned whenever he thought of the horrid threat of that prayer book, and resolved to do all in his power to avoid such an outcome.

Proceeding then, with the assurance of success, the first order of business was clearly the acquisition of a suitable equipage for Miss Wentworth's driving lessons. The Earl went to Tattersall's on the next sale day to look for a phaeton and pair. Unfortunately, all the carriages on the block there struck him as rather shabby. He decided none of them was quite what he had in mind, but he did buy a beautifully matched pair of chestnuts, warranted to be sweet-goers and complete to a shade. After leaving Tattersalls, he visited a coachbuilder in St. James Street, where he ordered a phaeton of graceful lines, to be stained chestnut brown with bright brass fittings. The proprietor faithfully promised him that it would be delivered to his lodgings by Thursday afternoon.

The Earl left the coachbuilder's greatly pleased with his new purchases. The phaeton and pair together would make a striking turnout. He had a passing thought of Alicia's cream and blue barouche. That was more eye-catching, without question, but it was also—put brutally—designed mainly for purposes of advertisement. Such a flashy rig was not in the best of taste, nor could it be thought appropriate for the conveyance of a *lady*. Moreover, there was no comparison at all between the performance of the two vehicles: one was purely for show, and the other was quality, a carriage the Earl would not have minded being seen driving himself. He decided with satisfaction that it would certainly outshine Miss Barrow's phaeton and flashy bays.

The Earl preferred not to spend too much time trying to analyze why he was going to such lengths to gratify Miss Wentworth's whim. He did, however, spend a fair amount of time envisioning how well she would look in the phaeton that had been so carefully selected to please her. Chestnut brown should suit her very well; it was almost the same color as the riding habit she had been wearing the other day in the park. At odd moments he found himself thinking of her as she had appeared that day, sitting in his curricle, her hair almost golden against the russet brown of her hat, and her eyes as vividly green—he kept coming back to that subject, too, somehow—as vividly green as emeralds.

Along with his excursions to Tattersall's and the coachbuilder, the Earl made a few other visits that week. He surprised a middle-aged spinster of his acquaintance by calling upon her and expressing a flattering interest in her affairs; if he deftly managed to bring the conversation around to the subject of her good friend Constance Wentworth, this manipulation went unnoticed. Lady Emily disgorged an amazing amount of information about Lady Wentworth, most of it quite irrelevant, but the Earl left Lady Emily's little house well satisfied. Based on information received from Lady Emily, he went on to set certain researches into motion. If everything worked out as he hoped, he thought he would be prepared to face the dragon in her lair when Thursday afternoon arrived.

Miss Wentworth, meanwhile, was very much divided in mind, trying to decide how best to mention the Earl's surprising offer to her mother, aunt, and cousin. Even to herself, she could scarcely admit how badly she wanted permission to drive out with the Earl of Stanford. She had a pretty good idea of the obstacles that must be overcome first, however, and was certain the Earl would be unsuccessful in convincing Lady Wentworth in spite of all the powers of persuasion he might possess. Miss Wentworth resigned herself, as she thought, to failure, but in the meantime she wavered between telling her aunt beforehand of the Earl's intended call, and the alternate plan of letting him come unheralded, giving him the advantage of surprise.

The decision was taken from her hands. On Monday afternoon, Henrietta had happened to let fall to Sir Richard that they had encountered the Earl in the park the week before. Sir Richard had in turn demanded an explanation from his cousin at the dinner table Monday night, and the whole story was dragged out of Miss Wentworth. Almost the whole story: she prudently made no mention of the wager, but merely said that the Earl of Stanford had offered to teach her to drive a phaeton and pair, and that he was coming to call Thursday afternoon with a view to doing so.

"Constance, what do you think?" appealed Mrs. Wentworth. "I'm sure I never would have thought it of Stanford, but it sounds harmless enough, with his coming to call first, you know."

Lady Wentworth looked grave. "I cannot like the idea, Amelia. It would look very particular, and give rise to the sort of talk that is best avoided."

"Yes. Yes, but he is still a very eligible *parti,* you know, when all is said and done," said Mrs. Wentworth, frowning. "The Collingwoods are an *excellent* family. And since he is disposed to admire Rebecca . . . though of course she is already engaged to dear Frederick. And I'm sure I wouldn't really trust Stanford, with the stories one hears, and if he knows Rebecca is betrothed to Frederick Russelton . . . does he know, Rebecca?"

"He knows, Mama."

"It is very puzzling."

"I myself will see Lord Stanford," announced Lady Wentworth in a voice of decision. "I will ascertain his motives. I fear they are doubtful, but I will inform him in any case that no matter how well intentioned, his attentions to Rebecca cannot be other than unwelcome. Once I have spoken to him, you may depend on it that he will see things in the proper light and take himself off."

Miss Wentworth feared her aunt was probably correct, but she continued to hope. On Thursday afternoon, she stationed herself in the drawing room with some needlework, her ears attuned to catch the sound of the Earl's arrival. She was not dressed to go out, for her confidence was not running high, but she was wearing a very pretty round dress of white muslin patterned in tiny green leaves, with a green ribbon threaded through her curls. Lady Wentworth was also in the drawing room, engaged in writing letters and looking her usual imperturbable self. Presently, the sound of wheels was heard in the street outside. There was a knock on the door. Miss Wentworth glanced toward her aunt. Lady Wentworth rose majestically to her feet as the Earl was ushered into the drawing room. "Leave us, Rebecca," she ordered.

Miss Wentworth left. She stole a look at the Earl as she passed out of the room. His eyes met hers, and she noted that he appeared perfectly self-possessed and also extremely elegant, in a blue coat cut by a master hand, an exquisitely arranged neckcloth, buff inexpressibles, and gleaming Hessians. He took in her own stay-at-home raiment, shook his head, and gave her a reproving look, his eyes merry.

Miss Wentworth looked back an apology before shutting the door behind her. She retired to the salon across the hall and waited with resignation to see the Earl summarily ejected by her aunt. If possible, she hoped to catch him on the way out and exchange a few words with him before he went out of her life forever.

Miss Wentworth fidgeted about the salon for some time. She rearranged all the ornaments on the mantelpiece; she flipped through the latest issue of *La Belle Assemblée* that was lying upon the sofa table; she examined her fingernails, and plaited and unplaited the tassels on the window draperies. It seemed to be taking Lady Wentworth a very long time to ascertain the Earl's motives.

Miss Wentworth left the salon and hovered uncertainly near the door of the drawing room. She could hear nothing of what was being said within.

She finally ventured to put her ear against the door, fearing every moment to be caught in this undignified posture by one of the servants. All she could hear was an indistinct murmur: her aunt's low, well-bred tones, interrupted occasionally by the Earl's deeper voice. It was maddening not to be able to make out what was being said.

Miss Wentworth returned to the salon and waited for another ten minutes, her curiosity becoming more unbearable by the moment. Finally, she resolved to go boldly into the drawing room and find out for herself what was going on. She could always claim she was merely retrieving her needlework, if an excuse was needed.

To Miss Wentworth's relief, her aunt did not seem annoyed by her reappearance. "That must be the Sussex Ramages, then," Lady Wentworth was saying, as Miss Wentworth entered the room and advanced toward her needlework lying atop the worktable. "I had heard that Rowena had married again. She was the second daughter, was she not?"

"Yes, I believe so," said the Earl, rising politely at Miss Wentworth's entrance and shooting her a look eloquent of triumph. The bits of conversation she had already heard, coupled with the Earl's triumphant demeanor, forced Miss Wentworth to acknowledge with respect that somehow he had managed to discover her aunt's Achilles' heel. Lady Wentworth barely looked up as her niece seated herself timidly on the sofa; she was too busy working out the ramifications of various families related both to herself and the Earl, emerging at length to announce that the Collingwoods and the Wentworths were related in some small degree.

"Yes, you are quite correct, Stanford, though of course the relation between the families is rather slight. More in the nature of a connection, I would say," said Lady Wentworth scrupulously.

"Oh, I am sure it merits a closer relationship than that, Lady Wentworth," protested the Earl, smiling impishly at Miss Wentworth. "I look upon the Wentworths as relations. When it was pointed out to me that Rebecca and I are actually related, I naturally—"

"Connected," said Lady Wentworth, but did not seem displeased by the implication that a closer relationship existed between the two families than was really the case. High stickler though she was, she was gratified to find herself connected—no, related—to the Collingwoods, who were, after all, a very good family. It was particularly gratifying that the scion of the noble family himself was disposed to recognize the relationship.

Indeed, with all this to recommend him, Lady Wentworth found she was easily able to overlook all the more lurid stories she had heard in the past concerning the Earl of Stanford. She reflected with satisfaction that she had heard no real ill of him in recent years; that unfortunate contretemps years ago with the Satterthwaite girl fell under the category of youthful peccadilloes and might be dismissed accordingly. He seemed now to feel just as he ought, on serious matters, and his opinions (coinciding, as they did, very closely with her own) she found to be both well formed and well expressed.

In the space of an hour, the Earl had risen so much in Lady Wentworth's estimation that she was now calling him familiarly by his title, while Miss Wentworth herself was being referred to as Rebecca by both parties and she could scarcely believe her own ears. It appeared that the subject of driving lessons had not yet been broached, but Miss Wentworth dared not interrupt the amicable relationship that was developing. She sat quietly on the sofa, setting stitches in her needlework and looking up every now and then to find the Earl's eyes upon her, dancing with amusement.

Presently, he made as if to rise, and then sat down again as though struck by a sudden thought. "By the by, Lady Wentworth," he said. "I had nearly forgotten one of my purposes in calling. When I made Rebecca's acquaintance some time back, I took the opportunity of delivering my felicitations on her approaching marriage. She chanced to mention that Russelton is a great admirer of female whips and was inclined to lament her own shortcomings in that area. I am accounted a fair whip myself; it occurred to me that I might properly offer my services as an instructor. Should Russelton present Rebecca with her own phaeton someday, it would be helpful if she had some familiarity with the principles of driving one. Then, too, we were considering it in the nature of a surprise for Russelton: Rebecca and I agreed it would be a prime joke to see his amazement and—er—delight, at finding his wife-to-be an accomplished whip, unbeknownst to himself." The Earl favored Lady Wentworth with his most blatantly charming smile. "Would you see any objection to such a proposal, Lady Wentworth? I had thought we might commence the lessons this afternoon, if you were agreeable to letting Rebecca accompany me for an hour or so."

"A groom would be accompanying you on the lessons, of course?" said Lady Wentworth gravely.

"Of course," the Earl assured her, with equal gravity.

"Then I can see no objection. But Rebecca, you are

not dressed to go out! Quickly, child, it is very kind of Stanford to take so much trouble on your behalf. Pray do not keep him waiting."

Dismissing her niece with a wave of her hand, Lady Wentworth turned back toward the Earl, her fine grey eyes kindling as she again took up her favorite subject. "I wonder, Stanford, are you acquainted with the Smith-Blessingtons, cousins of mine on my mother's side? No, not the Oxfordshire branch, but the—"

Miss Wentworth caught a last glimpse of the Earl's wicked grin as she meekly left the room once more. She sped upstairs to change her clothing. Soon she was re-entering the drawing room wearing a carriage dress of willow green muslin, topped with a spencer jacket of leaf green velvet. Her straw bonnet was lined with leaf green silk and ornamented with matching ribbons; a cluster of willow green ostrich plumes tipped with darker green finished off an article of headgear that several of her admirers had pronounced becoming in the extreme.

At Miss Wentworth's entrance, the Earl rose and took leave of Lady Wentworth, bowing over her hand with a nice mixture of deference and gallantry. Miss Went worth observed with awe that there was something very much like a simper on her stately aunt's face, and felt an increased respect for the Earl of Stanford as she laid her own gloved hand on his arm.

"That's a pretty bonnet," said the Earl, looking Miss Wentworth over with approval as he led her out the door. "But then, you have been admirably dressed every time I have seen you, Miss Wentworth. Allow me to say that your taste is excellent."

"Thank you, my lord," said Miss Wentworth. The look in his eye made her feel rather shy all at once, but she forgot her shyness when she caught sight of the shining new phaeton, harnessed to the pair of glossy chestnut horses. "Oh, is *that* your phaeton?"

"Yes, that's it," said the Earl, enormously pleased at her delighted face.

"But it looks quite new! I can't imagine why you don't wish to drive it yourself."

"I find I prefer my curricle and greys," said the Earl, avoiding his groom's eye. "Since you are just beginning to learn to drive a phaeton and pair, however, I thought you might find these chestnuts easier to handle than the greys. They're very well-behaved, but well-actioned, too. Certainly a cut above Miss Barrow's bays."

Miss Wentworth admired the chestnuts in extravagant terms while the Earl assisted her into the phaeton. Once they were both seated, she looked over at him and dimpled. "What a complete hand you are, my lord. I doubt Frederick will really be delighted to find me an accomplished whip, even if he is an admirer of female whips in general!"

"Yes, I fear I may have skated perilously close to falsehood there, though I congratulate myself that I made no statement that was actually untrue," said the Earl virtuously, his face alight with laughter. "But happily the dragon seemed to find it a believable idea! By the way, Miss Wentworth, I did not think her a dragon at all. Your aunt seems a very agreeable lady, if a trifle over-eloquent on the subject of her family tree."

"I cannot credit it, even now, that you actually got her permission to take me driving." Miss Wentworth shook her head in amazement. "But as you say, Aunt Constance has a great deal of pride in her family. Undoubtably it was finding out you were related to her that changed her mind, for she had every intention of sending you about your business, my lord. What a coincidence that the two families should be related."

"Not such a coincidence, really. Most of these old families are interrelated if you only go back far enough. Thank heaven for Rowena Ramage and her second marriage! I found out Lady Wentworth had a weakness for genealogy, put a man to work researching our respective families, and he was able to dredge up enough ammunition to enable me to—if I may phrase it so—slay the dragon! I did have another line or two I intended to follow up, if the family relation wasn't enough to overcome her scruples, but as you can see that didn't prove necessary."

"What a lot of trouble you have gone to, only to give me driving lessons," said Miss Wentworth, rather astonished.

"Ah, but the driving lessons were only a secondary consideration, as I may as well admit. Remember that little matter of our wager?" The Earl laughed aloud as a look of extreme consciousness spread over Miss Wentworth's face. "No, don't worry, I'm not going to demand payment today. I believe I'll hold the threat of it over your head for a while, like a sword of Damocles, so that you'll never enjoy an easy moment. Then, when you least expect it—"

"I'm not *afraid*, my lord," said Miss Wentworth with spirit. "I wagered and lost, and now I suppose I must play and pay, as Richard says. Oh, my, whatever will he say when he learns you are giving me driving lessons? He was a bit upset, the other night at the opera, when I—when you—"

"Since we are all relations now, your cousin can have no objection!"

"Not relations, my lord. Merely connections!"

"No, Miss Wentworth, I insist that we are relations. And that being the case, I think we can dispense with the formality of titles, don't you? Your aunt is already calling me Stanford, and here you are, still my-lording me. I would rather you called me Jack. That is how I am known to my friends, and we are friends as well as relations, I hope."

"Jack?" said Miss Wentworth doubtfully. "I don't think I can."

"Why not?" inquired the Earl.

"It seems very odd to think of calling you Jack, when you are an earl." The dimple flickered around Miss Wentworth's mouth. "I'm sure Aunt Constance would feel it was most irregular!"

"Ah, but I'm a most irregular earl, you know, and I insist that you call me Jack. And I will call you Becky, so we can be nice and informal all around." Miss Wentworth frowned. "What, does that offend you?" said the Earl in surprise.

"I have never cared to be called Becky."

"Why not?"

There was a short silence. "It sounds like a housemaid," owned Miss Wentworth, rather crossly.

The Earl grinned. "You don't look like one, never fear! For one thing, no housemaid would be wearing such a dashing bonnet. Yes, Becky it must be; Rebecca I find too formal for such close friends as we are destined to become." Miss Wentworth looked at him quickly, but he returned her regard with a bland smile. "I expect we will be seeing each other quite often now, since I have undertaken to teach you to drive," he explained.

"Oh, yes. I expect so, my lord," said Miss Wentworth, with the suspicion of a smile hovering on her own lips.

"Jack," said the Earl firmly.

"Jack," agreed Miss Wentworth, and promptly blushed.

While the driving lessons were in their early stages, it was jointly agreed that they would avoid the park and crowded West End, and seek out some quiet residential area where traffic was sparse. Miss Wentworth had no wish to parade her lack of skill in front of a crowd, and certainly not before the amused eyes of the *ton;* she felt it would make a far more impressive splash to appear in the park a full-fledged whip rather than drive there before her technique was perfected. The Earl agreed completely with this viewpoint.

"Miss Barrow, for instance, still betrays a little awkwardness in controlling her cattle. I've noticed her about a couple of times since we saw her last week, and it's my opinion that she could have used some additional tuition before making her own debut."

"Perhaps you can volunteer to teach her, when you are finished with me," suggested Miss Wentworth, with a daring smile.

"Devil a bit of it! I don't coach heiresses, only—" The word beauties was on the tip of his tongue, but he bit it back, afraid it might call to mind his association with various other beauties. For some reason, he suddenly felt sensitive on this subject around Miss Wentworth. "Only damsels in distress," he finished, after a tiny hesitation.

Miss Wentworth glanced at him, rather offended. The mention of damsels in distress made her wonder if the Earl pitied her. It was intolerable to think that he had suggested the driving lessons only because he felt sorry for her; even seduction would have been a preferable motive. "I suppose it will take up a great deal of your time, doing this for me," she said, watching him closely.

"Oh, I doubt you will be such a slow student as you fear. I'll wager that in a month's time you'll be driving at least as well as Miss Barrow." The Earl turned his face to smile at her. "What a gamester I am, laying wagers left and right! How about it, Becky? If you care to take me up on the matter, we could double the stakes and say—"

"I'll wager no more wagers with you, sir! After the unprincipled way you hoaxed poor Aunt Constance I've no illusions about the depths to which you will sink to gain your ends."

"Ah, well." The Earl heaved a philosophical sigh. "I can see I'll never make a gamester of you, Becky: you're too cautious by half! But I have no doubt I can make you into a creditable whip, if you're willing to apply yourself. This looks a quiet street. You take the ribbons now, and we'll begin our first lesson."

The Earl proved to be a far better teacher than Miss Wentworth's cousin had been. Lord Stanford did not wrench the reins from her hands at the slightest sign of trouble, or box her ears when she failed to remember his instructions, as Sir Richard had been wont to do. Instead, he lounged comfortably beside her, giving an occasional word of advice; even a near collision with a stray hackney coach earned her no more than a mildly-worded suggestion to mind her horses.

The Earl's groom was less sanguine. There was an occasional sharp intake of breath from the seat behind, and a full-blown sigh of relief when Berkeley Square was regained in safety, but the Earl gave it as his opinion that the first lesson had gone very well, upon the whole. Miss Wentworth thanked him, her cheeks pink with pleasure.

No one thought to mention the Earl's visit—or its outcome—to Sir Richard Wentworth. Sir Richard kept his own hours, and often dined away from home; consequently, it was several days and several driving lessons later that he first encountered the Earl of Stanford in Berkeley Square.

The Earl and Miss Wentworth were just leaving for another driving lesson as he came into the hall. Sir Richard looked stunned at the sight of his cousin's escort. He managed to stammer out a reply to the Earl's civil greeting, but they were out the door before he could think to inquire about their business. At the dinner table, however, he took his mother to task for what he called "letting Stanford run tame in the household."

"Dash it, Mama, you can't mean you let yourself be bamboozled by that fellow! There's no relation between the Collingwoods and the Wentworths."

It was the wrong thing to say, as Sir Richard was very soon brought to realize. Lady Wentworth drew her brows together, and for the next half-hour Sir Richard was dragged remorselessly through a tangle of cousins-thrice-removed and connections-by-marriage, until he was at last forced to admit that the Collingwood family tree and that of the Wentworths did indeed just touch each other, among the uppermost and outermost branches.

"But you can't call that being *related,* Mama. Dash it, the merest connection!"

"If Stanford chooses to call it a relation, then we need not scruple to do so," said Lady Wentworth reprovingly. "I spoke with him at length, Richard, and I believe you are putting yourself in a passion for nothing. It is merely a matter of a few driving lessons for Rebecca. There can be no harm in that, in an open carriage and with a groom along. And it is not as though Stanford believed Rebecca to be an unprotected girl, without a family to guard her honor."

Sir Richard looked a little blue at the idea of guarding his cousin's honor against the Earl of Stanford. Besides being uncommonly handy with his fists, the Earl was known to be a crack shot; Sir Richard had personally observed him culping wafers with deadly accuracy at Manton's Shooting Gallery only the week before. But from long experience, Sir Richard knew it was useless to argue with his mother. Instead, he took Miss Wentworth aside and attempted to instill a word of warning in her ear.

"And if he tries anything—anything at all—mind, you *tell* me," finished Sir Richard, with a harassed face.

"I thank you, Richard, but I believe I am very well able to take care of myself."

"Oh, no, you're not, my girl! You're not up to snuff yet, by a long chalk. If you knew some of the stories they tell about Stanford—"

"Belinda Satterthwaite, do you mean?"

"Dash it, Beck," exclaimed Sir Richard in high dudgeon. "I'd like to know who had the infernal gall to tell you about that!"

Miss Wentworth's dimple flickered, but she did not betray the good-natured Henrietta. "It is common knowledge, I believe," she said soothingly. "And did not all that happen a very long time ago?"

Sir Richard shook his head. "Maybe so, but I can't like it, Beck. And I don't know what Russelton's about. Dash it, he's supposed to be marrying you in June, and here he's letting you run all over town with a fellow like that—"

"It is none of Frederick's concern whom I drive with! You will notice that *he* is out driving with Clarissa Barrow at every opportunity."

Sir Richard regarded his cousin for a long moment. "This engagement of yours, Beck: it doesn't look to me as though things are going at all well," he said severely.

"No, you are quite right, Richard. But you need not bother yourself with my affairs. Really, I am perfectly well able to take care of myself," repeated Miss Wentworth, hoping that this would prove to be true.

Lord Russelton might have objected to the driving lessons had he known about them. Consorting with the Wicked Earl would have made a fine pretext for a quarrel, and a quarrel might in turn have led to an open rupture that would have ended Lord Russelton's inconvenient engagement once and for all. But Lord Russelton had been forced to retire to the wilds of Norfolk, owing to the state of his pocketbook and the importunings of his creditors. He left London the day after Miss Wentworth saw him in Hyde Park with the shipping heiress.

Miss Wentworth received a curt note informing her of her fiancé's temporary removal from London society, and was extremely pleased by the news. His absence would probably check some of the rumors that were flying about, concerning his fondness for Miss Barrow's company. By the time he came back to London, Miss Wentworth hoped to have thought of a plan for ending the engagement on her own terms, preferably while exacting some sort of revenge for past offenses. At the very least she could astound Lord Russelton and Miss Barrow by flaunting her newly acquired driving skills in front of their disbelieving eyes. Miss Wentworth was beginning to think this might be revenge enough. She was growing weary of keeping up a pretense of being happily engaged. The first sting of resentment had passed, and she now thought it might be better to make a clean break, accept whatever humiliation the break entailed, and get on with her life.

She finally determined to bring the engagement to an end just as soon as she made her appearance in the park with the Earl's phaeton. The idea of making a final gesture of defiance had captured her imagination; in any event, she told herself that this was why she was so eager to hone her driving skills. Honing her driving skills naturally meant seeing the Earl. Miss Wentworth was enjoying the hours spent in his company very much and was sorry to think that the driving lessons would have to end as soon as she had learned to drive well enough to outstrip the shipping heiress. There was no reason to think the Earl would have anything more to do with her, once the object of the lessons had been attained. Weeks went by, and Miss Wentworth felt she was not quite ready; Lord Russelton came back from Norfolk, and still she was unwilling to take the decisive step.

At last Miss Wentworth acknowledged to herself that she was putting off that final confrontation. She wondered what it was she was waiting for.

Chapter Nine

The Earl of Stanford was no longer under the illusion that chivalry played any part in his dealings with Rebecca Wentworth. What he had begun to suspect on the afternoon in the park, had crystallized into complete certainty as the weeks went by: he had lost his heart at last. The only uncertainty remaining was the question of what he was going to do about it.

There could be no uncertainty whatever about the feeling itself. In common with those people who escape common childhood maladies as children, only to suffer the same maladies later in life with devastating effect, the Earl's deferred case of first love proved to be an extremely serious one. He ate, slept, and breathed with the image of Rebecca Wentworth fixed firmly in his mind. She occupied his thoughts to the exclusion of such mundane matters as food and drink, removing once and for all any tendency toward avoirdupois. While in the grip of his obsession, he was apt to become rather preoccupied. His groom began to prophesy a speedy and humiliating expulsion from the Four-in-Hand Club after his master had three times unaccountably failed to note the presence of pedestrians in the path of his curricle, and once, a rather large mailcoach. The Earl only laughed and cheerfully advised his groom to hold his tongue. Mr. Deane held his tongue, but his position as groom during Miss Wentworth's driving lessons gave him every opportunity to observe the Earl's behavior while in that young lady's company, and he was not slow in drawing his own conclusions. Like most of the Earl's retainers, he had an affection for his erratic but good-natured master; Mr. Deane felt a strong sympathetic interest in the progress of my lord's love affair, but he also obtained a certain amount of enjoyment in seeing the cynical, heart-hardened Earl of Stanford behaving very much like a lovesick schoolboy.

Indeed, after a brief, half-hearted struggle to deny what was happening to him, the Earl had decided to surrender to the inevitable and was now bringing to the experience all the energy and enthusiasm that had once been devoted to dissipation.

He indulged in the usual lover's pastime of trying to trace the growth of his feelings, attempting to pinpoint the exact moment when attraction had blossomed into love. On the whole, he thought the night at the opera had marked the crisis. The words Miss Wentworth had unwittingly let fall that night had led him to reevaluate and finally reform his way of life. He could not claim to have done it for her sake, yet he had changed himself because of her, and he thought now that the change was likely to prove permanent.

There had always been a kind of invisible barrier across which he could not or would not step, a limit to what he would allow himself to do even at his most dissipated. He now recognized with rueful amusement that at heart he was really a good deal like his respectable father, all past behavior to the contrary notwithstanding;

the idea of mending his ways had been lurking unacknowledged in the back of his mind for some time. He had only wanted the proper motivation to point him in the right direction.

The Earl smiled to himself to think what a model of rectitude he was becoming, now that the proper motivation had appeared. He had ceased to frequent certain dens of iniquity where he was not unknown. His more disreputable acquaintances found themselves suddenly bereft of his company, and exclaimed over his absence for a week or two until fresh sensations absorbed their attention. The Earl had taken no new mistress since Alicia, nor had he renewed his pursuit of Lady Rosamund; he thought of his uncle's words once more, and gave those words a consideration they had not received at the time they were spoken. Giles thought it time he married and settled down. The Earl now agreed with him wholeheartedly, for since coming to know Rebecca Wentworth he had begun to feel that it was not a mistress he wanted, nor yet another married flirt, but a wife of his own.

In his extreme youth, he had sworn he would never lock himself into a narrow, respectable existence like that of his father. He had rather sneered at the thought of such a sober, settled style of living. Perhaps some day, when he was old, and life could offer no more pleasure, but certainly not while youth held, and London beckoned with a thousand enticements. Now the Earl found he had changed his mind. He would never choose to forgo London entirely, as his father had done, but the idea of spending most of the year at Stanford Park was beginning to hold a restful sort of appeal.

He could picture himself, in his mind's eye, attending to his estates, becoming a model landowner, enjoying the mild diversions of county society, the hunting and shooting, and above all coming home to spend the evenings with a wife of his own, and perhaps children, too, someday. In years past, he had never been able to see himself in such a role, but he thought it was one he could now enjoy very much, if Rebecca Wentworth was the wife in question.

Having made this momentous decision, the Earl began to face the difficulty of translating daydream into reality. He cursed himself for getting off on the wrong foot at the Seftons' ball. Although he could not really regret kissing Miss Wentworth, there was no denying that by doing so he had cast doubt on his intentions. Everything he did from now on was likely to be colored in her mind by his behavior that night. Regretfully, he decided he had better postpone the kiss she owed for their wager until she was free from her present engagement and there could be no doubt about his motives. With all the disadvantages of his disreputable past to overcome, it behooved him at present to maintain a strict propriety in his dealings with Miss Wentworth.

Her continuing engagement to Lord Russelton worried him not a little. Miss Wentworth had claimed her betrothal was no more than a charade, but she showed no signs of bringing it to an end as time went on, and occasionally the Earl found himself wondering if she still had hopes of marrying Russelton in spite of her avowed disgust of that gentleman's behavior. It had been understood that she would break her engagement once she had made an appearance in the park with the borrowed phaeton and chestnuts, as a final gesture to put her fiancé's nose out of joint. The Earl had agreed that this was a fine notion, and had aided and abetted her in it, but she was now quite a pretty whip, and the reasons she gave for waiting were sounding suspiciously like excuses.

The Earl felt his hands were tied by the present situation. He wanted to declare his intentions openly, in the approved way. Having decided to embrace respectability, he found that even such an enjoyable pastime as teaching Miss Wentworth to drive carried with it a faintly distasteful flavor, when said lessons were in truth a subterfuge to pursue a young lady who still technically belonged to someone else. Such conduct could not but raise doubts in Miss Wentworth's mind, assuming she was aware of his feelings.

The Earl had not yet said anything about his feelings, but he felt they must be becoming obvious by now; what were not so obvious were Miss Wentworth's own sentiments. Miss Wentworth was friendly, she was happy to flirt with him, and she seemed to enjoy his company, but he was often conscious of an element of reserve in her behavior. Doubt about his intentions would explain this reserve, but (the Earl made himself face the thought) it could equally well be a fundamental lack of interest in himself. How dreadful if the only woman he had ever loved failed to return his regard! The Earl resolved to go cautiously.

He was more than ever inclined toward caution by an incident that took place around this time. Since he had satisfied Miss Wentworth's family about the propriety of the driving lessons, it had not occurred to the Earl that other people might find anything amiss. The lessons took place outside the fashionable section of town, and he and Miss Wentworth had been quite successful in avoiding meeting anyone they knew on their drives. This secrecy had been necessary to keep Lord Russelton from hearing of his fiancée's doings before she was ready to put her plan into action, but it had also lent a rather clandestine coloring to the driving lessons, a coloring that would not have attended a more public intercourse. It came as a disagreeable surprise to the Earl when he discovered that word had definitely leaked out.

Looking in at White's one evening, he had wandered into the cardrooms. In one of them he found several of his acquaintances, who hailed him with delight.

"Jack! Well met, old fellow, we were just hoping to find someone to make up a fourth at whist," said Mr. James DeLacey, a slight, fair-haired gentleman with a prominent nose.

"Thought you were out of town, Stanford," said another gentleman at the table whom the Earl knew slightly, a stout, red-faced individual named Mr. Thomas Fairbanks. "Haven't seen you about lately."

"I have been rather occupied of late, but not out of town," said the Earl, taking a seat and accepting the hand of cards being dealt him. He nodded toward the lean, dark-faced gentleman at his right. "Good to see you, Hawthorne. Any luck at Newmarket last week?"

Lord Hawthorne grimaced. "Not a jot. Damned screw didn't even place. I haven't seen you about, either, Stanford, now that I think of it. Where've you been keeping yourself?"

"Or who's he been keeping?" said Mr. Fairbanks, with a sly smile.

Mr. DeLacey looked up from his cards. "That was a dashed pretty girl I saw you with the other day," he said. "Driving a brown phaeton, pair of chestnuts?"

The Earl only smiled, refusing to be drawn. "Your trick, I think, Fairbanks."

"By Jove, yes," said Lord Hawthorne. "Come to think of it, I saw you out in a phaeton a couple of weeks ago with . . . Miss Wentworth, wasn't it? Meant to ask you about it earlier, but it slipped my mind."

"What, the Green-Eyed Incomparable?" Three pairs of eyes regarded the Earl with lively interest.

"Thought you was sticking to married ones nowadays, Jack," said Mr. DeLacey, grinning broadly.

The Earl knew a sudden desire to bloody noses all around. "Miss Wentworth is related to me through her aunt, Lady Wentworth," he said stiffly. "I am teaching her to drive."

"Driving lessons, eh?" said Lord Hawthorne. "You want to watch yourself, Stanford, or you'll find yourself caught in parson's mousetrap yet. That's how they get you, my boy, mark my words: first it'll be driving lessons and then—"

"Miss Wentworth is already engaged to be married," said the Earl. "And if you would play your cards, Hawthorne, instead of—"

"That's right, she's booked to young Russelton," interrupted Mr. DeLacey, nodding. "Puffed off last Season in the *Morning Post.* I remember poor old Farnsworth's being so cut up about it at the time."

Mr. Fairbanks had been staring at the Earl very hard, and suddenly he let out a guffaw of laughter. "By God, Stanford, if that ain't just like you! Getting in your work beforehand with the girl, what?"

The other two at the table joined in his laughter, thinking this a very good sort of joke. The refrain was taken up with glee.

"He means to have the reversion of her, once Russelton's married her and made her eligible for his own attentions!"

"What a devil you are, Jack!"

"We'll have a wager on it," said Mr. Fairbanks, chortling with laughter and choosing to disregard the storm clouds gathering on the Earl's brow. He began to rise from his seat. "I'll ring for Ragget to bring the betting book. What do you say, Stanford? I'll lay you a monkey that you have her—"

A flurry of action erupted within the cardroom. Chairs were knocked aside and cards flung to the floor; Mr. Fairbanks found himself gasping like a landed fish as he was yanked to his feet and pinned against the wall. A pair of murderous dark eyes blazed into his own.

"I would take it very much amiss to have Miss Wentworth's name bandied about in such a way," said the Earl through clenched teeth. "The young lady is a relation of mine. You understand me, I hope?"

"Surely, surely," Mr. Fairbanks made haste to say. He was released and hesitated for a moment before he picked up his chair and sat down again. "No need to be so short-tempered about it, Stanford," he complained, rubbing the back of his head and eyeing the Earl askance. "Only having a bit of fun, don't you know."

The game was resumed, though there was little conversation at the table during the remainder of the play. When the game was over, the Earl stood up, collected his winnings, and left the cardroom.

"Well," said Lord Hawthorne, looking after him. "Well!"

"Never known old Jack to be so touchy about one of his little affairs," volunteered Mr. DeLacey, his face speculative. "Miss Wentworth, eh? I wonder."

"Sits the wind in that quarter, d'you think?"

Mr. DeLacey considered the idea. "Shouldn't think so," he said at last. "Mean to say, she's engaged to Russelton. Saw the announcement myself. No, must be because she's related to him, like he said. Fond of her; don't want talk bruited about."

"I never heard there was any relation between the Collingwoods and the Wentworths," said Mr. Fairbanks sulkily.

"Oh, those old families are all related," said Mr. De-Lacey, unconsciously echoing the Earl's words. "Very good *ton,* the Wentworths. Related to everybody, I shouldn't wonder."

After his temper had had time to cool, the Earl was able to see humor in his own ferocious championship of the proprieties, but he was also conscious as never before of the disadvantages of his reputation. Weeks of good behavior could not atone for years of dissipation. It was no wonder if Miss Wentworth failed to take him seriously.

In this he was quite correct. Miss Wentworth had no suspicion of the Earl's honorable intentions. Like most girls, she had been brought up to consider every unwed male acquaintance in the light of a possible future husband, but though she had thought several hundred times how wonderful it would be to be married to the Earl, she never for one moment imagined it was marriage he had in mind. His attentions toward herself she interpreted as chivalry, always with the dark, exciting possibility that he might be planning to seduce her someday. So far he had made no attempt to do so, unless one counted that kiss at Lady Sefton's. But it began to look as though that had been a freak incident, and one the Earl did not care to repeat; he had never even claimed the kiss she owed him for losing the wager.

As the weeks went by, Miss Wentworth became increasingly certain he had forgotten all about it. It was depressing that he showed such a lack of eagerness to claim his prize, and frustrating that she could not mention the matter herself without appearing unbecomingly eager, but there was always an off chance that he was only biding his time for some unfathomable reason of his own. Accordingly, Miss Wentworth remained very much on her guard. She felt a strong attraction toward the Earl of Stanford, no doubt about it, but she assured herself that this attraction would never lead her to succumb to his very considerable charm.

Miss Wentworth's nineteenth birthday was fast approaching. To celebrate the occasion, Mrs. Wentworth wanted to hold a large dinner party, with dancing afterward. Her daughter vetoed the idea.

"I would rather it was just us, Mama, a family party," urged Miss Wentworth. A large party would inevitably include Lord Russelton, who was now back in London after his stay in Norfolk.

"Well, if you would prefer it so, my dear." Mrs. Wentworth looked disappointed at first, but soon rallied. "It would be cozier with only the family present, to be sure. And naturally we will invite dear Frederick, for he is almost family now." Miss Wentworth's heart sank. She could only hope her fiancé had other plans for the evening, or would be obliging enough to pretend he did. "I'll write a note to Frederick this afternoon, inviting him to dinner," Mrs. Wentworth went on, taking her daughter's delight for granted.

"You might also invite Stanford," suggested Lady Wentworth. The Earl had become a great favorite with Miss Wentworth's aunt. He shamelessly courted her favor, too, coming to call now and then for the sole purpose (he said) of talking with her, thus rendering himself as agreeable to the formidable dowager as he had to the dowager's niece. "It would make an even number at the table if he were present."

"Yes, that would do nicely," agreed Mrs. Wentworth. "I'll send a note to Stanford as well."

"We must confer with Cook to plan a special menu," said Lady Wentworth. "Perhaps some of the roast chickens she does so nicely, and possibly a leg of lamb. It will be a very pleasant party, I think."

Miss Wentworth thought it sounded anything but pleasant. The idea of spending the evening with her fiancé was disagreeable enough, without having the Earl in attendance as well. His company, however enjoyable she might otherwise find it, was in this case likely only to aggravate an already uncomfortable situation; her feelings about the two gentlemen were complicated enough without sitting down to dinner with them both. Miss Wentworth could hardly voice such objections, but she found herself dreading the evening that was being planned for her especial pleasure.

On the day of her birthday, the Earl took Miss Wentworth out for a driving lesson during the afternoon. He made no reference to its being her birthday, nor did he mention the party that night to which he was invited. Miss Wentworth felt rather disappointed. Perhaps her mother had neglected to mention in the invitation that it was a party to celebrate her birthday. When the driving lesson was over, the Earl complimented her on her skill in handling the ribbons, but followed it up by saying bluntly that it was time for her to strike out on her own, a suggestion that made her feel even more despondent. Clearly he felt he had spent enough time on her. This thought, together with the prospect of an evening with Lord Russelton, served to send her spirits to a low ebb for the rest of the afternoon. She roused herself in time to make a careful toilette, however, and after arraying herself in a dinner dress of cream-colored gauze trimmed with blond lace, Miss Wentworth prepared to celebrate her nineteenth birthday.

The Earl was the first of the guests to arrive. He was announced, and made his entrance into the drawing room bearing a sizable bundle done up in silver paper.

"Oh, my," said Miss Wentworth, her eyes drawn at once to that intriguing parcel. The Earl, handsome in his black evening clothes, exchanged a few words with Lady Wentworth and then came over to where Miss Wentworth was sitting. He laid the parcel in her lap.

"A birthday gift for you, Becky," he said, looking down at her as she bent over the parcel, examining its size and shape with interest.

"You didn't have to get me a present, Jack," she scolded, smiling up at him with mock reproach. "But oh, I do love surprises! Whatever can it be?"

"Open it and see," said the Earl.

Miss Wentworth undid the wrappings and drew forth a rectangular box of rosewood ornamented with a pierced gold overlay. When opened, she found it to be a *nécessaire,* a sewing box beautifully outfitted with mother-of-pearl and gold-trimmed implements. There were scissors, thimble, bodkin, needlecase, and embroidery punch, all complete. Miss Wentworth lifted them out one by one, marveling at the workmanship.

"Oh, Jack, this must have been quite expensive," she said uncertainly. "I don't know if . . ." She glanced toward her mother and aunt, fearing she would never be allowed to keep such a lavish gift from a gentleman other than her fiancé.

The Earl saw her hesitancy and guessed its cause. "I

hope it is something you can use, Becky. Your aunt tells me you are a notable needlewoman, and of course I well remember the first time I called here. You sat on the sofa and sewed, while your aunt and I talked." Miss Wentworth looked again toward her aunt, and saw that Lady Wentworth was smiling benignly. "Lady Wentworth thought it would make a very appropriate gift," said the Earl, his voice almost humble. "I do hope you like it."

"It's beautiful," said Miss Wentworth. She was busy operating the gold-trimmed scissors, or she might have seen the Earl looking down at her with his heart in his eyes.

"It also has another function." He knelt beside her chair and pointed to a pair of gold knobs on the side of the box. "If you manipulate this control, so—"

Miss Wentworth listened, delighted, as music tinkled forth. "How pretty," she said. "A music box as well! What is the tune?"

"I thought you might recognize it," said the Earl, still watching her closely.

Miss Wentworth frowned in an effort to recollect. "It does sound familiar. I can't quite . . ."

"*Ah, taci, ingiusto core* is the title, I understand: the same aria you admired so much at the opera, back in April. I happened to see the box, and when I heard it play I immediately thought of you."

(This was a highly mendacious statement; the box had been specially ordered, at great expense, and had cost the Earl no small trouble from start to finish. The name of Nicoles-Frères meant nothing to Miss Wentworth's innocent eyes, however.)

"You remembered that?" said Miss Wentworth wonderingly.

"I have an excellent memory! I can remember every moment I've spent in your company, although some moments stand out more than others, of course. Do you remember that night at Lady Sefton's?"

Miss Wentworth tried to give him a reproving frown, but ended up smiling instead. The Earl dropped a light kiss on her cheek. "We are relations, you know," he explained, at her surprised look. "There can be no impropriety about a—ahem—brotherly kiss, on the occasion of your birthday." His eyes began to dance as he looked down at her. "But don't think this absolves you from paying your gaming debts, ma'am," he added, in a low voice. "No, I haven't forgotten, Becky, never fear!"

"Indeed, I am doubly in your debt now," said Miss Wentworth with a look of great innocence. "I shall work you a pair of slippers as my very first project with this beautiful sewing box. What color do you like, my lord?"

"Green," answered the Earl promptly, gazing into her eyes with an expression that threw her into some confusion.

The sewing box was passed around and admired. Both Mrs. Wentworth and Lady Wentworth had to try on the thimble and play the music; even Sir Richard, who had watched the whole proceedings with marked disapproval, grudgingly pronounced it complete to a shade. Miss Wentworth had finally regained possession of the box, and was in the midst of listening to the music once more, when Lord Russelton was announced.

"Ah, here is Frederick," said Mrs. Wentworth, smiling.

Miss Wentworth felt her heart sink. She set aside the sewing box and watched her fiancé greet Lady Wentworth. It had been some time since she had seen

Lord Russelton; looking at him now, as though for the first time, Miss Wentworth wondered how she could have ever thought she loved him. He appeared very young, and ridiculously overdressed, and he was barely civil to her family.

His brusque manner suffered a check when he caught sight of the Earl standing beside Mrs. Wentworth, however; Lord Russelton looked flabbergasted to encounter the Earl of Stanford in the home of the strait-laced Lady Wentworth. Introductions were made, and the two men greeted each other warily. The Earl's tall, broad-shouldered figure, in severe black, dwarfed Lord Russelton in his fussy, pinch-waisted blue coat and yellow pantaloons. The contrast would have made Miss Wentworth smile, had she not been assailed by a strong, unspecified discomfort at the sight.

At length, Lord Russelton made his way across the room to where Miss Wentworth was sitting. He kissed her hand in greeting, but his lips never actually touched her hand, and he let it fall afterwards as if he were relieved to have discharged such a tedious duty. A small package was dropped in Miss Wentworth's lap. "Happy Birthday, Rebecca," he drawled.

Miss Wentworth opened the package. It was a volume of poetry, a copy of *The Corsair.* "Mama thought you'd like it. She remembered your mentioning once how much you admired Byron's poetry. Never could see what all the fuss is about, myself."

"Thank you, Frederick," said Miss Wentworth in a colorless voice. She fanned through the leaves of the book and tried not to look toward a small gilt bookcase in a corner of the drawing-room, where a copy of *The Corsair* had reposed for many months. "I'm sure I shall enjoy it excessively. Pray thank your mother for me, if you will."

Presently, the party rose to go into dinner. The Earl took in Lady Wentworth, Sir Richard escorted Mrs. Wentworth, and Lord Russelton and Miss Wentworth brought up at the rear. Lord Russelton performed his duty carelessly, seating his partner with the same air of discharging a disagreeable chore. Miss Wentworth found herself shrinking from his touch. It was obvious he found her unappealing, even loathsome; she was made miserable by his presence. The situation did not bode well for the evening ahead.

Miss Wentworth sat beside Lord Russelton at dinner, with the Earl and her mother opposite, and Sir Richard and Lady Wentworth at the head and foot of the table. A tureen of soup *à la reine* was placed in front of Lady Wentworth, and she began to distribute its contents to the guests.

"And how is dear Lady Cassandra, Frederick?" asked Mrs. Wentworth, smiling at Lord Russelton. "We saw her last night, at a rout at the Maynards', but it was too great a squeeze to do more than exchange a word or two."

"My grandmother is very well, I believe," said Lord Russelton, addressing his soup. There was an expectant silence. He was forced to add, "I have been in Norfolk, and only got back to town last week."

"And how is dear Lady Russelton, your mother?"

"She is also very well."

Everyone finished their soup in silence. The soup plates were removed, and a dish of whiting with orange sauce was brought in.

"I suppose we will see your mother and grandmother soon," said Mrs. Wentworth, attempting to revive the flagging conversation. "At the ball, you know. I understand that Lady Cassandra is giving an engagement party for you and Rebecca, now that your family is out of mourning for your great-aunt."

"Yes. Yes, you will certainly see them then."

Miss Wentworth was aware that the Earl was looking at her from across the table. She could not bring herself to meet his eyes. What an awful party it was turning out to be, and how ashamed she felt to have the Earl here to witness Frederick's behavior. Her fiancé was acting like a sulky schoolboy.

"Since the families will be connected, we must all make an effort to become better acquainted," said Mrs. Wentworth, striving for a playful air. "Why, we haven't even seen much of *you* this last month or so, Frederick, I vow and declare!"

"I have been out of town," said Lord Russelton, after a brief hesitation.

The remainder of the first course was brought in. A leg of lamb, a fricandeau of veal, baked mushrooms, green beans *à la Quercynoise,* and a salad of pike fillets were served and eaten in almost perfect silence. Even Sir Richard Wentworth, not in general the most sensitive soul, seemed conscious of a chill in the atmosphere. Rising nobly to the occasion, he regaled the company with a story about an acquaintance who had recently purchased a horse, subsequently discovering that the animal possessed an unnatural appetite for ladies' parasols, which had only been discovered after a disastrous outing in Hyde Park. The story was received with an enthusiasm quite disproportionate to the occasion.

The second course was served, a duck with green peas, some truffled roast chickens, a timbale of macaroni, potatoes in white caper sauce, apricot fritters, and a claret jelly. The Earl turned to Lady Wentworth at his left and asked if she was in some way related to the Wentworth-Fitzwilliams of Northampton. For once, the complex genealogical disquisition that followed was welcomed. The mismatched company was relieved of the burden of conversation while the second course was disposed of.

Finally, only dessert remained. In honor of Miss Wentworth's birthday, a splendid specimen of the pastry-maker's art had been commissioned from the kitchens: a cake five layers high, with custard filling and snowy frosting. It was sensational enough to provide a fresh source of conversational material for the party, and together with a Rhenish wine cream and a strawberry-and-raspberry charlotte, the wretched meal was finally brought to an end.

After dinner, Miss Wentworth retired with her aunt and mother to the drawing room. They were joined soon after by the gentlemen, who had not cared to linger over their port in one another's company. Sir Richard was drawn into conversation with his mother; he pulled up a chair beside her and Mrs. Wentworth and joined their discussion of the latest play with the appearance of civility, if not enthusiasm. Lord Russelton dropped into a chair by the fireplace and gazed moodily into the fire. The Earl glanced at him, and then came over to sit beside Miss Wentworth on the sofa.

Miss Wentworth stole a look at him. He was regarding her with sympathy, but there was a quiver about his lower lip suggestive of laughter. Miss Wentworth's own sense of humor began to stir, and a faint chuckle escaped her. The Earl grinned.

"Do we look forward to more of the same animated conversation for the rest of the evening?" he inquired in a hushed voice. "Or does your aunt plan to set us playing cards?"

"Playing the pianoforte, more likely," said Miss Wentworth, plunged into gloom once more. "With me doing the playing."

"Why the long face, Becky? That does not sound such a depressing prospect. I can only speak for myself, but I would enjoy hearing you play very much. Do you sing as well?"

"I have not a voice," said Miss Wentworth tragically. "And I really don't think you would enjoy hearing me play, Jack. I am no more than an average performer. Less than average, I fear."

The Earl burst out laughing. Lord Russelton looked quickly in their direction and then looked away again.

"Poor Becky! Well, that's nothing to be in a flat despair about, but it does seem too bad to make you perform when you don't want to, and on your birthday, too. As birthdays go, I don't suppose this one will be anything you care to remember."

"I will be happy to remember what a lovely gift you gave me, at least," said Miss Wentworth, smiling at him shyly. "But oh, wasn't that the most dreadful dinner?"

"Not much festivity about it, certainly," agreed the Earl, his lip twitching again. "But if you do your duty nicely and play a few songs for us, perhaps your troublesome guests will take themselves off early."

"Oh, no," said Miss Wentworth, aghast at having given altogether the wrong impression. "I didn't mean to imply—it isn't *you* that—"

"You needn't explain," said the Earl. "I understand perfectly, Becky, indeed I do. But what with one thing and another, I can't think you're really enjoying yourself." He glanced significantly at Lord Russelton's back.

"It's the worst of manners to shab off so soon after dinner, but if I stay another half hour perhaps I can leave without mortally offending your aunt. And I rather think I could persuade Russelton to accompany me. He looks as though he would jump at any excuse to go."

The Earl's eyes flickered over Miss Wentworth's face, his expression inscrutable. "What do you think, Becky? Would you prefer to bring the evening to an early close? Much as I enjoy your company . . . well, I'm willing to forgo it, if it would bring you a shred of comfort."

"Would you?" Miss Wentworth wondered with a pang if the evening had served to disgust him with the entire Wentworth household, herself naturally included. It hurt to think he was already anxious to leave. On the other hand, it really was a wretched party, and she thought she could endure to sacrifice a few hours of the Earl's company in order to end what had been an evening of affliction for all concerned. "If you would not mind, Jack . . ."

"If it's what you want, I would not mind at all," he said, his eyes direct now and disturbingly intense.

"How kind you are to me." Miss Wentworth looked back at him for a moment. When she spoke again, her voice sounded a bit breathless to her own ears. "Thank you for everything, Jack. The sewing box and—everything."

He regarded her for a moment longer with that curiously intent look, and then smiled his familiar, heart-stopping smile. "You are welcome, very welcome, my dear. Come, shall we get the ordeal behind us? You can play, and I can probably manage to turn the pages for you, although my musical talent doesn't extend much further than that."

He stood up and gave her his hand. Miss Wentworth

took it, noticing at the same time what an attractive hand it was, the fingers long and well-shaped and ornamented with a heavy gold signet that flashed in the candlelight.

The Earl led her to the pianoforte, her hand still in his, and that odd feeling in the pit of her stomach reasserted itself, reminiscent of the first time he had smiled at her. She wondered if he realized he had just called her "my dear." He had never done so before. Miss Wentworth reminded herself that it was a common enough endearment, certainly no reason to make her heart pound in such a ridiculous way; she feared her performance at the pianoforte was likely to prove more than usually mediocre, given the agitation she was feeling.

The Earl conducted himself beyond reproach during the appointed time at the pianoforte. While Miss Wentworth played, he leaned over the instrument, turning pages and reproving her in a light-hearted way for attempting to hide her light under a bushel. "For you play very well, Becky. I have three cousins who are fashionable young ladies, and after enjoying—no, enduring—any number of their musical performances through the years, I think I may be accounted a competent authority."

"No, sir, but you may be accounted a rank flatterer, for telling such a whisker," Miss Wentworth returned, dimpling at him. "It cannot have escaped your notice that I missed that wretched sharp at least three times."

"Oh, as for that trifling deviation, I thought it a vast improvement. The composer himself would surely have sanctioned the change, had he but heard it performed so by *your* hands."

Miss Wentworth took him to task for voicing such

brazen falsehood, but was pleased nonetheless, the more so because the Earl's praise was not altogether unjustified. She found herself performing better than usual, even with the handicap of an audience that included a distinctly hostile element. Lord Russelton sat obstinately apart and refused to have anything to do with the impromptu musicale, despite his hostess's urgings. But the Earl was persuaded to sing a duet with Miss Wentworth, and joined quite a creditable baritone to her rather wavering contralto in a performance pronounced perfectly delightful, by the female half of the audience, at least. The male half manifested less enjoyment. Sir Richard looked bored, but also rather uneasy at the Earl's devotion to his cousin; Lord Russelton continued to brood in front of the fireplace and took no notice whatsoever.

The half hour spent in this fashion passed so agreeably that Miss Wentworth began to be sorry she had agreed to cut the evening short. The Earl was as good as his word, however. He made his excuses to Lady Wentworth and then turned to Lord Russelton. "I say, Russelton, I'm headed by way of Grosvenor Square myself. Perhaps I could give you a ride there, if you haven't your carriage."

Lord Russelton appeared to waver for a moment, and then accepted the offer with a stiff word of thanks. The two gentlemen made their adieux. Miss Wentworth thanked them both for her birthday gifts, but even while she was speaking to Lord Russelton her eyes continued to follow the Earl about as he took leave of her mother and aunt, and it was upon his figure that her gaze lingered as the gentlemen left the room together.

"Well!" said Mrs. Wentworth a trifle offendedly, also looking after the departing guests. "I'm sure there was no need for them both to rush off like that. Stanford had another engagement, to be sure, and that I can understand, but there wasn't any reason why dear Frederick couldn't have stayed a bit longer. I'm afraid Stanford may have made him feel he was overstaying . . . hurrying him off in that harum-scarum way. Why, you and Frederick had no chance to talk at all this evening, Rebecca."

"Lord Russelton did not appear to be in the best of spirits tonight," said Lady Wentworth, making this monumental understatement with her usual air of grave consideration.

"Yes, he was rather quiet, wasn't he? Perhaps he had the headache," said Mrs. Wentworth charitably. "That would explain why he chose to leave so early. With the wedding so near, I expect he has his affairs a great deal on his mind—"

"I think I will go up to my bedchamber now," said Miss Wentworth, with great presence of mind. "Good night, Mama. Good night, Richard. Good night, Aunt Constance. Thank you for the dinner, and for the gifts."

"Good night, my dear."

"'Night, Beck."

"Good night, Rebecca. I trust your nineteenth year will be a happy one."

"Thank you, Aunt Constance." Miss Wentworth put the second copy of *The Corsair* into the bookcase beside the first, tucked her sewing box tenderly beneath her arm, and went up the stairs to bed.

Chapter Ten

In the days following her birthday party, Miss Wentworth's thoughts and feelings grew more disordered than ever. The London Season was at its height, and she was kept very busy attending every species of diversion capable of being devised by the *ton's* enterprising hostesses, but there was no day so busy that Miss Wentworth did not find time to sit examining the sewing box the Earl had given her, playing the music over and over again and wondering.

She wondered why he had bought her such a lavish present. If it was all part of some plan for her eventual seduction, then she thought she could see why he had been so successful a rake, with a long string of conquests to his name. Any woman would find it difficult to resist a gentleman who went to such lengths to please, especially when this was combined with an extremely handsome appearance and the nicest of manners. The way he had won over Lady Wentworth was proof enough of his charm, if any were needed. Miss Wentworth was growing increasingly certain that further proof was not at all necessary. She knew she was coming to feel more strongly about the Earl of Stanford than was either wise or prudent.

Her feelings for him had already complicated matters immensely. She chose to endure her false engagement to Lord Russelton, and all its attendant miseries, because to end it was certain to affect her relationship with the Earl.

Almost imperceptibly, the hours spent driving with him had become the focus around which her days centered. Once she had cut her dash in the park with his phaeton, however, she would be obliged to break her engagement as she had pledged herself to do; she would have no further need of driving lessons, and without the excuse of the lessons it seemed probable that she would see very little of the Earl. This prospect was bad enough; the other, more disturbing possibility was that she had mistaken his character entirely and would find the Earl had been only waiting all along for the end of her engagement, to move beyond a merely friendly footing.

Miss Wentworth did not dare consider this possibility too closely. It was easy to resolve to be strong-minded in the privacy of her own bedchamber, but she had shown herself to be weak as water where the Earl of Stanford was concerned, on the occasion of their very first meeting—and since then her feelings for him had grown rather than diminished. Miss Wentworth feared respectability would stand no chance if brought into direct confrontation with the promptings of her own heart. It seemed wisest to put off such a confrontation as long as possible.

Accordingly, Miss Wentworth let the days slide by and tried to think as little as possible about the future. Having reached the conclusion that the end of her engagement would be attended either by the loss of the Earl's companionship, or, alternately, by the revelation that he was indeed a heartless libertine with designs on her virtue, she chose rather to do nothing, letting the situation go on as before. There was nothing wrong with this solution, as far as it went, but it was a solution that could only be temporary at best. Already it was May, and her wedding set for June. Miss Wentworth knew she must do something soon, whatever the outcome.

Lady Cassandra's approaching engagement party was a source of much woe for Miss Wentworth. Lord Russelton's grandmother had not given a party when the engagement was first announced, owing to a death in the family some months before; the Russelton household had been in half-mourning until quite recently. Now that the mourning period was over, however, Lady Cassandra proposed to give a party in the engaged couple's honor, and to Miss Wentworth's dismay it was not a dinner party or a rout party that was planned, but a full scale ball. As prospective guest of honor, she felt highly uncomfortable about the situation. Dissimulation was one thing when it affected only herself and Lord Russelton, but quite another when it began to put other people to great trouble and expense, all to celebrate an engagement destined to end in the very near future. The only possible source of comfort was that the expense on this occasion was being borne by Lady Cassandra, who would eventually leave her money to her grandson Lord Russelton, and thus it would be the culprit of the whole sorry affair who would be footing the bill in the long run. This was scant consolation, however.

By the time the evening of the ball arrived, Miss Wentworth's state of mind bore a strong resemblance to that of a prisoner preparing for imminent execution. Her gown, new for the occasion, was of white gauze over satin, with pearl buttons clasping the bodice. A drapery of white lace entwined with pearls trimmed the overskirt, and more of the same lace was set to drape over the neckline. Her front hair was arranged in loose ringlets, with the back dressed low, and she wore her borrowed pearls once more. She looked the part of a lovely bride-to-be, but she felt terrible: deceitful and petty-minded, to be putting so many people out for the sake of her pride. No amount of revenge was worth it. Since matters had gone this far, she felt obliged to continue the deception for a few hours more, but as soon after the ball as possible—maybe even tomorrow, if she could manage it—she must absolutely, positively bring the whole farce to an end. The idea of a final gesture of defiance, as represented by the plan to drive the Earl's phaeton in the park, all at once seemed futile, almost childish. What did she care for the opinions of Frederick Russelton and Clarrissa Barrow, after all? She wished only to live out the rest of her life without the need of being on terms of more than common civility with them both.

As for the Earl of Stanford . . . Miss Wentworth thought sorrowfully of the pains the Earl had taken for her sake, and the likelihood that she would be striking the death knell of their acquaintance. It was a saddening reflection, but even for his sake she could not bring herself to continue the deceit any longer. The time for resolute action seemed to have come at last.

In company with her mother and aunt, Miss Wentworth arrived at Lady Cassandra's house in Grosvenor Square, an impressive residence that she had once thought to be her future home. She had no regrets about losing it now; she only regretted the necessity of entering it again under such false pretenses. Feeling herself a perfect Judas, she was greeted by Lady Cassandra, resplendent in yellow satin and plumes, and by Lady Russelton in blue sarcenet, insignificant beside her flamboyant mother-in-law. Lord Russelton was there, too, of course, swathed to the ears in a bulky neckcloth and wearing a blue coat of the extreme cut he favored.

Miss Wentworth, regarding him dispassionately, decided he looked ridiculous. Only his extreme youth saved him from looking a regular counter-coxcomb; really, the Earl was right about Frederick being little removed from schoolboy estate!

The thought brought a ghost of a smile to her lips and enabled her to conceal the agitation that swept over her every time she looked at the lavishly appointed ballroom, banked with flowers; the orchestra tuning their instruments in the gallery above; the brilliant costumes of the ladies intermingled with their more soberly clad escorts, all testimony to the selfish pride of Rebecca Wentworth.

With his grandmother and mother looking on expectantly, Lord Russelton formally requested Miss Wentworth's hand for the first dance. She accepted, as in duty bound, and thought that with luck she might never be obliged to dance with him again.

She and Lord Russelton took their places on the floor for the first dance, a minuet. A great many eyes were upon them, and a little murmur of approval went round the room at the sight of the supposedly happy couple, so soon to be wed. Miss Wentworth's erratic spirits dipped lower still. Not a word was exchanged between the leading couple during the dance; Lord Russelton never even looked directly at his partner. His eyes were above her, or beside her, or—Miss Wentworth caught sight of a sturdy figure in pink muslin—on Clarissa Barrow, dancing nearby.

After the minuet ended, Lord Russelton silently escorted Miss Wentworth back to her mother and aunt. There was a gentleman sitting beside Lady Wentworth, and when he turned his head to look at her, Miss Wentworth's overburdened heart seemed to stop for a minute.

"What are you doing here?" she exclaimed and then flushed, realizing how unfriendly she had sounded. "I mean . . . I did not expect to see you here, my lord."

"Jack," said the Earl, rising to his feet and regarding her unsmilingly. "I have been Jack to you for several weeks now, and I refuse to be demoted to my lord once more. As for what I am doing here . . . why, I am here because I was invited by our hostess, of course. Even such a ramshackle character as mine would not dare to appear at one of Lady Cassandra's parties without an invitation." He gave Miss Wentworth a searching look and bowed. "Do you care to dance, Becky? There is a waltz beginning, and if you have no other partner—"

"Oh, yes! Yes, of course I will dance with you." She laid her hand on his arm, and he led her out onto the floor. A moment passed, and then another, with nothing but the lilting music of the latest waltz to break the silence between them. The Earl seemed indisposed to reopen the conversation, and Miss Wentworth was busy regretting her hasty words and trying to put her tumultuous thoughts in order.

"I'm sorry I sounded so uncivil, Jack," she ventured at last. "It was only that I was surprised. I didn't expect to see you here."

"I don't think you wanted to see me, either," said the Earl. "You've never so much as mentioned this party to

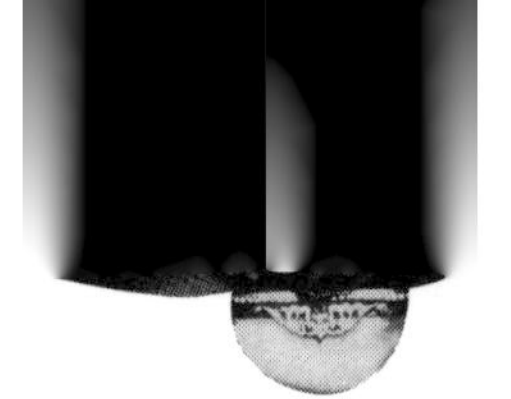

me, which I think you might have done, Becky. And the look on your face when you saw me . . . have I offended you somehow?"

"Oh, no! Not at all, Jack. I didn't mention it to you because I know you don't usually attend such parties."

"But your engagement party, Becky! Surely you don't think I would have missed that?" he said quizzically. There was a humorous quirk about his mouth, but his eyes held a rather watchful expression.

"I had hoped that you would—oh, that everyone would," said Miss Wentworth, drawing a deep breath. "I didn't mention it to you because I've been feeling dreadfully ashamed about it all. Oh, Jack, I am so miserable! All this trouble for an engagement I don't intend to go through with in the least. And Lady Cassandra and Lady Russelton have been so kind to me . . . I am quite cast down when I think of it."

The Earl looked at her for a moment. "Then end the engagement," he said. "Do it tonight."

"Tonight? Do you think I should?" Miss Wentworth looked up at him. His dark eyes glowed, and he was smiling now, a strange, reckless smile.

"Yes," he said deliberately. "To hell with—the devil fly away with revenge. Russelton looks miserable enough now. Why should you be made miserable, too, at his expense? I wish you would put an end to this May-game, Becky. I've felt so for some time, only you seemed so set on the notion of revenging yourself. Cut your losses, my dear: he isn't worth it, and we will go on a great deal better without him."

"You're right," said Miss Wentworth, conscious that her heart had given a leap at that word *we*. "I'll find a way to speak with Frederick tonight, and—and end it. But of course it will mean your labors have been for nothing, Jack. What a pity to waste all those driving lessons." She smiled uncertainly.

"Oh, I don't feel they were wasted," said the Earl, looking down at her. "Not wasted at all."

Miss Wentworth's heart gave another flutter. Waltzing in his arms was heaven, pure heaven, and suddenly she felt a conviction that the end of her engagement could not arrive a moment too soon. Since coming to London, Miss Wentworth had gained experience enough to recognize the difference between a gentlemen intent on diverting himself, and one whose feelings were genuinely engaged; the tone of the Earl's voice, the look in his eyes, even the way his hand rested upon her waist all betokened a certain warmth of feeling that did not accord with her notions of a gentleman performing a social duty, or one indulging in mere flirtation. The waltz was finished in silence, but it was a very different kind of silence than had accompanied the opening minuet. The sense of expectancy and suppressed excitement in the atmosphere was so strong that it was almost tangible.

As guest of honor, Miss Wentworth's hand was much in demand for the dances that followed. She danced them all, and always the Earl of Stanford was there when she returned to her seat. While Miss Wentworth was being twirled about the floor by a succession of admiring gentlemen, the Earl conversed amiably with Lady Wentworth, but whenever Miss Wentworth looked in his direction—as happened with some frequency—she found his eyes upon her. There was an expression in those eyes that sent her spirits soaring.

Her feet seemed to possess wings; she danced, and made lively conversation, and even the unavoidable references to her approaching nuptials with Lord Russelton could not spoil the mood of elation that was bubbling over inside her. She looked so convincingly happy that Lord Russelton, watching her from across the room, began to feel seriously alarmed. Nor was he the only one to be affected thus; as Miss Wentworth was leaving the floor with her partner after a country dance, she was waylaid by no less a personage than Miss Clarissa Barrow.

"I beg your pardon? Oh, Miss Barrow!" For a moment, Miss Wentworth felt as though cold water had been dashed over her. Then she remembered that the tie that bound her to Lord Russelton, like Cinderella's enchantment, was due to end tonight; that knowledge, together with the Earl of Stanford's very gratifying behavior, made her decide she could feel benevolence even toward the shipping heiress. "Good evening, Miss Barrow. What a lovely dress you are wearing tonight," said Miss Wentworth warmly, with the friendliest smile she could muster.

The other girl regarded her for a moment with narrowed eyes. An unconvincing smile appeared briefly on Miss Barrow's round, flushed face, her naturally high color even ruddier from the exercise of dancing. "Good evening, Miss Wentworth. I just wanted to wish you happy," said Miss Barrow, her tone of voice conveying the exact opposite intention. "I'm sure you're very fortunate to be marrying Frederick. Such a fine gentleman . . . the wedding is quite close now, isn't it?"

"Oh, it's still nearly a month away," said Miss Wentworth, entertained by the anxiety betrayed by her rival's words. Then she noted that the shipping heiress was looking almost disconsolate and felt a rush of sympathy. It was quite possible that Miss Barrow's heart was genuinely involved; Miss Wentworth felt a generous impulse to relinquish all claim to Frederick Russelton then and there, but was restrained by the reflection that it would be more seemly to inform the gentleman himself first.

"Thank you, Miss Barrow," she said, laying a hand on Miss Barrow's plump arm encased in a pink kidskin evening glove. Miss Barrow looked at the hand on her arm as if it had been a snake. "I do appreciate your good wishes, Miss Barrow. It is most kind of you." Giving the shipping heiress a smiling nod, Miss Wentworth took her partner's arm and went on her way. Miss Barrow looked after her for a moment, turned on her heel, and marched off in Lord Russelton's direction, a set expression on her face.

Miss Wentworth made no mention of the encounter when she reached her seat, but she drew a sigh of relief as she sat down beside the Earl. He smiled, took possession of her fan, and began to fan her with it.

"Thank you, Jack. How hot it is in here, to be sure!"

"You do look flushed," he said, his eyes wandering over her face and then, in the most nonchalant way, skimming over her person as well. "Beautiful, but flushed. Don't tell me poor old Farnsworth's been putting you to the blush! If that puppy's been making a nuisance of himself, I'll knock him down."

"Oh, Mr. Farnsworth would never dream of saying anything to make me blush," said Miss Wentworth demurely. "Unlike certain other gentlemen of my acquaintance . . ."

"Ah, I expect you're thinking of the Earl of Stanford, who had the infernal impudence to make you blush the very first time he spoke to you! That's a different matter altogether, my dear, and you may have noticed I've mended my ways lately . . . but even so, I reserve for myself the exclusive right to make you blush. You are forewarned, Becky! May I get you some champagne?"

"Yes, please," said Miss Wentworth. "Infernally impudent or not, you are very good to me, Jack." Her eyes followed him as he made his way through the crowd toward the refreshment room. He returned with the champagne, and Miss Wentworth, overcome by heat and excitement combined, dispatched it without delay. The Earl raised his eyebrows at her empty glass.

"I'll get you more if you want it, Becky, but you'll find yourself on the go if you're not careful," he cautioned with a smile. "There's something downright intoxicating in the very air tonight, have you noticed? No telling what could happen with an excess of champagne on top of it all—"

"Perhaps it will give me courage! You don't know how I dread talking to Frederick. Well, not so much him, I suppose; he'll be delighted. But when Lady Cassandra finds out . . . oh, dear! I'll need all the courage I can get."

"Dutch courage, perhaps, but I suppose it can't hurt." The Earl refilled her glass and his own as well. He felt reckless: half intoxicated already. The knowledge that Rebecca Wentworth would be free within a matter of hours had been running like an undercurrent through his thoughts all evening. She had never appeared more lovely, or more desirable, and unless he was very much mistaken she was not wholly indifferent to his suit, if suit it could be called.

In keeping with his resolution, he had preserved a complete silence on the subject up till now. It had been a struggle, however, and he was set on wasting no time once Russelton was finally out of the way. It might be rushing matters a trifle to declare oneself to a lady minutes after she broke off an engagement with another gentleman, but the circumstances were unusual in this case. He was damned if he would wait one moment longer than actually necessary to make his feelings clear. In the meantime, he was having a very good time, thank you very much.

"More champagne?"

"Why not?"

They sat out the next dance together, laughing and talking, and all the while the Earl felt certain stirrings within himself which several glasses of champagne did nothing to help. He had behaved himself with great restraint for weeks. Surely he was entitled to some small reward, he rationalized. There was still a slight formality remaining, in the form of her prior engagement; he could not yet approach the crux of the matter, but even so . . .

"Will you come with me, Becky?" he said abruptly, standing up and offering Miss Wentworth his arm.

She rose at once. "Where are we going?" she asked, with mild interest.

"There's a matter of a gaming debt that I feel ought to be discharged." The Earl laughed as Miss Wentworth's eyes widened. "No, I'd not forgotten—you knew better than that, didn't you? But I find I have the strangest scruples about kissing engaged ladies! Well, Russelton may not know it yet, but his engagement is over, and,"—the Earl took her firmly by the arm—"debts of honor must be paid, my dear, however distasteful the process may be!"

The champagne was coursing through Miss Wentworth's blood, and she felt stirrings of her own. "Play and pay," she said in a mournful voice, shooting a mischievous look at the Earl. His lips twitched appreciatively, and he tightened his grip on her arm, leading her out of the ballroom and down a paneled hallway lined with doors. The Earl looked into a few of the rooms opening off the hallway.

"Ah, the library," he said. "This should do nicely. We require a modicum of privacy." He led Miss Wentworth into the library and then shut the door behind her. The key was in the lock, and he turned it. "Privacy," he said again, as she gave him a startled look.

Lady Cassandra's library was a long, narrow chamber decorated in the Gothic style, with a preponderance of dark wood and crimson hangings. Bronze busts of philosophers stared down from atop bookcases ornamented with spires and urn-shaped pediments. In front of the fireplace stood a sofa and several chairs upholstered in crimson leather; a massive table was drawn up beneath a chandelier suspended from the center of the ceiling. The Earl stood near the door with his back against the bookcases and watched Miss Wentworth with an expression of amusement on his face. She looked back at him questioningly.

"I am waiting, Becky," he said in a tranquil voice, after a minute or two had passed in silence.

"Waiting?"

"Waiting for you to kiss me. That was the wager, you know: a kiss from you against a prayer book from me."

Miss Wentworth regarded him with resentment. There was something intimidating, almost embarrassing, about kissing a gentleman who merely stood there grinning at one and not helping in the least. She flew up to him, pressed a kiss on his cheek, and retreated. "There, my lord," she said, dimpling at him. "You have your kiss."

The Earl looked injured. "It must be a real kiss," he

said reproachfully. "Come, Becky, I know you can do better than that!"

The mockery on his face was quite simply intolerable. Miss Wentworth felt an urge to remove that irksome smile once and for all. She stepped forward and kissed him, as real a kiss as she knew how to give. Thanks to her experience on Lady Sefton's terrace, she had a pretty good idea of what was expected. The Earl seemed a trifle caught off guard by the determination of the attack, but he was not slow in taking up the challenge, and when Miss Wentworth stepped back from him at last, she was pleased to see that the offending smile was no longer there.

"Is my debt paid now, sir?" she demanded.

Little flames seemed to dance in his eyes. "There is still some interest owing," he said in a husky voice, and drew her back into his arms. Miss Wentworth showed no unwillingness to return there. She put her arms around his neck and submitted to the embrace that crushed her breathlessly close; she felt again the warmth and sensation of melting as his mouth on hers undermined resistance in the most insidious way. He kissed her fiercely, hungrily, and his hands ran up and down her body, molding her against himself. One hand worked its way around to the bodice of her gown.

"No," she whispered, turning her face away but making no accompanying effort to free herself. This unconvincing display of reluctance was treated with the contempt it deserved; the Earl merely took advantage of her averted face to kiss her neck instead, sending a wave of tingling sensations through her body. She gasped, and shuddered, and found herself being maneuvered toward the sofa in front on the fireplace. The pressure of the Earl's lips and arms bore her relentlessly down upon the sofa, until he was lying on top of her. Dimly remembered warnings and half-comprehended scraps of conversation fell suddenly into place, and a sense of imminent danger arose, only to be lost in a fresh tide of sensation: the intimacy of his body on top of hers, urgent, demanding, and irresistable.

The Earl's lips trailed down her neck, and again his hand fumbled with the pearl buttons that fastened her bodice. This time he encountered no resistance. Miss Wentworth had only the sketchiest idea about what was likely to happen next, but the way in which the generalized aching desire within her body had begun to focus in several specific areas was a revelation in itself. The Earl's hair tickled the delicate skin of her neck and breast as his mouth moved lower and lower. She ran her fingers through his hair and drew a long shuddering breath as his lips just touched the cleft between her breasts.

It was at this interesting moment that the library door rattled, as though someone were trying the knob from outside. The Earl raised his head and looked toward the door. Miss Wentworth opened her eyes, feeling disoriented and vaguely annoyed; she, too, turned her face toward the door. It rattled again, and the knob turned.

"You locked it, didn't you?" she whispered.

He nodded, but there was an ominous jangle of keys that made them both spring to their feet. The Earl looked about the library for places of concealment. He considered and rejected the table, the heavy mahoghany desk, the davenport drawn up before an armchair, the rows of bookcases.

"The window, Jack," hissed Miss Wentworth. "There's a window seat, I think." They hastened across the room to the library window. The Earl yanked the crimson velvet draperies aside, revealing a window seat set into the embrasure. Miss Wentworth lifted her skirts and gracefully vaulted onto the seat, revealing a pair of very pretty ankles as well as a fair amount of pretty leg, which the Earl did not fail to notice despite the urgency of the situation. He stepped onto the window seat beside Miss Wentworth. The draperies had barely swung back into place before they heard the grating of the key in the lock and the sound of someone entering the room.

They sat together on the narrow window seat, facing each other. The Earl was forced to stoop, as the embrasure was low; he was crouching rather than kneeling, and his position gave him an admirable view of Miss Wentworth's *décolletage.* Obviously unaware of her unbuttoned bodice, she knelt, leaning forward a bit, trying to peer out through a crack in the curtains. A good deal of her chemise hung out, and the swell of her breasts was clearly visible. Upon a gentleman of hot blood and impetuous temperament, aggravated by a course of rigorous celibacy and inflamed by the events of the past half hour, the sight served only to increase the discomforts of the situation. Miss Wentworth let out a sudden stifled gasp, and for a moment the Earl thought she must have noticed his preoccupation. She was not looking at him, however, but was staring between the parted curtains. A smile hovered on her lips.

"Look!" she said, in the barest breath of a whisper.

Reluctantly, the Earl tore his gaze from Miss Wentworth's bosom and applied an eye to the peephole. He discerned a commanding figure in yellow satin that could have been no one but Lady Cassandra Russelton. Lady Cassandra's back was to the window seat. She stood before a small mahoghany cabinet, twisting the lock back and forth with a ring of keys. At length, she removed a bottle from the cabinet and began to drink from it, without benefit of cup and glass.

"What's she doing?" whispered Miss Wentworth, trying to work her head in beneath the Earl's.

"Brandy," said the Earl, with a quiver of suppressed laughter. "Oh, Lord!" Lady Cassandra took another draught from the bottle and belched loudly, sending the fugitives in the window seat into silent convulsions. Then she replaced the bottle, locked the cabinet, gave a hitch to her petticoats that sent her observers into another fit of convulsions, and left the library. The door had scarcely shut behind her when gales of laughter burst forth from the window seat. The Earl shoved the draperies aside, and Miss Wentworth tumbled out of the window seat and collapsed onto the sofa, shaking with laughter. The Earl sat beside her, and for some time they were unable to speak at all; their narrow escape, combined with the ludicrous sight they had witnessed, left them giddy with laughter and relief.

"Straight from the bottle, by God!"

"Frederick always said she is often very cross in the mornings! I would never have believed it of Lady Cass."

"And that final little adjustment to the hoopskirt . . ." The Earl's shoulders shook. They sat savoring their enjoyment for several minutes more. The Earl's hand, lying along the back of the sofa, stole out to play with a curl that had escaped from Miss Wentworth's coiffure. She turned her face toward him and smiled.

"Oh, Jack, how terribly funny . . . and what a pity I can never tell anyone about it. Owing to the circumstances, you know." Her expression became embarrassed, and a little mischievous. "I suppose we ought to go back to the ballroom now?"

"Undoubtedly," said the Earl, smiling back at her. "But before we do, I would suggest that you adjust the—er—bodice of your gown. I can't think how such a thing came to happen. . . ."

Miss Wentworth looked down at her *décolletage* and blushed. With great tact, the Earl stood up and pretended to inspect the volumes of Plato on the library shelves while the necessary adjustments were made.

"There," she said. "You may turn around now, Jack." He turned around to see her standing before him, with a confiding air that he found wholly adorable. "Does my hair look all right?"

The Earl surveyed her gravely. "It looks charming, my dear . . . but not, I fear, exactly as it did earlier. The back part seems to be coming adrift."

"Bother," said Miss Wentworth, attempting to repair the damage.

The Earl watched her struggle for a moment. "Perhaps I could play lady's maid," he suggested. Miss Wentworth handed him half-a-dozen hairpins and turned around trustfully. He set the hairpins with care in the glossy coils of her hair. It was silky smooth and sweet-smelling, and the sight and scent of her at such close range made him forget once more all about his good intentions. He put his arms around her, pulling her against himself and nuzzling her neck; Miss Wentworth gave a startled gasp and found herself to be in worse case than before. His hands were free to range up and down the front of her body, while the disturbing warmth of him pressed against her from behind, and his mouth was on her ear, arousing truly incredible sensations. "Oh," said Miss Wentworth faintly, giving herself up for lost.

The doorknob rattled again. "Damn," swore the Earl. With by now well-rehearsed smoothness, they were both up and into the window seat, with the draperies in place, before the door opened again, and someone—it sounded like more than one person—came into the library.

This time, Miss Wentworth was acutely aware of being in a precarious position, in every sense of the word. She was stooping rather than kneeling on the window seat, balancing on her toes and trying to keep her skirts from tripping her up. If she were to fall backward, she would land practically in the Earl's lap, and she felt instinctively that it might be wiser to avoid such a position. In trying to keep her distance, however, she overbalanced. Miss Wentworth teetered forward, tried to catch herself, and fell back against him.

The Earl's arms caught her. He pulled her close, dropped a kiss on her neck, and automatically began to consider with interest the logistics involved in making love upon a window seat. Honorable intentions, he reminded himself, honorable intentions. Miss Wentworth was not making it easy for him to remember his intentions; finding herself in his arms, she had relaxed there, laying her face against his chest and closing her eyes. Her eyes flew open, however, as voices were raised in the library without.

Chapter Eleven

"How much longer do you think to keep me waiting, Frederick?" demanded a strident female voice. "I'm sure you've said a hundred times it'd all be over months ago. And now here she is tonight, looking like butter wouldn't melt in her mouth, and your mama telling everyone—"

"Only a little longer, Clarissa," pleaded a masculine voice, sounding extremely harassed. "She doesn't really intend to go through with it, I'm sure. Fact is . . . well, I'm thinking I went about this business the wrong way and set her back up. She's angry now, and keeping me on the string to spite me, but she won't actually go so far as to marry me, you may be sure."

"I'm not sure, not by any means. I think she plans to have you in spite of everything, unless you buckle down and do something about it yourself!"

"But my dear, I can't do that." The masculine voice sounded agitated now, as if the speaker was pacing up and down the room. "That kind of thing simply isn't done. I'd be cut dead by half the *ton* if I jilted her. And it wouldn't suit you if your husband was an outcast, would it, my darling?" wheedled the voice.

There was a brief silence while the female speaker seemed to be considering the question. "No, though I don't suppose it'd really come to that. But there must be some way to hurry things along, just the same. I expect it's really your money she's after; her papa's nothing but a country parson when all's said and done. Maybe she could be bought off. To my mind, it's worth a try, and I'm willing to approach her about it myself if need be. I'm not afraid of Rebecca Wentworth, even if you are, Frederick!"

The Earl felt Miss Wentworth's body stiffen within the circle of his arms. With a strong sense of inevitability, he realized that the speakers were none other than Lord Russelton and Miss Barrow, and that the shipping heiress was taking Lord Russelton to task for the dilatory manner in which he was handling his affairs.

"No, no, you'd best let me do it, Clarissa. Perhaps if I got her alone and had a word with her, maybe here in a week or two—she still might decide on her own before then, of course—"

"That won't fadge, Frederick. You've been stringing me along for months now, and I'm not about to wait any longer. Why, by rights this should have been *our* party tonight! If you really mean all that talk about loving me and not being able to live without me, you'd better show me now it's not just words and go tell Miss Wentworth you won't marry her. The worst she can do is a breach-of-promise suit. I doubt she'd care to advertise herself like that, but if she does I'd be happy to pay the damages. It'd be worth it to me, to have all this shilly-shallying done with. I have fortune enough to pay a dozen breach-of-promise suits, if it comes to that."

"Yes, I know, but . . . dash it, the old lady would have my head. She *likes* Rebecca."

"What's your grandma got to say about anything, I'd like to know? She can't stop you."

"You don't know my grandmother, Clarissa. I'm still underage, and if she came down hard on Mama, there's no saying but what Mama might get in a dither and refuse to countenance the match. Poor Mama never could say boo to a goose. What's more, my grandmother'd likely up and leave her blunt to someone else if I pulled a trick like that."

"What do you care for her money? I have fortune enough for us both."

"Yes, but . . ." The Earl, listening with some amusement, felt himself sympathizing with Lord Russelton's predicament. While obviously wishing to propitiate his heiress, Lord Russelton was yet reluctant to lose the chance of acquiring his grandmother's fortune as well, and was searching for a means by which he might do both. "It's not just the money, Clarissa. There's also this house. Been in the family for ages, but it ain't part of the entailment, and it won't come to me without my grandmother's say-so."

Miss Barrow sniffed. "And a shabby old thing it is, too!" Her disdain was palpable even to the eavesdroppers in the window seat. "My grandpapa's house in Russell Square is twice as grand as this place. You don't need it, Frederick. I have fortune enough—"

"Her jewelry," said Lord Russelton, grasping at straws. "Did you see those diamonds she was wearing tonight? They aren't entailed, either. M'grandmother can leave 'em to whoever she pleases, and that won't be me if I jilt Rebecca."

There was a thoughtful silence. "The stones looked pretty good," admitted Miss Barrow. "But the settings was horrid: perfectly Gothic. We could have them reset, of course, but I don't know as it's worth it for a set of diamonds, no matter how good. Why, I have fortune enough to buy—"

Miss Wentworth sneezed. There was total silence in the library, and the Earl could feel eyes riveted on the draperies that screened the window seat from view. Miss Wentworth looked at him in dismay, one hand pressed to her lips.

"That's dished us, my love," murmured the Earl, smiling at her rather ruefully. "We may as well get it over with." He gently pushed Miss Wentworth out of his lap, stood up as far as the low-ceilinged embrasure would allow, and pulled the draperies aside. He had glimpses of two stunned faces before he turned to assist Miss Wentworth, who stepped regally from the window seat with her head held high.

The two couples regarded each other for a moment in silence. Lord Russelton gaped at the unexpected apparition of his fiancée as if he saw a ghost, his mouth at half-cock. Miss Barrow looked from the Earl to Miss Wentworth and back again, pleasantly scandalized.

"Well, I never," she gasped. "I never." Her eyes ran avidly up and down Miss Wentworth's figure, looking for signs of ravishment. "I never," she repeated, a sly smile spreading over her face.

Miss Wentworth heroically resisted an urge to glance down at her bodice to verify that all was well. Knowing her position to be indefensible, she took refuge in a strong offense.

"Really, Frederick," she said, addressing her fiancé accusingly. "Really, Frederick, if you need the money as badly as that, pray do not keep Miss Barrow waiting on *my* account." The Earl noticed with appreciation that, consciously or unconsciously, her manner had taken on a tinge of Lady Wentworth's hauteur. "You may consider our engagement to be at an end, as of this moment," Miss Wentworth went on grandly. "I will see that a notice to that effect is sent to the *Morning Post* tomorrow. Rest assured that after the way you have behaved throughout our engagement, and after what I have been privileged to hear tonight, I would not marry you, were you the last man on earth, Frederick Russelton!"

It was a performance worthy of Mrs. Siddons. The Earl felt like applauding. Lord Russelton opened and closed his mouth two or three times before he recovered his powers of speech. Pulling himself together at last, he blustered, "Really, Rebecca! You are criticizing me for the way *I* have behaved? What, pray tell, are you doing in here, alone with *him?*" Lord Russelton raised his quizzing glass and addressed it toward the Earl. The Earl's black brows drew together in an ominous manner; hastily, Lord Russelton transferred the focus of the quizzing glass back to Miss Wentworth. "Pretty behavior, upon my word," he said severely.

"It is none of your concern now, Frederick. I am no longer betrothed to you!"

"And a very good thing, too, I must say." Lord Russelton's sneer became more pronounced. "If playing the lightskirt with Stanford is more to your taste than—"

The Earl's fist caught Lord Russelton squarely on the face, sending him sprawling to the floor. He lay there, half stunned, as the Earl stood over him, fists at the ready. So obvious was it that the Earl was only waiting for him to stand up, in order to hit him again, that Lord Russelton prudently remained on the floor.

"You'd do well not to air such an opinion, Russelton," said the Earl in a deadly voice. "If one word of this goes beyond this room—one word—I'll see that you're called to account. Do you understand me?" Lord Russelton touched his nose, started to say something, hesitated, and finally nodded. "Make sure your lady friend, here, understands it, too," said the Earl curtly.

"How dare you?" Miss Barrow, red with anger, dropped to her knees beside Lord Russelton. Taking her handkerchief from her reticule, she attempted to staunch the flow of blood from his nose. Miss Wentworth observed in a detached sort of way that blood had already defaced the unsightly bulk of Lord Russelton's neckcloth; she found herself quite pleased by the circumstance.

"How dare you speak so, my lord?" said Miss Barrow again, looking up from her ministrations to glare at the Earl. "If it comes to calling anyone to account over this business, I should think—"

The Earl ignored her and began to steer Miss Wentworth toward the door. "I'll see that Lady Cassandra is informed of your—er—indisposition, Russelton," he tossed over his shoulder. Lord Russelton was attempting to sit up with the aid of Miss Barrow, and made no reply other than a resentful look. The Earl opened the library door for Miss Wentworth, followed her into the hallway, and shut the door behind him.

"You were magnificent, Jack," said Miss Wentworth, rather awed. "You sounded positively murderous! Do you think . . . do you think they'll really keep it all to themselves?"

"They would do well to do so," said the Earl grimly. He was busy envisioning the consequences if things came to an affair of honor between him and Lord Russelton. He thought he would not at all mind putting a bullet in the young fool, but the scandal that would accompany such a business made him hope it could be avoided. And angry though he was at Lord Russelton, he was angrier still at himself; he found it galling that his own actions had precipitated Miss Wentworth into a scene as sordid as it was unnecessary. What the devil had he been thinking of, to put her in such a compromising position? A wry smile touched his lips. The answer to that question, at least, was obvious: he had not been thinking at all. There had been a considerable amount of feeling, but very little thought involved in his actions tonight, which had contributed not a little to the hobble he and Miss Wentworth were in right now.

Rousing himself at last from his reflections, the Earl became aware that his companion was looking at him with concern. "You were rather magnificent yourself, my dear," he said, making an effort to lighten his voice. "I never heard a more cutting speech. Your aunt could have done no better!"

Miss Wentworth smiled wanly. She looked so worried that the Earl would have liked to have taken her in his arms, and would indeed have done so if a servant had not been passing down the hallway just then with a tray of wineglasses. The Earl took the man aside, instructed him to convey the news of Lord Russelton's difficulty to Lady Cassandra, and abstracted a couple of the wineglasses. The servant left, and the Earl led Miss Wentworth to an upholstered bench near the entrance of the ballroom. She sank down gratefully and accepted a glass of wine.

"What a dreadful evening," she said with a sigh. The Earl looked at her quizzically over the rim of his wineglass. She regarded him for a moment, and her color rose. "No, no, not . . . oh, Jack! That part wasn't dreadful. I didn't—I never knew kissing could make one feel that way."

"Neither did I," said the Earl, and was conscious of no incongruity about the statement. Kissing her had been like nothing he had experienced before in his previous dealings with the female sex. There was a part of him that had always stood aloof even during the most absorbing moments, aware of himself, his own actions, his own intentions; in the past he had rather prided himself on this attitude that allowed him to be cynically entertained without ever becoming truly involved.

Then he had met Rebecca Wentworth, and cynical detachment had been at an end. Tonight's events had proved it beyond all possible doubt. Never before had he been so caught up in sensation that he forgot himself entirely. He had meant to do no more than kiss Miss Wentworth once or twice, and yet he had come dangerously close to doing considerably more, in spite of intentions that were (for once) quite honorable. The mechanics of making love were nothing new to him, but his feelings for Rebecca Wentworth had opened up an entirely new perspective on the experience—he found it almost dizzying to contemplate.

The Earl looked at Miss Wentworth, sitting beside him on the bench. Although the ballroom was close by, and a pair of servants could be seen loitering at the far end of the hallway, he recklessly took her in his arms and proceeded to kiss her once more, just to confirm his findings on the subject. She returned his kiss with a passion that surprised him. He released her, and took one of her hands between his own; he opened his mouth to tell her that he loved her. Then he saw that there were tears in her eyes.

It had been a stressful evening for Miss Wentworth.

She had been forced to endure the best wishes of her friends and acquaintances, feeling herself a hypocrite the whole time; she had nearly been seduced twice, at her own betrothal party, by a man not her fiancé; she had broken off her engagement after a distasteful scene, during which a nose had been bloodied and perhaps even broken on her account. Any of these would have been sufficient excuse for melancholy, but it was quite another matter that brought tears to Miss Wentworth's eyes.

However much of a sham her engagement had been, it had still acted as a barrier between herself and the Earl: a slight barrier, indeed, but it had served to keep an element of detachment in her dealings with him. Now that the engagement was at an end, however, the barrier was gone, too, and the truth stared her in the face. She loved the Earl of Stanford to distraction. The thought of life without him was too awful to contemplate. In spite of Belinda Satterthwaite, and Lady Rosamund, and a host of warnings from her friends and family about his public and private depravities, she was no more able to resist him than those other women before her had been. She was not even able to deceive herself about wanting to resist him; what had taken place in the library tonight had shown her the truth beyond all possible doubt. The inevitable might have been postponed, but it could not be avoided.

Miss Wentworth felt she could endure the terrible price she would pay for loving him. Fiercely, she told herself that she would gladly forfeit all she possessed for his sake. But even as he was kissing her, there in the hallway, Miss Wentworth's cold common sense was whispering to her that the day would come when the Earl would tire of her, whereupon he would leave her for another, and that thought she could not bear. Tears came to her eyes at the very thought.

Seeing those tears, the Earl was struck by doubt. A moment's consideration was enough to make him realize that she had been through a great deal already this evening, and much of what she had gone through had been indisputably his own fault. It could not be said to be an appropriate moment for a declaration. He might think himself fortunate if she chose not to cut his acquaintance altogether, after this night's work. Doubtless she would need time to recover before she would be in any mood to contemplate another offer of marriage.

"You look done up, Becky," he said gently. "Under the circumstances, I think it might be permissible if you pleaded a headache and went home. Do you want to wait here while I get your mother?"

Miss Wentworth shook her head mutely. The thought of telling her mother about her broken engagement made her feel rather sick. It was going to be incredibly difficult to explain her actions without giving away details she had no wish to discuss; the truth would likely come out soon enough, but she wished to spare her family as long as possible. "No. No, if you will take me back to Mama and Aunt Constance, I think it would be best, Jack. I'll wait until we leave before I tell them about—about the engagement. I hope Mama won't scold too much. She always thought Frederick too young . . . oh, dear." Miss Wentworth sniffed and attempted to wipe away the tears with her fingers. Silently, the Earl offered her his handkerchief. "Thank you, Jack. Indeed, you are very good to me," she said, trying to smile at him.

The Earl felt himself a complete reprobate. The words he wanted to say—words that might have redeemed himself in her eyes—would clearly be out of place at the present time. He escorted Miss Wentworth back to her mother and aunt, and immediately took his own leave of the party, disgusted almost beyond endurance with the way he had bungled the affair.

Chapter Twelve

The remainder of that evening went on to fufill all Miss Wentworth's grimmest expectations. Her departure from Lady Cassandra's party proved not the least of her ordeals. The much-dreaded interview with her mother lay immediately ahead of her, causing her untold anxiety, and her conscience was not made easier by her mother's touching concern for her spurious headache. The carriage was called, and their departure hastened; there were many expressions of sympathy and regret that Miss Wentworth's indisposition should have arisen at so untimely a moment.

Concern soon changed to disapproval, however, once they were safely in the carriage and Miss Wentworth had haltingly related the news that her engagement was at an end.

In the inquisition that followed, Miss Wentworth refused to give specific details. She would only say stubbornly that she and Lord Russelton had decided they would not suit each other after all. "I've suspected it for some time, Mama," she made the mistake of adding.

"Then why have you said nothing before now? Being a baroness is nothing to sneeze at, my dear. You're not likely to do better, this late in the season. And with your wedding less than a month away! It's very thoughtless of you, Rebecca: downright capricious. If you don't earn yourself the reputation of a jilt, it's more than *I'll* hope for."

Upon reaching Berkeley Square, Miss Wentworth withdrew to her bedchamber, still pursued by her mother's recriminations. She maintained a semblance of composure while the maid helped her change out of her ballgown and into her nightdress, but after the maid left, her pillow was the recipient of a good many tears.

Because she had been too proud to accept rejection at the onset, she had embroiled herself in a web of deceit and made any true explanation of her actions impossible. Miss Wentworth could see it all now, with the clarity of hindsight. If only she had broken the engagement weeks ago—months ago—when she had first become aware of Lord Russelton's change of heart, her mother's censure would have been much milder, and much less deserved. But though the present atmosphere of disapproval was difficult to bear, Miss Wentworth knew it would be as nothing compared to her mother's reaction if the real story of what had transpired in Lady Cassandra's library became known. Mrs. Wentworth's daughter had been on the verge of committing an enormity against which a broken engagement was a mere drop in the bucket.

Try as she might, Miss Wentworth could not feel remorseful about this part of her behavior. She recognized that such behavior was wrong, but it had certainly not felt wrong. Not wrong at all . . . thinking about those moments alone in the library with the Earl made her feel hot and cold all over, and filled her with a kind of exultation. She loved him; she had been willing then, and was willing now to give him whatever he wanted without counting the cost to herself. The thought of having him only to lose him someday was dreadful, to be sure, but it would be far worse to live out her life without ever having had him at all.

Miss Wentworth had reached this point in her cogitations when a new and even more dreadful thought struck her. What if her tears and vapors had disgusted him so that he no longer wanted her? Such thoughts were not conducive to repose. Miss Wentworth's eyes were heavy when she arose the next morning, feeling far from refreshed.

The Earl's night passed with scarcely less misery. He tossed and turned, as the tenor of his thoughts ranged from darkly despondent to wildly exultant and back again. He could not help feeling a sort of guilty gratification at the remembrance of what had happened in the library between himself and Miss Wentworth. He knew he'd had no business to let things go as far as they had—as later events had shown only too clearly—yet surely it showed she felt the same attraction toward him that he felt toward her? At one moment, the Earl was certain that she returned his feelings; at another, he wondered if he was making too much of a purely physical response. With a pang, he told himself that of all people, the Earl of Stanford ought to know how often love could be completely absent from the so-called lovemaking process.

The Earl's mood would have been far more confident had it not been for Miss Wentworth's tears, following as they did the scene with her ex-fiancé. To the Earl, they came as a confirmation that she still cared more for Lord Russelton than she was willing to admit. Her engagement had been doomed in any case; that was a foregone conclusion, but the Earl found himself wishing he had played not quite so active a role in bringing it to an end. His own part in the proceedings had been such an ignoble one that he decided the best thing he could do was to stay away from her for a week or two and give her time to recover. But by four o'clock that afternoon, he could endure it no longer. He gave orders to have the chestnuts put to, and drove around to Berkeley Square, his thoughts a jumble of hopes and fears. There was no fixed plan in his head. He hoped his reception today might provide a clue as to the best way to proceed with his mismanaged courtship.

Miss Wentworth was in the midst of drafting a notice to the *Morning Post* informing the polite world of her betrothal's end. She was not sorry to be interrupted at this melancholy task, and when the Earl's name was announced, and he came in just as usual, with the news he had come to take her driving, she was surprised into smiling and exchanging greetings with him in very much her normal manner.

"I suppose you know, Stanford, what this child has taken it into her head to do," said Lady Wentworth in a low voice, shaking her head regretfully.

"About her betrothal? Yes, I was sorry to hear the news, of course, but Rebecca had already confided to me that she had doubts about the match. Perhaps it may be for the best," said the Earl. His eyes rested on Miss Wentworth's face, downcast now at the reminder of her disgrace. "I suspect it might do her good to come out for a while, don't you think, Lady Wentworth? I have my phaeton outside, and it's a beautiful day."

"An excellent notion, Stanford," approved Lady Wentworth. "Rebecca, if you would care to have me finish that, I believe it would be as well for you to go out with Stanford. Nothing could be worse than to seem to be moping at such a time, you know."

"Would you finish it for me, Aunt Constance? Thank you!" Miss Wentworth gave her aunt the half-completed notice and ran upstairs to put on her pelisse and bonnet.

Once she was seated in the phaeton, however, she found herself shy in the Earl's presence. He gave her the reins, and she drove for a time in silence. She wondered if he would take advantage of their time together to make some sort of assignation with her. She was ignorant of the usual procedure in such affairs, but it seemed obvious that his intention in coming today was to carry forward what had been interrupted last night. It was only the details of his intentions of which she stood in doubt; did he mean to set her up in some sort of irregular establishment, publicly proclaiming her as his mistress, or was he planning to carry on a clandestine relationship under her aunt's roof? She could hardly ask him outright.

"I was quite surprised to see you this afternoon, Jack. After what happened last night—after ending my engagement with Frederick, I no longer have any need to impress anyone with my driving, you know. I had supposed the lessons to be ended."

Miss Wentworth waited to hear what he would say in reply. She felt she had done her best to bring matters to a crossroad of sorts. If he wanted to abandon her at this point, he had a suitable pretext; if not, it was up to him to set the basis on which the relationship would continue. She looked at him anxiously, hoping and yet dreading to hear him put in plain English what it was he wanted of her.

"Why should the lessons be discontinued for that reason? I enjoy driving with you very much, Becky. And you are welcome to use my phaeton whenever you please, if you still want to cut a dash in the park."

Heavens, was it possible he was going to pretend that nothing had happened? The Earl of Stanford might possess such sang-froid, but after the business in the library last night Miss Wentworth felt she could keep up the appearance of mere friendliness no longer. It would be easier not to see him at all rather than pretend an indifference she was far from feeling.

She spoke hesitantly, "Now that my engagement with Frederick is over, and I have had time to—to think, I believe I would feel uncomfortable borrowing your phaeton and—and pretending it to be my own, as we spoke of doing. I daresay it was improper to talk of doing so in the first place . . . if I had not been so angry, that day in the park, I don't believe I should have thought of such a thing. But oh, Jack, you must not think I am not very grateful for—for your help. You are a splendid driving teacher." She smiled at him, a sorry little smile that died stillborn. "Perhaps you can find another damsel in distress to help, now that you are finished with me."

The Earl felt as though he had been slapped. "Are you saying, then . . . I take it you have no further use for me, now that your engagement's over?"

"No, Jack! That's not true at all. Only I thought perhaps you . . ." Miss Wentworth shot him a fleeting look. "It is only that things have changed," she said helplessly.

"Yes, I am aware that things have changed." Growing more alarmed by the minute, the Earl abandoned all thought of proceeding with caution. He decided to hazard everything on a single throw. "Since you are no longer engaged to Russelton, have you ever thought . . . do you think you might like to marry me instead?"

Miss Wentworth was so astonished that she let the reins drop from her hands. The chestnuts broke into a canter. If the Prince Regent himself had asked her hand in marriage, she could not have been more surprised. By the time the horses were under control again, she had recovered her wits to some extent, but she could hardly believe she had heard the Earl aright. She reined the horses in and looked at him searchingly.

The Earl was unhappy with her reaction. His title and fortune made him an eligible, even illustrious *parti,* in society's reckoning, at least, and he had hoped Miss Wentworth was coming to care for him. He was hurt by her shocked face. Certainly his reputation was bad, but he was proposing marriage, for God's sake. "I'm sorry, Becky. I didn't think you'd find the idea so appalling. Don't think I—"

"No, no. Only you took me by surprise, Jack! Of course I will marry you." Miss Wentworth still felt dazed, but a great happiness was welling up in her heart. How she had misjudged him! She blushed with shame to think of the suspicions she had been harboring only moments before.

The Earl wished he knew the thoughts going on behind those wide green eyes. He wondered if he had been too precipitate. Still, she had accepted him. . . . "You might look happier about it," he suggested, with a faint smile.

Miss Wentworth laughed. "Oh, Jack, I—" A chilling thought caused her to break off the assurance she had been about to make. Was it possible that this, too, was chivalry? Perhaps he felt obliged to offer for her, after what had happened last night. "Jack, you mustn't think you *have* to marry me. I mean, after what happened last night—"

"I beg to differ with you! My behavior last night was inexcusable." The Earl felt he was demonstrating to Miss Wentworth what a reformed character he had become. The effect of his words, however, was to convince her that a sense of obligation had prompted the offer she had just received. There was an awkward silence. The Earl seemed on the verge of speech half-a-dozen times, before at last he spoke again. "I know I don't have the reputation of a saint, but I wouldn't have—er—behaved the way I did last night, unless I had intended to offer for you, Becky," he said contritely. "I was waiting for your engagement to Russelton to be over . . . and then, what with one thing and another, I may have anticipated matters a trifle." His eyes slid around to hers with an expression of guilty mischief.

Miss Wentworth badly wanted to believe him, but she was still dubious, and another difficulty had just occurred to her. "My marriage portion is quite small, you know," she said hesitantly.

"Do you think me a fortune hunter as well as a libertine? I am a wealthy man, my dear. I can afford to marry for—" The word love stuck in his throat. He was not at all sure Miss Wentworth loved him. The way she kept making excuses was definitely worrisome; it almost seemed as though she had thought better of her acceptance and was trying to turn him off. "I can afford to marry you, even if you are quite penniless," he said, trying for a light note. "Like the rich Miss Barrow, I have fortune enough for the both of us!"

Miss Wentworth burst out laughing. "Oh, I'm not quite penniless, Jack," she said, and her voice carried a note of happiness that reassured him. "Even if my papa is nothing but a country parson!"

"Well, that's settled, then! You have made me very happy, my dear." The Earl laid his hand over her own for a moment, and then went on, in a businesslike voice, "There are a few matters we'll have to decide that we might as well get out of the way now. The notice of our engagement, for one. Coming on top of the other announcement, it can't help but cause a stir, but it might be better to get it done with now and have all the fuss over with in one dose. And just think how effectively it will eclipse Russelton and Miss Barrow's betrothal announcement!" More chivalry, thought Miss Wentworth. "I expect it'll be a regular nine days' wonder, what with ending your engagement to Russelton, and then engaging yourself to me instead. And for me to be getting engaged at all . . . well, I suspect there'll be some shocked faces to see my name as your prospective bridegroom. More like a twenty-seven days' wonder, at the very least! Can you stand the nonsense, Becky? I don't know that it's worth it, just to be married to me."

"Oh, I expect I can stand it," said Miss Wentworth demurely. Married to him! Amid all her doubts and fears, she realized some small part of what marriage might be like with the Earl of Stanford. The dimple began to flicker.

The Earl regarded it with approval. "Well, then, we seem to be agreed. There's—er—just one more thing . . . would you mind very much, getting married right away? As you've probably realized, my dear, I'm not much of a hand at waiting." He shot her another sidelong look, eyes dancing with mischief, and Miss Wentworth felt herself blush.

"Yes, Jack," she said, her blush deepening. "I, too, would like to be married soon!"

The Earl leaned over and gave her a light kiss, in the vicinity of her ear. "I don't dare kiss you properly here," he apologized. "There's a gentleman in a frock coat over there who's already looking our way with great disapproval. It's my turn to be in debt now: I must ask you for easy terms, and promise to give you a real engagement kiss the first moment we find ourselves alone!"

The Earl took the reins, and they drove back to Berkeley Square. There was a slight constraint between them, owing to mutual uncertainty and the change in their relationship, but they were both feeling gloriously happy nevertheless. The Earl helped Miss Wentworth down from the phaeton.

"Shall I go in with you and announce the glad tidings? I look forward to seeing Lady Wentworth's face when she learns we are to be twice-connected!"

"No, I think she and Mama were going to the dressmaker's this afternoon. I will tell them myself, and take particular note of Aunt Constance's face. But I can already tell you that she will be delighted. You've made a complete conquest of her, Jack; this will make her very happy, I'm sure."

"I hope it will make you happy as well, my dear." For a moment they stood on the doorstep looking at each other. "I'll write your father tonight, Becky, seeking permission after the fact, as it were! But of course there's the matter of settlements to be arranged. May I come tomorrow and speak to your mother?"

"Of course," said Miss Wentworth. The Earl kissed her hand, started to leave, and then came back and took her in his arms, kissing her quite thoroughly despite the presence of his groom and half-a-dozen interested passers-by.

"There," he said. "Mind you, it's still not what I would call a proper engagement kiss, but—"

"But it will have to do for now, my lord," said Miss Wentworth with a saucy smile. The Earl's eyes narrowed and he took a purposeful step in her direction. Laughing, she whisked through the doorway, almost into the arms of her aunt's butler. Taking refuge at once behind this respectable individual, she called out in a sweet voice, "I will look forward to seeing you *tomorrow,* Jack." The Earl grinned, raised his hat in token of defeat, and took his leave.

Despite her overall mood of elation, Miss Wentworth found she was also feeling a certain amount of trepidation about the reception her news was likely to receive in the bosom of her family. Her concern was not with Lady Wentworth, for her aunt had been fully won over some time ago by the combined force of the Earl's charm and connection to the family. Miss Wentworth's mother showed surprising flashes of independence on the subject, however. Though usually ready enough to follow Lady Wentworth's lead, Mrs. Wentworth persisted in mistrusting the Earl and was still in the habit of delivering an occasional warning lecture about plausible villains to her long-suffering daughter. As for Sir Richard Wentworth, he had maintained a disapproving attitude all along. Miss Wentworth hugged her secret close until dinner time. When the dessert course was set on the table, and the servants out of the room, she decided the time had come. Fixing her eyes on the solemn painted countenance of the late Sir Thomas Wentworth regarding her from the opposite wall of the dining room, Miss Wentworth took a deep breath.

"Mama? Mama, Lord Stanford has asked me to marry him. And I . . . have accepted."

Lady Wentworth looked up from her plate, an arrested expression on her face. "I beg your pardon?"

"Stanford?" exclaimed Mrs. Wentworth, dropping her fork.

"Well, I'll be damned," said Sir Richard profoundly.

"Richard!"

"Sorry, Mama." Sir Richard regarded his cousin with awe. "But I mean to say, Stanford! How in the world did you manage to—seems to me you've been playing a deep game, Beck!"

"I do not know what you can mean by saying such a thing, Richard. Stanford has always shown a marked partiality for Rebecca."

"So attentive." Mrs. Wentworth nodded wisely. "Of course, he had no thought of marriage while she was engaged to Frederick Russelton—"

"I'll just bet he didn't," said Sir Richard in an undertone.

"—but now that she is free, he was emboldened to speak."

"Are you sure it was *marriage* he—sorry, Beck. If you say it's so, then I'll believe you, but I never thought to see such a thing. Lord, won't the gossips have a time of it when it's announced!"

"Jack—Stanford—thinks it should be announced immediately. On account of my other engagement ending, you know. He feels it would be better to get all the talk over with at once, rather than to draw it out."

Lady Wentworth and Mrs. Wentworth both frowned. "There's something in that, to be sure," said Mrs. Wentworth thoughtfully. "An announcement that she is betrothed to the Earl of Stanford would more than make up for that unfortunate affair with Frederick Russelton. If the engagement were announced now, and the wedding set for next Season—"

"Next Season? Oh, no, Mama, we want to be married very soon. I had thought, since I was planning to be married next month anyway—" Miss Wentworth paused. Her mother and aunt had exchanged glances and were shaking their heads as one. "Why ever not? I already have most of my bride-clothes."

"Out of the question, my dear," said Mrs. Wentworth, in a tone of voice that brooked no argument. "Since it is Stanford, you know, it would look so very . . . not that anyone would believe . . . but even so, no need to give the impression . . ." Caught amid a tangle of half-sentences, she looked to her sister-in-law for help.

"It would present a very odd appearance, Rebecca," said Lady Wentworth austerely. She regarded Miss Wentworth's rebellious face with quite a kindly eye. "I daresay it does seem hard to have to wait, but it would be altogether a much better thing to postpone the ceremony until the Little Season at the earliest. September, if you like, but certainly no sooner."

"That will show them," agreed Mrs. Wentworth obscurely.

It was a heavy disappointment to Miss Wentworth. She hoped the Earl would not be too much displeased by the wait. He came to call the next day and threw her aunt and mother into confusion by kissing them both in honor of the occasion ("Since we will all be doubly related now!"). Lady Wentworth in particular was moved to display a vivacity quite foreign to her usual self-possessed manner.

"Well, Stanford, I need hardly say how delighted we

are," she said, smiling broadly. "You and Rebecca should suit very well, I think."

"I think so, too," said the Earl, seating himself beside his betrothed. Miss Wentworth was looking rather rosy, as she, too, had been kissed in the general excitement. He shot her a smile and went on, addressing himself to Mrs. Wentworth. "I've already written to Mr. Wentworth, and as soon as I have his answer back we can proceed to the marriage settlements and such details. Lawyers' work . . . there will be a deal of paperwork involved, I'm afraid, what with the entail and all that nonsense. But I trust we may still have things tied up by the end of June."

A stillness fell over the drawing room. Miss Wentworth opened her mouth, shut it again, and looked helplessly toward her aunt.

"Rebecca has agreed that, while the engagement may certainly be announced immediately, it would be better to wait until the Little Season for the ceremony itself," explained Lady Wentworth.

"I see," said the Earl, after a brief, strained silence.

He was dreadfully disappointed, and fresh worries sprang up to torment him. Was his bride-to-be already having such doubts that she wanted time to reconsider her decision? The Earl supposed it was a reasonable request; he strove to hide his disappointment. "I expect that will do very well," he said carefully, "if that is what you would prefer, Becky?"

"Mama and Aunt Constance think it best," said Miss Wentworth, giving him an apologetic look. The Earl did not see it; he seemed to be occupied in examining the gloss on his Hessian boots.

"Well, then, we are all agreed," said Mrs. Wentworth vivaciously, conscious that the mood of gaiety had somehow gone flat. "I think this calls for a glass of sherry to celebrate, don't you, Constance? And perhaps you'll stay to dinner, Stanford?"

The Earl was forced to refuse. He had, in fact, a perfectly legitimate excuse, having arranged to dine at his aunt's house for the purpose of disclosing his engagement to his own relations. He did not mention this circumstance, however, and his manner was so withdrawn during the latter part of the call that Miss Wentworth became worried, and she soon began to wonder what he thought more important than spending the evening with her. A vision of the blond girl she had seen in the park promptly arose before her eyes. It was a small thing, but a seed of doubt was planted in her mind, and her imagination was quick to encourage its growth.

After the Earl left the house, Miss Wentworth thought back over everything the Earl had said and done during their acquaintance; the terms in which his proposal of marriage had been worded; the implication, unspoken but strong, that he had felt obliged to offer for her after what had happened on the night of the engagement party. She was unable to rule out the possibility that it was actually some sort of marriage of convenience he had in mind. Under such an arrangement, he would naturally feel free to continue his relations with the beautiful blonde incognita, or whoever else might have taken her place in the interim. Miss Wentworth wondered that she had failed to see it sooner. There was nothing to prove that a marriage of convenience was what the Earl contemplated, but likewise there was no proof that he contemplated anything more.

As for the idea that he had offered for her because he loved her—a possibility that had actually been her first thought, once the shock of his proposal had subsided enough for her to think at all—the idea now seemed fatuous beyond belief.

For less than a day Miss Wentworth had been happy in her engagement. She had thought marriage to the Earl of Stanford a fair approximation of heaven on earth. Now she began to suspect there might be a certain amount of hell in the prospect as well.

Chapter Thirteen

The announcements that appeared a few days later in the *Morning Post* caused every bit as much furor as the Earl had predicted. Speculation was rife in London concerning the facts behind those formal paragraphs. Someone was held to have been very clever indeed; opinions varied as to who this someone was. Lord Russelton's attentions to the shipping heiress had been an item of gossip long before the news broke about Miss Wentworth and her latest conquest, but the latter was definitely a more spectacular piece of news. The gossips were the more perplexed because all four of the parties involved seemed to have benefited in some way.

There could be no denying that the trick had been turned very neatly. Lord Russelton was now free to marry his heiress and repair his fortunes. Miss Barrow had found a suitable lord to make her "my lady." The Earl of Stanford had successfully made off with another man's fiancée, and this was thought to be very typical of him, in that he could not even do something as respectable as getting married without causing a minor scandal. Miss Wentworth was generally agreed to have achieved the greatest coup, however. She had captured the elusive

Earl of Stanford, despair of every matchmaking mama in London for nearly a decade, and her triumph was all the greater because she appeared not only to have captured him but to have tamed him as well.

Acquaintances who had never noticed his absence at the time suddenly began to realize that the Earl had not been near his more disreputable haunts in months. He had turned off the notorious Alicia long ago, and nobody recalled seeing him with any other Cyprian since. The gaming hells in Pall Mall and St. James Street had felt the loss of his patronage for some time. Cynics predicted that such virtue could not last; romantics thought it the prettiest possible illustration of the power of Love; wits declared it was as good as a play to see the Earl of Stanford playing propriety in Almack's Assembly Rooms with his pretty fiancée.

He conducted himself well there, dancing only the two permitted dances with Miss Wentworth and dividing his attention thereafter with well-bred impartiality. The other young ladies at those select gatherings shamelessly courted his favor, until it was remarked that he consistently sought out the plainest damsels in the room to dance with. The situation promptly reversed itself, and it came to be a terrible insult to be chosen as a partner by the Earl. Women fled the room when they saw him coming; one young lady even went so far as to burst into tears at his approach, until Lady Sefton put her foot down at this excess of virtue and undertook to personally supervise the Earl's choice of partners. He submitted to this with such lamblike meekness that Lady Sefton declared his betrothal would be the making of him. That lady had already come in for a good deal of reflected glory, as the person responsible for introducing the Earl to Miss Wentworth, and Lady Sefton annoyed her fellow patronesses very much by her insistence on taking full credit for the match.

Notwithstanding his fluctuating popularity at Almack's, there were a great many ladies in London who felt they would have been happy to have taken a hand in the Earl's reformation, had they only known him to be reformable. No one felt more strongly about the matter than Lady Rosamund.

Her reaction to his betrothal announcement is best passed over. Once her initial fury had exhausted itself, however, she settled down to consider what could be done about the situation. The Earl's abrupt loss of interest had been a terrible blow to Lady Rosamund's pride. Sure of herself and her own attractions, she had rejoiced in her power over the Earl; she had played him in the manner of an angler playing a trout, and had even—prematurely, as it had turned out—boasted of her skill to a couple of her closest friends.

From the moment she had made his acquaintance, Lady Rosamund had formed the intention of taking the Earl for her lover, but she had also the firm intention of making him work for his victory. It would never do to give in too easily. Full surrender would not take place until the Earl was firmly hooked, and Lady Rosamund became even more set on this policy as time went on, and her heart as well as her pride became involved.

Soon the idea of a mere amorous liason was no longer enough. Lady Rosamund had no actual objection to such affairs in principle, but it was her practice to have an eye to the future, and as her acquaintance with the Earl developed, so too did her ambition. Her present husband's state of health, always precarious, had been growing steadily worse. One of his physicians had personally assured her that he could not last another year.

Having married for money the first time around, Lady Rosamund thought she would marry to please herself the second; she had hoped to keep the Earl on the line long enough to make herself a widow and then, after the obligatory decent interval, she might manage to make herself Lady Rosamund Stanford.

Nothing had worked out as she had planned. The Earl had refused the bait altogether, not even sampling her charms before spurning them. Lady Rosamund comforted herself as best she could with the thought that it was she who had brought the affair to an end, and that the Earl had given up only because he despaired of winning her, but she knew perfectly well she hadn't been nearly as discouraging as that. The Earl had simply thought her not worth the bother. In consequence, hers was all the fury of a woman scorned.

For him to be marrying at all was bad enough, but Lady Rosamund found it particularly offensive that Stanford had shown the bad taste to fall in love with his fiancée. Lady Rosamund had initially dismissed the match as a marriage of convenience, but the first time she saw the Earl with his bride-to-be, the moonstruck expression on his face made it clear that he actually loved the girl. His changed behavior also bore this out, and that was another source of annoyance.

Months ago, when the Earl had first begun to dangle after her, Lady Rosamund had hinted in the most delicate way that she might be more open to his attentions if he were to end his liason with the infamous Cyprian known to be in his keeping. She had received such a blistering set-down on that occasion that she had never attempted to mention the subject again. Now all her so-called friends made a point of telling her what a reformed character the Earl had become. "They say he's broken off altogether with that blond creature that drives in the park—you know who I mean, my dear, I'm sure; you and Stanford used to be so close back then, before little Miss Wentworth took him in hand. She's certainly accomplished miracles. Why, they say Stanford didn't even attend the Cyprian's ball this year, if you can believe it," tittered one of these Job's comforters, who also happened to be Lady Rosamund's sister-in-law.

"I wouldn't dream of disbelieving you, Cecile. No doubt you have the information first hand," snapped Lady Rosamund, with a toss of her head.

With the lack of logic usual to those in her position, Lady Rosamund had chosen to direct most of her fury toward her unoffending rival rather than toward the gentleman who might more justly have been considered the real culprit.

Soon after the engagement was announced, Lady Rosamund sought out Miss Wentworth and found a mutual acquaintance to perform introductions, on an occasion when the Earl himself was not present. Miss Wentworth was dismayed to meet a lady whom she knew to have figured in her betrothed's scarlet past. She managed to conduct herself creditably, but she felt she had been summed up and dismissed as negligible by those flashing black eyes.

Had Miss Wentworth only known it, the dismay in Lady Rosamund's heart was far greater than that residing in her own. Lady Rosamund was forced to admit that Miss Wentworth was beautiful, as beautiful as herself (if you liked that insipid coloring), and Miss Wentworth also possessed the advantages of youth and freshness: Lady Rosamund's mirror had been telling her for some time that she was gradually losing both. She watched Miss Wentworth throughout the evening, and was struck with fresh dismay to see how gracefully Miss Wentworth danced and how well she conducted herself. It was no comfort for Lady Rosamund to tell herself that Stanford would soon tire of a green girl. Even if he did, the green girl would still be irretrievably married to him, effectually ruining Lady Rosamund's cherished plan.

She did her malicious best to make trouble for the affianced couple. She put it about that the Earl had been her lover for months, and was her lover still, and that he regarded Miss Wentworth merely as a necessity for the production of heirs in a marriage of convenience. Her gossip backfired. It was readily accepted that the Earl had been Lady Rosamund's lover, but she was pretty generally thought to have been jilted by him some time ago; no one had seen the Earl come near her in months. Her troublemaking efforts were received with amusement and carried no weight against the other, stronger evidence provided by the Earl's altered behavior. Lady Rosamund's spite did no more than add an extra zest to the story, though of that particular kind of zest there was no noticeable lack: Lady Rosamund was not the only lady made unhappy by the announcement of the Earl's engagement. The gossips were enjoying themselves immensely over the whole affair.

It was unfortunate, yet understandable, that the very gossip that would have reassured Miss Wentworth never reached her. No one saw fit to swell her head by telling her how successfully she had reformed the once-notorious rake, and she was left in a state of uncertainty about the Earl's feelings. Miss Wentworth was too busy to have much time for worrying, however. The last weeks of the Season passed in a whirl of excitement. After her engagement to the

Earl was announced, she was pointed at, whispered about, and all at once an object of interest to people who had never noticed her before. The Earl was taking his new responsibilities seriously and escorted her faithfully to the *ton* parties she attended.

All this was very gratifying, but she seldom had any time alone with him; she was chaperoned more strictly now than had been the case during her engagement to Lord Russelton. Lady Wentworth and Mrs. Wentworth saw this as a necessity, owing to the suspiciously short lapse of time between the end of Miss Wentworth's first engagement and the commencement of her second, but the constant presence of a third party made real conversation with the Earl next to impossible. Even her drives with him had been curtailed. She would have liked to ask him about some of the things that were worrying her, but there never seemed to be more than a moment or two of privacy at a time. Knowing her mother or aunt would shortly be re-entering the room kept her silenced even during such rare moments of privacy as did occur.

Miss Wentworth was a modest girl, brought up to make little of her own attractions. Any tendencies toward conceit engendered by her initial success in London had been quenched by the disastrous outcome of her first engagement. Since then, she had grown increasingly diffident and doubtful of herself. It was always in the back of her mind that the Earl had offered for her because he felt he had ruined her. Certainly there were times when she was with him and thought she sensed an attitude of more than mere chivalry, but she could not be certain. He had never mentioned love when he had asked her to marry him. On one hand, Miss Wentworth reasoned that if the Earl loved her, he would surely have said so; on the other, she remembered that Lord

Russelton had told her before, during, and after the proposal how much he loved her, and that had meant nothing at all. It was impossible to know what to think, in the face of so much conflicting evidence.

More than anything else, Miss Wentworth wondered if the Earl meant to continue his rakish pursuits after their marriage. She did not dare ask him. It was not a subject that could be approached while dancing together, or during a moment of snatched privacy. Miss Wentworth observed with relief that the Earl was now giving her his company in the evenings as well as the afternoons, but as soon as he left her side she was prey to doubts once more. If she could have seen the Earl at White's, good-naturedly enduring the ribaldry of his friends on the subjects of cats' paws and apron strings, she might have felt a great deal easier; unfortunately, the only talk that reached her ears was calculated to increase her worries rather than soothe them.

Lady Cassandra had contributed a good measure to her unhappiness. The great lady, in company with her mouselike daughter-in-law, had come to call soon after the ill-fated engagement party. Miss Wentworth flinched a bit when these particular callers were announced. She would have much preferred to have declared herself not at home, but a sense of duty, together with some lingering traces of guilt about her own behavior, forced her to go downstairs and face the Russelton ladies. Only the remembrance of Lady Cassandra, observed unawares on the night of the party, enabled her to face that formidable dame with anything like equanimity.

The interview went off better than Miss Wentworth had expected. She had no way of knowing what explanation Lord Russelton had seen fit to give his mother and grandmother for the abrupt end to his engagement, but it was clear he had given no very detailed account. Lady Russelton, with sighs and gentle reproaches, conveyed only mild disbelief that any young woman could dream of preferring another *parti* to her darling son; Lady Cassandra, in far more robust tones, took it quite for granted that Miss Wentworth had broken off the engagement with her grandson in order to wed the Earl of Stanford. Far from disapproving, Lady Cassandra stunned Miss Wentworth by congratulating her on this sensible behavior.

"I don't blame you for bettering yourself, my dear. I've about washed my hands of that grandson of mine myself, if it comes to that." Lady Russelton began to make little sounds of distress, but her mother-in-law waved her aside irritably. "Nonsense, May, you know as well as I do that he's been making a cake of himself for weeks, running after that whey-faced Barrow gel. After the dressing down I gave him at Sefton's, I fancied we'd heard the last of it." Lady Cassandra fixed Miss Wentworth with an accusing eye. "Only what must the jackanapes do, Miss Wentworth, but turn around and offer for the chit, as soon as ever you jilted him! She's rich as Croesus, they say, but I can't like the match: family smells of the shop. Or the shipyard, rather!" Lady Cassandra snorted and slapped her knee, delighted at her own jest. "I don't doubt you'll be better off with Stanford, m'dear. He's a handsome devil . . . why, I'd try for him myself, if I was thirty years younger!"

Miss Wentworth smiled and tried to look gratified.

"Yes, indeed: been a bit of a wild blade, if half the *on-dits* are true, but better a rake than a milksop, you know, and I don't doubt he'll settle down to make you a good husband. As good as any of 'em can be, the brutes! You'll have to turn a blind eye to his little affairs, of course. If I was you, my dear, I wouldn't let myself get too fond of him, I expect you know what I mean. Mistake, that; leads to nothing but heartache. I've seen it happen time and again." Lady Cassandra stopped for breath and looked Miss Wentworth up and down appraisingly. "You're a pretty girl, well-bred . . . just what Stanford would look for in a wife, though of course he might have looked higher, and why he had to cut out that grandson of mine . . . ah, well, it can't be helped. No doubt it's your pretty face that caught Stanford's eye, but at his age you can be sure he's thinking about getting himself an heir. With nothing but that rattle of a Giles Collingwood in line for the succession, stands to reason! You give Stanford a son or two, and likely he won't mind if you amuse yourself how and with whom you please. Although sometimes those rakes make the strictest husbands . . . well, I suppose that stands to reason, too, when you think of it!"

Naturally, this conversation added nothing to Miss Wentworth's comfort. She was even more dismayed to have the same information more or less confirmed by her own mother, though Mrs. Wentworth's warnings were couched in language considerably less frank.

"But I don't understand, Mama," said Miss Wentworth rebelliously. "I've driven out with Jack—Stanford—dozens of times, before we were engaged. Even Aunt Constance thought it was perfectly proper. And I drove out with Frederick Russelton the whole time I was engaged to *him.* Why won't you let me go with Stanford anymore?"

"You know I had doubts about letting you go with him in the first place, my dear, though certainly it has turned out for the best . . . but in any case, all that was before you caught him. Now that you have him, you must be careful to do nothing that might give him a disgust. No matter how he himself may have behaved in the past, Rebecca, you can be sure that Stanford expects his future wife to come to him with her reputation undamaged. I'll admit that he has conducted himself quite well thus far, but you must not encourage him to . . . that is, if you were to let him take liberties with you now, before you are actually wed, you would find he would be the first to condemn such conduct. Men are very odd, my dear."

"Oh, Mama, I don't think he—" Miss Wentworth fell silent, thinking of that fateful evening in the library. She had certainly allowed the Earl to take liberties with her upon that occasion, and by doing so had deprived herself forever of the chance to learn if he had intended to offer for her freely. It was true that he had never condemned or reproached her in any way, but how could she know what he really felt?

Mrs. Wentworth saw her daughter's face grow thoughtful and pressed home her advantage. "In any case, it is as well for you not to spend too much time in each other's pockets, either now or later. You know, my dear, you must not be expecting Stanford to dance attendance on you constantly, after you are married. If you find he chooses to . . . chooses to . . . well, the fact is that men have needs that women cannot understand. You will simply have to learn to look the other way. I think Stanford cares for you, Rebecca, and he will not purposely mean to hurt you, but if he discreetly goes elsewhere for . . . for . . ."

"You mean he will have mistresses, Mama."

Mrs. Wentworth frowned at this plain speaking. "It is quite a common thing among men, I fear," she said repressively. "They do not see things just as we do. You will find that most of them see nothing amiss in—"

"Mama! You don't mean that *Papa* ever—"

"No, no," said Mrs. Wentworth hastily. A little smile played briefly about her lips. "Your father, I am happy to say, is—well—different. But then, he was only the younger son of a baronet, of course, and being in the church he had naturally to look to his reputation. Although I don't believe your papa would ever—but there, what I mean to say is that Stanford's position in society is quite a different matter, and likewise a different standard of conduct is considered acceptable. Do you understand, Rebecca?"

"Yes, Mama," said Miss Wentworth sadly.

Chapter Fourteen

The matter was never far from her mind during those last few weeks of the London Season. Every feeling revolted at the idea of marriage on the terms described by her mother and Lady Cassandra. Miss Wentworth found it difficult to believe that such an arrangement was what the Earl had had in mind when he asked her to marry him, but it seemed even more unlikely that after years of being pursued by ladies both well-born and beautiful he should have settled upon her own self to fall in love with. She was inclined to humbly accept the superior wisdom of her elders and resign herself to a loveless marriage of convenience. Enough doubt remained, however, to make her desirous of consulting someone else on the subject, preferably someone close to her own age who was better-versed than she in the ways of the *haut ton.*

In the past, she had often looked to the Honourable Miss Ingleside for advice. It seemed to Miss Wentworth that Henrietta might well be the proper person to consult about this, her latest *crise de coeur,* as well. An opportunity soon arose. Lady Ingleside and her daughter came to call a few days after the visit from the

Russeltons; during the call an *al fresco* party was mentioned, to which both Henrietta and Miss Wentworth were invited on the following week. The occasion was to be one of the last great *fêtes* of the season and was deemed of sufficient importance to merit a new dress for Miss Ingleside. Without any prompting at all, Henrietta was moved to invite Miss Wentworth to accompany her upon the expedition to buy material for the new dress. The invitation was quickly accepted. Miss Wentworth, too, had an excellent excuse to go shopping; her father had recently sent her five guineas, along with a letter acknowledging her engagement to the Earl.

Miss Wentworth had wept a good deal over that letter. In the kindest way, her father had assured her that any bridegroom she might choose would be quite acceptable to him, but he had also stressed that she was equally welcome to remain beneath the parsonage roof for as long as she might require its shelter. She was urged not to marry for merely worldly considerations, and if pressure was being brought to bear upon her (Mrs. Wentworth was not actually mentioned, but the inference was strong), she was to remember that her father, at least, would always stand by her, even if her decision was to return to Derbyshire unwed. Miss Wentworth hastily dashed off a letter of reassurance to her father, revealing as much as she dared of her real feelings about her future husband, but the five guineas still remained to be disposed of.

Notwithstanding the number of hats and bonnets among her accumulated bride-clothes, Miss Wentworth had determined to spend her money upon another hat. She was given to understand that the hats in her trousseau were unsuitable for her present unmarried status, and sacrosanct as well until after the wedding ceremony.

This being the case, and given the fact that the Earl was to accompany her to the upcoming *al fresco* party, Miss Wentworth felt she could not lay out her money to better advantage than upon a new and spectacular hat. Henrietta expressed complete sympathy with this viewpoint, and when Mrs. Wentworth mentioned that her daughter's yellow mulled muslin needed new ribbons it was agreed that no further excuse could be necessary to justify devoting a few hours to the delightful exercise of shopping. Henrietta promised to come around to Berkeley Square on the following afternoon, and Miss Wentworth looked forward to unburdening herself upon one whose wisdom she had come to trust.

The expedition got off to a promising start. Henrietta was accompanied only by a maid, which augured well for Miss Wentworth's hopes of a *tête-à-tête*. The ladies' first destination was in Pall Mall, where resided the establishment of Harding, Howell and Company's Grand Fashionable Magazine.

"For I need gloves as well as the material for my new dress, and if I should not find quite what I am looking for at Harding's, we may always look in Bond Street later," explained Henrietta, after giving the direction to the coachman. A disgruntled look settled over her plump, pretty face. "It's a great pity the Season's so near to being over. I won't get a chance to wear the dress more than once before we leave town. Imagine being exiled in Suffolk all summer, my dear! Really, it is too bad. I might wear my oldest rags there, and no one blink an eye. But at least I shall look well for the Manions' *al fresco* party—though I daresay Richard won't blink an eye, either," she added, with an air of resignation. "It always takes him an age to notice that one is wearing a new dress, and another age to decide that it does not make one look a perfect quiz after all."

Miss Ingleside smiled, a softened look upon her face. "Dear Richard . . . you mustn't mind my grumbling, Rebecca, for we shall go on very well, you know, Richard and I. I suppose it seems very odd and unromantic to you, after the way Lord Stanford swept you off your feet—"

"Oh, no," said Miss Wentworth, quite pink. "Oh, no, Henrietta. I have always thought you and Richard to be very well-suited."

"Well, I think we are," said Henrietta, in a large-minded way. "But it does seem strange to think that you will be marrying Lord Stanford months before I marry Richard, and Richard and I engaged nearly a year now. I'm sure anyone would think we were dragging our heels abominably over the business." With a glance toward the maid sitting opposite them in the carriage, Henrietta leaned over and said, in a confidential tone, "To think of how Lord Stanford carried you off, practically under Frederick Russelton's nose! It makes me laugh now, to think of the way Frederick behaved when we were all at the opera that night. You know, Rebecca, I wondered even then if Lord Stanford did not have you in his eye. Richard would have it that it was nothing but a flirtation, but I had my doubts. It seemed so particular, his singling you out in such a manner. And the way he looked at you . . ."

"Really, Henrietta?" said Miss Wentworth wistfully.

"Well, of course, you goose! One can always tell. I'm sure I'm very happy for you, my dear: you're definitely the most envied girl this Season, and I am only glad that Richard and I are not marrying until next spring, for otherwise your wedding would quite cast ours into the shade!"

"Oh, Henrietta, that reminds me. I had wondered if you might stand my bridesmaid," said Miss Wentworth, a little hesitantly. "I know your mama said you were not coming to town for the Little Season, but Suffolk is not so very far away—"

Henrietta at once declared herself delighted to fufill the office of bridesmaid. "My dear, I would not miss it for anything. The wedding of the season, imagine! There will not be the slightest difficulty to bring Mama and Papa down for a week or two, you may depend upon it. And what's more," said Miss Ingleside, her voice becoming exultant, "what's more, it gives me a splendid excuse to buy material enough for *two* dresses today, for of course I must have a new dress if I am to be your bridesmaid." In an access of affection, Henrietta embraced Miss Wentworth and vowed eternal friendship, along with the more immediate intention of sparing no expense to avoid making a shabby appearance at her friend's wedding.

The premises of Harding, Howell and Company being reached, the two ladies disembarked from the carriage and sallied forth to accomplish their several errands. They spent some time among the furs and fans, admired and criticized the jewelry and ornamental articles in ormolu, and at length arrived in the haberdashery department, where Henrietta thought she might reasonably expect to find a muslin appropriate for the *al fresco* party.

After much discussion, a rose-pink jaconet was decided to be both suitable and becoming. The material was measured, cut off, and wrapped, while the ladies satisfied themselves that there was nothing among the many bolts of fabric sufficiently striking for the bridesmaid's dress; Miss Wentworth was forced to exercise great self-restraint and barely escaped with her five guineas intact when a canny shopkeeper cast before her the shimmering breadths of a beautiful *eau-de-Nil* zephyrine silk, which he declared might have been expressly designed with her in mind.

She and Henrietta then proceeded to the ribbons and laces, where they found the ribbon needed to rejuvenate the yellow mulled muslin. Henrietta purchased as well two pairs of Limerick gloves, and the ladies left the store with the intention of visiting next a certain milliner in Bond Street.

"For though Harding's has a very fine millinery department, to my mind there is nothing so elegant as Madame LaLande's bonnets," explained Henrietta, and Miss Wentworth solemnly agreed.

The carriage set them down some blocks from Madame LaLande's shop. "We may as well look into a few mantua-makers', too, as long as we are in Bond Street," said Henrietta, arranging her unfurled sunshade over her shoulder with the appearance of airy unconcern. "After all, we have not yet definitely settled what I am to wear for your wedding. I come to think that crepe at Harding's was perhaps a trifle dear."

In point of fact, both ladies were happy enough to have an excuse to stroll along and inspect the merchandise displayed in Bond Street's wonderful shops, a pastime that would have been discouraged had either Lady Ingleside or Mrs. Wentworth been present. Certainly the progress of two very pretty, modish, and unescorted damsels occasioned no little interest among the scores of gentlemen who loitered along Bond Street for the sole purpose of inspecting every feminine passer-by through the medium of the quizzing glass.

"I know Mama does not like me to walk here without

her, but with both of us, and Martha as well, I cannot see that there is the least impropriety," said Henrietta virtuously, trying to look unconscious of a quizzing glass being leveled at her by a lanky gentleman got up in a canary-striped waistcoat and bottle-green coat.

"Oh, no, I'm sure it cannot be improper," agreed Miss Wentworth, with a fair assumption of Henrietta's unconcern. As the maid was lagging a good half block behind them, however, and showed a disposition to encourage the flirtatious advances of any beau inclined to make them, Miss Wentworth did rather wonder how much protection Martha's presence ensured. As it happened, she need not have worried; Miss Ingleside had been three Seasons in London and was quite equal to the situation.

A pair of young gentlemen with bad complexions and exceedingly high shirt-points were lounging against a shop front as the ladies passed. One of these gentlemen, in the most casual way, extended a booted foot, further adorned with a wicked spur, at an angle calculated to snag the flounce of Henrietta's fawn-colored walking dress. Henrietta neatly sidestepped both foot and spur, at the same time bringing the ivory handle of her sunshade smartly against the gentleman's knee. A roar of pain issued from his lips.

"Oh, I do beg your pardon, sir!" Henrietta's voice was drenched in sympathy, but the look she shot her companion was more expressive of glee. "Really, I have no patience with those creatures," she told Miss Wentworth, once they had put a little distance between themselves and the wounded dandy. "What's he doing now? If he dares to follow us—"

"No, I don't think he will," said Miss Wentworth,

casting a look over her shoulder. "He seems to be walking away—no, limping away—in the other direction."

"Good," said Henrietta with satisfaction. "Ah, here is Madame LaLande's."

Miss Wentworth had been regretting that she had as yet found no opportunity to speak to Henrietta of the serious matters weighing on her mind, but she straightway forgot all else amidst the fairyland of entrancing headgear displayed in Madame LaLande's shop.

The conversation naturally turned instead to such crucial matters as the set of a bow or the angle of a brim. Miss Wentworth soon declared herself unable to decide between two of Madame's creations, one a large leghorn straw trimmed with peach-colored satin ribbons and a bunch of summer flowers; and the other, a bonnet of white corded *gros de Naples* with a low crown and large brim, finished with a fall of white lace and adorned with a full-blown yellow rose surrounded by clusters of rosebuds.

"Everything looks well on you," said Henrietta, wrinkling her nose at her own mirrored face, which was crowned at the moment by an unlikely headdress composed of a rose, an aigret, and a wisp of veiling. Miss Ingleside had not the intention of actually buying anything in Madame LaLande's shop, but finding herself there, she felt obliged to try on a few hats herself, merely to keep Miss Wentworth company.

"Does not this suit me admirably, Rebecca?" she inquired a moment later, smiling from ear to ear and presenting for Miss Wentworth's inspection a tall evening toque of bright yellow satin, with an outsize crepe flower and stiff plume of ostrich feathers set squarely above her right eye.

"It would suit Lady Cass a great deal better," said

Miss Wentworth, laughing. "And I don't think Richard would much care for it!"

Putting the bonnet she was wearing aside, Miss Wentworth set in its place a confection of white satin edged in green-and-white plaid silk, trimmed with a large bow of the same plaid and three green ostrich feathers. "Oh, dear! I love this one, too," she wailed, with a despairing look in the mirror. "Which do you think, Henrietta? I had thought to wear my yellow muslin to the *al fresco* party, but I could wear my ivory just as well, and it would go splendidly with that pretty leghorn with the flowers. Or if I were to wear my green sprig muslin I might wear this bonnet I have on now, though I do have a green bonnet already . . . I suppose it ought really to be either the leghorn or the bonnet with the roses, but I can't decide which."

"Buy both," advised Henrietta, critically examining her own appearance in a French walking hat of straw-colored plush.

"I can't afford both," said Miss Wentworth, sighing. "Mama would like the bonnet with the roses, I'm sure, and it would look lovely with my yellow muslin, but this leghorn is so very pretty . . ."

Henrietta shot a shrewd glance at Miss Wentworth, and another at the milliner's assistant hovering helpfully behind her. "I daresay Lord Stanford would think them both very pretty," she said meaningfully. "And since you will be marrying in September and have your bride-clothes to buy . . ."

"But I already have—oh!" A poke in the ribs made Miss Wentworth stop short. She looked at Henrietta reproachfully. "You know perfectly well I already have most of my bride-clothes, Henrietta," she whispered. "I was to be married to Frederick this month, and nearly everything was ready but my wedding dress, weeks ago. Why did you—"

"Hush," said Henrietta. "Don't you see, ninny, Madame LaLande will sell you those hats for a song if she knows you're buying bride-clothes. Particularly if she knows it's the Earl of Stanford you're marrying. Didn't you see the girl hurry off when I mentioned his name, and your wedding in September? You'll see, Madame will come in and offer to make a lower price, if only you will agree to mention to your friends that you bought the hats in her shop. It is very often done," she explained condescendingly, at Miss Wentworth's astonished face. "When my older sister married Lord Anthony Rolande three years ago, Mama got the shopkeepers to take a little off the price of nearly everything, and *he* was not an earl, you know, but only a younger son."

The notion of such self-aggrandisement made Miss Wentworth open her eyes, but Henrietta proved to be perfectly correct; the five guineas purchased both of the hats Miss Wentworth had admired, and she left the milliner's shop enormously impressed by her friend's worldly wisdom.

"I never would have thought of such a thing, Henrietta," she confided, as the bandboxes were loaded into the carriage. "However did you dare?"

"Oh, my dear, you should see Mama at the game! I daresay she would have got the white satin with the plaid trimming included as well. Mama is a great one for bargains," said Henrietta, with simple pride. "At first, it does seem a little odd, to bargain with the tradespeople, but only think how many people will see you wearing those hats. I expect a great many ladies will ask where you bought them. You need do no more than say, 'at Madame LaLande's,' and probably you will sell a dozen more for her. With your looks, I'm sure she couldn't ask for a better advertisement. Especially since your engagement to Lord Stanford was announced . . . really, I think we might have got the white satin as well," said Henrietta, looking back toward the shop as though she contemplated doing further battle with the milliner.

"Oh, no, no," said Miss Wentworth hastily, still a trifle uncertain about the propriety of trading on her future position for such a purpose. "But thank you very much, Henrietta. Now I may wear the bonnet with the roses to the Manion's, and save the leghorn for another time. It will do nicely this summer, when we go to Brighton."

"Yes, and I am very glad I went ahead and bought that perfectly lovely French walking hat. It will run me over my quarter's allowance a bit, but I can always talk Papa around," said Henrietta, bending an affectionate look upon the bandbox containing her own new headgear. "Do you want to look farther down Bond Street, Rebecca? We still have not settled upon a material for my bridesmaid's dress, though there is no great hurry about that, of course."

"Perhaps a little farther," assented Miss Wentworth. Now that most of the shopping was done, she realized there was little time remaining for the serious discussion with Henrietta she had hoped for. The two ladies walked down Bond Street, Miss Ingleside keeping up a lively commentary on the merchandise in the shop windows, and Miss Wentworth trying to think of a way to bring the conversation around to the subject of marriage.

Henrietta obliged her by mentioning it herself. They had entered a draper's shop, still in quest of the material for the bridesmaid's dress. "Do you think pink, Rebecca? Mama will always have me wear pink, because of my dark hair, but I believe blue might make my eyes look bluer. Although Mama holds that brunettes don't look well in blue . . ."

"That color of blue looks very well on you, Henrietta," said Miss Wentworth, scrutinizing her friend's form against a drapery of cerulean blue gauze. "I think it would make up beautifully. If you decide to buy it, you may tell your Mama that I particularly wanted you to wear blue. In case she does not like it, you know."

"Oh, I wouldn't be so unhandsome as to pin the blame on you," Henrietta assured her, flitting away to examine a bolt of cherry-colored sarcenet. "Mama won't mind one blue dress, I'm sure. But how much more comfortable it will be when I am a married woman and may choose my gowns to please myself! It is very tiresome, always to be told that whatever one likes is too daring, or the wrong color, or not at all suitable for an unmarried girl. Won't it be lovely, being married?"

This aspect of married life had not previously occurred to Miss Wentworth, but she felt the force of Henrietta's arguments and agreed that greater freedom in the matter of dress was nothing to be despised.

"Yes, and as Countess of Stanford you will have any amount of pin money. Lord Stanford is very rich, they say. Does he mean to live in town a great deal, after you are married? Only think of coming to London for the Season and buying dozens of new gowns every year! My sister does—my married sister, Lady Anthony, that I was telling you about earlier. Of course, she prides herself on being all the crack, but I daresay you will be, too." Henrietta hunched her shoulders in resignation. "Naturally, Richard must needs want us to bury ourselves in the country all the year round, but I expect we'll get to London once in a while, even if it's only for a few weeks of the Season."

"Do you mind very much, Henrietta? I know Richard is always saying he has no opinion of London."

"Oh, I shan't mind living in Derbyshire most of the year, as long as we come to town every now and then. Richard may not be excessively fond of *ton* parties—well, I know he is not—but I shall insist on an occasional trip to London, never fear!"

Listening to this speech, it occurred to Miss Wentworth that her cousin was likely to find in his bride a certain resemblance to his mother. There was little superficial likeness between the two, but something about Henrietta's buoyant self-assurance reminded her irresistably of Lady Wentworth. "I don't suppose Richard will really mind, if you want to come to London now and then, Henrietta. You seem to have the knack of managing him very neatly." Miss Wentworth hesitated. "I don't think I'd dare try to tell Jack—Stanford—how to go on, as you do Richard."

"Oh, but you must, my dear! Not actually dictate, of course, but it's as well to take a stand with men right from the beginning and then stick to it. If one can make a thing seem like their own idea, so much the better, but the poor dears go on a great deal better with a firm hand on the reins."

Miss Wentworth wondered if she were capable of taking a firm stand on the subject of mistresses and feared she was not. "I expect it is different for you and Richard," she said, repressing a sigh. "You have known each other longer, and—and have had time to grow accustomed to dealing together."

Miss Wentworth decided she had been mistaken in

thinking Henrietta a proper confidante. Marriage to the Earl seemed unlikely to bear much resemblance to the comfortable, if prosaic relationship Henrietta was describing; Sir Richard Wentworth, too, was an entirely different style of bridegroom from the Earl of Stanford—not likely to deviate from the path of rectitude in any case.

"It's true that we've known each other longer." Henrietta looked meditative. "But I knew the minute I saw Richard that I wanted to marry him. It was very odd: I remember seeing him across a room—it was at a rout party, when I first came to London—and it simply popped into my head all at once—'that's him!' " finished Miss Ingleside impressively if ungrammatically. "Is that how—did *you* know, the first time you saw Lord Stanford? Oh, I beg your pardon, Rebecca, of course it would have been different for you, being already engaged to—forgive me, I didn't mean to be tactless."

"Not when I first saw him," said Miss Wentworth, a little shy but not at all offended. "The first time he smiled at me, I think."

"He does have a very handsome smile," said Henrietta feelingly. "My little sister could talk of nothing else, after that time we met him in the park. Oh, and Emma is terribly jealous of you, Rebecca! I think she had her heart set on marrying Lord Stanford herself, just like half the other women in town. There have been dozens of caps set at him; you can have no idea, my dear. They say Lady Catherine Billingsley tried to take poison when she heard he was engaged, though I for one don't believe she would have done any such thing without first making sure there was somebody by to wrest the bottle from her hand."

"Lady Catherine?" said Miss Wentworth, round-eyed. "The Duchess of Billingsford? Why would she—oh, you don't mean that *she*—"

"Oh, no! Not that I—that is, I never heard there was anything between her and—and Lord Stanford," said Henrietta, looking greatly embarrassed. "She only did it to make herself interesting, I daresay. You know what a silly creature she is."

Soon after this a want of spirits began to be felt by the shoppers. They decided to quit Bond Street, leaving the material for the bridesmaid's dress to be purchased another day.

"Mama will probably be wanting the carriage in any case," said Henrietta, still looking rather uncomfortable and as though she would have liked to say more. She and Miss Wentworth arranged themselves and their purchases within the carriage, and Henrietta gave the direction of Berkeley Square.

Traffic was heavy on Bond Street. The coachman was able to proceed only at a snail's pace. Looking idly out the window, Miss Wentworth espied some distance away a curricle drawn by a pair of greys and driven by an extremely familiar-looking gentleman with dark hair.

"Oh, there's Jack," she exclaimed, forgetting the gloom that had descended upon her at hearing her future husband's name linked with that of yet another beauty. "How vexing that there should be so much traffic. I'll never get his attention from here."

"Shall I give orders to drive back around the block?" inquired Henrietta solicitously.

"No, don't bother, Henrietta. He is to call later today, I believe, and I have nothing to say that cannot wait until then. Only it is so ridiculous to see him and not be able to—"

Miss Wentworth suddenly became aware that the Earl's attention was turned in quite a different direction. A barouche, occupied by a dashing lady with auburn curls, had maneuvered into position beside the Earl's curricle. The Earl's back was to Miss Wentworth; she could not see his face, but she could see the lady greet him with an alluring smile, coquetry in every gesture of hand and tilt of head. A moment, and the Ingleside carriage had moved on, leaving the sight behind, but to Miss Wentworth, settling disconsolately back against the squabs, it seemed only a further confirmation of her fears.

Chapter Fifteen

The Earl, meanwhile, was experiencing doubts of his own. In his official status as Miss Wentworth's fiancé, he saw a great deal of her, and made a point of escorting her as often as possible to the parties she attended. Short of being actually wed to her, this should have afforded him the utmost gratification. Unfortunately, he soon discovered that her aunt, or mother, or some other chaperone always accompanied them wherever they went, as a matter of course. It was a situation the Earl settled down to endure with what patience he could muster. September would come soon enough—although the Earl felt strongly that it could not come nearly soon enough for him—but in the meantime he found it annoying that he and Miss Wentworth were permitted less privacy now than had been allowed before their engagement.

The Earl missed their drives together. The comfortable relationship that had been developing nicely during the driving lessons had suffered a definite setback since the night Miss Wentworth had broken her engagement to Lord Russelton. The Earl could not help thinking of that night, and he often wondered if she had accepted his own offer the next day while still motivated by pique. Possibly she regretted losing Russelton . . . the Earl found himself downright jealous of that young gentleman, the first to touch Miss Wentworth's heart. He fell into the habit of watching her sharply whenever her ex-fiancé was near, searching for signs of wistfulness. In light of all his experience with women, the Earl was really behaving with absurd uncertainty, but he was lacking in experience of being in love; he could not be sure if it was love he thought he glimpsed in his betrothed's face, or only the product of his own wishful thinking. He began to regret that he had not told her he loved her when he asked her to marry him. At least it might have cleared the air of misconceptions. But the moment for that seemed to have passed, and no new opportunities presented themselves as the weeks went by and the vigilant chaperonage continued.

Despite these nagging uncertainties and petty annoyances, the Earl still managed to be happy in his engagement. Even Almack's Assembly Rooms, or the dullest *ton* party, was tolerable when he was with her, the woman he loved. Dancing together, he and Miss Wentworth could enjoy at least a few minutes of semi-privacy, and sometimes, when their eyes met, he became quite sure that she loved him. The Earl told himself grimly that even if she did not, he would marry her anyway and somehow force her to love him. It struck him from time to time that there was something rather humorous about the Earl of Stanford's being reduced to such measures, but he felt he was almost desperate enough to consider carrying Miss Wentworth off by main force if necessary, after the example of one of his more disreputable ancestors. Having come this far toward marrying her, he had no intention of letting her get away.

The Season was drawing to its end. In the excitement of departures for Brighton, Bath, and sundry country estates, the fashionable world was at last showing signs of losing interest in the Earl of Stanford's amazing engagement. Miss Wentworth was caught up in preparations for her own departure; Lady Wentworth had hired a house in Brighton, and Miss Wentworth was looking forward to her first summer at the famous resort. Alas, there was a fly in the ointment: the Earl was not going to Brighton that summer, but rather to his estate, Stanford Park.

The Earl found himself in something of a quandary. He had written to his bailiff on the same evening he had written to Mr. Wentworth, before the idea of a June wedding had been vetoed. At that time, he had fully expected to spend the summer at Stanford Park with his new bride. He had made no arrangements to hire lodgings in Brighton as he usually did each summer; now, with the change in plans, he was sorely tempted to go to Brighton anyway, taking whatever shelter he could find there in order to be near Miss Wentworth. But he had already received a letter from his bailiff in answer to his own, expressing such relief and gratitude that the Earl could not bring himself to renege. He knew he was needed at Stanford Park—had been needed there for some time—and there was an incentive as well in the idea of setting the place in order before he brought his countess home. He finally compromised by making arrangements to visit Miss Wentworth several times during the summer, and before the Wentworth family removed to Brighton, he invited them all to Stanford Park for a short visit.

Sir Richard refused the invitation: his plans were for a summer in Derbyshire at his own estate, and he was already in the midst of preparations for his departure. But the other members of the household were eager to accept, and the Earl left London in mid-June to put all in readiness for his guests' arrival. Lady Wentworth's carriage left Berkeley Square on the following day, carrying within it Mrs. Wentworth, Lady Wentworth, Lady Wentworth's dresser, and an excited and thoroughly nervous Miss Wentworth.

It was a journey of a little more than two hours from London to the Earl's home. Most of the conversation during the drive was provided by Lady Wentworth, who chose to beguile the tedium of the journey by reciting the names of every individual bearing the slightest degree of relation to herself, residing in the towns and villages listed on the signposts they passed. Mrs. Wentworth placidly tatted lace, responding to her sister-in-law's monologue with an occasional word of agreement whenever Lady Wentworth paused for a response. Miss Wentworth stared out the window and daydreamed. She was going to see her future home for the very first time. It was difficult to know what to expect, for the Earl had preserved a maddening reticence on the subject. When questioned about Stanford Park, he would only say that parts of it were very old, and other parts very ugly, while still other parts were both old and ugly, and that on the whole he preferred to let her see it for herself and draw her own conclusions. "Though don't think for a minute that I'll allow you to cry off if you decide you can't bear to live there," he had told her, jokingly, but with an underlying note of seriousness in his voice. "It's not necessarily a part of your marriage vows, and we don't have to go near the place if you take it in dislike."

This had sounded rather ominous, but Miss Wentworth was eager nevertheless to see the Earl's home, if for no other reason than that it was his, and therefore a matter of interest to her. She amused herself during the journey by picturing the house in her mind from such hints as the Earl had let fall and from snippets of conversation picked up here and there in company.

It occurred to her that she might have consulted a guidebook; as a nobleman's seat and a place of some antiquity, it would surely have received mention in one of the many guides listing places of interest to sightseers. Then she decided it was as well she had not. It seemed preferable somehow to approach Stanford Park with an open mind, especially since the Earl himself appeared to entertain such misgivings on the subject.

By and by, the travelers came to a village, where the coachman stopped to make inquiries. From the village, their way led down a country lane, green with the approach of summer. For several miles they drove on, passing cottages and fields, until they reached a gateway bearing shields, set between a pair of handsome gateposts.

"This must be it," said Mrs. Wentworth, leaning forward to look.

The carriage was admitted through the gates. Miss Wentworth, bracing herself for the moment of truth, caught sight of towers above the trees. In a moment more of the house itself came into view. As the carriage drew closer, Miss Wentworth could see that it was of red brick, three stories tall, with twin octagonal turrets flanking the central part of the building. Each turret bore four tiers of arched windows, and a frieze of quatrefoils and shields ran above the upper windows. Attractive it certainly was, but Miss Wentworth was surprised to see that it was of quite a reasonable size for a nobleman's home. It was a good bit smaller than the Squire's house back in Derbyshire, which had always represented the ultimate in size and splendor to Miss Wentworth; she had been feeling intimidated at the thought of being mistress of a great mansion and was relieved to see her fears were groundless. "How very pretty," she said happily.

"Yes, a fine example of an early Tudor gatehouse," agreed Lady Wentworth. "The terracotta work beneath the parapet is some of the best to be found in this country, I understand."

"Gatehouse?" Miss Wentworth's lips formed the word, but no sound came out. She searched her aunt's face for signs of humor. There were none; Lady Wentworth was gazing admiringly at the terracotta work, unaware of her niece's incredulous regard. Miss Wentworth turned to look again at the fine early Tudor gatehouse. The carriage was rapidly leaving it behind, lending further credence to the truth of Lady Wentworth's words. Miss Wentworth sank back against the squabs of the carriage and began frantically to revise her estimates about the size of an estate where the mere gatehouse was larger than her whole home back in Derbyshire.

The carriage rattled through a wooded park, somewhat overgrown, but (as Lady Wentworth pointed out) full of fine timber. The drive twisted and turned. At last it emerged into the open and straightened itself to become an elm-lined avenue, with a vast pile of brick at the end of the avenue that could conceivably have been called a house, although castle was the word that sprang unbidden into Miss Wentworth's mind. She stared at the vista of towers, battlements, and columns spread before her. The afternoon sun was caught and reflected back from a hundred windows; brick and stonework, column and carving were thrown into high relief, presenting an awe-inspiring vision of antique splendor set amidst green lawns and gardens. *This will be my home?* thought Miss Wentworth incredulously.

"There's a lake behind the house," said Mrs. Wentworth with an air of pleased discovery, folding away her tatting.

"That would be the remains of the moat, no doubt," said Lady Wentworth.

Tantalizing glimpses of formal gardens were visible through the trees as the carriage rolled into the court before the main entrance. Miss Wentworth put her hands to her bonnet and wished nervously for a mirror to check her appearance. Even her wildest flights of fancy had fallen short of the grandeur she saw around her. *I am to be a countess, and this will be my home,* she told herself. She could not make the notion seem real.

It began to seem a little more real when the Earl arrived on the scene. He had been out riding and came cantering up just as the ladies were stepping down from the carriage. His blue frock coat was open, showing him to be clad in the country gentleman's customary buckskins and topboots, but the tailoring of these garments—and their wearer's physique—declared him to be something quite out of the common run of country gentlemen. So thought Miss Wentworth, watching horse and rider clatter across the stone-paved forecourt. Sunlight gleamed off the Earl's dark head as he swung himself down from the saddle; a groom appeared out of nowhere to take the horse and lead it away to the stable block behind the house. There was warm approval in the Earl's eyes as they rested upon his betrothed's face, and more than a hint of mischief as well. "Welcome to Stanford Park, Becky," he said. Coming forward to take her hands, he smiled down at her, inquiring in a voice of exaggerated anxiety, "Do you like it? Or will you refuse to be saddled with such a millstone? I refer to the house, of course, not myself: you are stuck with me in any case!" The grip on her hands tightened. "Don't keep me waiting for your verdict, my dear. Now that you have seen Stanford Park, folly of the Collingwoods, for yourself—"

"It's so big," said Miss Wentworth, regarding him reproachfully. "You have been leading me sadly astray, Jack. I had not expected your home to be so grand!"

The Earl's smile became a little incredulous. "I will allow that it is big, but as for being grand . . . well, I have never thought the combination of Norman, Tudor, and Palladian to be a happy one! It's that belated touch of Palladio that did the mischief." He glanced toward the house and shook his head. "That south wing's always struck me as a great mistake. My great-grandfather apparently felt forty bedchambers weren't enough, and decided that as long as he was rebuilding the Dower House he might as well throw another wing onto this place while he was at it. I think sometimes he would have done as well to have treated it as he did the Dower House: tear the whole thing down and build it up to match."

Miss Wentworth saw he was only half joking. "Oh, but it is magnificent, Jack," she protested. "I do not think it ugly at all."

"You haven't seen the inside yet! But at least it's

comfortable—the newer parts anyway. And this is the best time of year to see the place, with the gardens in bloom." The Earl continued to look down at Miss Wentworth for a moment, his face meditative. "But then, they'd hardly dare do anything else, would they? Why, as long as *you* were here, I expect the flowers would burst into bloom even if it were November." Having quite overcome Miss Wentworth with this pretty speech, he took advantage of the situation by attempting to kiss her, but encountered the brim of her poke bonnet and had to content himself with chastely saluting her cheek.

"Dratted milliner's gear," he grumbled, surveying her with discontent. "Pretty, I'll admit, but what use is a hat that keeps a man at arm's length?" His eyes crinkled with laughter. "As if we didn't always have two or three people around to do that anyway!" He flicked the brim of her bonnet with one finger, grinned, and turned to greet Lady Wentworth and Mrs. Wentworth.

While the Earl was exchanging greetings with her aunt and mother, Miss Wentworth studied Stanford Park's sprawling facade. A closer inspection showed there to be some excuse for the Earl's disparagements. The south wing's Palladian front of white stone and red brick, set with fluted pilasters and Corinthian capitals, was in itself quite beautiful; unfortunately, it presented an awkward and rather incongruous appearance in combination with the main body of the house, a vast Tudor manse bristling with gables, chimneys, and battlemented towers of all heights and sizes. Offset slightly from the Tudor house stood the grim Norman tower, rising grey above the jumble of rose-red brick, a formidable structure whose slitted windows bore mute testimony to days when defense outweighed considerations of comfort and aesthetics. Taken altogether, the effect was impressive rather than beautiful.

"What, still lost in admiration?" The Earl smiled and took Miss Wentworth's arm, leading her up a flight of shallow balustraded steps to the porch of the Tudor house. He personally shepherded his guests through the front door into a small anteroom, brushing aside a stout butler who attempted to take them in charge. From the anteroom, they entered into the great hall.

"Oh, my," said Mrs. Wentworth.

"Magnificent," said Lady Wentworth.

"Yes, it's impressive, isn't it?" The Earl watched with amusement as Miss Wentworth's eyes widened, taking in the enormous hall with screen and dais, and the great dais window behind, rising to the height of the hammer-beam roof. "Not the coziest room in the house, of course, but definitely impressive. There are actually two halls here at Stanford Park; there's an older one in the tower as well. I believe we keep them only to impress visitors, for really they're not much use otherwise." The Earl paused, but as Miss Wentworth continued speechless, he prodded, "Your proper response would be to exclaim at the room's size, or at least to comment on the workmanship of the ceiling. All visitors are obliged to do so . . . at least, they never fail to say something of the sort! I don't think you're properly impressed, Becky. Don't tell me you haven't always nursed a secret desire for a great hall or two of your very own?"

"No, Jack," said Miss Wentworth, shaking off her introspection and making an attempt to enter into her betrothed's clearly frivolous mood. "But now that I am here, of course I can see what a convenience it would be." Her eyes sparkled with mischief as she looked from the dais to the Earl and back again. "Why, I can just envision you up there in your rightful place as Lord of the Manor, Jack, administering justice to your people, distributing alms—"

"Touching for the king's evil?" suggested the Earl with a grin. "I've often thought I was born several centuries too late. It's not nearly as much fun to be an earl nowadays! Do you see yourself on the dais as well, Becky?"

"Naturally. I should sit beside you, properly dressed in my farthingale and ruff, and devote myself to keeping you properly under my thumb! Those Tudor ladies were very autocratic with their menfolk, you know. Queen Elizabeth, and Bess of Hardwick—"

"You terrify me, my dear," said the Earl, sounding much alarmed but looking as though he was enjoying himself. "I can see all this Tudor business is going to go to your head. Before long, I'll be finding myself a poor creature without an ounce of spirit, reduced to begging my lady for permission to lift my finger. But I should have known how it would be when I engaged myself to such a termagant." He followed up this speech by putting an arm around the indignant termagant's waist and squeezing her nearly breathless. "My spirit isn't broken *yet,*" he explained, grinning at her.

As they turned to leave the great hall, the Earl noticed with resignation that at least a dozen of his retainers had found excuses to come into the hall and adjoining gallery while he had been speaking to his bride-to-be. Several kitchenmaids had dispensed with excuses altogether; from a vantage point in the passage leading to kitchen and butteries, they were inspecting with great interest the person of Miss Wentworth. Catching his butler's eye, the Earl made a brief but eloquent motion of his head. The kitchenmaids vanished; the hall began to empty, and the Earl led the way to a drawing room situated to the right of the hall, toward the back of the house.

"You will find this more homelike, I trust," he said. "The Tudor element's missing, but I think it rather a pretty room."

"Yes," said Miss Wentworth, looking about the drawing room. "Why, it is perfectly lovely, Jack."

"My mother had it redecorated not long before she died. It's the closest thing to modern we have at the Park; everything else is more or less uniformly Gothic. I'm afraid I've done very little with the place since inheriting the title." The Earl smiled at Miss Wentworth. "But I mean to start fresh, now that I'm to be a sober married man," he said, and Miss Wentworth returned his smile, her heart in a flutter. "I won't bore you with any more sightseeing now. I expect you're all tired from your journey and would like tea and some time to rest before dinner. I'll send for Mrs. Merryman, my housekeeper, to show you your rooms." The Earl bowed and withdrew, leaving them sitting in the drawing room.

"A very pleasant room," said Lady Wentworth approvingly, looking at the blue-and-white striped walls, the Axminster carpet, and the graceful gilt furniture upholstered in blue plush. "Most attractive, and the view quite attractive as well."

Miss Wentworth rose and went to one of the windows. She observed that the drawing room opened onto a terrace, with a yew-enclosed garden beyond. There were peacocks on the terrace. "It's like a fairy story," she said, stroking the blue damask draperies as though they might vanish at a touch.

The Earl's housekeeper, Mrs. Merryman, was a stern-looking elderly woman clad in unrelieved black. She led them up the great staircase to a hallway lined with doors. Miss Wentworth was shown into a spacious bed-chamber, a pleasant enough room, although the furnishings inclined toward the dark and heavy, and the hangings were undeniably a trifle shabby.

"His lordship has been meaning to redecorate all these rooms for I don't know how many years," said Mrs. Merryman, looking around the bedchamber with an air of censure. "I'm very sorry, miss, that things don't look as they should, but if his lordship had given us all a bit more warning that you was coming, something better might have been contrived."

Miss Wentworth was secretly rather frightened by Mrs. Merryman, but she had had enough experience with upper servants to know how fatal it would be to show it. "Don't be sorry, Mrs. Merryman," she said, in a voice she hoped was friendly without being either patronizing or subservient. "It all looks lovely to me. Certainly it is beautifully kept."

This at least was no more than the truth. The chamber radiated cleanliness, and the dark furniture had been polished until it shone with a mirrorlike glass. Mrs. Merryman merely bowed in acknowledgement, but she regarded Miss Wentworth with something close to approval on her stern face as she left the bedchamber.

Miss Wentworth removed her bonnet, fluffed her hair, and wandered about the room inspecting the pictures on the walls. The windows of the bedchamber looked onto the lawn, with the sparkling waters of the lake in the distance. She was far too excited to rest. Presently, a maid came to offer Miss Wentworth her services in dressing for dinner. The girl looked her up and down with interest, making Miss Wentworth a little uncomfortable, but she knew such interest to be natural and thanked the girl for her help.

"Thank *you,* miss. You look lovely, miss," said the maid admiringly, giving a last twitch to the folds of Miss Wentworth's pink-flowered muslin dinner dress. Miss Wentworth gathered up her shawl and went down the stairs to dinner, her heart beating rather fast.

The formal dining room at Stanford Park was a gloomy apartment of noble proportions. The walls were wainscoted halfway up, and nearly covered with portraits above the wainscoting, but in spite of these adjuncts the chamber bore an unfortunate resemblance to a barracks room, a resemblance that even a magnificent display of dazzling plate and snowy damask could not quite dispel. The mahogany table was ridiculously large for such a small party, as the Earl acknowledged once they were seated.

"I meant to give orders that we dine in the breakfast parlor—it's much smaller and pleasanter than this room. But I think the staff is wanting to show off for you, Becky. I hadn't the heart to disappoint them this time, but naturally we needn't dine in such pomp when we eat alone." The Earl smiled ruefully at Miss Wentworth from his place at the head of the table, some twelve feet away.

"But you must know that pomp is what I enjoy of all things," she returned, dimpling at him. "To be obliged to shout at you from the other end of the room, in order to carry on a conversation—"

"If you enjoy pomp, then the Countess's apartments should please you! I will take you all around the house after dinner."

"This is excellent fish, Stanford," remarked Lady Wentworth. "You have a good cook, I see. French?"

"No, actually a local woman. I haven't spent much time here in the past few years, and in London I have always lived in lodgings. But I suppose I'll have to look into hiring a chef if Becky and I decide to entertain on a grand scale."

The food was both well cooked and well served, but when the meal was over Miss Wentworth could not have said what it was she had eaten. Her head was spinning in an effort to cope with the steady stream of surprises that had confronted her since her arrival, and in the process, her original conception of married life with the Earl had undergone drastic revision. The size and style of Stanford Park was rather dismaying, but this was counterbalanced by the presence of the Earl himself; to hear him speak casually of such things as dining together and entertaining made their approaching marriage seem altogether more real and possible. Miss Wentworth studied her future husband anew as she rose to leave the dining room with her aunt and mother after dinner. Since the Earl chose that same moment to wink at her, she was saved from becoming unduly solemn about the prospect.

As promised, the Earl gave his visitors a tour of the house after dinner. They began with the oldest parts comprised within the Norman tower.

"I'll show it to you, but there's not much to see, I'm afraid," said the Earl apologetically. "We seldom use these rooms for anything but storage nowadays."

They descended to make a hasty inspection of the lowest level of the tower, which was dim and vaulted and served as a kind of lumber room. On the level above was the medieval great hall which, being both dark and empty of furnishings, did not long engage their attention. From the hall, they followed the Earl up a winding stone staircase with steps worn hollow by centuries of use. The floor above the great hall was divided between a chapel and a solar chamber, and here they lingered for some time. The upper rooms of the tower had not been subjected to such stringent security measures as were required on the ground floors; the windows, set within containing arches, were larger and allowed more light within the rooms than the narrow slits that served as windows in the chambers below.

"Oh, Rebecca, your father would so much enjoy seeing this," said Mrs. Wentworth in a hushed voice, as they looked about the chapel. Murals decorated the chapel walls, grave-faced saints and apostles whose eyes seemed to follow the visitors about with a fine, high, otherworldly incuriousity. Time had dealt kindly with those painted figures. The colors of their robes were as bright, their ascetic, haloed faces as sharply drawn, as if the medieval painter had just laid his brushes aside from his finished labor. Mrs. Wentworth and Lady Wentworth began to make a minute inspection of the murals, their voices pitched low in instinctive response to the chapel's atmosphere; the air of almost oppressive antiquity that hung about the place seemed to demand an attitude of reverence. The Earl noted that his betrothed was looking rather overwhelmed and led her over to one of the chapel windows. They perched themselves side by side on the windowsill; it made a very acceptable seat, owing to the immense thickness of the tower walls.

"I can't tell if you love it or hate it, Becky," said the Earl, scrutinizing her face. "Or is it merely too much antiquity in one dose?"

Miss Wentworth shook her head and traced with one finger the crest and motto carved in the stone beneath the chapel window. "I'm glad I didn't know it was like this, or I don't think I would have dared agree to marry you," she said, looking him full in the face with an expression of bemusement. "And you don't seem at all proud of it, Jack! I'm sure I would be as toplofty as—as Countess Lieven, or Mrs. Drummond Burrell, if I owned such a place. To think all this belongs to you . . ."

"Yes, I am very rich in great halls and solar chambers," agreed the Earl, hoping to make her laugh. He succeeded, but her face resumed its pensive expression as she continued to trace the motto on the windowsill with her finger. "*Avec Dieu et Mon Bras Droit:* a fine, pious sentiment, I have always thought," said the Earl, noticing her occupation. "They were hedging their bets, you observe, with both God and the strength of their swordarms for security. Although there was considerably more of *le bras droit* than of *Dieu* about their doings, in the early years of the barony, at least!" This earned him a fleeting smile. The Earl regarded his betrothed with exasperation. "Now, don't be getting blue-deviled on me, Becky! It makes a fine-sounding story, this talk of ancestry, and I am proud of it, I suppose, but it's not all glory and nobility by any means. There've been some curst rum touches littering the escutcheon along the way! Wait until we get to the portrait gallery, and I'll introduce you to some of them. The third Earl, for instance: there's a loose screw for you. If even half the stories about him are true, he was a sight worse than—than anyone else you might care to name," said the Earl, looking rather self-conscious.

Miss Wentworth dimpled. "Is your picture there, too?" she inquired innocently.

"No, ma'am, it is not! And let me say that I don't particularly care for your association of ideas," said the Earl, shooting her a sideways smile. "But my father and mother are both there, and a portrait of my grandmother, done by Reynolds." He regarded Miss Wentworth with fresh interest. "Now why didn't I think of it before? We'll have to have a portrait of you commissioned, as soon as possible. That will do more to improve the appearance of this place than anything else I'm likely to accomplish this summer."

"You ought to have one of yourself painted as well."

"Oh, Lord, you wouldn't do that to me, would you? Condemn me to hang with all the loose-screws and other riffraff we've picked up through the years?"

"You want *me* to hang there."

"Purely for aesthetic purposes," said the Earl firmly. "You'll easily take the shine out of our other countesses, not to mention all the other assorted females who've ended up in the gallery one way or another. There's a daughter of one of the sixteenth-century earls whom I've always thought a taking little thing, but even she can't hold a candle to you!"

Miss Wentworth smiled. "You are looking at it only from the masculine point of view, sir," she said. "I can tell you that your female descendants will much prefer to look at your face rather than mine. That is, if I . . . if we . . . if you have female descendants, you know." Miss Wentworth was conscious of having strayed onto dangerous ground. The Earl's eyes were dancing, and he looked to be on the verge of saying something outrageous. Fortunately, he was forestalled by Lady Wentworth, who announced in decisive tones that the light was fading. The group reassembled to go on with the tour.

One of their next stops was the portrait gallery. Here Miss Wentworth was sent into fits of helpless laughter when her mother took one look at the disreputable third Earl and pronounced him to be "the image of Stanford, here, I vow and declare." The present Earl, his dark hair fashionably windswept and his tall figure encased in severe black evening clothes, looked far from pleased at being compared with his ancestor, pictured as a handsome cavalier with beribboned lovelocks and plumed hat. He rolled a threatening eye toward his fiancée as she continued to shake with laughter. But noting that her merriment had destroyed the uncomfortably reverent atmosphere that had been developing, the Earl chose to endure the teasing in good part, merely threatening by way of retaliation to make room between a pair of sour-looking gentlemen of Jacobean vintage for Miss Wentworth's own portrait, whenever that yet-to-be created work might be available for display.

After the Earl had pointed out a few more of his ancestors worthy of notice, he led his visitors from the portrait gallery to view a seemingly endless series of rooms: summer and winter parlors, studies, withdrawing rooms, library and billiard room and domestic offices, ending up at last in the upstairs hallway of what the Earl informed them was the comparatively modern south wing.

"A regular rabbit warren, I'm afraid," he said ruefully. "But I've been saving the best for last. The Countess's apartments! You did say you liked pomp, didn't you, Becky?"

"Oh, dear," was all Miss Wentworth could find to say.

Someone, at some time, had apparently decided that the Countess's apartments should be decorated with an

Oriental theme. This had been done with a vengeance, and the effect was like nothing so much as an opium-eater's nightmare. Crimson and gold were the colors favored, and they figured largely throughout the suite of bedchamber, sitting room, and dressing room. The Oriental motif found its strongest expression in the bed itself, an enormous structure surmounted by a dome of gilded fretwork on which sat a pair of dragons regarding each other fiercely. The hangings were of crimson brocade, heavily fringed in gold and elaborately draped and festooned. Upon the headboard of the bed was depicted a little scene in carved and gilded wood: a chubby Buddha sat within a small temple surrounded by Oriental-looking foliage, with a few more dragons thrown in for good measure. As had been the case throughout the house, these chambers, too, bore the appearance of having been freshly cleaned, but a mustiness discernable above the smells of camphor and turpentine suggested that the Countess's rooms had been uninhabited for a very long time.

"You don't care for dragons, I take it." The Earl laughed outright at his betrothed's speaking expression. "It is pretty appalling, I must admit. High time these rooms were redecorated. I don't suppose anyone's been in here except to clean since my mother died. No, she didn't die here, Becky, never fear," he said, smiling a little at the alarm on Miss Wentworth's face. "No ghosts at Stanford Park, only dragons. Would you like the room better if I got rid of them?"

"Oh," said Miss Wentworth, struck by compunction. "If it was your mother's room, you wouldn't want to change anything, of course."

The Earl laughed again. "As a matter of fact, my mother didn't care for dragons, either! The chinoiserie was my grandmother's idea, as I recall. Very proud of it she was, too, and the old girl was such a Tartar that even after she'd removed to the Dower House nobody dared change a thing. I think my father and mother must have agreed between themselves to let it go until after she died . . . and then she ended up outliving my mother by nearly a decade. No, I have no sentimental attachment to the dragons, Becky. And now that I think of it, I don't believe I like the way that fellow up there on the headboard is looking at you. Sort of a leer on his face, don't you think? That settles it: no half-naked man is going to leer at *my* wife in her bedchamber—"

"Jack!"

"—unless the man happens to be me, of course—"

"Jack!"

"—but I flatter myself I cut a better-looking figure than *that* fellow. Oh, I've made you blush! It's been a long time since I've done that, hasn't it? But you must admit I owed you something for all that hilarity at my expense, back in the portrait gallery! Yes, yes, I'll behave myself, I see your mama looking at me, wondering what I've been saying to you . . . about the rooms, then. I'll have everything redone, however you please. What do you like? Sphinxes? Cherubs?"

"I don't know," said Miss Wentworth, looking about the gaudy bedchamber rather helplessly. "I really hadn't thought. Oh, anything you choose would be fine, I'm sure. Except sphinxes, perhaps; I believe they might be as bad as dragons."

"Well, I'll have it redone, and if you don't like it we'll consign the whole works to one of the guest bedchambers and try again. Most of the other bedchambers could probably use refurbishing anyway, if it comes to that."

"Oh, but you mustn't go to so much trouble on my account," protested Miss Wentworth, secretly much gratified.

"Yes, I must! I want you to be happy here. Well, not just *here,* of course—" the Earl looked around the bedchamber and smiled. "But come to think of it, it's as good a place as any to start." There was a wealth of meaning in his voice, and Miss Wentworth found herself blushing once more.

Chapter Sixteen

The Wentworths' visit to Stanford Park proved a great success, and incidentally did a great deal toward removing certain reservations felt by both the bride-to-be and her prospective bridegroom. For Miss Wentworth, it was her first opportunity to observe her future husband in what might properly be called his native setting. She found herself both unsettled and oddly reassured by her observations. She had teased the Earl on the first day of her visit about playing Lord of the Manor, but after she had been a few days at Stanford Park she came to see the genuine respect and authority he commanded among his household and tenantry. He seemed at times quite a different person from the lazy aristocrat she had first encountered at Lady Sefton's ball. His responsibilities were real, and even during her short visit she saw how constant were the demands on his time and attention. The Earl abused himself loudly for the negligence in the past that made such intrusions necessary now; he apologized profusely whenever estate business forced him to leave his guests to their own devices, but Miss Wentworth used the time to become better acquainted with her future home, and she soon decided he was guilty of overstating the case. Stanford Park was far from being the crumbling eyesore the Earl's rather sinister hints had led her to expect. Neglect and decline might be apparent to his eyes, but to Miss Wentworth, Stanford Park seemed a thriving place of considerable beauty, and the Earl himself very much at home in the role of its manager. In the time Miss Wentworth was there, she came more and more to see and be impressed by this unexpected side of his character. It did him no disservice in her eyes. The careworn man of authority was only another facet of the gentleman with whom she had first fallen in love, whose smile could still make her heart beat faster, and whose irrepressible—and often irreverent—sense of humor did much to set her at ease among her unfamiliar and imposing surroundings. Such reassurance was needed, for Miss Wentworth often felt desperately inadequate when she surveyed the scope of her future responsibilities, but she thought she could be happy at Stanford Park. Some of her fears about the Earl's future conduct were set at rest to learn that a large part of their lives would be spent in the country. Miss Wentworth thought hopefully that he was less likely to stray there than amid the temptations of London society.

For his part, the Earl was pleased with every aspect of the visit. He thought Miss Wentworth's qualms laughable. Naturally she had no experience in managing a large household, but he was perfectly convinced she would come to do so with the ease and grace that distinguished all her actions. She expressed some doubts about this, but showed nevertheless a surprising willingness to take the job on. As one who had himself shrunk from assuming its burdens, the Earl would have found it less surprising if her qualms had led her to eschew

Stanford Park altogether. It had never formed part of his plans to wed a domestic paragon. If he had inadvertently acquired one in his chosen bride, so much the better, but he would in truth have been happy enough to have lived with her in London, or Brighton, or anywhere else she might have preferred. The frank enthusiasm she showed for Stanford Park was an unexpected bonus, and all that was needed to put the capstone on his happiness. The Earl had, at heart, a greater love for his ancestral home than he would openly admit; seeing it anew through Miss Wentworth's eyes made him value all the more the legacy he had taken for granted for most of his adult life.

Those few happy days at Stanford Park wrought a subtle change in the betrothed couple's relationship. Freed of the formalities of London society and thrown together throughout most of the day, they found the constraint they had both been feeling since the night of Lady Cassandra's party was beginning to subside at last. Soon they were upon much the same easy terms enjoyed previous to their engagement. To be sure, there was a new tension between them now, a heightened awareness, but it was the kind of stress natural to any soon-to-be-wed couple aggravated by ever-present chaperonage. As before, Lady Wentworth and Mrs. Wentworth could be counted on to be somewhere in the background wherever they went. The less formal atmosphere of country living offered greater opportunities for escape, however, and by keeping alert the Earl managed to elude Miss Wentworth's chaperones and got her away to himself for a time.

"Where is Mama?" asked Miss Wentworth, pausing in the doorway of the drawing room. She and her mother had gone out driving with the Earl that afternoon to make a tour of his property. Miss Wentworth had just changed her dress and had come downstairs to find her fiancé alone in the drawing room. He stood up when she entered and came forward to meet her with suspicious alacrity.

"I sent your mother and aunt off with my housekeeper to inspect the stillroom," he informed her in a conspiratorial voice, his eyes dancing. "Quick, Becky! We haven't a moment to lose. Come with me, I particularly wanted to show you the gardens while I have you to myself for a bit."

There was a look in his eye that Miss Wentworth thought she recognized, but she settled her shawl over her shoulders and obediently took his arm. They went out onto the terrace and down the steps to the lawn. Miss Wentworth paused for a moment to admire the view of the lake, but the Earl did not seem disposed to linger and look at it. He hurried her along, through a yew archway and into a small enclosed garden containing a fountain and a statue of a dancing nymph.

"Alone at last, thank God," said the Earl devoutly, and took her into his arms without further ado. Miss Wentworth found herself being kissed with a ferocity that would have been frightening, had it not also been thoroughly enjoyable. So enjoyable was it, indeed, that things began to show signs of getting out of hand, and might easily have done so had not Miss Wentworth (with an eye to the windows overlooking the garden) been moved to protest.

"No doubt you are right, my prudent Becky, but I don't see any reason to go back inside for a while yet. Mrs. Merryman's tour of the stillroom ought to be good for at least another half hour. Shall we sit here for a moment and enjoy the sunshine?" The Earl seated himself upon a stone bench beside the fountain and patted his knee invitingly.

Miss Wentworth, her dimple very much in evidence, refused the proffered seat and sat beside him on the bench instead. The Earl promptly put his arm around her shoulders. She made no demur, only moving closer and resting her head against his shoulder.

"I was really beginning to think I wasn't going to get another chance to kiss you until after the wedding! Is it my imagination, or has the chaperonage been stepped up a trifle in the last few weeks?"

"No, you are not imagining it, Jack. Aunt Constance and Mama feel that . . . well, on account of all the talk, you know, about ending my other engagement . . ."

"On account of my being the Wicked Earl is more like it, I expect! I suppose I'm not trusted to keep the line until September? Well, it does seem a long time to wait, but I'll try to behave myself until then. Meanwhile, my girl, you must kiss me again and give me something to live on, all those weeks."

Miss Wentworth, nothing loth, lifted up her face. His mouth came down upon hers; another kiss ensued, progressing rapidly to a mutual state of quickened breathing, with a noticeable disinclination to stop being felt by both participants. This time the Earl was the first to draw back, though the effort made him groan.

"Mm . . . September seems further away all the time! In the interests of propriety, I believe we'd better discuss some other subject. The weather's always safe, of course, or there's plenty of scenery for you to admire, if you prefer the beauties of nature—"

"The scenery is certainly very lovely. I have been meaning to say so, only you have given me no chance to talk at all, Jack! How beautiful it is here. I wonder you can bear to leave it."

"I've always taken it for granted, I suppose. If you could have seen it in my father's time . . . the truth is, I've been a bad landlord and let things go to the devil." The Earl reached out to break off a shoot of overgrown hedge. He rolled it between his fingers, a frown settling over his face. "Even the gardens aren't what they used to be. Things have gotten in a pretty bad way on the home farm, these last few years, and some of my tenants are in even worse shape . . . but I mean to change all that. By the end of summer, things should be in much better curl. There's a deuce of a lot of work to be done, though. Not to mention a fair amount of money to be spent." With a grimace, the Earl threw the spray of hedge at the feet of the dancing nymph.

"Oh, Jack, and you talk of spending more, only for my bedchamber! You needn't, you know. I can do with anything and be happy. Who knows, I may come to love those dragons in time."

"No, no, you shall have your bedchamber, my darling, never fear. That's the merest trifle. But when I think of how much I've dropped at the gaming table in the last year or two . . . enough to redecorate the whole house, I expect, and rebuild every fence on the place. Fortunately, I cut out the deep play a few months back." The Earl hesitated, rather wanting to mention a few other changes he had made in his lifestyle since then. Talking about one's own virtue seemed priggish, however; he reflected that in view of all the chaffing he had endured on the subject, she surely must have heard the news of his reformation by now. "It's a pity I wasted so much of the ready, but at least I never quite outran my income," he said lightly. "We won't have to make any retrenchments on that account. And there's no reason why the estate shouldn't bring in a good deal more than it does right now, if I buckle down and take a hand in things myself. Do you think you would mind living here for most of the year, at least for the first year or two? We'll go to London for the Season, of course, but—"

"Mind? Oh, Jack, I can think of nothing I would like more. I was brought up in the country, you know." Miss Wentworth looked around the garden with a thoughtful air, her eyes coming to rest at last on the bulk of the great house rising up beyond the gardens and terrace. "Although Papa's parsonage has not quite so much splendor about it, I fear," she said, with the same air of serious consideration.

The Earl laughed and stood up, pulling her to her feet. "Oh, Becky, I believe we are going to be very happy," he said, putting his hands on her shoulders and smiling down at her. "Very happy indeed. But for now, my dear, I believe you'll have to give me one more kiss . . . at *least* one more kiss, before September. Oh, Becky, I do—what is it, Hastings?"

"I'm very sorry, my lord." The man standing just inside the entrance to the garden tugged his cap and looked perseveringly at his own feet. "I'm very sorry, but the men was wishful to know which of them trees you wanted to come down in the park." He risked a quick, fearful look toward the Earl and then went on, rather diffidently, "Jervis would have it that those beeches near the Dower House was to go, but—"

"I suppose I'll have to go and show the idiots myself! Well . . ." The Earl looked at his patently embarrassed servitor for an indecisive moment and then at Miss Wentworth, herself scarcely less embarrassed. "Let me take Miss Wentworth back to the house, Hastings," he said heavily. "You may tell the men I'll be with them directly." Resigning himself with an inward sigh, the Earl led Miss Wentworth back out of the garden. The moment had passed again.

No further such opportunities arose during the remainder of the visit, but the time passed pleasantly nevertheless. The Earl, after diligent search, unearthed a prayer book that had been presented to him in his youth by his godmother. It was triumphantly displayed for Miss Wentworth's inspection. "There now, I told you I had a prayer book, ma'am! I hope you're thoroughly ashamed of yourself for doubting my word, all these weeks?"

"It does not look much used," pointed out Miss Wentworth, examining the dusty book with a critical eye.

"That's only because I've always taken such good care of it," the Earl assured her, with his familiar look of guilty mischief. "Well, I can see you don't believe me, Becky, but my upbringing was really very proper, I'll have you know. And if you're willing to take me in hand, I may yet turn out to be a credit to my name." He took the book back from her and began to brush the dust away in a rather gingerly manner. "I suppose now that I've found this, we really ought to put it to use and gratify the village by appearing in the family pew tomorrow. Should you mind? It would probably please old Phelps, though of course the good people of the village will stare at you for all they're worth. Everything's news in a place like this."

"Of course I would not mind going to church."

"We'll do it, then. Wear your prettiest bonnet and don't let Phelps fill your head with stories about my wild boyhood. It's been a good long time since I've sat through one of the Reverend Phelps's sermons . . . in fact, I'm afraid I've been giving the family pew the same kind of—ahem—*careful* treatment as this prayer book! But since I'm going all respectable and getting myself properly married, I may as well go the whole distance and edify the villagers by showing up at church, too, don't you think? I only hope Phelps hasn't anticipated me and decided to preach on the prodigal son or some such thing. You may laugh,"—the Earl looked darkly at Miss Wentworth, who was indeed laughing—"but Phelps has a nasty trick of picking out all the bits of the Bible you'd rather not hear about. When I was a boy, he never failed to deliver a thundering scold from the pulpit, whenever I'd got myself into some particularly outstanding piece of mischief: naming no names, but making it pretty clear all the same who he was talking about."

"It sounds as though you got into mischief rather often, Jack!"

"Not at all: the rarest thing in the world," said the Earl virtuously. "Why, if you like, I'll take you and your aunt and mother around to visit my old nurse tomorrow after church. Dear old Hetty will talk your arm off, telling you what a perfect angel I've always been—"

"Losing her memory, is she?" said Miss Wentworth sympathetically.

"Baggage!" The Earl's eyes danced. "I come to think what we need around here is a stiff sermon on proper wifely behavior. Didn't St. Paul say something or other about wives being submissive—"

"Ephesians: chapter five, I believe," said Miss Wentworth condescendingly. "But I am creditably informed otherwise by a friend of mine, who tells me that men go on better with a firm hand on the reins. I intend rather to follow the Tudor example, as I believe I mentioned the other day. Bess of Hardwick—"

"No, there I must draw the line. I refuse to be bullied like poor Shrewsbury. You will find me a biddable enough creature in the main,"—there was a gleam in the Earl's eye at odds with the meekness in his voice—"but it will have to be a light hand on the reins, ma'am!" He put the prayer book under his left arm and offered Miss Wentworth his right. Together they went down the stairs in perfect amity.

The visit to church took place on Sunday, the last full day of the Wentworths' visit. As the Earl had foretold, there was a tremendous amount of excited whispering together with a good deal of craning around of necks as the party from Stanford Park filed decorously into the great family pew. The Earl and Miss Wentworth shared a hymnbook, and the Earl daringly held Miss Wentworth's hand during the sermon; the Mr. Reverend Phelps chose for his text the story of the young man with many possessions ("Verily, I say unto you, That a rich man shall hardly enter into the kingdom of heaven"), which, as the Earl whispered to Miss Wentworth, was pretty much what might have been expected. When the service was over, they paid a call upon the Earl's old nurse, a tiny and incredibly wrinkled old woman who persisted in addressing the Earl exactly as though he were still in short coats and who enchanted Miss Wentworth by giving her a great deal of advice on the management of her future husband.

After a light nuncheon, the betrothed couple—and their inevitable chaperones—went for another drive around the Earl's holdings. This occupied the greater part of the afternoon, and then the dinner hour was suddenly upon them, bringing with it the awareness that this was to be the last evening preceding a separation of several weeks. In honor of the guests' departure on the morrow, the dinner that evening was an especially fine one. Every delicacy that the Earl's succession houses, dairies, orchards, forests, stock-ponds, poultry yards, and kitchen gardens could yield, and his cook prepare, was present upon the table. Despite all this largess, the Earl himself made but a poor meal, and Miss Wentworth a not much better one; it earned a warm commendation from Lady Wentworth, however.

The Earl rejoined the ladies in the drawing room soon after dinner. At her mother's urging, Miss Wentworth submitted unenthusiastically to playing the pianoforte for the company, modifying—as the Earl assured her—the works of Haydn and Clementi to great effect. When the hour of ten o'clock arrived, Lady Wentworth rose and announced her intention of retiring early in preparation for the journey the next day. Mrs. Wentworth hesitated, and then stood up herself.

"It is growing late—not late for London, to be sure, but travel is so fatiguing. I believe I will go up now myself. Rebecca?" (With a minatory eye on her daughter.)

"Please, Mama, may I not stay a little longer? That last bit with the left hand, on that sonatina I just played—" Miss Wentworth spun around on the pianoforte stool and began industriously to address the passage in question. "I would like to practice it over again, if I might. Only fifteen—twenty more minutes?"

Mrs. Wentworth looked from her daughter at the pianoforte to the Earl lounging on the sofa nearby, his expression guiltless of anything more than polite interest. "Five minutes," she announced grimly, and stalked from the room. If she had chosen to linger near the door, she might have heard a little shriek and a confused clash of chords, followed by a complete and absorbing silence.

On Monday morning, the Wentworths exchanged farewells with their host, climbed into the carriage, and began the journey back to London. The Earl accompanied them on horseback as far as the gates. Miss Wentworth's final view of Stanford Park was of the Earl, one hand raised in farewell, sitting atop his big black gelding beside the gates bearing his family shields. The kiss he had given her in parting still tingled upon her lips ("Chaperones or no chaperones! I'm not going to see you for *weeks*—"), and there was a tingling sensation along her spine as well. When next she passed those gates, it would be as the Earl's wife. The realization gave her plenty to think about on the drive to London.

The transfer of the Wentworth household from London to Brighton was accomplished shortly after their return from Stanford Park. Miss Wentworth soon found herself in the midst of a whole new round of diversions unique to Brighton. Promenading on the Steyne of a morning, sea-bathing, visits to Donaldson's library and, in the evening, parties in the Assembly Rooms or going to the Theater on the New Road were among the activities that made up her days. She was invited to one of the Prince Regent's parties at the Pavilion, and stared at the Oriental splendor she saw there; she dined, and danced, and dressed, and paid calls with her aunt and mother. With her still-talked-about conquest of the Earl of Stanford resting on her brow like an invisible laurel wreath, Miss Wentworth enjoyed a greater social success than ever before. She found only two things amiss in Brighton that summer: the Earl was not there with her, and Lady Rosamund was.

Lady Rosamund, accompanied by her aged and infirm husband, had come to Brighton that summer as was her annual custom.

It was not long before she learned from acquaintances that the Earl was at Stanford Park. It was a pleasant surprise to find he was not planning to spend his summer dancing attendance on Miss Wentworth, but Lady Rosamund knew his coming nuptials probably obliged him to put his home in order, and she did not get much satisfaction from the circumstance. It was true that for a time she considered turning it to account and paying an unannounced visit to Stanford Park. The only thing that stopped her was her uncertainty as to her welcome there; she was unwilling to risk a second rejection at the Earl's hands. After so many months of virtue, he certainly ought to be ripe for the picking, but on the whole Lady Rosamund thought it best to try to remove Miss Wentworth from the picture first, and then to present herself as an agreeable substitute.

Lady Rosamund knew that from a strictly worldly viewpoint the Earl's rank and wealth were sufficient to outweigh almost any amount of past, present, and future misconduct, but she was confident that Miss Wentworth cared for the Earl himself far more than for the prospect of being Countess of Stanford. Lady Rosamund's jealous eyes had long ago descried Miss Wentworth's true feelings; she would, in truth, have been greatly surprised to have found Miss Wentworth indifferent toward her future husband. Even Lady Rosamund's armored heart had proved vulnerable where the Earl of Stanford was concerned. Losing him would never have upset her half so much if she had not begun to care for him in good earnest, with perhaps the sincerest affection she had felt since embarking on her career as *première intrigante* of the Upper Ten Thousand.

It was Lady Rosamund's opinion that a schoolroom miss with a headful of romantical notions ought to be easy to overset. She began to set in motion a subtle persecution. For the most part, the two ladies moved in different circles; Lady Rosamund and her husband were of the older, faster set that hung about the Prince Regent, while Miss Wentworth attended only the larger parties at the Pavilion, to which everyone went. But whenever poor Miss Wentworth found herself in the same room with Lady Rosamund, she was equally sure to find a pair of malevolent black eyes following her wherever she went. The little nods, whispers, and half-audible remarks that accompanied Lady Rosamund's fixed regard were like so many pinpricks in Miss Wentworth's heart, yet she ignored them as best she could, and succeeded so well that Lady Rosamund was forced to proceed to open warfare. One night, at a ball given by a local hostelry, Lady Rosamund chose to confront her rival head-on.

Miss Wentworth had gone to the ladies' retiring room to pin up a torn flounce on her dress. There was nobody in the retiring room except a maid, who obligingly helped with the repair. Satisfied, Miss Wentworth thanked the girl, picked up her reticule, and prepared to go back to the ballroom. Before she could do so, the door to the retiring room swung open. Lady Rosamund stood before her, clothed in gold brocade and looking rather like a dark angel, with her black eyes flashing and her mouth set in a scornful smile.

"I beg your pardon," said Miss Wentworth, lifting her chin the least little bit and taking a step toward the door.

Lady Rosamund made no move to stand aside. She stood blocking the doorway, looking Miss Wentworth up and down with great contempt.

"I suppose you think Stanford loves you," said Lady Rosamund, coming directly to the point. She chose to ignore the presence of a third party, though the maid was gaping at this unexpected turn of events. "He doesn't, you know. I hope you haven't been fool enough to fancy that yours is a love match, no matter what Stanford may say."

Miss Wentworth regarded Lady Rosamund levelly. "I don't see that it's any of your concern, really," she said. "If you would kindly let me pass—"

"Let me give you some advice, Miss Wentworth. I've been . . . *friends* with Stanford for longer than you've even known him! If you think he means anything more by you than a—a brood mare, to get him an heir, you'll find yourself sadly mistaken."

By now, Miss Wentworth was so angry that she stood immobile, gripping her reticule and not saying a word. The only things she could think to say would put her on the same level as Lady Rosamund; she was determined to control her temper and withstand the urge to respond in kind. She itched to slap Lady Rosamund's face, but this urge she also managed to withstand.

"Well?" said Lady Rosamund impatiently. She had expected tears and recriminations, and was secretly a little disturbed by Miss Wentworth's reaction.

"I have nothing to say to you," said Miss Wentworth, with an air of dismissal that Lady Rosamund found intolerable. Her eyes flashed, and she took a step forward, her beautiful face contorted with fury.

"Fool," she snarled, almost spitting the word into Miss Wentworth's face. "He's mine, you know, in the only way that matters. You can ask anyone! All this time, when he's been pretending to be your devoted fiancé, where do you think he goes when he leaves you?" Lady Rosamund looked Miss Wentworth up and down once more. "All the time you've been engaged to him, Miss Wentworth, and don't think he's likely to stop after you're married. Why, he was telling me, just a few weeks ago—"

"I'm sorry, Lady Rosamund, but I'm really not interested in what you have to say," said Miss Wentworth coldly. "And if you'll pardon me for saying so, I can't imagine why you would tell me such a thing. Even assuming it were true, it hardly reflects to your credit, you know."

Lady Rosamund gasped as though she had been stung. "Marry him, then, you little fool, and see what you get! I thought I would do you a favor, Miss Wentworth, and tell you what all London knows. Don't you realize how they're all laughing at you behind your back? And you so smug, thinking you've reformed Stanford! Pardon *me* for saying so, but I can't imagine what you think you have that would attract him in the first place—apart from your function as a brood mare." Lady Rosamund gave a scornful laugh and swept out of the retiring room in a whirl of gold brocade.

Miss Wentworth found she was trembling. Angry tears prickled behind her eyes, and she felt as though she might be sick to her stomach. The maid eyed her with concern and came over to her, leading her to a chair in the corner of the retiring room.

"Just you sit down for a minute, miss," said the maid kindly. "The nerve of her, lighting into you that way! Plain as the nose on your face that it's jealousy. Why, anyone can see what *she* is, for all her airs."

Miss Wentworth hardly heard the girl's soothing words. She sat, dazed by the intensity of the attack, struggling to collect herself. Then it occurred to her that the longer she remained in the retiring room, the more cause Lady Rosamund would have for considering herself the victor in the encounter. The thought was a spur to Miss Wentworth's pride. She promptly decided she was composed enough to return to the ballroom, but her face was so wan that her mother took one look at her and asked if she had the headache. Miss Wentworth was not too proud to seize gratefully upon this excuse to leave the ball. She was soon back home in her bedchamber, though sleep proved impossible; after a time she gave up all idea of sleeping, lit a taper, and sat up in bed, hugging her knees and thinking.

Remarkably, the half hour's concentrated thought that followed did more to soothe her than all her struggles to avoid thinking about the scene that had taken place that evening. The first shock soon passed; Miss Wentworth found herself in agreement with the retiring-room maid and was much inclined to dismiss Lady Rosamund's words as jealous spite. If Lady Rosamund was really the Earl's mistress, she might have an excuse for jealousy, but she could hardly expect to keep him from matrimony by such tactics. Miss Wentworth knew Lady Rosamund to be married. She could gain nothing by attacking the Earl's future bride, for the Earl could never have married Lady Rosamund in any case, even if he had wanted to. Remembering the scene she had witnessed at Lady Sefton's ball, Miss Wentworth thought it highly unlikely that he wanted to do any such thing. She concluded that the Earl had indeed been Lady Rosamund's lover at one time—there seemed little enough reason to doubt that—but the connection had almost certainly been severed some time ago, probably around the time of the Seftons' ball. Lady Rosamund was only trying to cause trouble now. While it was distressing to be confronted with evidence of her betrothed's past, Miss Wentworth's confidence was still buoyed up by the memory of her visit to Stanford Park. She resolved to put the incident out of her mind and succeeded reasonably well.

Chapter Seventeen

The Earl of Stanford was very busy that summer. He plunged with his usual wholehearted enthusiasm into the role of model landowner, attempting to undo years of neglect in the space of a few months. While Miss Wentworth was trying not to worry about the misdemeanors he might be committing in her absence, he was falling into bed dog-tired at night, lonely for his wife-to-be but in some measure consoled by the satisfaction that comes from hard work. And he found no lack of hard work as the summer wore on; he was busier than he had ever been before in his life. Apart from his work about the estate, he also made time to accept a few invitations to dinners and other such mild amusements extended by some of the families whose estates ran with his own. He had had little to do with county society in the years since his father's death, but being on good terms with his neighbors had a new importance now, in view of his approaching marriage. The Earl looked forward to the days to come when he and his wife might return their neighbors' hospitality. For the present, however, it was the anticipation of his visits to Miss Wentworth in Brighton that enabled him to endure an otherwise tedious and lonely summer.

Those visits, though keenly anticipated, he soon discovered to hold almost as much frustration as pleasure. Miss Wentworth was chaperoned as closely as ever; the Earl seldom enjoyed a moment alone with his bride-to-be, and the social whirl of Brighton did not lend itself to any real or satisfying discourse. The days of his visits slipped by all too quickly, and he invariably found himself taking leave of Miss Wentworth, full of dissatisfaction that their brief time together had been spent at parties where they could dance with each other twice, at most, or in such closely chaperoned surroundings that every word they exchanged was subject to being overheard. It was frustrating, but even the most frustrating, tedious, or lonely day brought September another day closer. The Earl's mind was tolerably at ease, looking forward to the day when he could have his bride to himself at last.

In contrast, Miss Wentworth's mind was anything but easy. When the Earl was with her in Brighton she felt reassured, and the optimism she had felt at Stanford Park returned, but as soon as he left again she fell prey to her own imagination. For one breathless moment, she had thought the Earl had been about to tell her he loved her, that day in the garden at Stanford Park. But the words had remained unsaid, and as time went on Miss Wentworth became increasingly fearful that she might have been mistaken. She worried that she was marrying a man who might not love her and almost certainly could not be faithful to her; then her imagination took things a step further and she began to wonder if her second engagement was destined to go the way of her first. After all, Lord Russelton's feelings had undergone a complete change in the space of a few weeks spent away from her. What if the Earl was already experiencing a similar revulsion of feeling? Miss Wentworth hid her doubts as best she could and went mechanically through the unceasing round of balls and parties that made up the summer days at Brighton, an object of envy and admiration to people who never suspected the true state of affairs behind her smiling face.

The combined strain of worry and waiting, and the continuing petty persecutions of Lady Rosamund took their toll, however. Miss Wentworth soon began to show visible signs of strain. Being a gradual process, it went unnoticed by those around her, but when the Earl made what was to be his final visit to Brighton, in August, he was startled at the change that had taken place since his visit only a few weeks before. The Earl himself was looking rather lean and brown from being out-of-doors so much; his betrothed greeted him shyly but had soon relaxed enough in his company to quiz him about his weather-beaten appearance.

"Oh, I'm not quite a blackamoor, surely," he objected with mock indignation. "But it's no wonder if I look a bit like one, as much as I've been in the fields of late. We've been getting in the harvest, you see, and while I haven't actually gone so far as to wield a scythe myself, my presence is definitely obligatory. I suppose that while I've been getting up at five o'clock to deal with the hay, and the fences, and the roofs, you've been revelling in your usual whirlwind of gaiety?"

"Yes, we have been very gay. Brighton is a wonderful place." Miss Wentworth hesitated and then added, rather sadly, "I wish you had been here, too, this summer."

"So too do I, but I'm paying the piper now, for all those years of dancing! Speaking of dancing: you look as though you've been trotting a bit too hard, Becky." The Earl's voice was teasing, but his eyes examined her with some concern. She looked paler, he thought, and there were faint shadows under her eyes.

"Perhaps I have. We've been out every evening for weeks, I think."

"We attended one of the Regent's parties just the other night," put in Mrs. Wentworth impressively. "I suppose you're familiar with the Pavilion, Stanford, but Rebecca and I had never seen it before this summer. Such a magnificent place! I admire it of all things."

"What about you, Becky? Did it take your fancy?"

"I don't think it did," confessed Miss Wentworth. "Certainly it is very magnificent, but," she smiled at him, "there are too many dragons for my taste!"

The Earl grinned. "It's a mercy you haven't changed your mind and developed an affection for them. I've already redone the Countess's rooms, and it would be rather a blow to hear you wanted dragons after all."

"What does it look like now?" inquired Miss Wentworth, with liveliest curiosity.

"It's a surprise," said the Earl sternly. "You left it in my hands, remember? I don't intend to tell you a thing about it. You'll just have to wait to see it in September."

"May I not have even a hint?"

"Not even a hint. You told me you loved surprises once, if you'll recall. I'm afraid you'll simply have to curb your impatience somehow, my dear, just as I've been curbing mine, all these weeks . . ."

Mrs. Wentworth, disliking the trend of the conversation, plunged into speech once more. "Rebecca has had quite a success, here in Brighton," she said brightly, with a fond look toward her daughter. "The Prince Regent himself complimented her on her dancing, and His

Grace, the Duke of Clarence, stood up with her twice at a ball last week. She has received a really flattering amount of attention. But there, I expect it is her future status as Countess of Stanford that may be thanked for that."

"Oh, I can't take credit for her face, Mrs. Wentworth, and you may be sure that's where the real attraction lies. Prinny and Clarence, eh? I can see I need to keep a tighter rein on you, my dear. That's flying pretty high!"

"Everyone has been very kind," said Miss Wentworth, rather embarrassed.

"Indeed they have," agreed Mrs. Wentworth vigorously. "If I've heard it said once, I've heard it said a hundred times what a beautiful countess she will make. Even Mrs. Drummond Burrell has condescended to remark upon it, in a most amiable way."

The Earl lifted one eyebrow. "Amiable, indeed! But the Drummond Burrell has no great opinion of me, you know. I suspect the boot is on the other foot: more likely she is consoling you for having been inveigled into permitting such a *mésalliance.*"

"If she does not approve, you may be sure that it's only because she dislikes the idea that Rebecca will outrank her, once she is married to you," insisted Mrs. Wentworth.

Miss Wentworth saw that the Earl was looking displeased and made an effort to ease the tension. Smiling at him, she said, "That reminds me, Jack: I find there are advantages to this countess business, advantages I never suspected. The modistes are actually fighting over the privilege of making my bride-clothes, which they never did when I—when I was engaged to Frederick before, you know. Madame Arnot and Evangeline each assure me that the other is worse than incompetent and will make shambles of my wedding dress. I never dreamed there was competition for such a thing."

The Earl smiled, but he was made uncomfortable by these repeated references to rank, and more uncomfortable still by Miss Wentworth's blushing mention of Lord Russelton. He thought she looked unhappy, despite her smiles, and he wondered if she were having doubts about the engagement but was being made to go through with it all the same because Mrs. Wentworth was ambitious to see her daughter a countess. The Earl looked again at Miss Wentworth's pallor and shadowed eyes. Something undoubtably ought to be said, but if his surmise was correct he could hardly speak out before Mrs. Wentworth, and it was quite obvious that Mrs. Wentworth was not about to quit the room while he remained in it. The Earl continued to make small talk, but there was a faint crease between his brows. He made up his mind to seize the earliest opportunity of speaking privately with his bride-to-be.

The Earl and all three Wentworth ladies attended a ball in Brighton that evening. Their party arrived as a waltz was beginning, and the Earl led Miss Wentworth onto the floor. For a time they waltzed in silence, just looking at each other. They were both thinking of the first time they had danced together, at Lady Sefton's, and of how much had come about through that chance encounter.

"Becky, my dear," said the Earl at last. "I don't mean to keep implying that you look an antidote—far from it." His eyes warmed as they flickered over her graceful figure clothed in gauzy white muslin and her face framed by clusters of glossy ringlets. She wore a wreath of white roses on her head, much like she had been wearing the first time he had seen her. "You look . . .

beautiful . . . but it seems to me that you've lost some of your color, and you look a bit thinner, too, now that I come to think of it. Is something troubling you, my love?"

Waltzing in his arms, Miss Wentworth discovered that all her doubts and fears had magically melted away. "If I've lost my color, then you seem to have gained enough to make up for it," she said, smiling. "No, nothing is wrong, Jack, really. It's the—well, the waiting, I think."

"I understand perfectly," said the Earl with strong feeling. "In fact, I am grown so tired of waiting that I'm tempted to kiss you, right here and now, and the devil fly away with anyone who says nay!"

Miss Wentworth gave a gurgle of laughter. "Jack, you mustn't! Mrs. Drummond Burrell is already looking at us very disapprovingly. I think she must be shocked at the sight of an engaged couple enjoying each other's company. If you kiss me, she'll never allow either of us inside Almack's again."

"If it comes to a choice between kissing you and going to Almack's, Mrs. Drummond Burrell can go hang, too! Thank God September's almost here. If I'd known in the beginning how much waiting I was letting myself in for, I believe I'd have abducted you straight off and made for Gretna Green. What a pity I didn't think of it sooner. I wouldn't be the first Collingwood to acquire a bride in an unorthodox manner; we don't usually put the story about, but the third Earl is supposed to have carried off his bride while she was actually in the midst of being married to someone else. He then incarcerated the poor girl at Stanford Park until she—ahem—consented to make the change of bridegrooms official. Just think of how much time and trouble it would have saved, had

I only done the same." The Earl regarded Miss Wentworth quizzically. "Can you imagine Russelton's reaction at seeing his bride carried off during the wedding ceremony? Though I'd be more inclined to fear Lady Cassandra's reaction myself."

"Oh!" Miss Wentworth looked surprised and a little embarrassed. "Oh . . . but you know I was not really going to marry Frederick in any case, Jack. Even that night when I first met you . . ." She blushed rosily. "I would never have gone out on the terrace with you as I did, if I had really considered myself betrothed to Frederick."

The Earl regarded her with severity, though his lips were twitching. "Fine words, my dear, but you're alarming me to no end. All this time you've been betrothed to me, I sincerely hope you've been considering yourself *really* betrothed and not thinking yourself free to slip off to the terrace with just anyone."

"Jack! As though I—oh, you are joking me. Of course I would never do such a thing. In the general way, that is," she added hastily, as his grin widened. "That evening at Lady Sefton's was . . . different."

The Earl looked down at her for a long moment. When he spoke, his tone of voice was offhand, as though he were musing to himself. "This ballroom is deucedly hot," he said. "Do you suppose there might be a terrace around this place somewhere?"

"I think not," said Miss Wentworth, dimpling.

"A library, then?"

As the waltz came to an end at that moment, Miss Wentworth was saved from answering and merely gave him a quelling look as he led her off the floor. The Earl delivered her back to her mother's side, where she was promptly claimed for the next dance. He then began to stroll about the room, looking for a young lady without a partner. Before he could find one, he had the misfortune to fall into the clutches of Lady Pendleton, an elderly dowager who had been well-acquainted with his mother. Lady Pendleton was of a garrulous disposition. Several dances went by while she regaled the Earl with a lengthy account of her own wedding, which his approaching nuptials had called to mind. He was just meditating a desperate dash for freedom when a hand in a white kid glove was laid upon his arm.

"Stanford," purred Lady Rosamund. "You must allow me to congratulate you upon your engagement. Miss Wentworth is such a pretty little thing! I'm sure she will make you an admirable wife."

"Thank you, Rosamund," said the Earl warily. Lady Pendleton had paused in the midst of her story and was regarding the interloper with surprise, surprise changing to disapproval as she took in the extreme *décolletage* of Lady Rosamund's wine-colored velvet gown. Lady Rosamund nodded coolly toward Lady Pendleton and took the Earl's arm with a proprietary air.

"Lady Pendleton, please excuse us. Stanford and I are old friends, and we have a great deal to discuss. You are promised to me for this waltz, you know, Stanford."

The Earl could not in courtesy contradict her, and he was glad enough to get away from Lady Pendleton, but he felt a stab of annoyance as he accompanied Lady Rosamund onto the dance floor. He wondered what the devil she was up to. Her display of good nature struck him as being very much out of character; she had frozen him for weeks after the night of Lady Sefton's ball. It seemed a pity she had decided to thaw tonight. He was uncomfortably aware from the expressions of those around him that he and his partner were the objects of a certain amount of speculative interest.

"I doubt we have much to discuss, Rosamund," he said pointedly, as they joined the other couples circling the floor to the lilting music.

Lady Rosamund pouted. "Oh, Stanford, don't be so terribly stiff-necked. I only wish to congratulate you—"

"You've done that."

"—and tell you how charming I find your bride-to-be. She has made a great success for herself here in Brighton, you know; they say Clarence is quite *épris*. Take care, Stanford, or you may find yourself cut out, as you cut out poor young Lord Russelton."

"Your concern is touching, Rosamund." The Earl smiled at her sardonically. "Touching, but misplaced. I can be trusted to take care of my own affairs."

Lady Rosamund bore this snub with a smiling face. She thought she had seen Miss Wentworth's eyes widen at the sight of the Earl and herself dancing, and she meant to exploit the situation for all it was worth. "Unkind, Stanford," she chided gently, arranging her features into a beguiling pout once more. "Only a word of warning, from an old friend—"

"I don't think we were ever *friends*, Rosamund."

Despite the Earl's discouraging attitude, Lady Rosamund kept up a stream of animated chatter, stealing glances from time to time toward Miss Wentworth to see how she was reacting. The Earl also looked toward his betrothed with some anxiety. It was a damnable situation, and he knew it looked bad, but fortunately Miss Wentworth did not seem to be noticing. She was very busy laughing at something said by Mr. Fanton, her partner in the waltz.

After the waltz, the Earl dealt brusquely with Lady

Rosamund's attempts to keep him beside her, removing her hand from his arm without ceremony and making his way back toward Miss Wentworth. He led his betrothed out for the next dance, a quadrille. She seemed to be in spirits—almost unnaturally vivacious spirits, in fact—and she made no mention of Lady Rosamund. The Earl opened his mouth to explain and then changed his mind. Possibly Miss Wentworth had heard gossip concerning his past dealings with Lady Rosamund: she might well be unhappy to see him dance with a lady popularly supposed to be one of his inamoratas, but the ballroom was really no place to discuss such a topic. He decided to save his explanations until a more propitious moment.

But there was no time that seemed propitious, that evening or throughout the rest of his visit. By the time he left Brighton, the matter had faded in importance, and he ended by shrugging it off altogether. The wedding was now so close that explanations might more profitably be postponed until afterwards; the Earl felt he could demonstrate his real feelings very convincingly, once he and his bride-to-be were no longer hedged in by all the conventions surrounding them both at present. His conscience was clear where Lady Rosamund was concerned, and he attached no particular importance to the incident.

For Miss Wentworth, seeing the Earl dancing with Lady Rosamund had served to confirm her worst fears. She had not realized how painful the sight of Lady Rosamund in his arms could be. And he had not said a word about it afterwards, though half the room had been abuzz at the sight and he must have realized how particular it would appear. Miss Wentworth began to fear there might be some truth after all in Lady Rosamund's boasts, and her misery rose to new heights. After the Earl's visit ended, and he had left Brighton for Stanford Park once more, she sat down and made herself face the situation.

In spite of his reputation in the past, and the present evidences of his faithlessness, Miss Wentworth came up against a solid wall of internal resistance when she tried to make up her mind to break the engagement. Faithless or not, she simply could not live without him. That being the case, there was obviously nothing to be done except to go through with the marriage and prepare to turn a blind eye, as Lady Cassandra had recommended. She knew herself to be the worst kind of fool; undoubtably she would be fitly punished for her weakness in due time, but she could not endure the pain of losing the Earl, even to save herself from more pain later on. It was with these and similar cheerless thoughts that Miss Wentworth ended her summer at Brighton and made preparations to return to London and be married.

The Earl had brought his estate into the best order possible, given the time and means at his disposal. It was now only a little over a week until his wedding day. Miss Wentworth was back in London, and he drove up to visit her there. He found his betrothed in a rather nervous state, but attributed this to the same anxiety that he himself was feeling over the approach of such a momentous occasion.

"Not thinking of crying off at the last minute, are you, Becky?" he inquired, with a quizzical smile.

"Oh, no, Jack," said Miss Wentworth quickly, with more vehemence than seemed called for. She flushed and then smiled back at him. "Why do you ask? Don't tell me you're having second thoughts yourself?"

"Second and third and fourth thoughts, mostly at the

notion of meeting your father. I'm shaking in my boots; don't I look it?"

"Indeed, it was very good of you, Stanford, to volunteer to bring Charles down from Derbyshire," said Mrs. Wentworth. "I know he is looking forward to meeting you. And I must confess that I breathe easier, knowing he is traveling with someone else. I fear Charles is inclined to be a wee bit absentminded."

"I look forward to the trip," said the Earl politely. "And I am also looking forward to seeing your home." Mrs. Wentworth smiled graciously and withdrew to the other end of the drawing room to fetch her workbag. The Earl turned back to Miss Wentworth and went on, in a low voice, "But as I said, I'm a bit daunted at the idea of telling your father that I'm the scoundrel who's stealing his daughter away. What does he make of such a black sheep seeking entrance to his respectable family?"

"Oh, Papa will like you, I'm sure. And I'm sure you will like him, too. Everybody does," said Miss Wentworth simply.

"Yes, but he's a clergyman. He may have views about me and my—er—chequered career!"

Miss Wentworth dimpled, momentarily forgetting all her fears. "You need not worry, Jack. As a clergyman, he looks upon himself as shepherd to his flock, and like a good shepherd he 'rejoiceth more of that sheep that has gone astray and then returned to the fold, than of the ninety-nine which went not astray.' I expect that applies even to black sheep." Then her heart gave a lurch, as she remembered the uncertainty about this particular black sheep remaining within the fold for any length of time.

The Earl, unaware of these reflections, only laughed.

"I'll comfort myself with those words, ma'am! Kindly write down chapter and verse for me, along with any other useful texts you might recall. Perhaps I can undertake to impress your father with my scriptural knowledge if he fails to recognize my desirability as a son-in-law in any other way! Mind you do it soon, though; I'm leaving tomorrow and should be in Derbyshire within three days if all goes well. In the meantime, do you have time this afternoon to come around with me to Manchester Square, Becky? And you, too, of course, Mrs. Wentworth," he added, as Mrs. Wentworth rejoined them. "There's a house there that I'm considering taking a lease on. I'm putting up at the Clarendon for now, but we'll need someplace to stay in town after we're married, and my bachelor lodgings wouldn't do, of course. We'll want to come up for at least part of the Little Season so Becky can be presented at court, and I don't want to buy a house until we've had a chance to look about. My agent tells me this place should serve nicely. It's furnished and all, so we needn't worry our heads about buying furniture right away, either."

"Oh, I'd love to go, Jack, but I've a dressmaker's appointment in less than an hour," said Miss Wentworth regretfully. "The last of my bride-clothes, you know. I hope you have arranged for a large wardrobe in my rooms at Stanford Park? Mama and Aunt Constance seem to think a very great number of clothes are necessary to being a countess."

"Still fishing for hints about your rooms, are you?" teased the Earl. "You're out of luck, my dear, for I mean them to be a surprise. There's no shortage of space at Stanford Park, though; I expect we can find room for your clothes somewhere." Smiling, he rose to take his leave. "Since you can't come with me to look at the house, do you trust me to take it without your even seeing it? I don't think there'll be another chance before the wedding. By the time I've gone to Derbyshire and back, there won't be any too much time to spare as it is."

"Of course, Jack. If you think the house suitable, then I'm sure I shall, too." Miss Wentworth looked conscience-stricken. "It's asking a great deal of you to take care of all these details. And then, to have to go all the way to Derbyshire and back in the space of a week . . ."

"Your papa could not like to leave his church for very long," said Mrs. Wentworth in a commiserating voice. "It's a pity he cannot make a nice long visit while he is here in London, but at least he will be able to come for the ceremony. So fortunate that he managed to get Reverend Oakes to come in for him. He was greatly relieved to be able to leave his flock in such good hands."

"I only hope I can convince him that his daughter is in good hands as well," said the Earl feelingly. He kissed his betrothed, made his adieux to her mother, and took his leave.

Meanwhile, Lady Rosamund was preparing to make a last-ditch effort to prevent the Earl's nuptials. After his disobliging behavior in Brighton, she had decided that she despised him and no longer cared if she got him for herself; revenge was her goal now, and the idea had become an obsession. She set one of her footmen to keep watch on the Wentworth house in Berkeley Square. One afternoon soon after the Earl's departure for Derbyshire, she received word from her spy that both Lady Wentworth and Mrs. Wentworth were out, while Miss

Wentworth remained at home. Lady Rosamund put half-a-dozen artistically forged letters in her reticule and ordered her smart barouche to take her round to Berkeley Square.

Fortunately for Lady Rosamund's plans, her quarry was sitting in the drawing room and had no time to flee when her name was announced. Miss Wentworth raised a startled face and made as if to leave, but Lady Rosamund had not waited upon ceremony and entered the drawing room hard upon the heels of the butler who had announced her.

"No, don't go, my dear," she said, coming forward to lay a compelling hand on Miss Wentworth's arm. "I don't mean to behave as badly as I did in Brighton, truly I don't." Lady Rosamund summoned up a gentle, apologetic smile. "You must forgive me for what I said that night. I was sadly overwrought, and I fear I let my emotions get the better of me."

Miss Wentworth sat back down, but she did not return Lady Rosamund's smile. "What do you wish to see me about, Lady Rosamund? Only to apologize for calling me—a brood mare, was it not?"

Lady Rosamund bit her lip. "As I said, I was overwrought at the time. But I come to you as a friend today, Miss Wentworth. I could not let you go through with this marriage, without making known to you the truth about the man you are marrying. No, sit down! When you have seen my proofs, then you may do as you please. The reason I was so terribly upset that night was that I had just found out that Stanford was playing me false—playing us both false, as it were. He is, I believe, quite incapable of being faithful to any woman for long. I was furious when I found out! My only thought was to revenge myself upon him in the way I thought would hurt him most. Through you, Miss Wentworth," said Lady Rosamund impressively. "I wished to hurt him through you. I believe Stanford cares for you, as much as he is capable of caring for anyone, and I know he truly wants to marry you, my dear." Lady Rosamund's voice had become very gentle. "But I cannot believe that you would want to marry him, knowing the truth."

She waited expectantly, but Miss Wentworth only went on sitting, regarding her steadily with an expressionless face. Lady Rosamund resumed her story. "After I had had time to calm myself, I realized that we are in much the same position—you love him, too, do you not?—and that perhaps I owed it to you, to show you frankly how matters stand." Lady Rosamund drew the forged letters from her reticule and spread them before Miss Wentworth. "Here are six letters, written by Stanford to me within the last few months. These five are love letters, but this one . . . this one he sent to me after the last time we—when he was in Brighton in August, you know. He wrote that he was tired of me and my reproaches, and that he preferred the other lady to myself. Oh, but he can be cruel, Miss Wentworth! Read it—you recognize his handwriting, do you not?"

"It is like his," said Miss Wentworth.

She had no intention of reading the letters, but though she refused to take the letter lady Rosamund was holding out to her, her eyes were caught and held by a phrase from one of the other letters lying on the table, a phrase that seemed to leap out at her from the paper. The Earl had written Miss Wentworth a number of letters throughout the summer: playful, affectionate, even loving letters, but nothing like those scorching words.

Feeling suddenly ill, Miss Wentworth pushed the letters away and stood up.

"You have done your duty, Lady Rosamund. Now I must ask you to excuse me." Miss Wentworth moved blindly toward the door of the drawing room, determined not to give way before the other woman. Lady Rosamund stared after her and then rose to her feet, stuffing the letters back into her reticule.

"You will call off the wedding now, will you not?" she demanded eagerly. Miss Wentworth was already out of the room and did not answer. Baffled, Lady Rosamund followed her and stood irresolutely in the hallway, looking up the stairs after Miss Wentworth's retreating figure. She would have liked to have pursued her further, but the butler reappeared, and Lady Rosamund was forced to leave the house, uncertain of having accomplished her mission.

Miss Wentworth went to her bedchamber and lay down upon her bed. No tears came. She felt stunned, as though a stifling weight was pressing upon her chest. The letters Lady Rosamund had shown her had hurt her so badly that she saw the situation with an odd, dispassionate clarity, and what she saw appalled her: she could never marry a man who could write such things to one woman while being engaged to marry another. What she had just gone through with Lady Rosamund was a fair sample of the kind of thing that would inevitably happen again and again throughout a lifetime spent with the Earl of Stanford. There was only numbness when she thought of life without him, but to feel numb was surely better than the agony she was feeling now. Her mind was suddenly quite made up. Miss Wentworth rose, dressed for dinner, and went downstairs to tell her mother and aunt what she had decided to do.

Chapter Eighteen

"Stanford and your father should be in London tomorrow," remarked Mrs. Wentworth, helping herself to a dish of jellied poached chicken and then passing it on to her daughter. "Rebecca, you've scarcely eaten a thing. Do try some of this chicken. You must keep up your strength, my dear; it wouldn't do to fall ill now, so close to the wedding. Only think, in three more days you will be the Countess of Stanford!"

Miss Wentworth squared her shoulders. "I am not going to marry Lord Stanford, Mama."

Mrs. Wentworth regarded her daughter with the kind of incredulity usually reserved for the ravings of heretics or madmen. Lady Wentworth's eyebrows rose, and she set her wineglass carefully beside her plate.

"Why, whatever do you mean, Rebecca?" exclaimed Mrs. Wentworth. "Surely you don't—"

"I mean that I shall not marry him," said Miss Wentworth, lifting her chin defiantly. "I have changed my mind."

"But surely Stanford can know nothing of this," said Lady Wentworth.

"No. No, I only just decided today." Miss Wentworth

hesitated and then, in a burst of confidence, added, "But I have been troubled for some time, Aunt Constance."

"Nerves," said Mrs. Wentworth firmly. "I'm sure I never had a spasm in my life, but the morning I was to marry your father, I felt certain I'd succumb then and there. You will find yourself to be quite comfortable and happy once you are actually in the church, my dear."

"I'm not going to be in the church! I'm not going to marry him."

"Do you expect one of the royal dukes to offer for you instead?" Mrs. Wentworth smiled a rather tight-lipped smile. "The idea, jilting first poor Frederick Russelton—a baron, after all, and a very good family—and now to talk of jilting the Earl of Stanford! Don't be ridiculous, Rebecca. Of course you will marry him."

"I won't!"

"Perhaps it would be as well if you went to your bedchamber and lay down for a time, Rebecca," said Lady Wentworth, glancing from her niece's flushed face to her sister-in-law's determined one. "And I expect it would do no harm if you took a few drops of laudanum to help you rest. When Stanford arrives tomorrow, I daresay you will be able to resolve whatever is troubling you, to your own satisfaction."

"I will not change my mind," said Miss Wentworth mutinously. "In fact, I never want to see him again. We can send the announcement to the *Morning Post* tomorrow. And as for—"

"Rebecca!" There was a hint of steel in Lady Wentworth's voice now. "Do you really think it fair to Stanford, that he should read about your change of heart in the *Morning Post?* No one can force you to marry anyone, child, but if you are indeed set upon ending your engagement, you owe your prospective bridegroom the courtesy of telling him so, face to face, along with your reasons for taking such a drastic step."

"Oh, no! No, I don't want to see him. Couldn't you tell him for me, Aunt Constance?"

"Certainly not. To break an engagement is a very serious matter, not something that should be left for others to do, and certainly nothing that should be decided on the spur of a moment."

"But couldn't I write him just as well as tell him? I don't see why I need—"

"Rebecca, I think it would be best if we put the subject aside for the time being," said Mrs. Wentworth briskly. "Until Stanford arrives, there is really nothing that can be done. I suspect, too, that by morning you will find things looking altogether different. It is not in the least unusual to have these nervous fits before one's nuptials, my dear."

All Miss Wentworth's protests were in vain. She was unable to make any headway against the unyielding attitude adopted by her mother and aunt. They refused to take her change of heart seriously and persisted in believing that the Earl's arrival would set all to rights. Under protest, Miss Wentworth was dosed with laudanum and sent to her bedchamber as though she had been a naughty child.

Disturbingly, the Earl and Mr. Wentworth failed to arrive on the following day. Neither Lady Wentworth nor Mrs. Wentworth felt this was any cause for alarm, however. Sir Richard arrived from Suffolk, where he had been visiting Henrietta, and added his own reassurances to those of his mother and aunt.

"Daresay they ran into some kind of trouble on the road," he said cheerfully. "Sort of thing that happens all the time—why, I came within amesace of being ditched myself on the trip down! Ten to one, they broke a trace or something of the sort and find themselves cooling their heels in a posting house for a day. No need to get in a pelter, Beck."

"Or perhaps your papa wandered off at one of the stops," suggested Mrs. Wentworth. "Do you remember that time we all went to Derby to do some shopping, and he became so engrossed in that old book he found in one of the shops there, that he completely forgot to meet us back at the inn for nuncheon?"

"Whatever the delay, you may depend upon it that Stanford and your father will arrive in good time," said Lady Wentworth comfortably. "Stanford is really a most capable individual, Rebecca, and you are exceedingly fortunate to be marrying him."

"I'm not going to marry him," repeated Miss Wentworth, through clenched teeth.

The travelers did not arrive on the next day, either. By the time dinner was over, both Lady Wentworth and Mrs. Wentworth were looking rather worried, and Sir Richard announced his intention of ordering out his curricle and making a round of the London posting houses in search of news.

"Perhaps Papa forbade the banns," suggested Miss Wentworth hopefully, after her cousin had left on his errand.

"Nonsense, Rebecca! You know perfectly well that it is no such thing. The match has your father's full approval . . . why, I showed you the letter myself. And the marriage settlements have already been agreed upon . . . and Stanford so very generous . . . no, there can be no difficulty there. I feel quite certain that it is as Richard says, and they have encountered some sort of trouble on the road. Perhaps it is raining up north. I'm sure it's been gloomy enough here in London all week," said Mrs. Wentworth, sighing.

"But the wedding is tomorrow, Mama! We must let the guests know as soon as possible that there will be no ceremony. I'll write the notes myself, and we can have one of the footmen take them around—"

"Not until you've spoken to Stanford." The little smile on Mrs. Wentworth's face infuriated her daughter. "Constance is quite correct in saying that he must be told first, my dear."

"There will be no time to notify the guests if we wait any longer! Oh, this is intolerable." Miss Wentworth began to pace up and down the drawing room.

"I believe I hear a carriage outside," remarked Lady Wentworth, looking up from the firescreen she was working in gros point. "Perhaps it is Richard, with some news for us."

Miss Wentworth flew to the window. "No, it's them," she announced tensely. "There's Papa, and there's—oh, I can't see him, Mama. You must tell him for me." She ran from the room just as the knocker sounded on the front door.

The Earl of Stanford arrived in Berkeley Square on the eve of his wedding, two days later than planned and in no very good humor. A series of mischances had plagued the travelers on their journey south. They had been delayed a full day in starting because a sick parishioner had requested the Reverend Charles Wentworth's presence at his bedside. The conscientious cleric could not bring himself to leave while he was needed by one of his flock.

The Earl had endured the wait in good part. An object of immense interest to the parsonage maidservants, he had wandered about the house, taking note of the books and belongings left there by his bride-to-be, on the whole quite pleased to have this unlooked-for opportunity of learning more about her by examining firsthand the home in which she had grown up. The delay was annoying, but it did not worry him. They could make up much of the time lost, once they were on the road, and even with the delayed start there was an extra day to spare.

When an axle on the chaise broke during the second day of their travels, the Earl's attitude was much less nonchalant. While the Reverend Mr. Wentworth sat peacefully in the parlor of a nearby inn perusing a hefty theological tome he had brought to while away the journey, the Earl of Stanford stood over the unfortunate wheelwright and personally supervised the repairs, doing rather more harm than good; the man was made so nervous by his impatient manner and glowering countenance that the work went very slowly. It was more than another half-day's wait before they were able to resume their journey.

Finally, on the second-to-last stage before London, one of the wheelers went lame. The chaise limped into the next posting house at a bare walk. Only the presence of the Reverend Charles Wentworth kept the Earl from venting the full measure of his wrath upon anyone and everyone within range; the ostler who came up to take the old team in hand caught a glimpse of the Earl's face and scurried off to complete the change of horses in record time. Such a dangerous-looking individual should assuredly not be encouraged to linger upon the premises!

The Earl was tired, hungry, and travel-stained by the time the outskirts of London came into view, but he felt in better spirits as they neared their destination. Tomorrow was his wedding day . . . he directed the postboys to Berkeley Square and hoped he might be in time to see his beloved for a few minutes, before returning to his hotel and trying to snatch some badly needed rest. He had scarcely slept the night before, through fretting over the delays.

After Miss Wentworth fled the drawing room, she went to her bedchamber and rang for the maid. With the girl's help, she hastily undressed her. No one could make her go down to the drawing room if she was already in her nightclothes, she reasoned triumphantly. She wrapped her dressing gown around herself, extinguished the candles, and stood by the window to catch a last glimpse of the Earl of Stanford before he left Berkeley Square, never to return.

There was a knock on her bedchamber door. Miss Wentworth spun around in dismay and looked at the door. They were going to try to make her go downstairs, then. Perhaps it would be better to pretend to be asleep and ignore the summons. She made a move toward her bed. Before she reached it, the knock was repeated, more emphatically, and the door swung open. The Earl's figure stood there, silhouetted in the light from the hallway.

Miss Wentworth drew in her breath sharply. Conscious of her state of undress, she took a step backwards and nervously tried to tug the folds of her dressing gown further over the nightdress underneath. The Earl was frowning, his eyes adjusting to the dim room. Then he saw her and came forward to where she stood. He was still wearing his many-caped topcoat; to Miss Wentworth's eyes he appeared very tall and formidible, an appearance that was intensified by the grim set to his mouth.

"What are you doing here?" she said in a voice little more than a whisper.

The Earl smiled, but the smile did not reach his eyes. "We're to be married tomorrow, remember? Your aunt said you were distraught about something, and with rare good sense she agreed we might dispense with chaperonage on this occasion. What the devil is going on, Becky?"

"I cannot marry you, Jack. I would—I should have told you before tonight, but—"

"You cannot marry me?" repeated the Earl. His mind felt dull with fatigue, but he was conscious of exasperation, or something stronger than exasperation, welling up inside him.

"I have changed my mind," said Miss Wentworth bravely.

"Why?"

It was an awkward moment, surpassing all previous awkward moments in Miss Wentworth's life. She had not given thought to how she would explain her decision to the Earl. Seeing him so fierce-looking made the task doubly intimidating. "Your lifestyle . . . your habits . . . I am persuaded we should not suit. Oh, I know my own behavior has been very much at fault. I led you on to think—to think—"

"My habits?" interrupted the Earl. "You refer, I collect, to my libertine habits?" His voice was neither loud nor angry, but something in it made Miss Wentworth take another step backwards. She could not keep from giving one frightened glance toward her bed, looming uncomfortably close at hand.

The Earl observed the look and was suddenly furious. The injustice of the accusation stung him. He had done his best to reform his way of life and had endured any amount of ridicule from his peers for doing so. Now the woman he loved was behaving as though he was a monster of depravity. The fear in her eyes made him more furious still, with a sort of savage impulse to confirm her bad opinion for all he was worth. Miss Wentworth saw his face change. She darted toward the doorway, but the Earl caught her around the waist and flung her down upon the bed. Miss Wentworth found her hands pinned above her head and the Earl's eyes inches from her own, glittering with an emotion that was anything but loverlike.

"Let me go," she gasped, truly terrified by his expression. "Oh, let me go. I shall scream—"

For answer, the Earl's mouth came down hard on hers. She struggled, but he only tightened his hold and kissed her with bruising force. Yet even as he kissed her, his anger dwindled away. He felt hurt, deeply hurt, by her distrust and was all at once weary rather than angry. He broke off the assault on Miss Wentworth's mouth and looked down at her frightened face.

"You little fool," he said, his voice rough with emotion. "If I was really such a libertine, do you think I would have asked you to marry me? Damn it, I love you!" He was aghast as soon as the words were out of his mouth. I didn't mean to tell her like this, he thought with dismay. Oh, what have I done? This wasn't how I meant it to be at all.

Miss Wentworth had stopped struggling and was staring up at him, her eyes wide. "What did you say?" she whispered.

"I said I love you," said the Earl, rather fearfully.

"Well, I love you, too," said Miss Wentworth, and burst into tears.

The Earl laughed. He felt suddenly light-headed and

light-hearted. Standing up, he pulled Miss Wentworth to her feet and wrapped her in his arms. She sniffed and laid her face against his chest, bedewing his topcoat with her tears. "Oh, Becky," he said, stroking her hair. "Oh, Becky, I've loved you ever since that day in the park. Maybe before then, only I didn't recognize it."

"And I think I've loved you ever since you first smiled at me, that night at Lady Sefton's. Oh, it was such an odious smile, Jack! I could see perfectly well you thought I was setting my cap at you, but I couldn't help the way I felt, no matter what they said about you."

"No doubt they said plenty. I wish I could say there wasn't a grain of truth in it, but . . . oh, my dear, I truly don't think I'm as black as I've been painted, though God knows there are episodes in my life of which I'm not proud. Was it . . . did someone tell you something about me, to make you change your mind about marrying me?"

Miss Wentworth stiffened. "I almost forgot," she said in a flat voice. "Lady Rosamund . . ." She found herself unable to go on.

"Rosamund told you something about me?" The Earl frowned, looking down at Miss Wentworth's rigid expression. "Well, I suppose I shouldn't be surprised; she doesn't love me, you know. What did she say?"

Puzzled, Miss Wentworth searched his face. "About . . . your being lovers."

"Rosamund said we were lovers?" said the Earl incredulously. The situation struck him as exquisitely humorous, and he began to laugh again. Miss Wentworth regarded him with doubt, uncertain whether to be reassured or offended. "Becky, whatever else may be laid in my dish, on that score I can plead innocence. Rosamund and I *never*—that is, I don't deny that there was a flirtation between us at one time, but nothing more." The Earl's face assumed a look both reminiscent and rather wicked. "Why, you and I went a deal further than that, the very first evening we met! Not to mention that time in Lady Cassandra's library . . . no, my dear, I can vouch that you yourself are—ahem—better acquainted with me than Rosamund could ever claim to be."

Miss Wentworth felt her cheeks grow warm, but it went unnoticed in the dark room. Her dimple was beginning to flicker. "But Lady Rosamund showed me some letters," she said hesitantly. "Love letters you wrote her."

"Well, that just shows she made it up out of whole cloth. I make it a particular point—that is, in the *past* I've always made it a particular point to avoid writing letters to married women. Not so much on moral grounds as for motives of self-preservation; I've never had the inclination to embroil myself in a divorce suit."

"They looked like your handwriting."

"I expect Rosamund forged them. Now that I think of it, I believe I did send her a note or two, early in our acquaintance. Nothing incriminating, you understand: little notes given to her maid, signed only with a single cryptic initial. Oh, dear, I hope I'm not giving you a disgust with all this talk of past intrigues? It's shameful stuff to have to admit to, but I can assure you it never came to anything, even if it suits Rosamund's purposes to say otherwise. You're not disgusted with me, are you, love?"

"No, Jack. Actually it is very interesting, for of course I have heard of such things and have often wondered how they were managed. Now that I know—"

"Now that you know, you had better forget all about it! I plan to be a very jealous husband, my love. I'll certainly beat you if I catch you carrying on in such a way!"

"But I might *need* to make you jealous," explained Miss Wentworth, all wide-eyed innocence. "In case you should begin to pay too much attention to someone else—"

"There will be no one else. The only woman who will receive my attention will be my wife. All that other business is behind me, I promise."

"Like that blond girl in the park?"

"Look here, what do you know about—" The Earl broke off, regarding his betrothed with comical dismay. She dimpled at him, and he smiled ruefully. "Becky, you wretch! I hope you don't mean to throw all my past follies in my face? That's ancient history, over and done with by the time you came along. I'm quite a reformed character nowadays. Just ask any of my friends . . . why, they've been talking at White's about putting in my name as a suitable candidate for a monastery! You must be the only one in town who hasn't heard, my love."

Miss Wentworth sighed happily and laid her face against his chest once more. The Earl held her tightly for a moment and then began to speak again, picking his words with care. "Such follies as the girl you mentioned are common enough among bachelors—and some who aren't bachelors, sad to say—but I've truly turned over a new leaf in that direction and mean it shall stay turned. Had I known I could feel about someone, as I feel about you . . . oh, my dear, I might have done differently. But I can't undo the past. Do you love me enough to marry me anyway, with the understanding that I will go on differently in the future?"

"Yes," said Miss Wentworth simply.

"Thank God!" There was heartfelt relief in the Earl's

voice, but his eyes were dancing. "I must say, it's as well you agreed, because I'm afraid I've compromised you pretty thoroughly. Entertaining a man in your bedchamber is not at all the thing, my love."

Miss Wentworth gave a watery chuckle. "It is very shocking," she agreed. "I never would have believed Aunt Constance would allow it."

"Your aunt is a woman of great good sense. I become more convinced of it every day."

"You only say that because she likes you!"

"She has great discernment of character as well! Oh, Becky, I do love you. Do you think you could tell me that you love me, too, one more time? Just to tide me over until tomorrow, you know."

"I love you, Jack," said Miss Wentworth obediently. Since it seemed possible that further proof might be needed, she put her arms around his neck and drew his face down to her own. The Earl's embrace tightened. They kissed, and his mouth drew from hers a growing response, which was promptly returned, multiplied tenfold. At last, the Earl took a deep breath and disengaged himself reluctantly.

"Look here, I'd better go before—I'd better go!" he said, smiling down at her. "I'll tell your mother and aunt that you've changed your mind and decided to marry the brute after all." He took her face between his hands and kissed her again, very gently. "And now you must get some sleep, my dear . . . and so too must I . . . but I will be seeing you tomorrow at ten o'clock, St. George's, Hanover Square." He paused with his hand on the doorknob. "I love you," he said once more, looking back at her. The unaccustomed words came awkwardly to his lips, but once they were spoken he wondered how he could have made such a piece of work about the business. It seemed the most natural thing in the world: to love her and tell her so.

"I love you, too, Jack," said Miss Wentworth, smiling mistily.

Chapter Nineteen

The sun shone brightly on Miss Wentworth's wedding day. That morning, just before the hour of ten o'clock, the Earl of Stanford arrived within the sacred precincts of St. George's, Hanover Square. He was accompanied by his uncle and groomsman, the Honorable Mr. Giles Collingwood. Supported by the Honorable Miss Henrietta Ingleside, the bride made her appearance soon after, and was given away in marriage by her father with all due ceremony. The Reverend Charles Wentworth had dignified the occasion by appearing in a fine new coat of blue Bath cloth, although he had inadvertently worn his oldest boots as well.

Everyone agreed there had never been a lovelier bride. The ex-Miss Wentworth was an ethereal vision in white, robed in layer upon layer of filmy drapery sheer as cobweb, worn over a form-fitting satin undergown. A white gauze veil was draped over her head and fixed in place with a wreath of white roses. The women present (when not sniffling into their handkerchiefs) divided their time pretty evenly between admiring the bridal toilette and the person of the bridegroom. The Earl's coat of blue superfine set off his broad shoulders to perfection, and the glow in his dark eyes when he looked at his bride made the ladies sigh and universally declare him to be still quite the handsomest gentleman in London.

After the vows had been exchanged, and the couple pronounced officially wed, there was a regular stampede for the honor of saluting the new countess. In the flurry of promiscuous kissing that ensued, she was made pink as a peony by the enthusiasm shown by certain gentlemen in claiming this privilege. The Earl endured it with good-humored resignation, limiting himself to a brandishing of fists in the direction of the worst offenders and a few sinister predictions about the fate of any gentleman who, not content with a single kiss upon this occasion, might attempt anything of the sort later on.

He himself kissed Lady Wentworth, Mrs. Wentworth, Henrietta, and two or three other ladies who just happened to be standing nearby and who showed signs of becoming mortally offended at being passed over. The Earl made Lady Wentworth blush by calling her Aunt Constance; Mrs. Wentworth alternately sobbed and smiled at the sight of her newly married daughter; the Reverend Charles Wentworth engaged the acting minister in a scholarly discussion on the Gospel of St. John and was only removed from the church at last through the united efforts of his wife, daughter, and son-in-law.

A splendid wedding breakfast followed at Lady Wentworth's house in Berkeley Square. After everyone had eaten and drunk a great deal in honor of the occasion, and had admired the bride's beauty, and the bridegroom's elegance, and the general taste and perfection that characterized the whole of the proceedings, the Earl and his countess were packed into their carriage. Every good wish was showered upon them; they were also the butt of a vast number of the sort of jokes that gentlemen consider appropriate on such occasions, making the bride turn pink again. At last the horses were set to. The carriage rattled out of the square, headed toward the newlywed couple's honeymoon destination, Stanford Park.

The Earl spent the first few minutes of the journey disposing of the sheaves of grain and other similar tokens that his friends had thoughtfully arranged within the carriage. This he did through the simple expedient of hurling them out the door, to the consternation of several unwary pedestrians. The Countess looked on indulgently.

"There's a bit more of it, caught in the hem of my pelisse—no, not my flowers, Jack! I want to keep those." The Countess watched her husband pitch the last of the wheat straw out the door. "I can't imagine why your friends wanted to fill the carriage with such rubbish."

"DeLacey tells me it is an ancient custom among the villagers in the North country, where his family hails from." The Earl gave her a look sparkling with mischief. "I understand it's meant to ensure fertility." He shut the door of the carriage, dusted off his hands, and sat down beside his wife on the banquette. "That's a pretty hat you're wearing, Becky," he said, looking her over appreciatively.

"Do you like it?" The Countess was wearing a broad-brimmed straw gypsy hat, turned up in front and trimmed with an exuberant plume of green ostrich feathers. "I hoped you might. I think it quite the prettiest hat I have ever owned."

"I like it very well, but I wish you would take it off."

"I think I would do better to leave it on," said the Countess, eying him mistrustfully.

"Take it off, madame wife!"

"But I prefer to leave it on, my lord!" The Countess retreated to the far end of the banquette as the Earl rose and advanced on her. A brief scuffle ensued, during which the Earl rapidly gained the upper hand; the offending hat was tossed on the banquette opposite, and the Earl proceeded to kiss his new wife with deliberation and some attention to detail. To the Countess's relief, he showed no signs of carrying matters further than that. He merely pulled her close, with one arm about her shoulders and her hand held tightly in his own. By the time they reached open country, however, the Countess felt the pressure of his hand slacken. She turned her head and discovered that her husband had fallen asleep.

The Countess settled herself so that his head might rest comfortably upon her shoulder, and then began to study once more the face of the man she had married. In sleep he looked young, and innocent, and rather vulnerable, the lines on his face smoothed and softened, and his lashes lying peacefully against the tan of his cheek. Something about the sight aroused a protective, almost maternal feeling in her breast. Carefully, so as not to disturb him, she rolled up one of the window shades to watch the passing scenery and sat there, feeling grown up all at once and profoundly happy.

They reached Stanford Park late in the afternoon. When the carriage turned between the gateposts, the Countess reluctantly decided that the time had come to wake her husband, but he began to stir as their pace slowed to negotiate the winding drive. The Earl stretched himself, yawned, and opened his eyes.

"Becky! Have I been asleep all this time?"

"Yes, I hadn't the heart to wake you. You must have been quite worn out, Jack. Papa told me this morning all about that terrible trip down from Derbyshire."

"That's no excuse for being such a tedious companion. Good God, what a slow-top I am. You mustn't let word of this get out, my dear, or my reputation's gone forever. To have had you to myself for two hours, and then not to have improved the time! But I'll make it up to you." The Earl went on to make it up to her very agreeably during the time it took to drive from the gateposts to the courtyard in front of the house.

Then there was the terrifying ordeal of greeting all the servants to be got through. With her husband at her side, this proved less daunting than the Countess had expected. A word or two from the Earl, a smile and greeting from herself, and the thing was done. Mrs. Merryman, the Earl's severe housekeeper, came forward after the gauntlet of servants had been run, to take the new countess in hand.

"If you will come this way, my lady, I will show you to your rooms."

"I'm coming with you," announced the Earl, his hand already on the newel post of the staircase.

Mrs. Merryman turned to fix him with an icy stare. "That you will not, my lord," she said sternly. "Her ladyship will wish to change her dress and perhaps rest for a while, before dinner."

"Yes, of course, but I want to see how she likes her rooms first."

"You may trust me to see that her ladyship has everything she needs, my lord. If you will go to the small parlor—"

"By God, this is *my* house, and I'll—good Lord, I sound just like my father." The Earl blinked in surprise. "Must be something to do with the wedded state . . . assuming the yoke of duty and all that. Don't I sound like the old Earl, Merry?"

"To the life, my lord. Now if you will go to the small parlor—"

"Don't scowl, Merry. I don't intend to pester Lady Stanford with my attentions, but I've spent a deal of time fixing up her rooms, and I want to see how she likes them. After that, you may toss me out as soon as you please."

"As you wish, my lord." Mrs. Merryman led the way up the staircase, her back ramrod straight and disapproving in her black bombazine gown.

"Isn't she terrifying?" whispered the Earl. "I used to go in fear of her, in my boyhood. I'm not sure I don't even now . . . when she looks at me, I feel as if I were still about six years old and had just been caught with my hand in the jam pot."

The Countess was betrayed into an unladylike giggle, but she pinched her husband's arm and did her best to arrange her features into a suitably dignified, matronly expression. The expression changed, however, when she walked through the doorway of her newly decorated bedchamber. She stood gazing about the room, her eyes wide.

"Do you like it?" asked the Earl, watching her face jealously.

The Countess nodded, too overcome to speak. Gone were the dragons and gilt and red brocade. The walls had been stripped of paper and painted cream color, and the wall opposite the bed had been overlaid with a trellising of green lathwork, made to let the creamy wall beneath show through the openwork of trellising. The new furniture arranged within the room was simple, almost severe, in design, veneered in golden satinwood. The canopied bed had curtains of flowered chintz patterned with green leaves on a cream background and lined with plain green material. Draperies of the same chintz hung at the windows. The sofa and some of the chairs were covered in green, and other chairs and cushions were pink and yellow to match the flowers in the pattern of the chintz. Green painted flower stands of basketwork were set in the corners of the room; pinks and daisies filled the stands, and in a place of prominence upon the satinwood dressing chest stood a jardinière of blush-pink roses, scenting the room with their perfume.

"It's beautiful," she said at last. "It looks like a garden, Jack!" The Earl found his wife suddenly in his arms. It seemed only logical to kiss her, and this he did, until Mrs. Merryman stepped in.

"It's time you left, my lord!"

"She started it," said the Earl defensively.

"That's as may be, but it's time you left all the same." Still protesting, he was driven from the room by his implacable housekeeper.

There was no question of lying down for the Countess that afternoon. She went about her new rooms, examining the adjoining dressing room, opening the doors of the wardrobe, exploring the contents of writing desk and dressing table, and admiring the silver-backed brushes she found there, engraved with her new monogram. Presently, a maid arrived to help her with her toilette for dinner. The Countess was awakened to her wifely duties, which included the immediate duty of looking as beautiful as possible for her husband at their first dinner *en famille.* She bathed, and dressed in a dinner dress of emerald green silk with a low, square neckline. The maid assisted her in dressing her hair in soft curls around her face with a psyche knot in back. The Countess had just given a final tweak to a stubborn curl over her right ear when there was a tap upon the door joining the Earl's bedchamber to her own.

"May I come in, my dear?" The Earl stood smiling at her from the doorway. "I have something else in the way of a surprise for you." The Countess observed that he was carrying a black plush-covered box under his arm. Coming forward to where she sat before her dressing table, he laid the box on the table. "How appropriate that you should be wearing green tonight. I believe I've just what you need to complete your toilette."

"Oh, Jack," said the Countess. "Oh, Jack!" Reverently, she lifted a necklace of emeralds set in gold from the case.

"The Stanford emeralds. They're yours now, and in all the years they've been in the family I don't think they've ever belonged to anyone who became them better. See, there are earrings, too, and a tiara. There's also some other jewelry belonging to the estate that you can look over later, but I thought tonight—would you wear the emeralds for me tonight? Humor me, my love: I've been imagining how they'd look on you ever since that night I saw you at the opera!"

"A tiara is a bit formal for a family dinner," pointed out the Countess, her dimple flickering. "Highly irregular!"

"Yes, but I'm a highly irregular gentleman, you know, and likely to prove dangerous if I don't get my way." The Earl drew his brows together and regarded her with a mock-menacing glare. "By God, woman, will you wear that tiara, or will I have to—"

"Yes, my lord," said the Countess with great docility. The maid helped her set the tiara upon her head and put the earrings in her ears. The Earl himself clasped the necklace about her throat. She shivered a little at the touch of his fingers; her thoughts flew ahead to consider what still lay before her that evening. Looking up, she found her husband was watching her in the mirror. The same awareness was in his eyes, but he only smiled and wordlessly offered her his arm. Together they went down the stairs to dinner.

The Earl and Countess of Stanford dined that evening in the breakfast parlor, a much smaller apartment than the great formal dining room. Neither of them was seen to eat much of the excellent dinner set before them. They both drank a couple of glasses of wine, however, and sat smiling at each other from opposite ends of the table: the Countess in her green dress, emeralds glittering in her hair and at her throat, and the Earl in black evening clothes, his eyes never straying far from the vision of his wife sitting across from him. When dinner was over, the Countess very correctly removed to the drawing room. The Earl was left to drink his port in solitary state, but he soon followed his wife into the drawing room with the decanter in his hand and drank his port in front of the fireplace, with his wife perched informally upon his knee.

"Ah, married life," he said, draining his glass and setting it aside. "My own fireside, my own wife . . . what more could a man desire?" He reached up to play with a curl lying loose upon his wife's shoulder. The Countess turned her head to smile at him, and he touched the earring that hung from her right ear, making the jewel suspended from it swing and send out flashes of scintillating green fire. "My beautiful wife," he said with satisfaction, and kissed the ear.

The Countess looked gratified, but faintly uncomfortable. "The servants," she said, glancing toward the door of the drawing room. "Should we . . . should I . . ."

"Damn the servants," said the Earl amiably, and kissed her ear once more, lightly. Then he pulled her into his lap and kissed her several more times, not lightly at all. "Oh, Becky," he said indistinctly, his face against her neck. "Oh, my dear. Run along to bed, love, and I'll be up before long."

Knowing what she would see in his eyes, the Countess could not bring herself to look at him, but she stood up and dropped a kiss upon his brow. "I love you, Jack," she whispered, and hurried from the room.

During dinner, the Countess's gowns and other belongings had been unpacked and put away in her new rooms. A fire burned in the fireplace, and the bedclothes had been turned down for the night. The maid who had helped her dress for dinner was waiting in her bedchamber; the Countess was made extremely self-conscious by the knowing look on the girl's face as she helped her mistress undress for bed. Once the Countess had changed into her nightdress, the maid brushed out her hair until it rippled smoothly over her shoulders, the shining waves glinting with red and gold in the candlelight. "Thank you, Sally, that will do," said the Countess. "You may go now." The girl left the room, with a last look of curiosity mingled with sympathy that made the Countess's cheeks burn.

When the door had shut behind the maid, the Countess started to lie down upon the bed. Then she changed her mind and seated herself instead on one of the chairs in front of the fireplace. The information her mother had given her concerning what would take place on her wedding night had been both alarming and very vague. The experience in Lady Cassandra's library had given her a much clearer idea what to expect, but she was altogether pitiably nervous about the prospect. When the Earl came into her bedchamber a little later, she looked so scared that he set aside the bottle of wine he had brought with him and straightway took her in his arms.

"Oh, my love," he said, holding her tightly. "Don't be frightened, my love. It's only me, and I shan't force you to do anything you're not . . . ready for." He was conscious of being the world's greatest hypocrite as he spoke, already aroused at the sight of her in the thin nightdress with her hair loose. He closed his eyes to shut out temptation and was forcibly struck by the sweet smell and feel of the exceedingly feminine body he was holding in his arms. The Earl opened his eyes again. Making a supreme act of will, he began, "If you would rather I stayed in my own room tonight—"

"No, Jack." The Countess shook her head resolutely. "No, don't go." She raised her face to look at him. He kissed her then, gently at first, but soon gentleness was at an end; his mouth took possession of hers while his hands ran over the curves of her body. She was aware of growing warmth, the pressure of his body and the corresponding relaxation of her own as fear and resistance melted away. Her hands began to caress his back and shoulders. The hard muscles beneath the fabric of his shirt felt strong and solid, satisfyingly masculine. At her touch, he made a noise like a groan, gathered her in his arms, and carried her to the bed. After laying her upon the counterpane, he turned to extinguish the candles. The room grew dim, lit only by the glow from the fireplace.

He began to strip off his shirt. The Countess watched for a moment, shocked and fascinated to see his bare chest and shoulders, broad and well muscled with a patch of dark hair upon his chest; it was her very first glimpse of a bare male torso and such a disturbing sight that she felt unable to sustain further revelations and shut her eyes.

He finished undressing. She felt him lie down beside her, his body pressing against her. The feel of his skin was warm and comforting, but exciting, too, as she reached out to embrace him.

He began to kiss her neck: light little kisses that sent trickles of sensation through her. She gasped and half-sobbed as his mouth moved lower. He gently drew the nightdress over her shoulders and down to her waist. She heard him catch his breath and opened her eyes to find his own eyes burning down at her.

"You're beautiful," he whispered. "So beautiful, my love." His lips touched her neck and again moved lower until at last his mouth came down on her breast. The shock of the sensation made her gasp; the vague, aching hunger that had been growing within her became sharper, nearly unbearable.

His hands stroked her breasts and shoulders, and one hand wandered lower until he unerringly reached the center of sensation. She protested with a little cry and tried to twist away, but the weight of his body, and his hands, gentle but firm, held her in place.

His fingers began to stroke her once more, awakening a response that made her back arch of its own volition, while his mouth on her breast intensified that intolerable, aching desire inside that cried out to be filled. She moaned, turning her head from side to side, seeking release. One hand fluttered out to touch his head at her breast. "Jack," she said, making his name a plea for what she could not put into words. "Oh, Jack."

The Earl paused. He shifted slightly in the bed while his hands worked to free the nightdress around her waist; then that last flimsy barrier was thrown aside and the weight and warmth and solidity of his body eased down on top of her. She opened her eyes. His face was level with her own, and she felt the pressure of him seeking entrance between her legs. The Countess took one swift look downwards at what was about to happen to her and fixed terrified eyes on her husband's face.

"Oh, my love," he whispered. "There will be some pain, I'm afraid, but only this once, I promise . . . never again . . . oh, Becky, I love you, my darling." Then he was inside her, and she cried out at the burning pain: pain as though she was rent in two, filled full beyond bearing.

"Oh, Becky!" Half-triumphant, half-repentant, the Earl regarded his wife. Her eyes looked enormous, gazing up at him, with her long hair fanned out on the pillow. "Oh, my love." He thrust again, and again pain filled her. Her hands tightened upon his shoulders. She shut her eyes and gathered her breath in a little gasp.

"It's all right, Jack," she whispered. "Go on."

He began to thrust steadily, and at first each thrust was fresh agony, but gradually the unfamiliar sensation of him within her body ceased to be painful. Then the feeling became oddly pleasurable; with some surprise, she heard her own voice urging him not to stop, and found her own body responding enthusiastically, obviously possessed of an instinctive knowledge of its own.

The sensation moved abruptly to a different plane altogether, becoming incredibly pleasurable, so pleasurable that she rather thought she would die if he were cruel enough to stop . . . and then she decided she was dying anyway, or experiencing something quite as momentous, so that it seemed natural to cry out to Maker and lover in the same breath as wave after wave of sensation broke over her. The Earl was so engrossed in watching the play of emotion upon her face that his own climax took him by surprise. He, too, cried out, and his body exhausted itself in a series of convulsive shudders. At last he came to rest, burying his face against her shoulder.

For a moment he rested there, inhaling the sweet smell of her hair. They were both silent for some time. The noise of their breathing and the crackle of the fire in the fireplace were the only sounds to be heard in the room. Somewhere in the house a door slammed; in the distance a dog barked, and was quiet, and barked again.

Finally, the Earl raised his head. His wife was looking up at him, her eyes filled with wonder.

"Oh, Jack, is it always like that?" she whispered.

The Earl wisely refused to be drawn into indiscreet comparisons. "It always will be with us, I hope," he said, kissing her eyes, her mouth, and finishing with the tip of her nose. She gave him a tremulous smile. Gently, he rolled himself off her, pulling her over with him until he was lying on his back with her lying beside him, her head cradled on his chest. He began to stroke the heavy silken mass of her hair. She shut her eyes and could hear the beat of his heart; the warmth of his body was comforting, and his arms the safest place in the world. Between the sound of his heartbeat and the soothing hand moving rhythmically upon her hair, she fell asleep at last.

* * *

Before falling asleep, the Countess's last thought was to wonder how one ever looked one's husband in the face in the morning after sharing an experience of such an intimate nature the night before. This did not prove to be a problem, however; when she opened her eyes the next morning, she found the Earl already awake and lying on his side, his head propped on one elbow. He appeared to be watching her intently. As she looked at him, his mouth curved into a smile both mischievous and suggestive. Remembrance flooded back into her sleep-fogged mind.

"Good morning, my lord," said the Countess, her dimple very much in evidence.

"Good morning, my lady! We're exceedingly formal this morning . . . quite unnecessarily so, in my opinion, given the terms we were on last night." The Earl's eyes roved with bold admiration over his wife's body. Suddenly aware that she was not wearing a stitch, the Countess pulled the counterpane up to her chin and tried to glare at him. He grinned back, and her face relaxed into an answering smile. She began to look about for her nightdress. It had unaccountably ended up some distance from the bed, making it necessary for her to sit up in order to retrieve it.

"Oh!" The Countess winced as muscles she had not known she possessed made protest. The Earl gave a snort of laughter as his wife retrieved the nightdress in a gingerly manner, and she looked at him reproachfully.

The cause of the discomfort was openly laughing at her now. Not only did he show a lamentable lack of repentance for what he had done; he went on to compound the offense by subjecting her to more of the same treatment, introducing one or two innovations that embarrassed his wife very much. Her shock at seeing herself so used did not noticeably impair her enjoyment, however, as the Earl felt obliged to point out afterwards.

"That may be so, Jack, but there is no need to talk about it!" The Countess spoke severely, although the tell-tale dimple flickering about her mouth seemed to indicate no very real or lasting displeasure. Finding her nightdress to have suffered irrevocable damage, she was making do by wrapping herself in her dressing gown. Her husband lounged upon the bed and watched her with lazy interest. "What had you thought to do today, Jack? Oh, you know what I mean! Are you going out or staying in? I need to know which dress to wear."

"If you feel you must dress—and pray do not feel obliged to do so on *my* account—then I would suggest something suitable for driving out. I was thinking of having the team harnessed to the phaeton and resuming your lessons. It's time you learned to manage four horses, my dear; I intend that you shall take the shine out of every other female on the road."

"Tyrant," said the Countess affectionately.

"On the contrary." The Earl rolled off the bed and threw himself at her feet. "I am your most abject slave and worshiper," he announced soulfully, and began to cover her feet with kisses.

"Jack, put on some clothes!" said his wife, affecting to be much scandalized but laughing nonetheless.

She observed with deep suspicion the upward trend of his kisses. "I thought we were to go driving?" she reminded him.

"In a little while . . ."

"But won't the servants—"

"The servants will come when I ring for them and not

before. I gave very strict orders to that effect before retiring last night!"

The Countess looked down at her husband and then over at the bellrope. Her eyes sparkled. She broke from his hold and made a dash for the bellrope. The Earl recaptured her easily. She shrieked with laughter as he threw her upon the bed, pulled open the dressing gown, and commenced operations in earnest.

"I thought you said you were my slave and worshiper, Jack!"

"Indeed I am, my dear. Why, I'm worshiping you this minute!"

"But your conduct is hardly slavelike, sir! If you were really my slave and worshiper—oh!"

"Yes, my love?"

"If—oh! Do stop that, Jack, I'm trying to talk to you—if you were really my slave and worshiper, it seems to me you ought to do my bidding instead of *pouncing* upon me in such a way."

The Earl raised his head and gave the matter his serious consideration. With ruffled hair and a look of conscious guilt spreading over his face, he had the appearance of a small boy caught out in mischief.

"Yes, love, you are perfectly correct," he said at last, contrition struggling with laughter in his voice. "I'll admit I may have been a trifle highhanded just now—the excitement of the moment, you know. But if you really wish me to stop—"

"Certainly not," said the Countess. "I have no objection to being worshiped; it's merely the *principle* of the thing. Now that you understand your position—" she shot a mischievous look at the Earl, whose eyes glinted dangerously, "now that you understand your position, sir, you have my permission to—to—"

"Worship?"

"Yes, worship!"

"Thank you, ma'am," said the Earl, very meekly, and then went on to demonstrate a complete lack of meekness in his subsequent behavior.

ABOUT THE AUTHOR

Joy Reed is a resident of Phoenix, Arizona, where she lives with her husband and daughter. She is a housewife and an avid reader, and attributes her interest in the Regency period to a copy of *VANITY FAIR* that fell into her hands at an early age. AN INCONVENIENT ENGAGEMENT is her first regency novel for Zebra Books. In April 1994 she will have a short story in Zebra Mother's Day regency collection: *A MOTHER'S JOY.* Joy is currently working on her next regency novel. You may write to her c/o Zebra Books. Please include a self-addressed stamped envelope if you wish a response.